KILKENNY COUNTY LIBRARY

KK467302

WITHDRAWN

BLOOD TORMENT

D1387243

Also by T. F. Muir

(DCI Gilchrist series)
The Meating Room
Life for a Life
Tooth for a Tooth
Hand for a Hand*
Eye for an Eye*

(DCI Gilchrist Short Story)
A Christmas Tail

*Written as Frank Muir

BLOOD TORMENT

A DCI Gilchrist Novel

T. F. Muir

Constable • London

Accession No: KK467302
Price: EUR11.01
75845
THE BOOK NEST LTD
160712

CONSTABLE

lished in Great Britain in 2016 by Constable

1 3 5 7 9 10 8 6 4 2

Copyright © T. F. Muir, 2016

The moral right of the author has been asserted.

All characters and events in this publication, other than those clearly in the public domain, are fictitious and any resemblance to real persons, living or dead, is purely coincidental.

All rights reserved.

No part of this publication may be reproduced, stored in a retrieval system, or transmitted, in any form or by any means, without the prior permission in writing of the publisher, nor be otherwise circulated in any form of binding or cover other than that in which it is published and without a similar condition including this condition being imposed on the subsequent purchaser.

A CIP catalogue record for this book is available from the British Library.

ISBN: 978-1-47212-116-5 (hardcover)
ISBN: 978-1-47212-115-8 (trade paperback)

Typeset in Dante MT by Hewer Text UK Ltd, Edinburgh
Printed and bound in Great Britain by CPI Group (UK) Ltd, Croydon, CR0 4YY

Papers used by Constable are from well-managed forests and other responsible sources.

MIX
Paper from
responsible sources
FSC
www.fsc.org
FSC® C104740

Constable
is an imprint of
Little, Brown Book Group
Carmelite House
50 Victoria Embankment
London EC4Y 0DZ

An Hachette UK Company
www.hachette.co.uk

www.littlebrown.co.uk

For Anna

CHAPTER 1

7.18 a.m., Monday, mid-April
Fisherman's Cottage
Crail, Fife

DCI Andy Gilchrist had just taken his first mouthful of sliced mango when his mobile rang – ID Jessie. 'Morning, Jessie. Hungover, are we?'

'Is that the pot nipping the kettle?'

He was indeed feeling a tad tender. Impromptu celebrations and a one-for-the-road *deoch an dorus* – or was it three? – in The Central had that effect on him now, but he said, 'Never felt better.'

'Cross your heart and hope to die? And I don't think. Listen,' she said, 'I've just caught a message being passed out on the radio from Control. We've got a Grade 1 priority. Missing child. Katie Davis. Two years old. Mother put her to bed last night, checked on her this morning, and she was gone. Mother's never married. Lives by herself.'

'Name?'

'Andrea Davis.'

The name meant nothing to him. 'Who's the father? Do we know where he is?'

'Don't know to both questions. But I'll get on to that. The Duty Inspector's getting a dog handler over to the house as soon as. Grange Road. You know it?'

'Branches off before the Kinkell Brae?'

'That's it.'

Gilchrist pushed his fruit to the side. 'Address?'

'Grange Mansion.'

'Mansion?'

'Yeah. She's well to do, by the sounds of it. Which might be a motive for kidnap. But there's no ransom note. Nothing.'

'That could come later.'

'I phoned the Duty Inspector,' Jessie said, her voice rushing, 'and asked her to check ViSOR for any RSOs in close proximity.'

The Violent and Sex Offender Register was a police system that kept tabs on RSOs – Registered Sex Offenders. From the rush in Jessie's voice, Gilchrist suspected they had their first solid lead. 'Keep going,' he said.

'A nasty paedo by the name of Sammie Bell moved into the area about three weeks ago.'

'Never heard of him.'

'Doesn't ring a bell, you mean?'

'Very funny.'

'He's just moved back from London.'

'Back?' he said. 'So he used to live here?'

'Family home's in Crail. Not too far from where you live. Parents dead. No siblings. Mother passed away last month, which might explain why he's returned.'

'To claim his inheritance?'

'Got it in one.'

'Address?'

Jessie gave it to him.

Anstruther Road ran south from Westgate on the outskirts of Crail, and was bounded by some nice property. 'Find out what you can on Bell, and get back to me.'

'Want me to pick you up?'

'I'll meet you there.'

'Oh, and one other thing,' she said. 'The Incident Officer's been assigned.'

Something in the chirpy tone of her voice sent a warning through him. 'Who is it?'

'DI Walter MacIntosh.' A pause, then, 'Isn't he a pal of yours?'

'Bring the coffee,' Gilchrist snarled, and killed the call.

DI Walter *Tosh* MacIntosh. It had been eighteen months since he'd last seen the man, the nastiest piece of police shit he'd ever tried to scrape off his shoe. After their last run-in, Tosh had been transferred to Lothian and Borders, then moved to Strathclyde HQ. But if he was now back with Fife Constabulary, he was too close for comfort. Gilchrist snatched his leather jacket from the back of a chair, and strode to the rear door.

Although his back garden was sheltered, it felt cold enough to have him blowing into his hands. By the wooden shed in the far corner, he checked the cat's dish, but its food was barely touched. He peered inside – empty – and jammed a stone at the foot of the door to keep it open. At least it would have a safe place to hide, if it ever came back.

Out the front door, in Rose Wynd, a cold wind had risen. He tugged his collar tight around his neck, stuffed his hands into his pockets. An empty plastic bottle of Irn-Bru rattled across the cobbles. He swung a foot at it, but a sudden gust of wind swept the Wynd, and he missed. Overhead, gulls stalled mid-flight, then wheeled off in windswept free-fall.

He beeped his remote fob, and his BMW winked at him.

The lease on his Mercedes had expired, so he'd gone for a BMW this time. His son, Jack, who'd never owned a car, never even taken a driving lesson – *Automation's what's wrong with the world now, we should all go back to shanks's pony* – had gifted Gilchrist four thousand pounds *in recognition of being an arsehole of a son for all these years*. It had taken much drunken persuasion for Gilchrist to accept, recognising that his persistent refusal would be seen as offensive. On one hand, Jack throwing money to the wind in defiance of materialism was a no-brainer. On the other, it worried him that Jack's sculptures and paintings were being priced so highly now – or, more to the point, what the hell was he doing with the surplus cash?

Gilchrist was about to turn into Westgate when a tradesman, clambering into his van with a sausage roll spilling crumbs, took his attention. The thought of a roll and bacon had his mouth watering, and on impulse he pulled left and parked.

He was crossing the road when his mobile rang – ID Force Control Centre.

'DS Janes asked me to call you about Mr Bell, sir.'

'Let's have it.'

'His full name is Samuel Johnson Bell, aka Sammie Bell, aka Jimmy Bell, aka Ding, born in '66. Has a string of offences from the age of thirteen – up in front of the sheriff for shoplifting, petty theft, card fraud; then moved to London in '85 and was prime suspect in a series of rapes in and around Romford from '87 through '95, underage girls – fifteen years, thirteen, and one twelve year old – but his alibis were bombproof. Then we move to the serious stuff, sir.'

Something clamped Gilchrist's gut. As if underage rape was not serious enough.

'Was charged by the Met in '98 with the kidnap and murder of two children from a council house in Dagenham. Never recovered the bodies, but was found guilty and sentenced to twenty years. But he served only six and was released on appeal in 2004. No other reported incidents since. A marker was added to ViSOR three weeks ago on his return to Crail.'

'How old were these children?'

'Two, sir. Both girls.'

Same age as Katie Davis. Gilchrist cursed under his breath. How anyone could harm a child, or take sexual satisfaction from someone little older than a baby, was beyond him. He stepped aside as an elderly lady exited the shop, gave her a grim smile and a good-morning nod, then pushed through the door.

'Anything else?' he asked.

'Yes, sir. He's been given an interim SOPO, but his solicitor's applied to the court to have that lifted on the grounds that he was wrongly convicted in London, and is no danger to any child. It also prevents him from working near children.'

Gilchrist ordered a bacon roll while his mind worked through the logic. With Bell just back from London, an interim Sexual Offences Prevention Order would have been granted within a few days of his return, notwithstanding his alleged innocence. But he worried that Bell's appeal had been successful. Here was a career sexual offender with a smart brain, or good legal advisors, or both.

'What did he do for a living?'

'School janitor.'

Bloody hell. Like giving a fox the keys to the henhouse.

'He'd been employed in a number of primary schools in and around Romford, sir. After his release he lived in rented accommodation in London, but never stayed in any place longer than six months. He returned to Crail when his mother passed.'

'Email me a copy of your report,' Gilchrist said. 'And copy Jackie Canning in on it.' He rattled off his and Jackie's email addresses, then ended the call.

Back outside, he bit into his bacon roll, its crisp, salty meat setting his saliva glands on overload. It was the first bacon roll he'd had in two weeks since Maureen had urged him to eat more fruit and veg. *You're eating all the wrong stuff, Dad. Your cholesterol must be through the roof.* He had reciprocated by urging her to eat bigger portions of what he ate – steak pie, chips, pizza – so that she might put weight back on. Three years earlier, she'd lost forty pounds in four months, and had not fully recovered. He often wondered if she ever would.

He dialled her number.

'Morning, Dad.' She sounded tired, but not disgruntled like Jack first thing in the morning. 'Why do you always call so early?'

'Because it's the best part of the day, and you shouldn't miss it.'

'What time is it anyway?'

'Close to eight.'

'Which puts it at about seven,' she said, 'if I know you.'

'Thought we could meet up during the week. Maybe share a fish supper, or two.'

'So the diet's taken a dive?'

'Wouldn't want to call it a diet, more like a change of subject matter.' He bit into his roll, as if to make his point.

'Let me get back to you, Dad. Got some finals coming up. I need to study.'

'Play catch-up, you mean?'

'You need to be more trusting,' she said. 'But I still love you.'

'Love you, too, Mo,' he said to a dead line.

Back in his car, he thought of his children. Now they were both living in St Andrews again, he had hoped to spend more time with them. But the sad truth was that they had their own lives to get on with, and being a DCI with Fife Constabulary did not exactly lend itself to knitting to pass the time.

Jack was doing well, showing his art in a gallery in South Street, making a name for himself in circles that mattered, or so he said. Which was always a worry. Gilchrist continued to have difficulty believing Jack. On the other hand, Maureen was as straight as the road was long, and told the truth, whether it cut him to the bone or not.

But it troubled him that he had not been entirely honest with them, and had yet to tell them he was about to become a father again. After much soul-searching, Forensic Pathologist Dr Rebecca Cooper had decided not to have a termination, despite protests from her soon-to-be-ex-husband, Max, who was now regretting his own infidelities and wanted to start afresh – *without someone else's bastard child*. Not that Max had any say in the matter, Gilchrist thought he understood that much, only that guilt was playing a part in the man's remorse.

He slowed down as he located himself from the street addresses, then pulled on to the pavement opposite Bell's property. The house surprised him, a substantial two-storey stone property that looked as if it had been maintained to within an inch of its life. Vinyl windows glistened like paint. Spotless slates reflected a grey sky. Only the garden looked unkempt, the lawn still stunned from its winter hibernation, and shrubs in need of a pruning, an indication as to how the house would decline now it was being looked after by the Bells' criminal son.

He dialled Jessie's number. 'Where are you?'

'Hold your horses. I've just got the coffee. You want to have it before or after you grill Bell's arse?'

'Before,' he said.

'That's better. I'll be there in ten.'

The line died, leaving Gilchrist to shake his head.

In the five months he had been partnered with Jessie he had come to understand that 'morning' and 'Jessie' were two words that should never be together. She had a bright mind and a quick wit, but personal problems with which she refused to let him help, and a driven desire almost as fierce as his own to bring criminals to justice.

So he waited for her arrival, and eyed Bell's house.

Had the upstairs curtains opened since he'd parked? He couldn't say. As if to reassure him, slatted blinds in the lower right front window flashed open, revealing the silhouette of a man's figure.

A pair of slats at head height widened as someone peered through them. Then they flicked shut, and the blinds rose with the steadiness of a stage curtain lifting, the windowsill low enough to reveal a naked man, arms blackened with tattoos for sleeves, thighs coloured like a Chinese painting, head shorn like a polished newel.

The man seemed unconcerned by his nakedness. But it was the manner in which he stood that Gilchrist found unsettling. He was being stared down, no doubt about it. 'That's the way to do it, sonny Jim,' Gilchrist whispered. 'You're trying to wind up the wrong guy.'

8

CHAPTER 2

Jessie parked her Fiat behind Gilchrist.

When she slid into his passenger seat, he said, 'You look flushed.'

'And you look like you've been out on the binge. Here.' She handed him his coffee. 'You'd better drink that before it gets cold.' Then her eyes widened as her gaze shifted over his shoulder.

Gilchrist followed her line of sight as he took a sip of coffee. Sammie Bell – if that's who the man was – had returned to stand at the window, still naked.

'Is that Sammie Bell?'

'That's his address,' he said, and took another sip.

'Swallow up,' she said. 'This I've got to see,' and stuffed her cup into the holder in the centre console.

He followed her as she took the garden steps two at a time. She'd been exercising, which he had to say was working, and her once chubby figure was beginning to recover its shape. By the time they reached the door, the man hadn't moved, just stood there, watching them with a dead stare. Jessie rang the doorbell, hardly out of breath, while Gilchrist flashed his warrant card at the window.

It worked. The man lowered the blinds.

Several seconds later, the door opened wide, releasing a waft of warm air and a heavy guff of stale food. The man stood before them. An open-mouthed red dragon entwined itself around and up his left leg, while an iridescent wide-fanged python squeezed his right, as if both creatures were striving to reach the easy prey of the man's penis – the effect striking enough for Gilchrist to have difficulty diverting his eyes. The man's arms were sleeved so thickly with tattoos that it looked as if he'd worn gloves and dipped his arms up to the armpits in tar. A pair of diamond studs pierced his right ear. His feet sported hairy toes and nails in need of a cut, and stood atop a carpet of unopened envelopes, brochures, spam mail, with Bell in the first line of the address.

'Mr Samuel Johnson Bell?' Jessie said, holding up her warrant card.

The man cocked his head.

'We need to talk to you.'

'Talk?'

'Can we come in?'

Bell stared at Jessie, silent.

It took several seconds for Gilchrist to notice that Bell's pupils were dilated, that he was likely high on drugs. 'We could drag you down to the Station, if you'd prefer,' he said. 'But I think you'd catch your death of cold. So why don't you invite us in so we can talk in the warmth?'

Bell's lips parted in a weak grin. 'Heating's not on,' he said.

'That's it,' Jessie said, and reached for her plasticuffs.

Bell's eyes widened at the sight of the cuffs, and he took a step back.

'These are going round your wrists or your balls, I don't care which.'

Gilchrist grabbed Bell's arm as he stumbled backwards, and managed to prevent him from falling. But Bell locked an out-of-focus stare on Gilchrist's hand, and said, 'Pi can't be expressed as a fraction.'

'Do you have a solicitor?' Jessie asked.

'It's an irrational number that never repeats—'

'How about repeating this? Do you have a solicitor?'

' . . . and never ends when written as a decimal.'

Gilchrist relaxed his grip on Bell's arm, and gave Jessie a tiny shake of his head. She got the message, and slipped her plasticuffs back into her pocket. 'Would you like me to make you a cup of tea, Mr Bell?' Gilchrist asked.

Bell seemed confused for a moment, then said, 'No kettle.'

Jessie tutted and pushed past him, towards a door that Gilchrist assumed opened to the kitchen. Bell turned and followed her, Gilchrist behind him.

Where the exterior of the house was immaculate, the kitchen was a different matter.

Pots and pans piled high in a scum-lined sink. Crusts of burned toast and the remains of other food littered the draining basin. Emptied tins of baked beans sat on the granite tops, some on their sides, dribbling the last of their contents down the cupboard doors. The air was thick enough to taste, and a smell that left a coating on the tongue had Gilchrist pressing the back of his hand to his nose.

'Bloody hell,' Jessie said, and snapped open a window.

Fresh air rushed in.

Bell stepped towards a circular oak table, bare feet squelching

KK467302

on sticky linoleum. An opened bottle of ginger beer lay on its side in the corner. He shoved aside a stack of books, and hastily scraped together a haphazard pile of loose papers. Then he looked at Gilchrist, papers hugged to his chest.

'Let's try the front lounge,' Gilchrist said.

Without a word, Bell walked from the kitchen.

In the lounge, other than the opening of the blinds, the room looked as if Bell had not set foot in it. Cushions sat plumped up on a crinkle-free settee, as if untouched since their last cleaning. Two crystal vases stood on a glass-topped coffee table, lily and rose petals scattered around them like crinkled scraps. On a shelf by the rear window, a devil's ivy drooped to the floor, its yellowed leaves as crisp as dried paper.

'How long have you lived here, Mr Bell?' Gilchrist asked.

Bell was standing at the window again. A fierce-eyed eagle spread its wings across his upper back, yellow beak open, talons splayed, feathers fluttering from the rippling of his muscles. Bell might be high on drugs, but he was in excellent physical shape.

Gilchrist let a silent ten seconds pass before saying, 'I don't like repeating myself.'

'A month,' Bell said, 'give or take.'

'These papers you're holding, Mr Bell. What are they?' He detected a tensing in Bell's stance.

Jessie took a step closer to Bell. 'Are you hiding something?' she asked him.

Bell turned suddenly, and held the papers out to Gilchrist.

From where Gilchrist stood, the pencilled triangles and trapeziums and numbers for angles reminded him of his geometry classes in secondary school. But he kept his arms at his sides. 'Studying maths?' he said.

'It took over three hundred years for Fermat's Last Theorem to be solved—'

'Where were you last night?' Gilchrist interrupted, and watched calculated cunning slide behind Bell's eyes.

'Why?'

'Just answer the question.'

Bell pulled his papers back to his chest. 'I was here.'

'Alone?'

'Yes.'

'Did you go out at all?'

'Where to?'

'That's what I'm asking.'

'I had a couple of pints.'

Like pulling teeth, Gilchrist thought. 'Where?'

'Golf Hotel.'

The Golf Hotel was at the other end of town, but an image of Bell seated in the lounge having a jovial pint did not materialise. 'The bar?' he asked.

'Where else?'

'What's that?' Jessie asked, and nodded to Bell's papers.

But Bell ignored her, kept his eyes on Gilchrist.

'Looks like there's some photos in that lot,' she persisted.

Bell tightened his grip on the bunched papers.

Jessie smiled. 'Head shots of Fermat, are they?'

Gilchrist eyed the papers, but from where he stood, all he could see were scribbled pages. 'Like to show us?' he said to Bell, and held out his hand.

Bell pulled the pages tighter.

'We can apply for a warrant,' Gilchrist reasoned.

Something seemed to settle over Bell at these words but, as he relaxed his grip, first one photograph, then another, slipped from the loosening pages. He tried to catch them, but only made matters worse as other scribbled pages and coloured prints fluttered to the carpet.

Jessie reached down and retrieved a photograph. She stared at it for several seconds, then said, 'What's this got to do with Fermat's Last Theorem?'

Bell gave her a dead-eyed stare.

'Did someone give you this, or did you download it?'

Silence.

She picked up another photograph, then one more, and said, 'We can take you to the Station as is. Or you can get dressed. But however you do it, I'm detaining you on suspicion of downloading images of underage children. You do have a computer, don't you?'

Bell lifted his gaze to the ceiling, and cocked his head as if some idea had come to him. Then he gave a weak smile, and said, 'I'll get dressed.'

'Not so fast,' Jessie said. 'Leave that lot here.'

Bell crouched down, and placed the papers on the carpet with care, revealing more images of what looked like child porn.

Gilchrist said, 'I'll come with you while you dig out your clothes.'

'I can manage,' Bell said, and turned to the door.

Jessie took a step to the side, blocking his way. 'You heard the man.'

Bell narrowed his eyes, as if seeing her for the first time.

'That's right,' she said to him. 'We'll be searching that computer of yours before you can delete a bloody thing.'

CHAPTER 3

While Jessie arranged transport to take Bell to the North Street Office, Gilchrist phoned Brenda McAllister, the Procurator Fiscal, and organised a search warrant for Bell's property. With the process started at least, Gilchrist walked upstairs, leaving Jessie to keep an eye on Bell. Strictly speaking, anything found in advance of the warrant could be deemed inadmissible in court, but Jessie would back him up, he knew.

Just as on the lower floor, upstairs was a dichotomy of cleanliness and disarray. He entered a front bedroom, the floor littered with clothes, bed-sheets, discarded beer cans, plates dirtied with hardened lumps of food. The walls, once neatly wallpapered, were pencilled from floor to ceiling in scribbled mathematical equations that ran for line upon line in the tiniest of writing, making Gilchrist wonder if Bell had been trying to solve Fermat's Last Theorem all by himself.

An opened laptop sat on the bed, screen half hidden by a filthy pillow which he eased aside. He ran a knuckle over the touch pad and the screen revived to an image of what looked like the lower half of a naked child, legs wide . . .

Gilchrist's stomach seized. He turned away as the urge to throw up hit him like a kick to the guts. He choked back a sliver of bile, ran the back of his hand over his lips, his mind screaming that he would have Bell, he would kill the man, he would . . . he would . . .

He took a deep breath to settle his heart, and forced his mind to think rationally. He accessed the images in sequence to confirm the child was female but, importantly, that she had a small birth-mark on her inner right thigh, which could help identify her. The corner of his eye caught what he thought was spillage on the bed-sheets. He leaned over for a closer inspection, and managed to stifle another spasm as his gut threatened to eject his breakfast.

But he gagged it down, and stumbled from the bedroom.

Jessie's eyes widened as Gilchrist barged into the living room.

Bell stood in profile, facing the window, lips curling with the tiniest of smiles. Then he turned and stared through Gilchrist, pupils no longer dilated. And Gilchrist wondered if Bell had not been on drugs but high on the sexual thrill of masturbating to children.

The smirk was too much.

One step, two steps, and he had his fingers around Bell's neck and his back thumped hard enough against the wall to send a mirror crashing to the floor.

'Who is she?' he snarled.

Bell's muscles flexed, then he launched himself from the wall and went for a head-butt. Gilchrist was ready, and pulled him off balance with a twist of his shoulders and a hook of his leg. Bell hit the floor and a knee thumped into the small of his back, emptied his lungs with a surprised grunt.

'Was that Katie Davis?' Gilchrist growled.

16

Bell bellowed in pain, but managed to grunt, 'Who's Katie Davis?'

Gilchrist pressed harder. 'I swear I'll—'

'*Andy.*'

Jessie's shout brought him back. He released his grip, pushed himself to his feet.

Bell rolled on to his side, and Gilchrist jerked him upright, thudded his back against the wall again, ready to send him to the floor if he so much as looked as if he was going to retaliate. But Bell coughed once, twice, then chuckled. 'You don't know,' he said, 'do you?'

'Don't know what?'

Bell shook his head with a smile. 'You just don't know.'

It took all of Gilchrist's willpower not to throttle the life from Bell. 'We'll ID her from the birthmark,' he said.

Surprise flickered across Bell's face.

'And if that's you on the screen, I'll make sure you spend a weekend in Cornton Vale before they send you to Barlinnie.'

Gilchrist knew his words were meaningless to a man like Bell. Being threatened by the law was no more hurtful than being sworn at. Nonetheless, he breathed a sigh of relief when a police Transit van pulled up on the pavement outside Bell's house – the uniforms to take Bell to North Street.

By the time the warrant arrived, Jessie had been through Bell's laptop, but found no more child porn. When the SOCOs turned up, Gilchrist and Jessie had their stories straight, and Gilchrist made a point of following Colin, the lead SOCO, into Bell's bedroom, where the laptop was discovered and bagged for removal. Gilchrist then instructed Colin to search the place from top to bottom, and left him to it.

As he and Jessie walked along the garden path, he said, 'Penny for your thoughts?'

'You can't afford them, the things I'm thinking of doing to that pervert.'

'We don't yet know that the man in the images was Bell,' Gilchrist reasoned.

'Just some pervert who needs his cock whacked off,' Jessie said. 'And I'll tell you what, for all the shit those dickheads for brothers of mine have done, they draw the line at that.' She scurried down the steps and stomped across the road to her Fiat.

Gilchrist could not argue with her. Tommy and Terry Janes might both have served time in Barlinnie, but Jessie's criminal brothers were just that – criminals, not paedophiliac perverts. He pressed his key fob. 'Let's leave Bell to stew for a bit in the Station—'

'*Stew?* I'd boil the bastard.'

Gilchrist opened the car door. 'Let's have a look at Grange Mansion first,' he said.

Grange Mansion stood in a wooded enclave on the east side of Grange Road, and was accessed through a stone gateway that looked as though age was doing what it could to pull it down. Dislodged stones lay in roadside piles overgrown by dandelions and nettles tall enough to sting your face. Police cars, Land Rovers, Transit vans with antennae spiking skywards, and an array of private cars, lined the opposite side. Police tape blocked the entrance where journalists milled like a market throng.

A TV crew went about its business of setting up cameras.

Gilchrist nosed closer, flashed his warrant card, and was permitted access.

The entrance driveway was little more than two worn tracks

in weed-riddled gravel, pot-holed and puddled. Rhododendron bushes brushed the car's wings as he eased through, its chassis bucking as he negotiated the dips and hollows. He found a spot by a derelict barn, which offered a narrow view across open fields.

Jessie parked her Fiat next to him.

He removed a set of coveralls from the boot. The wind had settled, and a white haar was gathering from the north. In the distance, a flat sea melded into a horizon as grey as slate. St Andrews lay off to the left but, from that angle, through the trees, only the harbour's stone pier and a snippet of the East Sands was visible.

The Crime Scene Manager was WPC Mhairi McBride, who had only just returned to the Constabulary the week before after being hospitalised. She signed them in, noting the time, and said, 'We've almost completed a search of the house and the outbuildings, sir.'

Gilchrist felt his gaze being pulled to the derelict barn, and two dilapidated buildings either side, which could both do with new roofs. Plenty of places for a child to hide.

'But Katie's not here. The SOCOs are working the back garden, sir, which is where they believe entry to the property was made. Over the boundary wall, sir.'

'How did he gain access to the house?'

'Used a glass cutter on the bedroom window, then undid the sash lock. No prints, so he was wearing gloves.'

Gilchrist stared along the side of the house, beyond a white Lexus that looked as if it could do with a cleaning. From where they stood, he could see the stone wall that bounded a property line thick with shrubs and bushes. In pitch darkness you could stumble about, maybe lose your bearings. Had the kidnapper known the layout? He felt his gaze drift back to the driveway. This far out of town, the kidnapper must have come by car, parked on Grange Road remote from the entrance, and maybe edged along the south boundary wall.

But the SOCOs would confirm that.

He turned to Mhairi. 'Do we have a list of friends, relatives, tradesmen; anyone who might have had recent access?' he asked.

'DS Baxter is collecting that information, sir.'

'Is he here?'

'Popped back to North Street, sir.'

Gilchrist eyed Grange Mansion, a two-storey stone structure that lacked any sense of architectural vision; just upper and lower windows either side of a dark front door. Like the outbuildings, it was in a poor state of repair. Paint peeled in blisters and flakes from rotted windows and fasciae. Weeds sprouted from rooftop gutters. Rainwater darkened the corner where a downpipe hung loose like a broken leg.

'Where's Ms Davis now?' Gilchrist asked.

'She's inside, sir. With Family Liaison. WPC Carlton.'

'Good. She'll handle her well.'

He was about to walk off when Mhairi said, 'Did you know that Ms Davis's father is the ex-MSP, Dougal Davis, sir?'

Gilchrist grimaced. From memory, Dougal Davis had been forced to resign from the Scottish Parliament after his third wife turned up at the local A&E with a fractured arm, and confessed to a series of incidents of physical abuse throughout her marriage.

Davis denied every one of them, and the Procurator Fiscal decided against proceeding with criminal charges in the end. The popular story at the time was that Davis had bought the PF's silence. But the damage was done, and Davis had to step down from a career in politics. Gossip was rife, with other stories of abuse surfacing for a moment, only to be squashed by solicitors representing the powerhouse businessman that Davis had since become.

'Did Davis ever remarry?' Gilchrist asked.

'Nobody'll have him, more like,' Jessie said.

'Maybe so. But we need to check him out.'

Gilchrist thanked Mhairi and was about to walk away, when he caught sight of Tosh at the corner of the barn, barking into his mobile phone like a field commander. He thought he looked fatter by about a stone, maybe three. Fat bulged around his neck, and his face look boiled. The only thing thinner about him was his hair, which sported a freckled patch at the back of his crown.

When Tosh saw Gilchrist, he turned his back on him and walked off.

Gilchrist resisted the urge to follow, and strode towards the house. 'See if you can get hold of Jackie,' he said to Jessie, 'and find out everything you can about Dougal Davis.'

Gilchrist stepped on to the front porch while Jessie walked off for better reception. He opened his coveralls and put them on. The main door creaked when he turned the handle, and he stepped into a dark hallway that smelled of damp wool and stale dust. Ahead, it widened to a staircase on the left, which rose to the upper floor. On the right, a narrower walkway led deeper into the house.

He caught the faintest echo of conversation, the distant sound of footsteps on wooden floorboards. He walked past the staircase, the voices becoming clearer. The ceiling lowered where the staircase above turned at the mid-landing. He bent his head, and stumbled down a couple of steps he failed to see in the dim light, beyond which the hallway ended at a door.

He pushed through, and entered the kitchen.

WPC Jenny Carlton sat at a kitchen table large enough to accommodate a party of ten, talking to a straggle-haired woman – presumably Andrea Davis – who sat with her back to Gilchrist, hands clasped to a tea mug. They both wore forensic coveralls.

The kitchen was redolent of coffee and burned toast, the air thick with the warmth of a homely Scottish welcome. A cast-iron range cooker nestled in an arched alcove that could have been constructed in the nineteenth century. A German shepherd lay on the floor in the cooker's heat, and gave Gilchrist an uninterested sniff before nestling its head on to its paws and closing its eyes. Through the window, the dark grey line of the boundary wall edged the property at the end of an overgrown lawn. A search team on hands and knees were working their way through the uncut grass in an almost perfect line.

WPC Carlton caught Gilchrist's eye, and rose to her feet.

'No need to stand,' he said, as he walked across the floor. At the hearth, he paused and scratched the dog behind its ears, estimating its age to be greater than ten – getting on in dog years.

'What's its name?' he asked the woman.

'Chivas,' Davis said.

'As in Regal?'

'Yes.'

'Sorry,' he said, and turned away from Chivas. 'I have a soft spot with animals.'

'You have a dog?' Davis asked.

He was about to say he used to, when his children were young, but stopped himself in time. Instead, he shook his head. 'Only an injured cat at the moment that turns up looking for food from

22

time to time.' He held out his warrant card. 'DCI Andy Gilchrist, St Andrews CID.'

She nodded. 'Andrea Davis.'

Gilchrist took the chair next to WPC Carlton and faced Davis. 'Do you mind if I call you Andrea?'

'If you like.'

He gave a short smile, then assured her that he would use all resources available to him in the search for her missing daughter, that it was crucial he learned as much as he could about events leading up to and after she noticed her disappearance.

'Your daughter's name,' he then said. 'Katie, is it?'

She nodded.

'Short for Katherine?'

'Katarina.' Although the name had been announced with authority, her voice sounded brittle, wounded. But Katarina intrigued him. Not your usual Scottish name, although it had been shortened to one.

'Any middle names?'

She shook her head.

'Just Katarina Davis?'

He thought it odd how, at the mention of the surname, she crossed her arms over her chest, as if chilled from a rush of cold air. 'It's an unusual name,' he said. 'Katarina. Sounds East European, even Russian.' He threw in that comment, just to gauge a reaction.

But Andrea said nothing, and gave an almost unnoticeable shake of her head.

'I'm sure you've been through this before,' he said, and waited until her gaze settled on his. 'But I'd like you to tell me what happened.'

CHAPTER 4

'I woke up just after six,' Andrea said.

'Why?' Gilchrist asked.

'Light sleeper.'

'Nothing woke you, I mean.'

'No. Most mornings I'm awake early.'

Gilchrist let his silence work for him.

'I didn't get out of bed, though,' she went on. 'Just read for a bit.'

'The newspaper?'

'Biography of Dickens. Been meaning to read it for ages.'

'So when did you get up?'

'Six thirty-eight.'

'Exactly?'

She nodded. 'I looked at the clock. That's why I knew the exact time.'

Gilchrist cocked his head at the sound of footsteps from the hallway. The others heard them, too. Together they turned as Jessie entered.

'Not interrupting anything, am I?'

Gilchrist said to Andrea, 'Do you mind if DS Janes joins us?'

'Would it make any difference if I did?'

Rather than answer, he nodded for Jessie to take a seat, but she chose to stand at the end of the table. He turned back to Andrea. 'So you got out of bed at exactly six thirty-eight,' he said, bringing Jessie up to speed. 'Did something make you look at the clock?'

He thought it odd the way her fingers tightened around her mug, how she took a quick sip of tea, then set the mug down. 'It was the silence,' she said. 'It felt different.'

'*Felt* different?'

'Nothing tactile in the correct definition of the word, rather that the silence was not as silent as it usually is, if you get my meaning.' Then she frowned. 'You're staring at me.'

'I don't mean to. Sorry,' he said, and continued to focus on her eyes.

She cleared her throat, looked down at her hands. 'I could hear birdsong,' she said. 'I can't normally hear that from my bedroom. And my bedroom felt colder, too. So I got up, and before doing so, I looked at the time.'

'Go on,' Gilchrist encouraged.

'I put on my dressing gown and walked along the hallway to Katie's room.'

'Were you wearing slippers?'

'Yes. Why?'

'You didn't say you put on slippers. Do you sleep with your door open?'

'Partly. Why?'

'You didn't say you opened the door.'

Andrea looked at Gilchrist, as if seeing him for the first time. 'Does it matter if I opened the door wider, or put on my slippers?'

She took another sip, fingers shivering with a tremor that threatened to bring tears to her eyes.

'It's important that you tell me everything,' he said. 'No matter how small. It'll give us a clearer picture.' He waited until she replaced her mug. 'Take your time.'

She took a deep breath, then exhaled. 'I reached Katie's bedroom door. It was open. It always is. And I just knew she was gone. Even before I looked inside, I knew she was gone.'

'How did you know?'

'It was cold. The window was open.'

'From the hallway, could you see the window was open?'

'No. Not there. I felt it. The coldness. And when I saw her cot empty, I realised the window was open.' She pressed her hands to her face, gagged a gasp.

Gilchrist waited several beats before saying, 'Did you notice anything else?'

She looked at him, puzzled. 'Like what?'

'Anything missing?'

She shook her head. 'Her blankets. He must have wrapped her up in her blankets.'

Gilchrist noted the reference to *he*, but it was the natural assumption – strength to climb over the boundary wall, break into the bedroom, remove the child, make off with her in his arms, carry her across a field, if he had to.

Instead, he said, 'Anything else missing? Toys? Dolls? That sort of thing?'

She shook her head as if lost for a moment, then livened. 'Yes. Her woollen Chivas. She always slept with it. Her bed's empty, so it's gone, too.'

He frowned. 'Her woollen Chivas?'

'It's a knitted toy dog. The same colour as Chivas.'

Gilchrist glanced at movement to the side, as Chivas raised his head at the repeated mention of his name, then returned to his slumber.

'My mother bought it for Katie.'

'Can you describe it?' he said. 'We can make a point of searching for it. Maybe it dropped from the bedclothes as they crossed the lawn, or climbed the wall. It could help us track the kidnapper's movements. Even help us ID Katie, if she still has it.'

'I think I have another one. Not the same colour, but the same style. Do you want me to get it now?'

'Later,' he said. 'So where was the real-life Chivas when this was going on?'

'Asleep.'

'Wouldn't Chivas have barked if he'd heard anything?'

'Chivas suffers from canine narcolepsy. He spends most of his time sleeping.'

Gilchrist felt his gaze drawn to Chivas by the range cooker. Head on paws, eyes closed, which he supposed gave new meaning to the phrase *dog tired*. He turned back to Andrea. 'When you realised Katie wasn't in her cot, what did you do?'

'I called the police and reported her missing.'

'You called on your mobile?'

'Yes.'

'Did you have it with you when you left your room and walked to Katie's in your slippers?'

'No. I keep it on my bedside table.'

'So you went back for it?'

'Yes.'

Gilchrist nodded to Jessie, who walked around the end of the table to face Andrea.

'Your 999 call to the Force Control Centre at Glenrothes was logged in at 07.07 this morning,' she said, 'and a priority alert was put out on all channels at 07.14.'

Andrea looked at Gilchrist, then Jessie, then back to Gilchrist. 'I don't understand.'

'Neither do we,' Jessie said.

Gilchrist returned Andrea's puzzled expression. 'Six thirty-eight,' he said to her.

'I . . . maybe I was mistaken.'

'You sounded so certain.'

'I . . . ' She shook her head. 'I can't explain it.'

Gilchrist tried another angle. 'Was anyone with you last night?'

'No.'

'Did you speak to anyone on the phone last night?'

'My mother called.'

'Anyone else?'

'No one.'

'We'll be checking your phone records—'

'Why?' she said. 'Don't you believe me?'

'We need to satisfy ourselves about the discrepancy in your story versus the time of your calls. We need to have a clear under-standing of what—'

'*Story?*' she snapped. 'Is that what you think this is? Some sordid little *story* that you can all have a laugh at back at the police station?' She rose to her feet. 'My daughter's been kidnapped and taken to God knows where. I don't even know if she's come to any harm, and you're talking to me as if I'm making up some kind of *story*.' Her lips whitened, then she shouted, '*Get out.*'

Gilchrist nodded to Jessie, then stood. 'WPC Carlton will stay with you—'

'I don't want anyone to stay with me. I just want Katie back. I want her back. Can't you understand?'

Gilchrist squeezed Carlton's shoulder. 'Call, if you need me.' Then he and Jessie walked from the kitchen, leaving Andrea sobbing opposite Carlton, shoulders heaving, and strangely, or so Gilchrist thought, not a tear in sight.

Outside, he puffed away a shiver. 'First thoughts?'

'She's not right in the head, is what I'm thinking. What the hell was that all about?'

'Do you believe her?'

'How long would it take to walk from her bedroom to Katie's and back, then call in a report? Best guess, three minutes max.'

'So we're looking at 06.40 until 07.07,' he said. 'Giving her the benefit of every doubt, plus or minus a minute or two either way, we're missing, what, twenty minutes?'

'Want me to take her to task on that?'

Gilchrist shook his head. 'She's hiding something. She was emphatic about the time, but it doesn't mean she's involved in Katie's disappearance, or not devastated as her mother. Let's give her the benefit of that doubt.' He looked off to the horizon. The skies had cleared, the morning greyness replaced by a blue sky that shuffled clouds as thin as cards. He caught the shimmer of the North Sea, a scattering of broken glass on a grey field.

Despite the cold, it could be a good day after all.

'So what did she do in these missing twenty minutes?' Jessie asked.

'If I was a betting man, I'd say she was on the phone. So check her phone records.'

'Maybe she had a lover staying over,' Jessie said. 'Giving her a morning shag—'

'So why check the time?'

'To see how long he lasted?' Jessie let out a guffaw, then said, 'I've just shot down my own argument. We're looking for twenty minutes, not twenty seconds.'

'But he'd need to get dressed and leave, which would take time.'

Jessie scowled. 'Are you winding me up?'

Gilchrist unzipped his coveralls. 'Let's go and see Jackie.'

He waited until Jessie started up her Fiat, before he went looking for Tosh.

He found him at the side of the barn, on his mobile, staring out across the fields.

Tosh turned at the sound of approaching footsteps, and slapped his mobile shut with a snarl when he recognised Gilchrist.

'I'm the SIO on this investigation,' Gilchrist said. 'Normally, I'd ask the Incident Officer to remain as a valued member of my team, but I don't believe you're up to it. So you're being kicked out of it.'

Tosh grunted a smirk.

'I want all statements and files obtained under your watch on my desk by midday.'

'Still playing the big-shot, I see.' Tosh's tight eyes danced for a few seconds, then he sidestepped Gilchrist and tried to push past him.

But Gilchrist grabbed him by the shoulder, only to have Tosh swipe at his hand, turn, and step in close enough for him to smell the man's bacon breath.

'Touch me once more, you smarmy bastard, and I'll fucking have you.'

'My desk,' Gilchrist said. 'Midday. Then you're out of it.'

'You know your problem, Gilchrist?' Tosh's eyes flared with an unhealthy wildness. 'You fancy yourself. You think shit doesn't stick to your shoes. But you're a loose cannon. You're reckless. If it wasn't for you, Stan the man would still be around.'

Gilchrist hit him, a straight-fingered jab to the solar plexus, which had Tosh gawping for breath like a landed fish, face turning a deeper shade as the ability to breathe failed him. A quick glance left and right confirmed that no one had seen the blow. He gave Tosh a friendly pat on the back, and waited for that first merciful intake of air to fill his lungs.

'Something catch in your throat?'

Tosh flailed his arms and broke free. 'Fuck you, Gilchrist.' His pinpoint eyes blazed. A vein pulsed at his temple, and his neck threatened to burst his shirt collar. 'I'm your worst fucking night-mare. You'd better believe it. I'll get you, I fucking promise. But you won't know when it's coming, or where. Just that it will be fucking coming. And it'll be lights out. Period.'

'Finished?'

Tosh stepped back, and tried a smile, but some part of his brain failed to compute as ordered, and he jerked a grimace instead. 'Sleep tight in that tidy little Fisherman's Cottage of yours, Gilchrist. And remember what I told you. Night-night. And lights out.'

'Midday,' Gilchrist said, and turned away.

From behind, he heard Tosh's forced laughter, the guttural coughing up of phlegm as he spat out his anger. He tried to downplay the incident in his mind, as if it was not worth the worry. But he'd crossed Tosh before, years earlier, only to be kicked unconscious by a pair of thugs a week later while walking

31

home from the pub. No one was found, no one was charged, and the incident faded into history.

But Gilchrist had known his beating had been instigated by Tosh.

You crossed Tosh, you took your chance.

He cursed under his breath and walked to his car, the ghost of Tosh's threat sweeping after him like an ice-cold backdraught that chilled the length of his spine.

CHAPTER 5

By the time Gilchrist drove through the pend and parked at the back of the North Street Office, he had organised a search of Andrea Davis's bank accounts, standing orders, direct debits, credit and debit cards, to help him understand why she could afford to live in a mansion – albeit a dilapidated one – alone with her daughter and a dog-tired Chivas. Maybe she had money of her own; a trust fund perhaps – good enough reason to initiate a ransom demand – but he needed that confirmed. If she thought she could brush him off with some fudged excuse about twenty missing minutes, she was sorely mistaken.

Once in his office, he accessed his computer and checked his messages – nothing urgent or relevant to the current case – and was about to head to Jackie's office, when his mobile rang – ID Becky.

'The weather's forecast to pick up later today,' she said, without introduction, 'so I thought you might like to unpack my new barbecue and set it up for me. And I've found a new recipe for a Caribbean marinade, which I'm eager to try out on you. But I suppose I should first ask if you're free this evening.'

'Good morning to you, too, Becky.'

She chuckled. 'Polite to a fault, Andy. Your most endearing and irritating trait.'

Their relationship was coming up for four months old and, despite her being pregnant, he felt as if he still didn't know her. They needed to spend more time together, but not that evening. 'Just been hit with a new case,' he said.

'Hopefully not the kidnapped girl.'

'Afraid so.'

'It's on all the news channels. The granddaughter of that vile ex-politician Dougal Davis. God, I hate the man and all he stands for. And so full of himself. You should hear him talk. He's already made a statement to the kidnappers—'

'Excuse me?'

'BBC Scotland. About fifteen minutes ago—'

'Let me get back to you.'

He hung up, and strode to Jackie's office – Jackie Canning, first-class researcher, who suffered from cerebral palsy and scurried around on crutches with surprising agility, but had a stutter so bad she had almost given up speaking.

Jessie was standing next to her, staring at her monitor.

'Log on to BBC Scotland,' he said to Jackie, 'and pull up a replay of Dougal Davis's speech.'

Jackie worked the mouse and keyboard like the expert she was. She opened her mouth to ask a question, but her stutter stumped her every time.

'It was on about fifteen minutes ago,' he told her.

Jackie's rust-coloured mop of hair bobbed as if sprung. 'Twe . . . twe . . . ' she tried.

'That's it,' he said, and almost knocked her crutches to the floor in his eagerness to see the monitor. He moved them out of the way, stood them in the corner. 'Turn up the volume.'

Jackie obliged, and the presenter's voice cut in.

' . . . over to Edinburgh, where ex-MSP Dougal Davis is set to make an announcement to the press.'

Gilchrist leaned closer as the scene shifted, and the camera zoomed in on two men standing on the steps to some office. He recognised Davis from when he'd been a regular on the news, spouting off political wisdom on matters from the need to remove Trident from the Clyde, to the state of Scotland's prison service. He thought Davis had aged. A florid face with jowls that seemed to sag over his shirt collar suggested too many business lunches. The man at his side, a manicured solicitor somewhere in his early forties, was speaking into the mic.

After thirty seconds of legalese, Gilchrist said, 'Fast-forward to Davis talking.'

Jackie obliged, overshot it, and backed up to Davis pressing closer to the mic.

'I will say this once, and once only.' His voice boomed. His eyes livened. 'Whoever you are and wherever you may be, if any harm befalls my granddaughter, Katie . . . ' He paused for effect, his wild gaze boiling the air, TV camera zooming in until his face filled the screen. ' . . . the world will not be big enough for you to hide in. I say to you, return my granddaughter unharmed today, and you will not be prosecuted. You have my word on that.'

The camera zoomed in until only Davis's eyes and the bridge of his nose filled the screen. He held his hard-as-steel stare at the camera, eyes displaying a mix of defiance and patriarchal outrage. Here was a man who would hound you to the far corners of the earth if you crossed him, and God help you if he ever found you.

Gilchrist pushed himself upright, stunned by what he had just heard. 'The man's a lunatic,' he said. 'And he's interfering with my investigation.'

'Don't you think it's interesting that he said return Katie to *me*?'

'The mighty Dougal Davis? Bugger that. Get on to the Beeb, instruct them to pull that recording. No ifs, ands or buts. Get it pulled. Then find out if he's been talking to anyone from the Office. And get me a number for that solicitor of his.'

With Jessie gone, Gilchrist instructed Jackie to find out Davis's personal and business worth, and likewise with Andrea Davis's mother. He'd received no ransom demand, but that might yet come. You could never be sure. A call from Chief Superintendent Greaves, with a demand to come to his office, cut his tasks short.

'Just email me what you find,' Gilchrist said to Jackie; by the time he left her office, her fingers were back to tapping the keyboard as fast as a woodpecker.

Gilchrist knuckled Greaves's door, and entered on command.

It never failed to amaze him how free of clutter Greaves's office appeared. Three grey filing cabinets stood against the back wall. Two chairs faced a wooden desk on which sat a phone and a three-high filing tray, stuffed with papers. A laptop and printer stood on a table to the side, as if never used. It seemed as if all Greaves had to do was walk from the office one day and not return, and no one would know he'd ever existed.

'Just got a call from the Chief,' Greaves said. 'He's spoken with the elder Mrs Davis and given his personal assurance that we would find her granddaughter for her—'

'Chief Constable McVicar knows the missing child's grandmother?'

'They went to school together.'

'So he must know Dougal Davis, too, sir.'

Greaves face darkened. 'I believe they're no longer on speaking terms.'

Gilchrist almost nodded. The recently promoted Archie McVicar was too long in the tooth to be associated with someone as despised as Dougal Davis. The very instant then-MSP Davis's abusive history came to light, big Archie would have distanced himself from the man with the expertise of a disappearing illusionist. But it made you wonder how much he knew about Davis's marital abuse.

'Anything else I need to know?' Gilchrist asked.

Greaves gave a tight grin. 'How do I say this?' he said, and searched the ceiling for a long moment before levelling his gaze at Gilchrist. 'The Chief Constable's made it clear that in the event of even the slightest fuck-up, pardon my French, heads will roll.'

Silent, Gilchrist returned a hard stare of his own.

'If I were you, I would tread with extreme caution. Do I make myself clear?'

'You do indeed, sir.'

Greaves gave a dead smile. 'That'll be all.'

Gilchrist turned and walked to the door, expecting to hear some parting comment. But the silence that trailed him warned him that the disappearance of Katie Davis might be more than personal to Chief Constable McVicar.

Back in his office, he found a Post-it stuck to his computer monitor with the details of Dougal Davis's solicitor printed on it. One minute later, he had the connection.

'Hughes Copestake Solicitors,' the receptionist said.

Gilchrist gave his name and title, and asked for Simon Copestake.

37

'One moment, please.'

Andrea Bocelli's 'Canto Della Terra' was coming to an end for the second time in its perpetual loop when the receptionist came back with, 'I'll put you through now.'

The line clicked, followed by a sharp, 'Simon Copestake.'

Gilchrist went straight in with, 'You represent the Davis family—'

'Before I can disclose any details of my firm's representation, for security reasons you need to give me a number I can call you back on, or else we can meet in person.'

Gilchrist rattled off the phone number of the North Street Office, and said, 'Get your secretary to check it out and call me back straight away.'

The connection died.

Gilchrist replaced the handset, and noted the time on his computer monitor. It took a further eleven minutes before Copestake called.

'You must be a busy man,' Gilchrist said to him.

'How can I help you, DCI Gilchrist?'

'Firstly, by not wasting any more of my time. Secondly, by advising your client, Mr Dougal Davis, that his personal appeal on BBC Scotland this morning was unauthorised and contra-vened the 2005 Scottish Crime Recording Standard—'

'As Mr Davis's solicitor—'

' . . . and that a police spokesman will be following up later today with a statement to the media confirming that any and all offences in the matter of the missing child, Katarina Davis, will indeed be reported to the Procurator Fiscal, contrary to your client's misguided statement, and that charges will follow as appropriate—'

'I have to assure you that—'

'Thirdly, that if your client's statement turns out to be detrimental in any way to my investigation, he may find himself charged with obstructing the course of justice—'

'I really don't think that—'

'And fourthly, that I am the Senior Investigating Officer on this case, and any and all contact with the media with respect to this case *must* and *will* go through this Office, to be approved and vetted by members of my team, or by me personally, before being released to the media. Do you understand?'

Silence.

'Mr Copestake, do you understand?'

The line died.

Gilchrist replaced the handset, then logged on to his computer. He noted the postal address for Hughes Copestake Solicitors, then accessed the firm's contact email, drafted an email for the attention of Mr Simon P. Copestake LLB, confirming the content of their phone conversation, and advising that a formal letter on Fife Constabulary letterhead would follow.

He then printed out a copy and marked up the sections he wanted to include in a formal letter, and walked back to Jackie's room.

She was concentrating so hard on her monitor that she almost jumped when he handed it to her. 'Put this into a letter for my signature,' he said. 'And have you anything on Andrea Davis's mother yet?'

She removed a batch of papers from her print-tray, riffled through them, then handed him several sheets. He noted the current address in Perth, including a Google Maps printout, then went looking for Jessie.

CHAPTER 6

He found her in Interview Room 1, along with DS Ted Baxter.

Bell sat opposite, thumbing the cuticles on his nails, as if trying to work out whether or not to cut them, and by how much. Baxter had never been a smiler – thinning red hair and a high forehead over eyes too close together would put anyone's optimism to the test – but one look told Gilchrist that the interview was going nowhere.

Gilchrist called Jessie out of the room. 'Anything?' he asked.

'Other than what we saw on his laptop, we've nothing. He walked to the Golf Hotel last night, had three pints by himself, then went home alone. He's signed on the dole, but says he doesn't need the work or the money. We're checking it out, and I've arranged for door-to-doors. But nothing back from the Computer Crime Unit yet. Unless they can identify that wee girl being . . . the child on his laptop as Katie, then we've got sweet eff-all to link him to her disappearance.'

Gilchrist grimaced. The only reason they'd tackled Bell was because he'd moved into the area. Not exactly compelling proof. 'Charge him with possession of indecent images of children under

Section 52(a),' he said. 'Then release him on the undertaking to attend court at a date to be later advised. Anything we find in the intervening period, we can add to his charges. I'll meet you outside.'

'You sound in a hurry.'

'We're driving to Perth.'

In the car park at the back of the Office, he phoned his son, Jack.

After ten rings, Jack answered with a groggy, 'Yeah?'

Well, it was still this side of midday, which could be considered an early rise for his boy – boy being the operative word. Although twenty-four, Jack coursed through life like a perpetual student. Responsibility could be an alien concept. But the past few months had seen his artist son's impecunious lifestyle evaporate due to the sale of some of his paintings, with several having sold for five figures – although Jack had failed to say which end of the five-figure table they had gone for.

'You free during the week?' Gilchrist asked him.

'Free?'

'As in, you don't have any appointments or meetings?'

Jack coughed a chuckle, and Gilchrist knew – he just knew, from the phlegmy hack that barked down the line – that his son was back on drugs. 'When was the last time I had a meeting, Andy? I mean . . . ' Another cough, less raspy, but the seed was planted. 'Meetings are for people who try to justify their own sense of importance by organising others to come and listen to what they have to say, when all they're—'

'So I take it that's a No.'

'Capital N, capital O, double underlined. No meetings.'

'So you'll be free to have dinner with me this week. How does Friday sound? I'll book a table for three at the Doll's House for six

41

o'clock, so we can get the early evening menu. But unless something breaks on this latest case, I can't stay long—'

'Table for three? Who's coming?'

'You and Maureen.'

A pause, then, 'So what's the occasion?'

'Why does there have to be an occasion? Can't I take my children out for a meal once in a while? And it's on me. My treat.'

'You're not getting married, are you?'

Gilchrist laughed, although the idea had crossed his mind. Even though Becky was going through with the birth, every molecule of his being warned him that she intended to raise her child on her own. 'No, I'm not getting married,' he said. But he was going to be a father, which was why he wanted to meet Jack and Maureen, and tell them face to face. 'And why does everything with you have to have a reason?'

'Because it's been years since we've all been out together.'

Gilchrist caught his breath. Hadn't they had drinks together last month, well . . . two months ago, maybe three? And what about New Year? Or Christmas? As his memory came up blank, he realised Jack was right, that despite repeated promises to spend more time with his children now they were back in St Andrews, he had failed to keep them.

'Well, isn't that good enough reason for us to get together?' he said, but his words sounded false, as if any attempt at being a fatherly figure was doomed from the outset.

'Just Maureen and me?'

He thought Jack could be hinting at bringing along one of his girlfriends, so he said, 'Preferably,' and was saved by Jessie crossing the car park, gathering her scarf to ward off an icy wind that gusted through the pend. 'Listen, Jack. Got to go. Catch you Friday.' He killed the call before Jack could object.

The door burst open to, 'Bloody hell. Where's spring when you need it?'

He waited until Jessie clicked on her seat belt, then slid into gear and eased away.

'I tell you, the weather in Scotland would drive you to drink,' Jessie said. 'As if we need an excuse. So what's on in Perth?'

'Vera Davis. Andrea's mother.'

'So she's still Mrs Davis? Not remarried?'

'Unless she has, but chosen to keep the name.'

'After being married to that plonker?' She shook her head. 'Some women, I tell you.'

Gilchrist turned left on to North Street, and depressed the accelerator.

'Here's what I've got,' Jessie said, opening a folder on her knee, and reading from a printout. 'No calls were made or received by Andrea Davis's landline or mobile phone this morning, until her 999 call to FCC at 07.07. So, if she wasn't getting a good-morning shag, what was she doing for these twenty minutes?'

A fresh thought struck Gilchrist, and he groaned, 'If her bedside clock was slow by twenty minutes, that would explain it.'

'Already checked it. It's bang on.'

'Not just a pretty face.' He accelerated past the Old Course Hotel, and left the town limits hitting seventy.

When they neared Perth, Gilchrist tapped the centre console. 'Directions are in there.'

Jessie unfolded Jackie's printed map, taking a few minutes to work out where they were. Then she said, 'Take the next left on

43

to South Street and cross the Tay,' and called out further directions in good time, guiding him without flaw to a detached stone house off Glasgow Road, large enough to convert to four flats.

A Bentley Convertible with a private registration of two letters and one number told Gilchrist that Mrs Vera Davis had more money than she knew how to spend – one more reason for a kidnapping ransom?

He pulled on to the paved driveway, and parked behind the Bentley. A white-painted garage, which looked as if it had been built on the property as an afterthought, sat off to the side, separate from the house, its door open wide enough to show the polished paintwork of a Range Rover, the image of *concours d'élégance* spoiled by mud-splattered wheel-flaps.

'Looks like they're in,' Jessie said.

Gilchrist strode to the front door, its porch shining with wood that could have been treated with marine varnish. A lawn with stripes you could set a straightedge against spilled down a shallow incline to a stone wall on which sat a hedge trimmed to perfection.

At the side of a pair of outer doors, a brass doorbell looked polished smooth.

Gilchrist pressed it, and a melodic chime echoed from within.

'Should we take our shoes off?' Jessie said to him.

'Why are you whispering?'

Jessie cleared her throat and nodded to the garden. 'That looks like a weed.'

'Thank God for small mercies.'

Beyond the glass-panelled inner door, a silver-haired man approached. He clicked the handle and opened the door.

Both Gilchrist and Jessie held up their warrant cards. 'We're looking for Mrs Vera Davis,' Gilchrist said.

The man nodded, held out his hand to Gilchrist. 'Sandy Rutherford. How do you do?' The grip was dry and firm. 'Is this about Katie?' he asked.

'Can we come in?'

'Of course, yes, sorry, I'm forgetting my manners. Such a dreadful state of affairs. Don't know which side is up or down. Been in a fuddle all morning. Vera's devastated, poor girl. Follow me.' And with that he turned and strode along the hallway, leaving Jessie and Gilchrist to close the door and follow.

The house smelled of polish and flowers. Vases sparkled. Woodwork glistened. The carpet felt as thick and soft as Egyptian bath towels. They passed a staircase with brass rods that shone like gold. A wooden banister gleamed all the way to the upper level. Through a lounge with furniture that looked as if it had never been sat upon, and into a conservatory at the rear of the structure.

A blonde-haired woman looked up at them as they entered.

At first glance Gilchrist put her in her forties, an older version of Andrea Davis, with sharp but handsome features softened by a lilac cashmere twin-set. Black silk trousers hid long legs tipped with faux leopard-skin slippers. The middle-aged image was spoiled by a creased neck that verged on chicken wattle. Plastic surgery could do only so much.

She did not stand when they entered the conservatory, instead stared at them with a frown, as if irritated by the violation of her private space. So much for grandmaternal grief.

'Have a seat,' Rutherford offered.

'I'm sure they'd rather stand,' Mrs Davis cut in. 'They won't be staying long.'

'We can arrange for you to attend our North Street Office in St Andrews later today, if that's what you'd prefer,' Gilchrist said to her.

45

'That won't be necessary,' she replied.

'I hope not,' Jessie added.

'And what do you mean by that, young lady?'

'Detective Sergeant Janes,' Jessie advised her.

Gilchrist could swear that the air around the two women just bristled with electricity looking for a place to short. But the harsh echo of CS Greaves's voice reminded him that Chief Constable McVicar and Mrs Davis went back a long way.

'If you could answer a few questions,' Gilchrist said, 'it could help us have a better understanding of what might have happened. I'm sure we won't keep you long.'

'I'm sure of that, too,' she replied.

'Tea? Coffee?' Rutherford said, just to keep the irritation level high.

'We're fine, thank you.' Gilchrist returned his attention to Mrs Davis. 'We're sorry to hear about Katie's disappearance, but I can assure you that we'll use every resource available to us in the search for her—'

'I wouldn't expect anything less.'

'You spoke to your daughter, Andrea, on the phone last night—'

'There's nothing wrong with that.'

Gilchrist pushed beyond the snap in her tone, and said, 'How did she sound?'

'She sounded fine. Just said she was tired.' She snorted. 'Tired doing nothing all day long, if you ask me. I told her just to take a pill and go to bed.'

'What kind of pill?'

'Sleeping pill, of course. What other pill would you expect her to take?'

'And did she take a sleeping pill and go to bed?'

'How would I know whether or not she did, for goodness' sake?'

'Well, did she say she would take one then go to bed?'

'Why? What difference does it make?'

'If she took a sleeping pill, it might explain why she never heard anyone break into her house and remove her daughter.'

Jessie nudged in with, 'And I'd like to ask her why she never mentioned anything about sleeping pills when we spoke to her this morning.'

'What exactly are you implying by that remark, young lady?'

'Detective Sergeant—'

'So we'll put that down as a No,' Gilchrist said.

'What down as a No?'

'That you don't know whether or not Andrea took a sleeping pill as you suggested, before she went to bed.'

'Mmhh.'

'When was the last time you saw Katie?' Gilchrist said.

'A month ago. No. Three weeks last Wednesday. It was my birthday. Sandy and I drove down for the day.'

'To see Andrea?'

'And Katie.'

'Of course,' Gilchrist said. 'And how did she seem?'

'How did who seem? Katie or Andrea?'

'Andrea,' Gilchrist said, becoming wary of the speed of her mind and tongue.

'Barely gave us the time of day, but Katie was wonderful.'

Even then, her face failed to break into a smile, as if she were saying one thing and thinking another. 'And why would Andrea

47

barely give you the time of day?' Gilchrist asked, and noted her gaze flicker at Rutherford.

'She's never approved of my relationship with Sandy.'

'Why not?' Jessie again.

'That's none of your bloody business,' she snapped.

Gilchrist thought it odd the way her gaze darted left and right, as if she was wary of showing some hidden inner emotion. 'Would it be fair to say that Andrea is unhappy that you and her father divorced?' he tried.

Her gaze settled on something on the floor. 'That might explain it. But who knows?'

He tried to pull his questioning back on track with, 'Can you think of any reason why anyone would remove Katie from her home?'

'Isn't that your job?' Her eyes were back on his, dancing with anger.

'We don't have all the answers,' Gilchrist said. 'Not yet. But it always helps if we know of any arguments, threats, anything of that nature; or if Andrea fell out with anyone, owed money to anyone – anything at all.'

She shook her head. 'No.'

Well, that was a quick response that seemed to cover all events with negativity. He turned to Rutherford. 'How about you, Sandy? Can you think of any reason why someone might take Katie away from her mother?'

Rutherford's forehead creased, his lips twisted, as if he'd been asked to calculate the square root of the nineteenth prime number. Then his face cleared, and he shook his head, and said, 'Sorry.' He might be physically fit, but he was bugger-all good at quick thinking.

Gilchrist studied Rutherford for a few more seconds before turning to face Mrs Davis again. 'How about money?' he asked her.

She frowned. 'What about money?'

'Could someone have kidnapped Katie and be holding her for a ransom?'

'Shouldn't you be answering that question? Have you received any demands?'

'Not yet,' Jessie said, which received another fierce look.

Again, Gilchrist diverted the hissy-fit with, 'Does Andrea have any money worries that you're aware of?'

'She shouldn't have. Her father spoils her. Her biological father, that is.'

Another glance at Rutherford, who lowered his head as if in shame, although it was not clear to Gilchrist what shame he felt. At not being a biological father to Andrea? Or not spoiling her with money despite living in obvious wealth?

'Do you keep in contact with Andrea's father?' he asked Mrs Davis.

'Good Lord, no. The man's a liability. And I have Sandy now.'

She almost smiled, which had Sandy raising his eyes from the floor in response.

Gilchrist continued with his questions, pushing here, prodding there, but learning not much more other than the fact that neither of them knew who had fathered Katie.

'Probably from a sperm bank,' was the first comment Rutherford freely offered.

Mrs Davis glared at him, and he shrunk back into his cardigan shell.

'Why Katarina?' Gilchrist asked. 'Why not Catriona, or Katherine?'

Rutherford shrugged in silence.

'What's wrong with Katarina?' Mrs Davis asked.

'Anyone in the immediate family with that name?'

'No. But with the names mothers give their children now, we should be happy she's not named after some tropical fruit or God knows what.'

Gilchrist caught Jessie's eyes, and nodded to her, but she shook her head.

'Looks like we've finished for the time being,' he said, and slid a business card on to a corner table. 'Give me a call if you think of anything that might help us.' Rutherford pulled himself to his feet, and Gilchrist said, 'We'll see ourselves out.'

But Rutherford followed them to the front door, even walked them to his car, as if to make sure they touched nothing on the way.

Gilchrist beeped his remote fob and was about to slide in behind the steering wheel, when he nodded to the Bentley. 'Must be nice to drive. Especially with the top down.'

Rutherford surprised him by saying, 'Wouldn't know. That's Vera's. I'm not allowed behind the wheel.'

Jessie said, 'Possessive, is she?'

Rutherford cracked a smile, gave a nervous glance over his shoulder. 'You don't know the half of it. I think that's what finished her and Dougal in the end—'

'Nothing to do with his being a wife-abuser?' snapped Jessie.

'Vera can hold her own. Rest assured. Just like Rachel.'

'Who's Rachel?'

Rutherford's face creased, as if regretting having let a name slip. 'Andrea's sister,' he said.

Gilchrist jerked a look at him. 'No one mentioned she had a sister.'

'That's because she's banned from the family *sine die*, for hitting her father, Dougal.'

'Any other siblings?' Gilchrist asked.

'No.'

'You have a contact number for Rachel?'

Rutherford shook his head.

'You know where she works?'

A pause, then, 'Lloyd's.'

'Lloyd's where?' Gilchrist asked, intrigued and irritated in equal measure by the man's apparent reluctance to impart information.

'London,' Rutherford said.

'Is she still Rachel Davis?' Jessie asked. 'Not married, is she?'

Rutherford said, 'Rachel Novo. She's up there. A director of something. Just ask.'

And with that, he retraced his steps, head down, as if anticipating being chastised for having given away one too many family secrets.

CHAPTER 7

On the return drive to St Andrews, Jessie confirmed that a Rachel Novo worked with Lloyd's Insurance Group in their London office, as Director of Investments Strategy, and had just returned from a four-day business trip to Beijing, China. She had the conversation on speaker in Gilchrist's car, and said, 'Can you put me through to her?'

'She's in a meeting.'

'I'm sure she is, but would you mind interrupting her?'

'I'm not allowed to do that.'

'Tell her it's urgent, and that she needs to call one of these numbers before midday.' She rattled off her own and Gilchrist's number, then ended the call. 'What the hell is it with these people? They're always in meetings.'

Gilchrist smiled. 'Meetings are for people who justify their own sense of importance by organising others to come and listen to what they have to say. Did you know that?'

'No.'

'The world according to Jack.'

'Jack who?'

'My son.'

'Oh, that Jack. How is he?'

'Fine, I think.' He tried to shift the topic by saying, 'How's Robert?'

'Eh?'

'How's Robert?'

'What's that?'

Gilchrist glanced at her, then chuckled at her joke. Her teenage son, Robert, was stone deaf, and Jessie was a loving and devoted mother who fiercely protected him from her own dysfunctional and criminal family. Robert wanted to be a stand-up comedian once he had a cochlear implant, but in the meantime worked on his comedic skills by writing jokes and humorous stories.

'Is he still writing?' he asked.

'Can't stop him.'

'What's he working on at the moment?'

'Some short story about two postmen. One's got a wooden leg, and wants to take up ice-skating, and the other's got one arm, and fancies himself as a snooker player.' She shook her head and chuckled. 'I read a bit of it last night, and it cracked me up. And he's written a couple of jokes about a deaf salesman.'

'Let's have them, then.'

'No, I'll spoil them for him. He's superstitious that way.'

Gilchrist knew not to push. He called the Office and got through to Baxter. 'Did you release Bell from custody?' he asked.

'We did, sir.'

'Did he sign the undertaking to appear in court?'

'He did, sir, yes, and a DI MacIntosh handed in an envelope marked . . . ' A cough, then, 'For your attention, sir.'

That would be Tosh's reports and statements, handed in before midday. Maybe Tosh was reforming. On the other hand, maybe the Pope was a Protestant. 'Anything back from the Computer Crime Unit yet?'

'No, sir.'

'Get on to them right now,' he snapped. 'We need something that connects Bell to the kidnapping. Otherwise we've got diddly.' He killed the call. 'Jesus,' he hissed, 'we can send messages around the world in nanoseconds, but it takes days to download a hard drive.'

'That's because there'll be passwords and stuff,' Jessie said.

'Is that it?' he said. 'The extent of your IT terminology? Stuff?'

'You're getting right nippy in your old age. Fancy something to eat? I'm starving.'

'*Hungry.*'

'Eh?'

'You're *hungry*. People dying in famines are starving,' he said as his phone rang. He made the connection with, 'Gilchrist.'

'I've just been given an urgent message to call back on one of two numbers.'

The woman's voice was English, not upper-class Scottish as he'd expected, which threw him for a second. But he recovered, and said, 'Rachel Novo?'

'This is she.'

He thanked her for calling back, introduced himself, then Jessie, adding, 'I have you on speaker-phone, and we would—'

'What's wrong?' Novo said. 'Has something happened?'

Gilchrist glanced at Jessie. 'Have you not heard from anyone in your family?'

'My family and I no longer speak.'

'So you haven't heard that your niece was removed from your sister Andrea's house in St Andrews this morning?'

54

'No. I haven't.'

Gilchrist waited, but that seemed to be the end of it. If he thought the matriarch of the family was ice-grannie, he was speaking with fifty-below-Novo.

'Is this why you asked me to call back?' she said.

Jessie gasped. 'Before you hang up from utter boredom,' she said, 'we'd like to ask you a few questions.'

'Like what?'

'Like why your niece's disappearance is of no concern to you.'

'I told you, I no longer communicate with my family.'

'So you never knew you were an aunt?'

'Of course I knew. That's a bloody stupid question.'

'I thought you no longer communicated with your family.'

'I was informed by a family friend, whose name eludes me at the moment.'

'When you remember who it was, give me a call, will you?'

Gilchrist took over with, 'Although you've not been in touch with your family for a while, would you have any ideas at all as to who might have taken Katie?'

'My father,' she said. 'Dougal Davis. He's made many enemies over the years, and is a ruthless man who tolerates nothing and no one. I wouldn't put it past him. I suggest you focus your investigation on him.'

'I thought he'd also distanced himself from his family,' Jessie chipped in.

'It's not about love with that man,' Novo said. 'It's about possession. His family is something *he* possesses. And anyone who dares to take one of his possessions from him will face his wrath head on.'

'Sounds like a lunatic.' Jessie again.

55

'He's been called much worse, I can assure you.'

The logic of Dougal Davis having kidnapped his own grand-daughter, then put out a TV appeal for her safe return, did not compute with Gilchrist. Novo was likely just putting his name forward for personal revenge. So he said, 'I've one question. Unrelated to Katie's disappearance. Why did you fall out with your family?'

'I wanted to preserve my sanity,' she said. 'Being suffocated by an abusive psycho for a father is detrimental to your mental health. So I hurt him where it hurts the most. I removed one of his possessions from his life. Me.'

Gilchrist caught the vitriol in her tone. 'You're saying he abused you?'

'He tried to. Once.'

When she offered nothing more, he said, 'What happened?'

'I woke him in the middle of the night with a kitchen knife to his throat, and told him if he ever tried that again I would slit his throat when he was asleep.'

Well, that would take the heat out of most men's loins, he supposed.

'When did this happen?' he asked.

'When I was twelve.'

Gilchrist frowned at the speaker. 'Where was your mother when this was going on?'

'She denied all knowledge,' she said. 'But she knew. She always knew.'

Gilchrist accelerated through the mini-roundabout and powered up North Street. He thanked Novo for her time, and asked her to call again if she thought of anything new.

When he ended the call, Jessie said, 'What d'you make of that?'

'I think we need to talk to this Dougal Davis, see if he can shed light on who hates him so much that they might kidnap his grand-daughter. And do some digging into his personal life. He's been divorced a couple of times. Find out why.'

'I used to think my family was fucked up,' Jessie said, 'but we're learners compared to this lot.'

Gilchrist could only nod, his mind dredging up memories of his own familial failings. Too many hours spent on the case of the week, not enough time with his children, or his wife for that matter, his family forced to take a back seat while he concentrated on his career. And look where that had got him. Stuck at DCI with no hope of promotion – until he retired, or was forced to resign.

He reached the Office and found a parking spot near the back wall.

Jessie got out and stretched. 'Seeing as how I'm so *hungry*, I'm going to spoil myself and have fish and chips in The Central. Want me to order a pint for you?'

'Let me pick up some notes first, and I'll meet you there.'

He stuck his head into Jackie's office, but her desk was empty and her crutches were gone, so he assumed she'd popped out for lunch.

He found Tosh's envelope lying on the middle of his desk. He picked it up and read the handwritten address in big black letters – *FAO: DCI Randy Gilchrist* – and tutted. The envelope felt too light. He ripped it open, and removed a CD with a Post-it stuck to it with a series of numbers that started with a zero – a mobile phone number.

He checked the depths of the envelope, but no notes, only the CD.

KILKENNY COUNTY LIBRARY

He sat at his computer and fired it up, trying to salve his feelings with the rationale that Tosh had been the Incident Officer for no more than several hours. Even if he'd handed over all he had, there could not have been much.

He opened the CD drive, placed the CD into it, then frowned as he realised it was a video recording. When the video came up, he clicked the Play arrow, turned up the volume, and maximised the screen.

The time bar along the bottom of the screen told him the video was 3:35 long, and he eyed the monitor as the sounds of breathing and rattling came from the speakers.

Then an image appeared, out-of-focus browns and greys that shifted to dull greens. Voices mumbled in the background, like the busy hubbub from an evening at the bar – people hustling, coughing; feet crunching, scratching; engines revving, rattling. The camera jerked and shifted, the horizon rocking for a moment, disappearing, then returning to steady itself into the shape of a stone house that zoomed in, then out again, as if the cameraman was trying to familiarise himself with the controls. He caught his breath as the camera swung along the boundary wall and focused on the nearest car, a dark green Land Rover, then shifted to two people standing at the side of one of the barns.

'You bastard,' he hissed, as the camera zoomed in to catch him and Tosh breathing hard, their breaths gushing in the morning chill. Gilchrist paused the recording, replayed it, stopping and starting in jerking motions, and came to see that at the exact moment he hit Tosh, the camera's focus was on the barn door, although he and Tosh were still in the frame.

He clicked the video forward frame by frame, until he and Tosh were in sharp focus. And there he stood, back half-angled to the camera, clapping Tosh on the shoulder, asking if something had caught in his throat. As if to satisfy his own curiosity, the camera zoomed closer until the back of his head and Tosh's face filled the screen.

The hatred in Tosh's face was impossible to ignore, whereas his own body language – tense, he knew – looked relaxed to an onlooker. He felt relief flood through him as he played the recording all the way to the end without seeing evidence of violence, then ran through it one more time.

This time he saw it, an out-of-focus movement as his arm shot forward. Tosh's body jerked, not much, but enough to have any half-decent solicitor argue the case. With a bit of work, any competent IT expert could clean it up and present it as evidence.

Gilchrist let out his breath in a defeated gush.

If Tosh charged him with assault, in the face of what could prove to be compelling evidence, Gilchrist could do little to deny it. But for someone as twisted as Tosh, there was always more to it than just straightforward revenge.

There was only one way to find out.

He eyed the number on the Post-it, then dialled it.

The call was answered with, 'You took your time calling.'

Gilchrist could not fail to catch the glee in Tosh's voice, and he focused on keeping his tone level. 'You were instructed to hand over all notes and statements regarding Katie Davis's disappearance—'

'Oh, listen to this. Instructed to hand over. I've already done that.'

'All I've got is an out-of-focus CD of you and me having a friendly chat.'

Tosh forced a laugh. 'Friendly my arse.' He cleared his throat, and grunted in what sounded like him gobbing to the side. 'You always were a smarmy bastard, Gilchrist. Well this time I've got you good and proper, yeah? I'm going to take you down—'

'And I'll be reporting you for deliberately withholding evidence in a—'

'I told you I'd handed everything over, but you're not listening, see?'

Gilchrist's thoughts stumbled. Had he missed something?

'I gave it all to Mhairi with the tidy tits, and told her to deliver them to you in person, before midday, like you said.' Another laugh. 'But I tell you what I'm going to do, yeah? I'm going to contact Professional Standards and let them know that some DCIs use physical violence against members of their own team.'

'I'm sure they'll be interested, too,' Gilchrist said, 'to learn that some DCIs receive death threats.'

Tosh forced another laugh. 'You're as slippery as they come, Gilchrist, and you'll try to find some way to deny it's even you on that CD. But remember what I told you earlier. Night-night. Sleep tight.'

The line died.

Gilchrist replaced the handset, then stared out the window.

The skies had turned a sullen grey, with brooding clouds low enough to touch. He didn't think it would rain, but in Scotland no one took bets on the weather. It troubled him that one detective would have the audacity to threaten another. Tosh was the kind of person who should never have been in the constabulary; someone who abused power, strode through life bullying others. And it struck Gilchrist that he had only one option.

The answer was simple.

He would have to end Tosh's career to save his own.

CHAPTER 8

Gilchrist's call to Mhairi confirmed that Tosh had indeed handed all his files over.

'Sir, he said you were coming back within the hour to interview Andrea Davis again, and that I was to hold them until you collected them. I'm sorry, sir. I should've phoned when you never turned up.'

'That's okay, Mhairi. Did DI MacIntosh, did he . . . was he rude to you in any way?'

'Not really, sir. Just that he's sort of sleazy, and gives me the creeps.'

Gilchrist gritted his teeth. Tosh would have stripped her naked in his mind's eye and nailed her to the floor in his dreams. But fantasising left no proof. He needed hard facts if he was going to have Tosh fired. Maybe an exploratory call to Strathclyde Police HQ was on the cards. If anyone knew what Tosh was up to, DCI Peter 'Dainty' Small would.

He thanked Mhairi, and told her he would collect the files from her after lunch.

Next, he called Dick, a retired policeman who made extra cash building websites, on the face of it, but in reality did anything and everything related to computers and IT, legally or illegally, a fact which Gilchrist kept to himself. For a fee, you could buy a copy of the US President's or the Queen's phone records, with everything in between, if you wanted to.

'Got a video recording I'd like you to look at,' Gilchrist said. 'Maybe you could advise me what to do about it, once you've checked it out.'

He delivered the CD to Dick's house, then set off to meet Jessie.

The Central Bar thrummed. Students, visitors, and some faces he recognised – caddies already back from a morning's work on the links, trying to spend their day's earnings in one sitting – had every seat in the place taken, it seemed. He found Jessie in a corner booth, and managed to squeeze in beside her.

'You look fit to be tied,' she said.

'Didn't know it showed.'

She took a forkful of chips, then shoved the plate his way. 'Here,' she said. 'Help me out. I can feel the fat doubling up with every mouthful.' She stabbed at a piece of white fish meat, and mouthed it.

Gilchrist fingered a chip, slipped it into his mouth, but whatever appetite he'd had was drowned in his thoughts of Tosh. He watched Jessie nibble her food for another couple of minutes, then said, 'I know an infallible way to lose weight.'

She looked at him, a loaded fork poised at her lips. 'What's it called?'

'Work.' He pushed to his feet. 'Let's go.'

Jessie caught up with him as he was easing the BMW through the pend. He held his foot on the brake as she clambered into the passenger seat.

'Bloody hell,' she said. 'What's got you so fired up?'

Tosh, he wanted to say. But he depressed the pedal and powered up North Street.

If anything, the throng at the entrance to Grange Mansion had thickened.

Journalists, photographers, and hangers-on stood like the spectators they were, eyeing the driveway, as if willing the mother of the missing child to venture out and have a chat with them. Gilchrist eased his car towards the entrance. One local hack – a scruffy little tubby man called Bertie McKinnon – recognised him and broke free from the scrum to jog alongside his BMW, hand slapping the roof.

Jessie lowered her window. 'What's your problem?'

'Have you found Katie yet?' McKinnon shouted to her.

'We're working on it, what do you think?'

'I think you're fucking it up like you always do.'

'Why don't you print that, then?'

'Oh I will, hen, don't you fucking worry about that.'

Gilchrist drove forward as a uniform – a young face he couldn't put a name to – lifted the police tape and waved him through. He eased along the gravel track, the car rocking and bucking through the potholes, and warned Jessie about the perils of talking to reporters, particularly wankers like Bertie McKinnon.

'Is that the first time you've come across Bertie?' he asked.

'And the last, I hope.'

'Be careful around him. He's a piece of shit who writes what he likes. He hates the police for some reason that no one understands.'

'Seems to be par for the course up here,' she said.

He nosed the BMW into the branches of an overgrown shrub, and parked.

They met Mhairi in the Mobile Incident Room, a 7.5-tonne vehicle parked next to the barn, which buzzed with the chatter of a busy office. Whiteboards sported black lines that ran like a genealogical chart, listing names, places, dates, times, phone numbers with occupations ranging from pizza delivery man to plumber. He scanned the names to confirm that neither Vera Davis nor Sandy Rutherford were listed, then added both to the whiteboard.

He compared Tosh's records against the notes on the whiteboards, handwritten notes of phone interviews – not surprisingly, only four in total; not quite as diligent a detective as Tosh would have you believe. Then he called the team together, and they spent the next hour exchanging notes, messages, expanding what little information they had. They did confirm that the bulk of Andrea Davis's income came from a personal trust fund valued at well over a million pounds.

'So she's a bloody millionaire?' Jessie gasped.

'Bloody millionai*ress*,' someone corrected, which brought a scowl to Jessie's mouth, and an under-the-breath, '*Fuck sake.*'

'And we still haven't received any ransom note?' Gilchrist asked, eyeing the group.

Their silence gave him his answer, which had him dreading the alternative – Katie had been taken for sex. Not good. Not good at all. He spent the next ten minutes assigning everyone to specific tasks, then said to Jessie, 'Follow me.'

They found Andrea Davis in the main lounge, sitting on a threadbare sofa with her feet tucked up beneath her, reading a book – Gilchrist caught Dickens on the cover. Chivas lay asleep on the floor, and could have been dead for all the attention he gave them.

Andrea looked up from her book, but neither stood nor spoke, and it struck Gilchrist that here was a woman as cold and emotionally distant as her mother and sister.

'We'd like to ask you a few more questions,' Gilchrist said.

'Have you found my daughter yet?'

'No.'

'Shouldn't you be out there searching for her, instead of in here pestering me?'

'We spoke to Rachel,' he said.

The name seemed to confuse her, and she tilted her head, as if catching the telltale sound of someone creeping up behind her. Gilchrist found his gaze following her line of sight as it settled on the bookshelves by the fireplace. Then she blinked, and faced him.

'How is she?' she asked him.

Chivas almost stirred – an ear twitched, a paw moved, then sleep stilled him.

'Why didn't you mention you had a sister?'

'Why should I? I haven't seen her in years.'

'When, exactly?'

'What difference does it make?'

'We're trying to build a picture of your and Katie's lives, see who might—'

'Rachel isn't in my life, and has never been in Katie's.' She slapped her book shut, placed it on the cushion by her arm. 'For God's sake, where are you people from? Why waste time talking to someone in London when Katie's gone missing from her home in Scotland?'

'How do you know Rachel lives in London?' Jessie asked.

'Please tell me you're not serious.'

'Oh, we're serious all right. You haven't been in touch with your sister for years. So how do you know where she lives?'

Gilchrist caught another flicker towards the bookshelf.

'I'm sure I heard it from my mother,' she said.

'We've spoken to your mother, too,' Gilchrist said.

'Oh, you *have* been busy little bees.' She pushed herself from the sofa and walked to the window, more to hide a flush that coloured her face, Gilchrist thought, than to check out the weather. 'So how is the bitch?'

'Concerned over Katie's disappearance.'

She turned to face them both, and something akin to anger tightened the set in her jaw. 'As concerned as you are?'

Gilchrist let a couple of beats pass. 'When did you last talk to your father?'

'What?'

'He's already been on the news, making an unauthorised personal appeal.'

'Well, he would, wouldn't he?'

'Why would he?'

'Other than the fact that Katie's his granddaughter, you mean?'

'Precisely.'

She glared at him for a long moment, then shook her head as she turned from the window. 'I don't believe this,' she said. 'I'll show you out,' and strode to the door, her hand sweeping something off the bookshelf, slipping it into her pocket.

Gilchrist nodded for Jessie to follow, and received a glare in response.

At the end of the hall, Andrea twisted the handle, and pulled. A cold draught chilled the hallway. She stood to the side, as if sheltering from the wind.

Gilchrist paused on the doorstep. 'You never answered my question.'

'Which one?'

'All of them,' Jessie snapped.

Gilchrist stepped in with, 'About when you last talked to your father.'

'I can't remember the last time I talked to him,' she said, and made a display of shivering off the cold. 'Why don't you check it on my phone records?'

'We will.' Jessie walked past her, and strode towards the barn.

Gilchrist gave Andrea a quick smile. 'We're doing everything we can to find Katie. But we can't leave any stone unturned. If that means touching on subject matter that might be too close for comfort, then I apologise for that.'

She returned a look as cold as slate.

'I may want to speak to you later,' he said, and crossed the threshold.

The door slammed behind him like a kick to the spine. But the memory of a nervous glance at the bookshelf, and a hand brushing something into her pocket, pulled up the ghost of another possibility.

CHAPTER 9

The first thing Gilchrist did was have one of his team go through Andrea Davis's phone records again, and check every number she'd called in the past couple of months. They were missing something, he was sure of it. For a mother whose child had been kidnapped, her behaviour was not normal. So he emailed Jackie as well, instructing her to check Andrea's phone records also, see if anything jumped out at her. Were these numbers new? How often were they called? Who did she phone the most? How and when did she pay her bills?

Leave nothing out. Check everything and anything.

Jessie wanted to bring Andrea to the Office for some hard questioning, but Gilchrist reminded her that she was the mother of a missing child, and it would be more considerate, even prudent, to put all thoughts of arresting Andrea to the side.

'At least for the time being,' he said, which seemed to appease Jessie.

Gilchrist and his team spent the remainder of the day tracking down, and talking to, everyone who had been at Grange Mansion within the past three months. But everyone to a person seemed to have a genuine and innocent reason for their visit.

By the end of the afternoon, he was no further forward.

He called the Computer Crime Unit, but they'd not been able to identify the wee girl on Bell's laptop. They had, however, uncovered a hidden file containing initials and phone numbers, which looked like a list of individuals to whom Bell had been supplying drugs. It pleased him that his impromptu visit to Bell's home that morning might have uncovered a link to a drug supply chain, but it was still only a tiny splash in a big ocean – jail every-one on that list, and another list would pop up the following week. They could be pulling weeds from a spring garden for all the good they were doing.

Although not yet connected to Katie's disappearance, Gilchrist instructed Baxter to detain Bell on suspicion of supplying Class-A drugs. Bell could spend the next several days behind bars while he waited for his court appearance.

But a phone call from Greaves, late afternoon, reminded Gilchrist that Chief Constable McVicar was keeping a close and personal eye on progress – or lack thereof – and demanding a press conference in time for the six o'clock news. 'We have to seek the public's assistance,' Greaves told him, no doubt regurgitating McVicar's exact words.

That evening in the Mobile Incident Room, Gilchrist watched himself on TV, standing at the end of the gravel drive, Grange Mansion silhouetted in the background, an image of Katie Davis staring over his shoulder in one corner of the screen. He thought he looked tired and defeated – leather jacket slack at the shoulders, hair greying, lips unsmiling. By his side, an alert DS Jessie Janes looked positively youthful.

Old footage of ex-MSP Dougal Davis was included in the news bulletin, with viewers reminded of his forced retirement from Scottish Parliament. A futile attempt to interview his solicitor resulted in a hand being shoved at the camera by a grim-lipped Simon Copestake, who bustled past a group of cameramen to slide into the back of a chauffeured limousine.

'Charming bastard,' someone said to the TV screen.

At the end of the televised conference, a phone number ran like a banner across the screen, which viewers were encouraged to call with complete anonymity if they had heard or seen anything remotely suspicious. Gilchrist ordered his team to work on for another hour, to follow up on any calls that might come in. But by eight o'clock nine calls had been received, two of which were identified as crank. Uniforms sent to check others had come back with no leads. To crown it all, Baxter reported that Bell had slipped surveillance and was not answering his door, and that all attempts to reach him had failed.

'Check up with the Computer Crime Unit for the latest,' Gilchrist said. 'Then find out where the hell Bell is. And when you find him, bring him in.'

By 8.20 p.m., Gilchrist had set up shifts through the night, and was ready to call it a day.

'Right,' he said to no one in particular. 'I'm off. If anything comes up, you know where to reach me.'

Jessie walked with him to their cars. She had parked her Fiat by the barn. Through the trees, open fields fell away to an invisible sea. Blushing clouds streaked a darkening horizon.

'Red sky at night, and all that,' Jessie said.

'I always check it out in the morning,' Gilchrist said. 'I'm going

70

to have a pint in the Golf Hotel, see if I can find out a bit more about Sammie Bell.'

'You don't still think he's involved in Katie's disappearance, do you?'

Gilchrist clenched his jaw. Right up to his drug-addled brain, he wanted to say. But if Bell was involved, Gilchrist and the rest of his team were missing the connection. He played it safe with, 'I'd like to interview him right now. But first we need to find him.'

Jessie beeped her remote, and the Fiat's lights flashed. 'I'd better head back home,' she said. 'Robert'll be wondering if he's still got a mum.' She opened her car door, and slipped inside.

By the time Gilchrist reached his BMW, Jessie had driven off. He slid in behind the wheel. Before firing the ignition, he called Cooper, only to be shunted into voicemail.

He left a message saying he was heading home, and if she wanted to call he would love to have a chat with her. 'If I don't hear from you, I'll call before I hit the hay, if it's not too late. Love you,' he added, then killed the connection.

At the entrance gate, he tried to keep his face deadpan as he drove through flashing cameras. Something thudded the roof of his car, and he forced himself to take no notice, just drive on. The last thing Greaves needed was one of his SIOs involved in a need-less fracas with local journalists. He turned on to Grange Road, depressed the accelerator and powered from the scene.

In Crail, he parked off Rose Wynd and locked his car for the night.

On the short walk to the Golf Hotel, he phoned Maureen. 'Hi, princess,' he said. 'How's your day been?'

'Better than yours by the look of you on TV. You need a haircut.'

He chuckled. 'Been a busy day,' he said. 'But I talked to Jack earlier, and we're going to meet in the Doll's House on Friday. Are you free?'

'Let me check with my secretary and get back to you.' A pause, then, 'Of course I'm free, Dad. What do you think I get up to at the weekends?'

He sent another chuckle down the line, just to let her know he found her response amusing. 'Thought you might be studying,' he said.

'Nope. All done. So, what's the occasion?'

'Friday. And the end of the week from hell.'

'Do you mind if I bring a friend along?'

He almost stopped. He could not remember the last time Maureen had gone out with anyone. In the past few years, it seemed as if she had lost all ability to develop relationships with her peers, male or female. 'Anyone I know?' he tried.

'Tom. He's a friend. A student at the university. We met in the library.'

'And does Tom have a second name?'

'Sorry. Yeah. Tom Wright. He's a local. Lives out by the Botanic Gardens. His dad's a lecturer. English, in case you're interested.'

Interested that Tom was a student? Or that his father was a lecturer? Again, he could never be sure, so he trod with care. 'I'm thinking of booking a table for the three of us for six-thirty, so maybe we could—'

'So you're saying No, is what you're—'

'No, Mo, I was going to suggest we meet Tom after—'

'What's wrong with inviting Tom to join us? I'll pay for him.'

Gilchrist eyed the length of High Street, and struggled to keep his tone level. 'I'm not asking you to pay for Tom, Mo. You know that. I'm more than happy to invite him along. But I've something I need to tell you and Jack in person, and I'd prefer if it was just the three of us.'

The line hummed with silence, long enough for him to think she had hung up. 'Please don't tell me you're going to get married, Dad. Not to that bitch.'

He caught his breath, stunned by the venom in her voice. 'Why say that?'

'She's so not good for you, Dad. You just don't see it.'

'Who are we talking about?'

'God, I hate it when you speak to me like that. Don't treat me like a child—'

'Then don't act like one.' He regretted his comment the instant it snapped from his mouth, and he held his breath, waiting for the click of a lost connection.

Instead, she said, 'I just . . . it's . . . I'm sorry, Dad, but it's so unfair.'

He caught the hint of a tremor in her voice, felt his heart stutter with an aching pain at the knowledge of what she was saying. Eighteen months had passed since her mother's death, but Mo was still hurting. He could see it in her eyes, hear it in her voice, whenever Gail was mentioned, or her memory threatened. He wished he could fill the void her death had left, but he'd barely been around for his children, and he could not shift the irrational thought that this was payback from Gail; that he deserved parenthood not to be easy.

'I'll reserve a table for four,' he said. 'Bring Tom along.'

'No, Dad, I didn't mean—'

'It's okay, Mo. Tom means a lot to you.' He listened to her silence, thought he caught a sniffle. 'And you don't have to worry. I'm not getting married.'

73

'So why didn't you just say that?'

'You didn't give me a chance. Remember?' He waited for her response. But the line had already died.

He closed his mobile.

His relationship with Maureen had never been smooth. Even as a child, she seemed to be able to work her way around him with a petted lip, or tearful wail. Of his two children, Mo was the one most like Gail – which had its downsides, he had to confess. But on the upside, her spirited nature could be taken as a sign that she was at last on the mend.

With that thought he smiled, slipped his mobile into his pocket, and entered the hotel's public bar.

CHAPTER 10

Although he'd missed lunch, Gilchrist hadn't felt hungry until the warm smell of food and the noisy clatter of a busy bar had his taste buds watering. With only five minutes until the kitchen closed for the evening, he ordered a Belhaven and eyed the menu. He thought of having only a starter, then surprised himself by ordering the home-made steak pie, with baked beans instead of veg.

By habit, 9 p.m. was too late for him to eat, but by the time his food came up, he was already on his second pint, the beer slipping down a treat. The gravy tasted meaty and salty, and when the waitress removed his empty plate, he found himself ordering one more pint – last one for the road, he promised. He chose to drink standing at the bar, so he could better engage the staff in casual conversation.

'What can you tell me about Sammie Bell?' he asked the barman, a white-haired man who looked to be in his seventies, with the friendly face and talkative charm of a Scotsman always looking to earn a wee dram for a tip.

'You need to do better than that, son.'

'Six foot? Shaved head? Two diamond studs pierced in his right ear?'

'You could be describing half the folks in Scotland nowadays, son. And don't even think about throwing in a tattoo. Don't know what they're thinking of. It used to be anchors and love hearts on your arm, and if you kept your shirt sleeves rolled up, that was your lot.'

Gilchrist sipped his beer, then said, 'He was in here last night and had a few beers. Fancies himself as a bit of a mathematician, working out equations and puzzles.'

The barman scratched the top of his head with his pinkie. 'Anybody working out equations here, they'd be calculating the odds on the horses.' He shook his head. 'Try asking Danny. He might know.'

At the mention of his name, a young barman pulling an Eighty Shilling looked over at Gilchrist, 'With you in a sec, pal,' and levered the pint until it filled to the brim with a creamy body. Then he let the pint settle, rubbed his hands on his jeans, and came over to Gilchrist with an upward nod with his chin.

'Bald head,' Gilchrist said. 'Pierced right ear, six foot tall, Samuel Bell?'

'That'd be mad Sammie,' Danny said. 'Hasn't been in here tonight. If you're trying to reach him, you might ask these guys in the corner. They were with him the other night.'

Gilchrist glanced at a table by the window, its surface glistening as wet as a puddle. He caught the eye of one of three youths who looked like they were spilling more beer than they were drinking. Then back to Danny. 'Last night?' he asked.

'No. Night afore, I think.'

'Why *mad* Sammie?'

Danny shrugged. 'Rhymes with bad?'

'Trouble, is he?'

'We don't have trouble in this bar. We don't stand for it.'

Gilchrist took another sip, duly chastised, then glanced at the corner table.

Three half-finished pints stood abandoned by empty seats.

He pushed his Belhaven away and strode from the bar.

Outside, a stream of cars eased along High Street, headlights sweeping deserted pavements. Ahead, the road ran out of town. To his right, Marketgate lay quiet. Back inside and heading to the Gents, down the stairs and through the door to a toilet with an opened window that drew in a cold breeze. No one there, and no way out. Back upstairs, a tight turn up and into the upper lounge, where the fire escape door at the far end stood open to a darkened car park. He reached the door, peered into the evening gloom, and fancied he heard the distant patter of feet running down Tolbooth Wynd – no chance of catching them.

He caught Danny at the bar again. 'These three who just left. You know them?'

Danny shook his head. 'They're not regulars. Just seen them with mad Sammie a few times. That's all.'

Gilchrist thanked him, finished his pint, then set off for the walk home.

Outside, he turned up his collar, wishing he'd brought his scarf. Summer solstice might be only two months away, but it was still cold enough to have teeth chattering. Although his cottage was no more than a few minutes' walk from the Golf Hotel, he chose to take the long way home, so he walked along the front of the hotel, then down Tolbooth Wynd.

The beginning of the Wynd was bounded on either side by stone walls that threatened to hem him in, then opened up on the right to the hotel car park. Ahead, the road seemed to shift with dull shadows cast by the light from two lampposts. Dimmer light spilled from adjacent buildings. The Wynd lay clear all the way to its expansive junction with Nethergate.

Whatever running feet he might have heard were long gone.

He slipped out his mobile, phoned Cooper.

She picked up on the third ring with a throaty, 'Hello.'

He thought she sounded tired. 'I'm sorry, have I woken you up?'

'No, I was dozing.'

'I'm on my way home. Did you catch the news on TV?'

'No.'

He tried to engage her by saying, 'So how was your day?'

'Bad.'

From her monosyllabic response and tone of voice he thought that Mr Cooper had perhaps returned to the marital home and was within earshot. 'Would you like me to call back?' he said. 'Or tomorrow?'

'I've just returned from the hospital, Andy.'

He slowed down. 'What's . . .?'

'I was trying to move your damn barbecue, and I tripped.'

Ice chilled his blood. He stopped, pressed his mobile to his ear. 'Are you all right?'

'I've had a miscarriage.'

He felt his breath leave him in a rush as he lifted his head to the sky, and watched the moon spin as he turned at the sound of running footsteps—

A blow to the side of his head sent him reeling.

He couldn't hold on to his mobile as he hit the ground and heard it clatter as a foot to the stomach booted his breath from him. Another kick scuffed the side of his face – proper contact would have loosened teeth. On his knees, struggling to his feet, while three wraithlike shadows rounded the corner and disappeared into Nethergate.

If he'd been twenty years younger, he might have had a chance of catching them. But even if he did, three against one was not good odds, cop or not.

He coughed, cleared his throat, picked up his mobile.

But the connection was dead.

He tried dialling Cooper's number again, but his mobile was shot. He cursed himself for taking the long road home, then gritted his teeth and settled into a steady jog.

He ran into Nethergate where it widened and branched into two separate roads.

The youths were nowhere to be seen. They could have run along either one of the branches, or more likely nipped down the side of an adjacent house to the beach. He jogged on, keeping to the centre of the road, senses alert for any shadows turning into men. But after fifty paces, all he heard was his own steady breathing and his blood pulsing in his ears.

Minutes later, he fumbled with his house key, and pushed his way inside.

In the kitchen, he lifted his phone from the handset and called Becky again, only to get the disconnected tone. He thought of trying her landline, but her imminent divorce from Mr Cooper had never been made clear to him, and he worried that Mr Cooper might pick up.

So he replaced the handset, resigned to calling her in the morning.

He slumped into a chair at the kitchen table.

The effects of the food and the beer were working up an exhaustion that swept over him like a wave. He was tempted just to lay his head on the table and let sleep take him. But he had a case to work on in the morning, and he forced himself to his feet. He slipped off his jacket and shoes, and managed to make it to his bedroom before falling on to the bed.

Sleep swamped him in seconds, the echo of Becky's voice reverberating through his mind in a wordless cry for help. But he could not help. He was being held down by three men who laughed and punched and spat in his face then ran off. The more he struggled, the more leaden his body became, until all he could do was let himself be pulled beneath the warm waves, little fingers clawing at his clothes, a child's voice whispering in his ears . . .

Help me . . . please . . . help me . . .

CHAPTER 11

Morning arrived to the sound of thunderclap.

Another clatter jerked Gilchrist awake.

He opened his eyes, wondered why his bedroom was so bright.

A noise like a tuneless racket thudded in the distance like some demonic echo. He pulled back the sheets, swung his feet to the floor, surprised to see he was fully clothed. He blinked at the window, confused by its brightness. Beyond, the sky shone a brilliant blue.

The thudding rattled again, coming from his hallway.

He groaned, pushed himself upright, and had to steady himself for a spinning moment with a hand slapped against the wall. He stumbled from the bedroom into the hallway, where the thudding became a sharper clatter, metal on metal, which rattled with all the consideration of a fire alarm.

He reached the door and pulled it open.

'Bloody hell,' Jessie said, 'I was just about to call for the big key.' She frowned as she eyed his crumpled shirt, ruffled hair, grazed face, then glanced past him as if expecting to see trouble at the end of the hallway. 'You all right?' she asked.

'Yeah. Late night.' He stood aside as she squeezed past him.

She entered the living room. 'So this is *chez* Gilchrist.'

He closed the door, followed her inside.

He faced her, raked his hand through his hair. 'What time's it?'

'Almost eight.'

When had he last slept past six? He worked spittle into his mouth, ran his tongue over dry lips, conscious of not having brushed his teeth, or washed his face; not to mention he was still wearing yesterday's clothes.

'You need to switch your mobile on. I can't get through.'

'It's . . . ' He shook his head, recalling falling to the ground, footsteps rushing past. He pressed his fingers to his cheek, felt the graze. 'I dropped it last night,' he said.

Jessie scanned the room. 'Don't you have a landline?'

'In the kitchen.'

'Does it work?'

'It should.'

'Don't you answer it?'

'Only when I hear it.'

She faced him then, her eyes alert, serious. 'I hate to tell you, but we've got work to do. I've been calling you for the past hour and a half. We've got a body.'

Gilchrist's chest shuddered. They must have found Katie. 'Was she—'

'It's a he. And he's a mess.'

His mind spun, his waking brain struggling to push its sleeping counterpart to the side. 'Who?' was all he could think to ask.

'Not formally ID'd yet, but I'm guessing Sammie Bell.'

It all came flooding back to him.

Baxter had not been able to find Bell. No reply at his house.

Slipped surveillance. Had Bell been dead by that time? If so, why? And who had killed him? Was his death unrelated to Katie's disappearance? Or not?

Too many questions sank a headache into the back of his eyes like a hot needle. 'Kettle's in the kitchen,' he said. 'Mine's a coffee. Strong. And give me ten minutes.'

The air hinted at the promise of a warm summer, although 'warm summer' could be an oxymoron in Scotland. Gilchrist walked down Rose Wynd, Jessie by his side. 'We'll walk,' she had told him. 'It'll sort you out.' He braved his face to the wind, relishing the brush of the sea breeze, the faint smell of kelp, the distant shriek of seagulls fighting over food. He'd brought a mug of coffee with him. It looked mud-brown, tasted bitter.

'What did you put in this?' he asked.

'You said strong, so I made it strong.'

'Did you empty the jar?'

'I left a spoonful.'

'Right.' Another sip, and he started firing questions.

'The body was found on the beach this morning,' she said. 'The call came in at 05:50. A Ms Jennie Crichton, out for her morning jog, said she almost tripped over it. She's in a bit of a state. Can't blame her.'

'You've seen it, the body?'

'No rest for the wicked.' She pressed on, as if determined to work up a sweat.

It was working. His breath rushed in his lungs, mouth dry, and he made a promise to get back into jogging now the worst of the winter was over. He went for another sip of coffee, but at that pace he was spilling more than he was drinking.

'I have to tell you, Andy, when you didn't answer your phone I was starting to think the worst. I mean Sammie Bell's murdered right on your doorstep? So I drove over, started knocking on your door. No answer. So I'm thinking you must be at the scene. But no one had heard a squeak, so I came back to batter the door down if I had to.'

'Glad you didn't have to.'

'It was a close call, let me tell you.'

'How was Bell killed?' he said, trying to shift the subject from his tardiness.

'Brutally,' she said. 'Face is . . . 'she sucked in, 'unrecognisable . . .'

'Positive ID?'

'Not yet. But I'm sure it's him all right. This way,' she said, and turned on to a grass-covered path that ran between the gable ends of two houses.

Gilchrist stopped.

Jessie had taken half a dozen steps before she turned to face him.

'Is it down here?' he said.

'About a hundred yards along the beach. Why?'

He eyed the path, then the road behind him, one of the branches of Nethergate, the memory of three running youths flickering through his mind. 'They could've run down here,' he heard his voice say.

'Who could've run down here?'

'My mobile,' he said. 'I dropped it. Three youths jumped me, then ran away.' He pointed, just to be sure of it himself. 'This way.'

'What time was this?'

'Close to eleven, or thereabouts.'

'We're putting Bell's murder at some time in the early hours. After two. Before five.'

Standing there, he took the opportunity to have another sip of coffee.

'Could you give a description of the youths?' she asked him.

'Didn't really clock any of them. But I know someone who might have.' He nodded to her mobile. 'Get the number for the Golf Hotel up the road,' he said, then set off again.

Within twenty seconds, they were walking along the beach together.

'Got it,' she said, and handed Gilchrist her mobile. 'It's ringing.'

Surprisingly, the call was answered. He asked to speak to Danny, only to be told he wouldn't be in until later in the morning. He killed the connection. 'Give Danny a call at midday,' he said, and stared off along the beach.

About forty yards in the distance, an area had been sealed off with crime-scene tape, fifteen feet or so back from the high-tide mark. An Incitent was already erected, and a group of SOCOs in white forensic coveralls huddled in conversation.

Several onlookers stood off to the side in silence.

Gilchrist felt a shudder of surprise when one of the coveralled group glanced his way – Cooper. She caught his eye, but he saw no happiness there, only a look of grim resignation. She said something, and the others glanced his way. Then she peeled her coveralls from her head, shook her mane of strawberry-blonde hair, more to loosen it than to rouse his attention.

He gave her a smile as he neared, but she ignored him and walked off in the direction of her Range Rover parked at the end of Nethergate South.

'You two not speaking?' Jessie said.

'Something like that.'

He gritted his teeth and strode towards the Incitent, conscious of others watching as he neared. He recognised the tall figure of the lead SOCO, Colin, who nodded a silent good morning to him, and said, 'Coveralls are over there.'

Gilchrist placed his coffee mug on the sand, and pulled on the coveralls. 'Thoughts on the body?' he asked, and glanced at Cooper over Colin's shoulder. She had stripped off her coveralls and had the door of her Range Rover open, about to drive away.

'Death by blunt trauma to the head.' Colin raised an eyebrow, shook his head.

'Any other injuries?' Gilchrist asked, tucking his hair in.

Colin scrubbed the back of his hand across his designer stubble. 'That's it.'

'Weapon?'

'Hammer. Lying beside the body.'

'Right. Let's have a look.'

'It's all yours.'

Gilchrist pulled back the tent flap, and stepped inside to a jaundiced silence. His first thoughts were of camping in the woods as a pre-teen with his brother, Jack. His second, that never before had he seen anyone beaten up so badly.

The body lay on its back, completely naked, spread-eagled as if its hands and feet had been pinned to the rocks. Ink-dipped arms. Red dragon and iridescent python wound around and up its legs, locked in perpetuity, as if caught in the act of trying to bite a penis that looked significantly deflated since he'd last seen it. The mess before him was Bell. If not for the tattoos, he would not have been able to identify him.

No one could.

He pressed a hand to his nose, all of a sudden caught by the smell of death, the hard metallic aftertaste of blood mixed with a guff of raw meat and . . . something else . . . battered brains. He fought back the overpowering urge to vomit, to step from the tent and breathe in clean sea air, and forced himself to study the scene of the crime.

He leaned closer, looking for injuries on Bell's legs, body, arms, but finding none. Even allowing for the layering of tattoo ink, Bell didn't appear to be bruised anywhere else. But where his head should have been, a splattered mass of blood and brains and a sprinkling of shattered teeth for rock salt lay like some Italian pie ready for the oven.

Again, he managed to choke back the bile, force himself to study the crime scene with dispassion, his eyes settling on a claw hammer lying no more than six inches from Bell's left hand. Nothing particularly interesting about the hammer, an all-in-one metal head and handle that you could buy from any B&Q, its black grip reddened with Bell's blood. Next to Bell's shoulder lay a bloodied shirt, the material thickened by being folded over, but ripped and torn and matted with gore, and Gilchrist came to understand that the shirt had been placed over Bell's face to mini-mise blood spatter from the hammering.

He eyed the rocks and sand by Bell's head. Bits of flesh and some indescribable grey stuff had been spattered there from the blows, despite the shirt. He tried to imagine the rage that must have been exhibited for someone to kill in such a fashion, but the feat was beyond him. Rather, it was easier to picture someone hammering Bell's head with complete and utter lack of compassion, happily counting out the blows – thirty-one, thirty-two, thirty-three – like Maxwell's silver hammer.

How many hammer hits would it take to batter a head like that?

Or, more to the point, he found himself asking, why would anyone have gone to the bother? With a hammerhead of approximately one square inch, how many blows would it take to flatten and crush every bone in the face? And he came to see that the act of facial obliteration must have been done for a reason.

Was the dead man not Bell, but someone else with the same tattoos? And, if so, had he worn the same studded earrings? Gilchrist got on to his knees, peered closer, resisting the urge to finger the mess in search of the two diamond studs. Would the killer have removed them before the killing? If not, they must be here. He eyed the mess, his subconscious working in the background, reminding him of Bell's hairy toes and nails in need of a cut.

He glanced at the body's toes, felt a flush of disappointment surge through him.

No doubt about it. This was Sammie Bell.

Gilchrist pushed to his feet. He'd seen enough. He stepped from the tent, avoiding eye contact with Colin, and stumbled down the beach to the water's edge.

A couple of deep lungfuls of sea air helped rid his tongue of the sensual aftertaste of gore, and a long look at the horizon diminished the mental image. He tried to clear his mind of its brutal recollections by forcing himself to think of everyday things – his cottage, his family, Maureen, Jack – but found his thoughts irritatingly being pulled back to Cooper.

A glance at the houses confirmed she had driven away.

He would call her if he'd had a mobile. Or should he wait for her to call him? But he suspected he would have to wait a long time before she would do that. He'd always regarded Cooper's coldness as self-protection from the brutalities of her job as a forensic pathologist, and from the often heartless comments of her misogynist husband, or soon to be ex-husband, Max. It had never struck Gilchrist until that moment that perhaps the only reason Cooper put up with him as a lover was because she had fallen pregnant with his child.

They say love is blind. Had he been blind to the fact that he was not the type of man she would ever consider marrying; that their relationship could never evolve beyond the most basic of attractions, sex? Had he been blind to the reality that her coldness was not to protect her from the needs of her profession, but was simply a reflection of her true feelings for him?

The echo of Maureen's voice hit him with renewed force.

Please don't tell me you're going to get married, Dad. Not to that bitch.

Had he failed to see that? Had he been truly blinded by love?

As he stripped off his coveralls, and stared out across the North Sea, the memory of Cooper's parting glance, the ease with which she'd avoided him, stung like a fresh wound. They would talk sometime soon. They would have to as a matter of professional necessity. As a registered sex offender, Bell's DNA would be in the system, so identification should be a simple matter. But it was not the question of Bell's ID that was now worming to the front of his thoughts; instead it was the method of Bell's murder, the fact that the hammer had been left next to the body, along with the bloodied shirt.

Why leave a critical piece of evidence for the police to follow?

He walked back up the beach, and found himself heading towards Jessie as his logic closed in on its conclusion. The hammer had not been left as a clue to assist in their tracking the killer. Not at all. It had been left as a signature mark.

He approached Jessie.

She frowned at him, and said, 'You look worried.'

'Phone Jackie and get her to search the PNC for anyone who's been murdered with a similar MO.'

Jessie gave a silent whistle. 'So what're you thinking?'

'That there could be some other reason for Bell to return to Crail.'

'Nothing to do with his mother passing?'

'Her passing was convenient, I'd have to agree. It gave him some place to stay. But I'm thinking that maybe Bell left London not by choice.'

Jessie turned her head to look at the Incitent. 'And they've followed him?'

'Could have,' Gilchrist said. 'We won't know until we hear back from Jackie.'

'I haven't spoken to her yet.'

'Exactly,' he said, and strode off.

CHAPTER 12

Gilchrist caught Colin's eye, and nodded with his chin – they needed to talk.

'Have you recovered any jewellery from the body?' Gilchrist asked him.

Colin grimaced, as if trying to work out the trick in the question. 'He wasn't wearing any clothes, so what you see is what you get. Not even a watch.'

'DS Janes and I spoke with Bell yesterday.' Gilchrist tapped his right ear. 'He had a pair of diamond studs in one ear.'

Colin's gaze drifted to the Incitent.

'Did you find any?'

'Not yet, sir. But we'll definitely have a closer look. Diamonds, you say?'

'Looked like diamonds.'

'If they were worth anything, maybe his killer took them.'

'Or maybe not.'

'But if they were cut glass, they could've been smashed to fuck, excuse the French,' he added, as Jessie joined them.

'Let me know what you find.' Gilchrist waited until Colin

entered the Incitent, then held out his hand to Jessie. 'In the absence of my mobile, can I borrow yours?'

She handed it to him. 'Jackie's on it.'

'Good,' he said, then called Glenrothes HQ and arranged for CCTV footage of High Street, Marketgate, Nethergate, and Crail in general, for evidence of three men suspected of being involved in, or having knowledge of, the murder of Samuel Bell. Their connection to Bell's murder was a bit of a stretch, he knew, but with a body on the beach, a request worded like that would be treated with urgency. He next assigned DS Baxter to liaise with the Anstruther Office and initiate the investigation into Bell's murder.

He thought of calling Cooper for confirmation of Bell's ID, but the memory of her lack of interest, and her apparent need to avoid him that morning, shut down all enthusiasm to hear her voice. He handed Jessie her phone. 'Call Cooper and tell her to speed up the ID. Bell's a registered sex offender, so it shouldn't take her long.'

'Tell or ask?'

He jerked a look at her. 'Ask.'

Jessie stepped to the side and stared out to sea, mobile already at her ear.

Gilchrist stuffed his hands into his pockets, feeling naked without a mobile. He could buy a new one, but just the thought of trying to figure out what make, model, whether to buy as you go, or pay monthly, had him thinking he should revert to using an airwave set. But that would be like stepping back in time. He watched Jessie out of earshot, and imagined Cooper talking in that cold tone of hers.

Then Jessie killed the call and walked over to him. 'Her Highness will do what she can,' she said.

He ignored her gibe. 'Where'd you park your car?'

'Outside the Co-op. I would've driven you here, but you looked like you needed to freshen up.'

'How do I look now?'

'Pissed off.'

'Right,' he said. 'Let's go.'

On the walk back, Gilchrist asked for her mobile again.

'You sure yours is buggered?'

'Positive.' He called the Mobile Incident Room at Grange Mansion and got through to Mhairi. 'Any updates?'

'Nothing major, sir. Except . . . ' A pause, then, 'Has no one been in touch with you this morning?'

'Only Jessie,' he said. 'What's up?'

'Liam from the Computer Crime Unit left a message, sir. His team's been working on Bell's laptop—'

'Hang on,' he said, and turned to Jessie. 'How do I put this on speaker?'

She took it from him, pressed a button, then handed it back.

'Carry on,' Gilchrist said, holding the mobile out.

'Liam says he's located hidden files on Bell's laptop, full of images you can download from just about anywhere nowadays, but none ever show any faces. So, we're going to be hard-pressed to ID that wee girl, or any of the others, sir.'

Gilchrist let his breath out. He'd been hoping for more, but in reality he'd got what he'd expected.

'And Liam thinks that the list of names and numbers they also found are people Bell was supplying drugs to.'

'Any way they're related to Katie's disappearance?'

'No, sir. He says he hasn't found any connection to that at all.'

'And this list of names? Anyone we know?'

'I couldn't tell you, sir. Liam left a message asking you to give him a call.'

Now they were getting somewhere. The list could double as a lead to someone who might know of Bell's past in London, maybe indirectly lead them to his killer. It might even include the name of the killer himself. Gilchrist felt a surge of excitement. This could break the investigation into Bell's murder wide open.

But he needed to prioritise and maintain focus on the missing child.

'If the list has nothing to do with Katie's abduction,' he said, 'I'm going to have DS Baxter talk to Liam first. In the meantime, I want you to locate Dougal Davis. Jessie and I need to talk to him. We'll be with you in about half an hour for a briefing on Katie's case, and you can tell me then.'

'Yes, sir.'

Gilchrist handed Jessie's mobile back to her. 'Come on,' he said. 'I'm hungry. Want a slice of toast?'

'Already eaten.'

'Half a slice?'

'Any strawberry jam?'

'No.'

'Good,' she said, and strode along Nethergate in a hard-paced walk that had Gilchrist struggling to keep up without breaking into a jog.

'In training?' he said to her.

'Promised Robert I'd lose a stone.'

'Why?'

'Why not?'

By the time they reached his cottage, Gilchrist's heart was racing.

'Bloody hell,' Jessie gasped. 'I'm getting fitter, but boy, it's tough.'

He opened the door, and let Jessie enter first.

'Never been in your house before,' she said, 'and now I'm making a nuisance of myself.' Without invitation, she entered the kitchen. 'Where's that mobile of yours?'

Gilchrist picked it up from the coffee table and handed it to her.

'The screen's cracked,' she said, 'and the back's loose. You tried fixing it?'

'I can do home DIY. But when it comes to mobile phones, forget it.'

But Jessie had the back off, and was too busy fiddling with it to comment.

He slipped two slices of bread into the toaster and removed a pack of cold cut meat from the fridge. For some reason, he felt livened. Maybe it was the hard walk from the beach, or the fresh sea breeze, but whatever it was, it had done him the world of good. His landline rang, and he reached over and lifted the handset.

'Hello?'

'The SIM card was disconnected,' Jessie said to him.

Gilchrist replaced the phone and gave her a tight smile.

She handed him his mobile. 'Do I get a gold star?'

'Two,' he said, 'and half a slice of toast.'

She shook her head, walked to the back lounge. 'Mind if I have a gander?'

'Be my guest,' he said, as she peered through the rear window.

'Nice little place.'

'Emphasis on little?'

'You should see mine. Robert and me stuffed into a box, more like. You're quite the gardener. Hedges trimmed. Grass cut. Where do you find the time?' she asked, then said, 'You never told me you had a cat.'

Gilchrist glanced at her. 'Is it black and scraggly looking?'

'And looks like it's been in a fight?'

'That's her. She's not mine. She turned up a week or so ago. I think she was attacked by a dog, or a fox maybe.' He looked out the window, beyond Jessie. By the open door of his shed at the far end of his narrow garden lounged a black cat, its fur clotted in scruffy tufts, its tail held low with an unusual kink that hinted of broken bones.

'Have you considered taking it to the vet?' Jessie said.

'She won't let me near her. All I can do is leave food and water out. But she's coming round. Slowly.'

'You got a name for it . . . for her?'

'Not yet. But I'm thinking of Blackie.'

'Well, I'll give you ten out of ten for originality.'

'Maureen's first pet was a cat called Blackie.'

'She's just gone back into the hut. Must have seen me eyeballing her.'

'She feels safe there. And I've laid out some blankets for her. Some food, too.'

With the cat no longer around to hold her interest, Jessie turned from the window and eyed an oil painting on the wall. 'Is that an original?'

'It is,' he said. 'Butter on your toast?'

'As long as it's light. Did Jack do this?'

'One of his girlfriends.'

'Impressive. Is she still with him?'

'No. I might have put too much milk in your tea,' he said, trying to change the topic.

'And these photographs are nice,' she said 'Eye-catching. Jack's, too?'

'Mine,' he said. 'Before digital everything took over.'

'Did you develop them yourself?'

'No. I liked taking them, not developing and printing them. I'd thought of building a darkroom, the DIY I was telling you about. But I kept putting it off. Then when digital cameras arrived, I lost interest.'

'They're striking compositions. You've got a knack. Who would ever have thought?'

'That I'm not just a pretty face?'

'Don't flatter yourself,' she said, and took a seat at the table. She sipped her tea. 'Not bad.' She replaced the mug to the table, eyed the plate as he put it down. 'Thought I was having half a slice.'

'You can cut it in two and eat one piece.'

She did just that – cut it in two – but the second piece seemed too good to pass up, so she tackled that, too. 'What's with this Dougal Davis?'

'I'd like to talk to him, see what he's got to say for himself.' His mobile came to life then, giving out a string of beeps as a number of text messages that had been suspended in the ether while his SIM card had been out of sync found their way to his message folder.

He was surprised to find three messages from Cooper, all within five minutes of each other, and just this side of midnight last night. He'd crashed out, and even if his phone had been working, he doubted he'd have had the mental wherewithal to carry on any sensible—

'I'd like to challenge him on his TV appeal,' Jessie said. 'Maybe even threaten him with interfering in a police investigation.'

Gilchrist placed his mobile to the side. 'You'd have the full rampant wrath of Simon Copestake LLB to deal with,' he said.

'Plonker.'

'Plonker he might be, but from what I gather he's got a reputation as a solicitor you don't want to come up against.'

'Eat up, and let's get on with it,' she said, and pushed her chair back. 'That list of names that Liam's uncovered,' she added. 'I'd like to hear what Baxter has to say about it sooner rather than later. It's a pity we can't ID that wee girl on the laptop.'

Gilchrist crunched into the last of his toast, swept it down with a mouthful of tea. The revolting image was likely only the first scratch at a filthy surface, and if there was one such image on Bell's laptop, there would likely be hundreds, if not thousands, more.

'Set up a meeting,' he said, 'and we'll see what Liam's got. In the meantime, I need a briefing on Katie's abduction.' He gathered their plates, placed them in the dishwasher, then removed a small jug of milk from the fridge. 'Give me a couple of minutes,' he said, 'while I top up Blackie's bowl. We'll take my car.'

Five minutes later, at the top of Rose Wynd, he beeped his remote fob.

Jessie reached for the door handle. 'Are you thinking that Dougal Davis could be the reason for the dysfunctional family?'

'He was bombed out of the Scottish government for marital abuse,' Gilchrist said. 'So if I was a betting man . . . ' He fired the ignition, eased his car forward. ' . . . I'd say the odds are on that.'

'He was brought down by his third wife,' Jessie said. 'Even though she didn't press charges. I've checked out her home

98

address. It's upmarket Aberdeen. She's never remarried, but she's doing all right for herself. You think Davis paid her off to keep her sweet?'

'Possible,' he said, and eased along High Street. As he turned on to St Andrews Road, the Golf Hotel on his right, he glanced towards Tolbooth Wynd, the memory of last night's attack still fresh in his mind. He hoped CCTV footage would help identify his attackers, and answer—

'So what do you say? You think we need to talk to her? Wife number three?'

'About what? We need to stay focused on Katie.'

Jessie stared through the window, as if snubbed, then said, 'Wife number two remarried, and lives in Glasgow. But she wants nothing to do with the man.'

Gilchrist powered up to fifty. The hard sound of the BMW's engine reverberated off the stone walls either side. 'Let's talk to Dougal Davis first. After that, we might want to talk to all of his exes and check out his story.'

'Make sure he isn't lying, you mean?' Jessie turned away and glared at the passing countryside, as if willing it to burst into flames. 'I hate bastards like that.'

CHAPTER 13

At the entrance to Grange Mansion, the scrum of reporters had thinned – yesterday's news of a missing child being trumped by today's of a battered body on a beach no more than ten miles away. But those who remained fired a barrage of questions at Gilchrist as he drove through the gateway in closed-window silence.

The white Lexus still sat at the side of the main residence. Curtains were drawn in all the windows, giving the aura of the mansion being closed for the day. Together, he and Jessie strode to the Mobile Incident Room,

The briefing brought nothing new to the case, other than the miserable fact that the Chief Constable, Archie McVicar, had made an impromptu early morning appearance and left ten minutes later, unimpressed by the investigation's progress, or lack thereof. By 10.30 a.m., Gilchrist had heard from neither Greaves nor McVicar, and every bit as worrying was the fact that his investigation was turning up more dead ends than a maze.

In an intensive effort by his team, everyone who had visited Grange Mansion in the last eight weeks had been interviewed

– surprisingly few, as it turned out. A pair of plumbers to repair a blocked kitchen drain. A number of delivery services: postal, fast food, laundry, and Co-op. A taxi driver who had delivered four tartan shawls from a kilt-maker in St Andrews – which all turned out to be genuine.

Friends seemed few and far between, with Andrea having been visited by a Mr Mark Davidson, who'd recently been laid off from the green-keeping staff at Crail Golfing Society, and who told the police that Andrea had just shouted at him one night to fuck off and never come back, for reasons he could not explain – *Fucking weirdo's what she is. I was just trying to chat her up, like, be nice to her.* One visit from Vera Davis and her husband, Sandy Rutherford, tied in with what they'd been told in Perth. But it seemed that Andrea rarely left the house, which had Jessie asking, 'Who looks after the fields?'

DS Curry looked up from his monitor. 'She rents the fields out, so I'd say it was one of the local farmers.'

'Let me repeat the question. Who looks after the fields? I want a name, and I want to know how much she gets paid for them.'

'Is that going to help us find Katie?'

Gilchrist stepped in with, 'We won't know until we get an answer. So, anything you can drum up would be helpful.'

'Yes, sir.'

Jessie glared for a long moment at the back of Curry's head, then turned to Gilchrist, and said, 'Are we about done here?'

'You got that address for Davidson?'

She tapped her mobile. 'Let's go.'

Outside, Gilchrist noted the curtains in the upper window of the mansion were open. He thought he glimpsed a woman's face through the pane, before it settled into the reflection of a passing cloud. The white Lexus was still parked at the gable end. Dog-tired Chivas was nowhere to be seen.

'You'd think she'd take the dog outside for a walk,' he said to Jessie.

'What does it do all day?'

'Eat and sleep, from the looks of things.'

'But is it house-trained, I ask myself?'

'I'm sure she must let it out to do its business,' he said.

'Hah. It'd probably fall asleep in its own shite.'

'Has anyone told you you've a way with words?'

'Talking of which,' Jessie said, 'I'm interested in hearing what shite this Davidson guy's going to cough up.'

They managed to track Mark Davidson down to a dishevelled cottage on the A917, north of Kilrenny, with an overgrown lawn that looked more like an abandoned scrapyard than a residential garden. Stripped washing machines, refrigerators, microwaves, parts of car engines, rusted wheels, all balanced in piles of ready-to-topple stacks next to sodden cartons of newspapers, magazines, books, that seemed to sprout from the grass like papier-mâché shrubbery.

Gilchrist parked in the short driveway, behind a tidy van with chrome bumpers that gleamed with polish and looked at odds with the ambient disrepair. A young man in his late twenties, who matched the description of Mark Davidson, was kneeling among the refuse, stripped to the waist despite the cold air.

He pushed himself to his feet as Gilchrist called out his name. 'That's me,' he said.

Gilchrist and Jessie showed their warrant cards, and Gilchrist realised that Davidson was in the process of trying to tidy the place up. 'You've got your work cut out for you,' he said, nodding to the mess.

'It's a toughie. Should 'ave it cleared by tomorrow night, though,' he said, and tugged his jeans up. Broad shoulders topped a lean body and pinched waist. Wide eyes that sparkled with intelligence stared from a handsome face spoiled by a flattened nose. 'So how can I help yous?'

'You know Andrea Davis?' Jessie asked.

'Are yous with the same crowd that talked to me last night?'

'Fife Constabulary, if that's who you're talking about.'

'Well, yeah, as I told them last night, I visited her a couple of times.'

'We have it down as four times in total.'

'Whatever.'

'What did you think of Chivas?' Gilchrist said, just to gauge a reaction.

'The dog?'

Gilchrist nodded.

'Could sleep for Scotland, is what I think.'

'And Katie?'

Davidson lowered his head, narrowed his eyes. Muscles rippled across his chest as he stripped off his working gloves. 'I'd nothing to do with her disappearance. I told yous lot I was working in Upper Largo. Building a garden wall. Never knew nothing about it until I seen it on the news.'

'And what about Andrea Davis?' Jessie asked.

'What about her?'

'Why'd she tell you to fuck off? Were you giving her one?'

Davidson's face grimaced in anger. 'Never touched her. I told them that. Never even shook her hand. No physical contact of any sort. None. Period. End of.'

'So what happened?'

'Fucked if I know. One minute she's smiling away, and the next she just flips and tells me to leave. I thought she was kidding at first, you know, having a joke—'

'So what had you done?' Jessie pressed.

'Nothing. That's what I'm saying.'

'Maybe it was the way you looked at her tits, the way you're looking at mine right now.'

Davidson blinked, then said, 'No way. She's a weirdo. I'm telling you.' He stabbed a finger to the side of his head. 'Loop-de-fucking-loop. Crazy as they come.'

'And where did you get your degree in psychology?' Jessie said.

'I know a nutter when I see one.'

'And so do I,' Jessie said.

Gilchrist stepped in with, 'How did you first meet her?'

'I knocked on her door and asked if she needed any work done around the place. It looked like it needed it. But she said she didn't. I thanked her, apologised for troubling her and left. When I got to my van, she shouted me back, and asked if I could come around the next day, she might have something for me. So I did.'

'And . . .?'

'And she did the same again – told me she had nothing, and asked me to come around the following week.'

'Did she invite you inside?'

'Not that time. But the following week she did.'

'Did you see Katie?'

He shook his head. 'Never even knew she had a kid. Thought she just lived by herself. She didn't look like a mother, you know

104

what I'm saying?'

'No,' Jessie said. 'Tell me.'

'She just seemed spaced out. But I didn't think she was on drugs, just acting stupid.'

'Did she come on to you?'

Davidson hesitated for a moment. 'Not really,' he said. 'Just giving me the eye. But I was having none of it.'

Jessie tutted.

Gilchrist said, 'Did you see anyone else when you were there?'

'No.'

'See anything that you thought was odd?'

'Odd?'

'Unusual,' Jessie said. 'Strange. You know, *odd*.'

He shook his head. 'I was just surprised when I heard on the news that her daughter had disappeared,' he said. 'That's what I thought was off. I never even knew she had a kid.'

'So what happened the last time you saw her?' Gilchrist asked.

'I thought I was being asked inside to fix a lock on one of her doors. I brought my toolbox along—'

'I'll bet you did.'

He looked at Jessie for a cold moment, then said, 'You know, maybe you're right . . . about the . . . the tits thing. She showed me the lock, but it seemed to be working fine. It was only after I told her that it was working okay that I noticed . . . ' He placed his hand to his chest. 'I don't think she was wearing a bra.'

Jessie burst out laughing. 'Get real.'

Davidson gritted his teeth, and a flush of sorts coloured his neck. 'You asked if I seen anything odd,' he said. 'And when I say I seen something odd, yous laugh. How about yous go and take a fuck to yoursels?'

'What's odd about not wearing a bra?' Gilchrist asked.

Davidson seemed surprised by the question. 'I didnae think she was that kind of a woman. I thought she was upper-class, yeah?'

'A lonely woman?' Jessie said. 'No man about the house? And in you come – ' she coughed – 'carrying your toolbox . . .?' A pause, then, 'So why don't you tell us what really happened?'

'Nothing happened. She told me to fuck off—'

'Exact words?'

'Yeah. That's what I keep telling yous. So I fucked off out of it.'

'And . . .?'

'And nothing. That's it. I've never went back.'

'Not even to get paid?' Jessie said.

'Paid for what? I done nothing.'

Gilchrist held out a business card. 'If you think of anything, give me a call.'

Davidson snatched the card from him, glared at Jessie, then stuffed it into the back pocket of his jeans. 'Aye, sure,' he said. 'I'll let yous know.'

Jessie stared at him for five hard seconds, then turned and strode off.

CHAPTER 14

Gilchrist reversed from the driveway, eying the lone figure of Davidson in his rear-view mirror as he accelerated away.

He waited until he hit sixty. 'You think he's lying?'

'All the way to the bottom of his toolbox,' Jessie said. 'Did you see the guy? Flexing his pecs like Mr Universe. And the way he kept looking at my tits?'

'Why, what's wrong with them?'

'Nothing's wrong with them,' she said, then chuckled when she got his joke. 'I tell you, Andy, that nose of his was probably flattened by some husband giving him a Glasgow kiss for nailing his wife.' She tutted. 'I mean, he comes round to her house on four separate occasions, then leaves without fixing a thing? Get real, for crying out loud.'

'Okay,' Gilchrist said. 'So, he's giving her one—'

'Giving her four, you mean.'

'So what does that do to help us find Katie?'

'Not a thing. But I tell you what, it makes me want to take that Andrea bitch down to the Station and cuff her to the wall until she tells us the truth.'

Gilchrist eyed the road ahead. In the five months he'd worked with Jessie, he'd come to understand that her volatility was her way of expressing herself. Although her words were spoken with anger, she rarely lost her temper. But she seemed particularly riled by Davidson. Sometimes difficult to understand, she was a solid detective with an intuitive sense second only to his own, and he thought of that now.

'So you think Andrea was having it off with toolbox Mark, then tired of him, and told him to eff off?'

Jessie snorted. 'I think we need to double-check the stories of every delivery man that visited the place, starting with the plumbers.'

'Why the plumbers?'

'Because plumbers are sexy.'

'Right.' He gripped the steering wheel. Well, there he had it. Plumbers over posties any time. He put his car phone on speaker, got through to Mhairi. 'I'd like you to go over the statements once more of everyone who's delivered, fixed, or sold anything at the mansion,' he said, and glanced at Jessie. 'Starting with the plumbers.'

'Anything I should be looking for in particular, sir?'

'The possibility that Andrea Davis was having sex with some or all of them.'

'Would you like me to question Ms Davis about—'

'Let's review the statements first,' he said, 'and if anything glares at you, bring them in again and ask them directly. And while you're at it, I want you to review all the printouts I've asked from Jackie.'

'Will do, sir.'

Gilchrist ended the call.

'Maybe we should just ask them directly first,' Jessie said.

Gilchrist said nothing. Jessie's belief that Andrea Davis was having sex was important only in that, if confirmed, then she'd been lying to them. Not unusual, he knew, but it struck him that Jessie's throwaway comment that an early morning shag was the reason for the missing twenty minutes might not be far off the mark.

'The more we look into this family,' Jessie said, 'the more we're seeing how fucked up they are. Rachel Novo threatened to kill her father at the age of twelve if he didn't stop molesting her? Yet we don't know if Andrea was molested by her father, too.'

'You're saying she's messed up because of what happened to her as a child?'

'I'm saying that this meeting with Dougal Davis could be timely. Maybe we should just ask him straight out.'

'As in . . .?'

'As in, have you shagged both of your daughters?'

'Not quite the words I'd use,' he said. 'But close.'

Gilchrist worked his way through the Edinburgh traffic and arrived at the offices of DBD Global Investments in Queen Street just before 1 p.m. It took another ten minutes of driving around before he managed to find a spot at a parking meter.

'Cost of parking would scare you shitless.' Jessie fingered deep into her purse, and slid three fifty-pence pieces into the meter. 'How come you never have any change?'

'Because I'm the guy who buys the beer.'

'What if I'm off beer?'

'I can't help that.'

They found DBD Global Investment offices on the top floor.

Four skylight windows spotted with bird-shit brightened an area that could only be described as drab – not quite what Gilchrist had been expecting of a *global* head office. A matronly reception-ist with a bun that went out of fashion in the fifties eyed him and Jessie as they approached.

They flashed their warrant cards in exchange for being shown grey teeth.

'We're here to talk to Dougal Davis,' Gilchrist said.

'Do you have an appointment?'

'No.'

'I'll see if Mr Davis is in—'

'He's in,' Jessie said. 'And we're going to talk to him, so save yourself the effort.'

'I'll see if Mr Davis is *available*, then.'

Gilchrist held up his hand to cut Jessie short. 'Tell Mr Davis we don't intend to take up much of his time.'

She took their names, writing them down with care. 'If you have a seat,' she said, 'I'm sure Mr Davis will be with you shortly.'

Gilchrist took Jessie by the arm, and led her to a sofa that lined the wall next to the entrance. A pile of magazines – *Smart Investor, Money Market, World Finance* – lay on a coffee table that could do with a lick of polish, or just binning. He picked up *World Finance*, flicked through it without reading anything, then replaced it. With nothing to invest, what was the point? A floorboard creaked. A beam ticked. A phone rang somewhere, then was silenced. The whole area had a sense of being run down.

Maybe this was what became of disgraced MSPs.

Jessie shifted by his side, texting Robert, as best he could tell, which reminded him of his own unread messages from Cooper.

He retrieved his mobile, feeling somewhat guilty that he had not given any more thought to her sad news. Three messages appeared on the screen as separate yellow speech bubbles that displayed the date and time to the nearest second, and each a short one-liner.

call me b xx

please?

need to talk

Gilchrist checked the times against each one.

The first was sent just over four minutes before the last, but with his mobile broken – or SIM card loose – he had not replied. Was that why she had ignored him that morning on the beach, believing his failure to reply was his way of saying he wanted nothing more—

'Mr Davis will see you now.'

Jessie almost jumped to her feet. 'About time,' she said, as a door to the side of the receptionist's desk opened and a white-haired man, with a face that looked more ruddy and bloated in the flesh than on the TV, stood in the doorway.

'I don't have much time,' Davis said to them.

'Neither do we,' Jessie said, and brushed past him.

In Davis's office, Gilchrist was surprised to find the well-dressed figure of Simon Copestake standing by the corner of the desk – which explained Davis's delay in meeting them; a quick call to Hughes Copestake Solicitors in the neighbouring building had brought his favourite solicitor running over.

Jessie stood next to one of two chairs that fronted Davis's desk, ignoring Copestake.

The door closed behind Gilchrist with a hard click.

'I understand you two have already met,' Davis said, his voice booming.

'Not in person,' Copestake said, and held his hand out.

Gilchrist shook it, then introduced Jessie as, 'Detective Sergeant Jessica Janes.'

Jessie ignored Copestake's outstretched hand while Davis slumped into a well-worn leather chair behind his desk. A slatted blind hung on the window behind Davis and offered a glimpse of a dark-stoned building on the opposite side of a narrow lane.

'I would hope you're going to tell me that you've found my granddaughter,' Davis began, 'and that you're here in person to apologise for taking so long to do so. But from the looks on your faces, I fear that might be somewhat presumptuous of me. Correct?'

'Correct,' Jessie said.

Copestake had repositioned himself by the corner of the desk, and now stood looking down at Gilchrist. He was not a tall man – maybe five ten – so standing gave him a sense of advantage. 'So what's the purpose of this visit?' he asked Gilchrist.

'To enquire if Mr Davis has any information that might help us locate his missing granddaughter.'

'So you're no further forward.'

'I didn't say that.'

'Well I don't have any information that could possibly help you,' Davis grumbled.

'We'll decide whether you have or not.'

Davis leaned forward, and lowered his head, eyes glaring as if his face was about to explode. 'I have to say, Mr Gilchrist, that in my view, if my personal television appeal had not been so eagerly overturned by your Constabulary yesterday, you might have had some more encouraging news to tell me today.'

'In our view,' Jessie snapped, 'you may already have compromised our investigation and put your granddaughter's life at unnecessary risk. Have you thought of that?'

Davis glared at Jessie, as if willing her to explode.

Gilchrist looked up at Copestake. 'I take it you've advised your client of yesterday's conversation and the contents of my email to you.'

'Yes, he did,' Davis growled, snapping his glare from Jessie to Gilchrist. 'And I didn't much care for your attitude.'

Gilchrist held Davis's rheumy stare, as loathing stirred within him. Here was a man who had abused his trust as a father, husband, MSP, and who had learned nothing from that experience. He resisted the urge to warn Davis that his unauthorised video appeal could be perceived as obstructing the police, or even attempting to pervert the course of justice, and instead said, 'Do you love Katie?'

'Of course I love her. What kind of a question is that, for God's sake?'

'And it's clear from yesterday's TV appeal that you would do anything within your power to get her back.'

'Which beggars the bloody question of why your incompetent lot withdrew it.'

Gilchrist held up his hand while Davis's outraged look evaporated. 'If you love your granddaughter, and would do anything for her . . . ' He watched Davis's eyes flicker with uncertainty, then he lowered his hand. 'Then help us find her.'

Davis harrumphed, glanced at Copestake as if searching for approval, then directed his stare back to Gilchrist. 'That's your

113

KILKENNY COUNTY LIBRARY

job. Not mine. And I suggest you bloody well get on with it, instead of wasting my time—'

'Jesus Christ,' Jessie said. 'You couldn't give a toss about Katie. Could you? All you want to do is get your face seen on TV.'

'What did you just say?'

'We've spoken to Rachel.'

'Who?'

'Your other daughter. She told us what happened when she was twelve.'

Davis pushed his seat back, brushed Copestake's hand from his shoulder. 'How dare you—'

'How dare I what? Listen to a woman tell us of how you molested her at the age of twelve—?'

'Get out—'

'How she had to threaten you with a knife to get you to stop.'

Davis struggled to his feet. 'Get out.'

Jessie stood. 'Did you do the same to Andrea? Is that why she's so fucked up—'

'Get out of my fucking office right now before I call the police and have you thrown out and charged with . . . with . . . '

Jessie leaned across the desk. 'We *are* the police. And we'll be taking a closer look into your daughter's allegations of sexual abuse. So why not take a few seconds to think about that?'

Davis put a hand to his forehead and turned to Copestake. 'Simon? Please?'

'I'll see you both out,' Copestake said, and strode from Davis's side.

Behind her desk, the receptionist was busy stacking one pile of papers on to another, tight-lipped, eyes fixed like beads. Copestake

114

led them to the main door, and stepped from the office, Gilchrist and Jessie behind him.

When Copestake closed the door, Gilchrist said, 'Would you like to talk outside?'

Copestake glanced over his shoulder, then shook his head. 'Here's fine,' he said. 'But don't be surprised when you receive a letter of complaint.'

'We *will* be looking into Rachel Novo's allegations against your client, whether or not he writes a formal letter of complaint. You understand that, I'm sure.'

Copestake took a deep breath, then let it out. 'These twins of his,' he said, shaking his head as if at the absurdity of it all. 'They've been the bane of Dougal's life. He's always said his life would have been different if he'd had boys instead of girls.'

'What, no one to touch up?' Jessie said.

Copestake snapped her a look. 'That tongue of yours is going to land you in trouble.'

'I'm sure it will.'

Gilchrist said, 'Twins?'

'Rachel and Andrea.' Copestake's eyebrows raised, and his lips pulled into a grin of feigned disbelief. 'You didn't know, did you? Oh my. Shouldn't even the most basic of investigations have found that out?'

Gilchrist could almost read the letter of complaint forming in Copestake's mind. 'Not if everyone's withholding information from us,' he said.

Copestake turned to the door. 'You'll be hearing from my client, no doubt.'

'Can't wait,' Jessie said, leaving Gilchrist to follow her to the lift.

CHAPTER 15

'I hate bastards like that,' Jessie said. 'You think he'll take it further?'

Gilchrist beeped his remote fob as he crossed the street. 'I'm sure he will.'

'Even though we'll be looking into his daughter's allegations of sexual abuse?'

'Maybe we won't be doing that.'

Jessie almost stopped. 'Jesus, Andy,' she gasped. 'Tell me you're joking.'

Gilchrist reached for the door handle. 'Confucius, he say, before insert spoon-load of shit into mouth, make sure Rachel telling truth.'

'That's going to be difficult. She might not want to talk about it.'

'Exactly,' Gilchrist said, slotting the key into the ignition. 'But I'm more pissed off that no one knew Andrea and Rachel are twins.' He shook his head. 'Made us look like a right pair of plonkers back there.'

Jessie grimaced and slipped on her seat belt.

Gilchrist received CS Greaves's call as they were crossing the Forth Road Bridge.

116

'Just had the Chief Constable biting my ear off,' Greaves said to him.

'How is he these days?' Gilchrist asked.

Greaves gave a dry chuckle. 'Always the smart comment, Andy. It never fails.'

Gilchrist tightened his grip on the steering wheel. One hundred and fifty feet beneath them, the dark waters of the River Forth slid towards the North Sea like some liquid titan.

'The Chief's received a lengthy phone call from an irate Dougal Davis who alleges that you accused him of molesting his daughter—'

'Both daughters,' Jessie chipped in.

A pause, then, 'Who's this speaking?'

'DS Jessica Janes, sir. And it was me who raised these allegations, sir, not DCI Gilchrist.'

Gilchrist said, 'I have you on speaker phone, sir.'

'Well, get me off speaker phone, damn it.'

Jessie said, 'Under the circumstances, sir, perhaps you should be talking to me, and not DCI Gilchrist. After all, Mr Davis's verbal complaint to the Chief Constable should be directed at me.'

'Are you trying to get yourself suspended, DS Janes?'

'No, sir. But in the course of our investigation into Katie Davis's abduction, we've uncovered evidence that Dougal Davis sexually abused one of his daughters, and we believe he may have abused both. He denied it, of course. Hence his obvious first line of attack by verbal complaint to the Chief Constable.'

Gilchrist glanced at Jessie, surprised to see her eyes welling. She was in so deep, she had no way of getting out. On instinct, he reached across the seat and squeezed her shoulder.

She glanced at him, and a tear spilled down her cheek.

Gilchrist sliced his hand across his throat in a say-no-more gesture, and said, 'What exactly did the Chief Constable say, sir?'

'What didn't he say, would be an easier question to answer.'

Silent, Gilchrist drove on.

'He wants a written report on your investigation into the Davis abduction on his desk by close of play today. Also a written report on your meeting with Dougal Davis. And don't even think about trying to soften it. He wants the truth.'

'And that's what he'll get,' Jessie said.

'I'm not finished, damn it.'

'Sorry, sir.'

'And he wants you to give him a call, Andy. Without delay.'

'I'll do that, sir.'

'Do you have his number?'

'I do, sir.'

'Good. And I want a copy of everything you send him.'

'Anything else, sir?'

'Is that not enough?'

The line died.

'Jesus,' Jessie said, and let her breath out in a heavy rush. 'I'm going to have to learn to keep that trap of mine shut right enough.'

'It wouldn't suit you.' Gilchrist smiled at her. 'Besides, we might never have found out about his daughters being twins if you hadn't worked them into a lather.'

Jessie looked away, and stared out the window.

Gilchrist waited for a clear stretch of road before calling Chief Constable McVicar. Despite Greaves's theatrics, Gilchrist knew McVicar to be fair; someone who would listen to all sides of the story, then come down like a sledgehammer on whichever party he deemed to be at fault, regardless of rank or personal history. Gilchrist had felt the heavy end of that hammer once before, and made a promise never to experience it again.

But sometimes stuff happens, and you just have to get on with it.

He made the call.

Introductions over, Gilchrist said, 'I'm driving, sir, and have you on speaker phone. DS Jessica Janes is in the car with me.'

'Very well, then, Andy. What can you tell me about Dougal Davis?'

'He's obstructive, argumentative, disrespectful, misogynistic, abusive, and walking on thin ice, sir?'

'Thin ice, Andy?'

Gilchrist explained the phone call with Rachel Novo.

'Good Lord,' McVicar said. 'The man's his own worst enemy. What do you intend to do with this information?'

Gilchrist could not fail to catch a softening in McVicar's tone, and decided to take the initiative. 'Now would not be the time to be seen bringing formal charges against a missing child's grandfather, sir. Not until we know more about the abduction.' He brought McVicar up to speed, and felt a nip of worry at the Chief's lack of comment – a telling sign that he was far from pleased. 'I understand you know the missing child's grandmother,' Gilchrist tried. 'Vera Davis, sir.'

The comment seemed to stun McVicar into silence for a couple of beats. 'I do. Yes.'

'Did you ever meet her daughters, Rachel and Andrea?'

'Only once,' McVicar said. 'When they were in their early teens.'

'What were they like as twins?'

'Can't remember much about them, to tell you the truth. But what I do recall, now you mention it, is that I don't think I'd ever before seen twins look so unalike.'

Gilchrist glanced at Jessie, who looked as confused as he felt.

'So, what's this about, Andy?' McVicar went on.

Gilchrist explained his concerns over Katie's mother not being truthful, but avoiding mention of possible sexual encounters. Although he sensed a shift in McVicar's attitude, by the end of the call he was left in no doubt that McVicar expected full reports on his desk by the end of the day – per CS Greaves.

Jessie said, 'Does he think we've nothing better to do than put pen to paper?'

'Call Mhairi,' Gilchrist said, 'and have her make a start on my report.'

His phone rang – ID Becky.

'You'd better take that,' Jessie said, then proceeded to call Mhairi.

Gilchrist lifted his phone. 'Yes, Becky, how are you?'

'Just had the blood results back on Sammie Bell,' she said, 'and he's got enough crack cocaine in his system to floor a horse.'

'Is that what killed him?'

'He was alive when they put a hammer to his head,' she said. 'But I doubt he would have survived the overdose.'

Even though this gave credit to his signature theory, he bounced another question off her. 'So if the killer knew that Bell had already overdosed, why hammer his head at all?'

'That's beyond my medical remit.'

'And what about DNA?'

'It's a match. It's Sammie Bell. I'll get back to you if I find anything untoward.'

The call died before Gilchrist could tell Cooper about his mobile not working last night. He replaced the phone to the car's system and eyed the road ahead. It seemed that his relationship with Cooper – maybe best to call it an affair – was on its terminal spiral. The tinny sound of a woman's voice to his side halted his thoughts, as Jessie mumbled repeated agreement.

The call ended abruptly with Jessie saying, 'No. Leave it with me. I'll tell him.'

Gilchrist glanced at his speed – seventy-five. Ahead, an articulated lorry indicated to shift into the overtaking lane. 'You know, these things never brake,' he said. 'They just pull out with no thought to anyone else on the road.' He waited for Jessie to comment, but after thirty seconds of silence, said, 'Anything you have to tell me?'

She let out a defeated sigh. 'Mhairi heard back from Baxter.'

'About?'

'Liam's report.'

The list of names on Bell's laptop. This could be their breakthrough. But Jessie's tone was all wrong. Something didn't fit. 'So what's Liam found?'

'You're not going to like it.'

Even as Jessie's words wormed through his mind, his logic was already working out the answer, telling him what he didn't want to hear. 'Oh for fuck sake, don't tell me . . . '

'Afraid so.'

His fingers crushed the steering wheel. 'Jack,' he whispered.

'Got it in one.'

CHAPTER 16

Gilchrist jumped to his feet and rushed into the water, pulled Jack free of the sucking waves. He picked him up, pressed him to his chest, felt his little body shivering with cold and trembling with sobs. I've got you, he said. You're okay. By the time he reached their beach-towelled spot, Jack's sobbing had subsided to little more than tremor-jerking sniffling. He towelled his son's skinny body dry, white and goose-pimpled, lips already turning blue from the cold. Do you want to go home? Jack shook his head, broke free from his grip, and ran back into the sea, only to be bowled over again.

'It's like he never learns,' Gilchrist pleaded. 'Jesus fucking *Christ*, he told me he was through with drugs. And like a fucking idiot, I believed him.' He gripped the steering wheel, felt white-hot anger flood his system, its fire like talons tearing at his guts. He could sink to his knees and scream to the skies. He could shake Jack's scrawny shoulders until that thick-nutted head of his bounced off. He could choke the living shit out of—

'Get him on the phone,' he snarled.

'No can do, Andy. You're a DCI, and Jack's father. You can't be seen to be—'

'Get him on the fucking phone, right *now*.'

'You're not thinking straight.'

Gilchrist gritted his teeth. Of course he wasn't thinking straight. How the hell could he when boiling blood was pumping through his brain? He took several deep breaths, tried to settle his thudding heart. But it was like trying to calm a broiling sea. Jesus Christ, Jack, what have you been up to? And Sammie Bell, a registered sex offender, for fuck's sake.

He glanced at Jessie, but he was getting no help there.

'Call him up on *your* mobile,' he said, struggling to keep his tone level. 'Put it on speaker. Tell Jack you're alone. Then ask him how in the name of fuck he knows Sammie Bell. Jesus fucking *Christ*.'

'Okay, okay, settle down before you give yourself a heart attack. But I'm going to talk to Baxter first, see how far he's taken this. And it's no use glaring at me like that. I have to do that. You just keep your eyes on the road, and let me do the talking. All right?'

Gilchrist stared at the road ahead, seeing everything, but taking in nothing. He pressed his foot on the accelerator, pulled out to overtake, and had to jerk back in as a Jaguar blasted past with its horn blaring.

'Want me to drive?' Jessie said.

'I'm fine.'

'Eyes on road.'

'Everything on speaker, then.'

'As long as you don't say a word. And I mean it, Andy.'

He nodded, pressed his head back against the headrest, and dropped his speed to the safer side of seventy. He said nothing while Jessie got through to Baxter.

'Been talking to Mhairi,' she said, 'and she tells me you've found Jack Gilchrist's name and number on Sammie Bell's computer.'

'I know, Jessie. The big man's going to go ape-shit. Can you talk?'

'I'm in my car, so I really shouldn't. But go ahead. Has anyone spoken to Jack yet?'

'Hang on a sec until I get out of here.' A moment of background rustling, then, 'No way. I'm not tackling that until I get clearance from higher up.'

'That's why I'm calling. I'm thinking maybe I could make that first call, see if I can glean something from him. It has to be a mistake, I'm sure of it. I'll keep you in the loop, of course. How does that sound?'

Another pause, then, 'Rather you than me. All I was asked to do was dig into Bell's computer.'

Gilchrist snapped his head to the side, and Jessie raised her hand to silence him.

'Okay, give me the number,' she said, and when she killed the call held her mobile up to Gilchrist. 'Is that Jack's?'

Gilchrist clenched his jaw, and nodded.

'Okay. Here goes. And stay quiet.'

Gilchrist eased his speed down a touch as he listened to the melodic beeping of Jessie dialling on speaker. He indicated left, braked hard, and pulled on to the hard shoulder. By the time Jack answered, he'd stopped the car, but kept the engine idling.

'Hello?'

Even from that one word, Gilchrist could tell his son was high on drugs.

'Jack, it's Jessie. You okay?'

'Yeah, yeah, I'm fine, Jessie. Sure. I was having a nap. Late night last night. Working on my latest and greatest.' A cough, then, 'So, this is a surprise. Why're you calling? Oh, no, don't tell me.' Wide awake now. 'Is the old man okay?'

'The old man's fine, Jack.'

'Jeez-oh, Jessie. For a moment there I thought you were going to tell me something had happened to him.'

'No, no, he's fine, Jack. He's fine.'

'That's good to hear. But I worry about him sometimes. He works too hard, but he won't listen to me. I keep telling him it's time to slow down, man, take it easy. I mean, it's not like the old man needs the money. He's done his thirty years, hasn't he?' Another throaty cough. 'He'll get a full pension. Besides, I can help him out now my stuff's beginning to sell.' He coughed again. 'So what's the occasion?'

'Have you heard anything from Sammie Bell?'

'Who?'

'Sammie Bell.'

'Who's he?'

'You don't know him?'

'Never heard of him.'

Gilchrist groaned, and received an angry glare from Jessie.

'You sure, Jack? Because he seems to know you.'

A sniff, then, 'Nope. But I'm pretty much hopeless with names. So who is he?'

'You mean, who *was* he?. He's dead.'

'Yeah?'

'He was murdered.'

'Okay.' Wary now, the word drawn out. 'So what's this to do with me?'

'I was hoping you might tell me,' Jessie said.

Jack chuckled. 'You sound just like the old man. No question's ever straightforward; always wrapped around something else, like he's trying to trip you up. Why don't you just come straight out and ask me?'

Jessie cocked her head. Gilchrist heard it too.

'Is someone with you, Jack?'

'Yeah. Tess. Say hi to Jessie, Tess.'

'Hi Jessie.' A woman's voice; tired, drunk, or just drugged, Gilchrist could no longer tell. He slashed his hand under his throat in an end-the-call gesture.

'Listen, Jack,' Jessie said, 'it's good to hear that you don't know Sammie Bell, but I've got to tick all the boxes. So someone from the Office'll come to your house and take a statement from you. They'll also ask you some questions about Sammie Bell—'

'Sure, send them along. I don't know a Sammie Bell, so that's fine with me. Heh, I can come along to the Station if you'd like, stick my head in and say hello to the old man, maybe squeeze a pint or two out of him.' He chuckled, coughed, then said, 'I can be there in thirty minutes if you'd like.'

'Let me get back to you on that,' Jessie said. 'Someone'll call to set it up.'

'Sure, Jessie. Say hi to the old man for me.'

Jessie disconnected, slapped her phone on to her thigh. 'What do you think?'

Gilchrist eyed her mobile, Jack's voice reverberating in his mind. 'I remember when Jack was eleven,' he said, 'and twenty quid went missing from Gail's housekeeping jar. She turned on him, and accused him of stealing it. But he denied it so convincingly that I believed him. It didn't convince his mum, though, and

126

she continued to hound him until a twenty-quid note magically reappeared in the housekeeping jar, and family peace was re-established. I'd always wondered if Gail had simply miscounted, believing she had twenty quid more in the jar to begin with, but it wasn't until years later during one of our drunken reunions in Glasgow that Jack confessed to me that he'd stolen the money.'

'But he'd returned it?'

Gilchrist shook his head. 'No, that was me. I slipped the twenty quid into the jar, just to keep the peace.'

Jessie frowned. 'And the moral of that tale is . . .?'

'If he has to, Jack can lie to his back teeth with the best of them. And when it comes to drugs, I've never fully believed him.'

'And you think he lied on the phone?'

'With Jack, I never know for sure. What I do know is, that his paintings are beginning to sell, and he now has more money than he's ever had. So, what's he doing with it?'

Jessie held his gaze long enough for him to feel a need to turn away. 'You could be wrong,' she said.

Gilchrist raised an eyebrow in disbelief. 'In what way?'

'Just because Jack's name and phone number's on Bell's computer, it doesn't mean he's taking drugs—'

'Correct. He could be distributing them.'

'Why do you always see the negative in Jack?'

Jessie's words hit him like a slap to the face. Was he now so steeped in the day-to-day criminality of life that he no longer saw honesty in people? Was it now beyond him to trust his son, ask a question and take his answer as the truth? Should he not be giving him the benefit of every doubt instead of—

'Why don't you let me chase Baxter on this one?' she said, just as his mobile beeped with an incoming message from Jackie.

He read it once, had to read it again to make sense of it.

Then he turned to Jessie. 'Listen to this from Jackie. Rachel Novo's phone records list calls from and to a Tesco mobile number contracted in the name of . . . ' He looked at Jessie. 'Go on, have a guess.'

'Santa Claus.'

'Try Katarina Davis.'

Jessie mouthed a *What the fuck?*

Gilchrist helped her out with, 'It's Andrea's other mobile. The one she used before she reported Katie's disappearance to the FCC yesterday. That's why no other numbers showed up on her records. She's taken it out in her daughter's name.'

Jessie's eyes hardened. 'Does Jackie have details of the times of calls?'

Gilchrist read on. 'Full records in office, but a call lasting twenty-two minutes and ten seconds was made to Novo on Monday the seventeenth of April, logged in at 06.42.'

'Hah,' Jessie slapped her hand on the dashboard. 'I knew it. I tell you, that bitch has got some explaining to do. Let's get her.'

Gilchrist slipped into gear. 'You're forgetting McVicar's call.'

'Bloody hell, tell me you're kidding.'

'Reports first,' he said as he floored the pedal, taking the car to sixty in a matter of seconds then easing into the inside lane. Too many questions, not enough answers. It felt as if his head was spinning, that no one ever spoke the truth, that life was nothing more than an infinite stream of lies stretching out ahead of him.

Who to believe? Who to trust?

These were the basic questions.

Experience had taught him to trust his gut instinct, and his gut was telling him that the answer to Katie's abduction lay right before him – in the home of Andrea Davis, and the call to her twin sister, Rachel.

'Get Rachel back on the phone,' he said to Jessie.

He eyed the road ahead, and listened to the echo of her call being answered, the hard rush of Jessie's voice as she introduced herself, then asked to speak to Ms Rachel Novo.

Lies, lies, and more lies.

As a Detective Chief Inspector, Gilchrist faced lies on a daily professional basis. But his private life seemed overrun with lies, too. Cooper lying about their relationship, about how she felt for him, when all along he had only been someone with whom she could salve the emotional pain of her marital failings.

It seemed as if there was never an honest answer to any question.

But he prayed he was wrong about one.

He prayed that Jack was telling the truth.

If not, there really was nothing he could do to help his son.

CHAPTER 17

Novo's voice cracked from the speaker like a pick breaking ice. 'What do you want?'

'When did you last talk to your twin sister?' Jessie asked.

A pause, then, 'So you've spoken with the mighty Dougal.'

'We have, but strangely he failed to mention that you and Andrea were twins.'

'So who told you?' she snapped back.

'Would you like me to repeat the question?'

'You have a short memory,' Novo said. 'My family and I no longer communicate. Now, if you've no other questions, I'll get back to—'

'Before you do,' Gilchrist said, holding up his hand to keep Jessie out of it, 'I would remind you that we're investigating the abduction of a young child, your niece you allegedly never see, and that any false or misleading information you provide might be construed as obstructing the course of justice and could—'

'I'll get my solicitor to call you back.'

'When he does, make sure you let him know of your twenty-minute phone call with your twin sister, Andrea, yesterday morning.'

Jessie eyed the speaker phone, as if willing the next lie to ignite the dashboard.

When it seemed as if Novo was silenced, Gilchrist said, 'We can continue to have a sensible conversation by phone, or we can arrange for someone from the Met to take you to your nearest station and hold you there until I fly down tomorrow.'

'I don't think you can do that,' she blurted.

'Believe me, I can. But if I have to fly down to arrest you in person, it won't bode well for police relations, if you get my meaning.'

'I'm inclined just to let you do that,' she said, 'but I really don't have the time to waste.' She let out a sigh of exasperation, and said, 'What do you want?'

'You can start by telling me when you last spoke to your twin sister.'

'I'm sure you already know this, but she called me yesterday morning.'

'Why?'

'Katarina was missing,' she snapped. 'Isn't that what this is all about?'

'But why did she phone you?'

'She trusts me.'

'And she's on for twenty minutes?' Jessie sounded incredulous.

'She was crying for most of the call. I thought she'd been smoking dope again.'

'So why didn't you hang up?' Jessie asked.

'I wanted to make sure she called the police.'

Gilchrist said, 'You could have done that for her.'

'Let me repeat – my family and I don't talk.'

131

'Except that you do,' he said, 'when Andrea calls.'

'That's different.'

'In what way?'

'She . . . my sister needs serious psychological help. She's not a well person. She has . . . she has mental health issues, and no one to help her.'

'By no one, you mean close family?'

'Yes.'

'You're her close family.'

'And I keep telling you that we don't communicate.'

Gilchrist held up his hand, and Jessie clamped her mouth shut. 'We seem to be going round in circles,' he said. 'You say you don't talk to your family, yet you talk to your sister.' A pause, then, 'What am I missing?'

'I don't talk to *them*. But sometimes Andrea calls to talk to *me*.'

'So, before yesterday, when did Andrea last talk to you?' He waited as silence filled the line, then added, 'You should be careful how you answer, as we'll have it verified from phone records.'

'Why ask me at all, then?'

'To make sure you're telling the truth.'

'Oh for goodness' sake, of course I'm telling the truth.'

'You didn't tell the truth this morning when we spoke,' Jessie snapped at her.

A couple of beats, then Novo said, 'Tenth of March.'

Gilchrist glanced at Jessie. 'Why do you remember that date?'

'It's Katarina's birthday.'

He frowned at the phone, troubled by something that eluded him, like the remnants of a fading dream. Then he thought he had it. Why would Andrea phone to tell Novo that it was her daughter's birthday? It would surely be the other way round. Or would Novo press on with a lie. 'Did she phone you, or did you phone her?'

A pause, then, 'I phoned her.'

'Why?'

'The same reason I phoned at Christmas, and New Year.'

'Which is?'

'If you can't answer that for yourself, then I don't hold any hope for you.'

Jessie glared at the phone. 'Are you for real?'

'If you have no more questions,' Novo said, 'then I'll—'

'Just one.' Gilchrist listened to silence stifle the line. 'When did you last see Andrea in person?'

'I can't remember.'

'One month ago? Longer? A year? Two years? More?'

'I really can't remember.'

'Roughly.'

'Why don't you ask Andrea? I'm sure she'll have better recall.'

'Why say that?'

'I'm being sarcastic, for God's sake. Don't you people have any sense of humour?'

'Only when it's funny,' Jessie said.

'If you've no more questions, I really must get on.'

'We may want to speak to you again,' Jessie said.

'Take a note of this number,' Novo said, and rattled it off, too fast for either Gilchrist or Jessie to write it down. 'That's my solicitor, Ellie Stevenson. We won't be talking again unless she's present.'

The connection died.

Gilchrist turned to Jessie. 'Can you remember your solicitor's number?'

'You're joking. Can you?'

'That's my point. Who can?'

He slowed down as he eased past the cathedral ruins into North Street, his mind stirring alive with possibilities. Katie Davis had been abducted, and his investigation was being carried out without a body, without which there was no point in taking samples for DNA, as they would prove nothing. Or would they?

But Katarina. That's what was troubling him.

Why would Novo call her niece by her christened name?

Why not Katie?

It was after 9 p.m. when Gilchrist decided to call it a day.

He and Jessie had completed their reports for McVicar, sent them off, but had heard nothing back. He had also heard nothing more on his son, Jack, which he supposed was about the only good news he'd had by close of play.

Jessie had finally got hold of Danny, the barman in the Golf Hotel, but he was unable to ID the three youths who had assaulted Gilchrist the previous night. And DS Curry had also confirmed that the fields adjacent to Grange Mansion were rented out to the McDonalds, who owned a farm on the other side of Crail, all for less than two thousand pounds a year.

'That's not a lot of money,' Jessie observed.

'That's because she's a millionairess,' Curry said, 'who doesn't need the dosh.'

Colin called to confirm that they'd not recovered any diamond studs or earrings from Bell's body, which had probably been stolen by the killer, or killers.

The day's debriefing uncovered nothing, either. Katie Davis was no closer to being found than on the morning she'd gone missing, a fact that Gilchrist had difficulty presenting with any kind of positive spin to the baying media circus. An imaginary shot of Dougal Davis with his hand to his head, talking to McVicar, burned itself into his memory banks with the indelibility of a white-hot branding iron.

With Grange Mansion being on the outskirts of St Andrews, CCTV footage turned up nothing in close proximity around the time of Andrea's 999 call. He was as unsuccessful with his request for footage in the backstreets of Crail around the time of Bell's murder. They did catch a sighting of three youths scurrying down Tolbooth Wynd, and of Gilchrist following shortly thereafter, but the youths never reappeared on any other CCTV footage around town. They could have split up as a group, then made their way home in separate cars. They could have gone anywhere. By the end of the evening, Gilchrist felt as if they probably had.

'I'm having a pint,' he said to Jessie. 'Thirsty?'

'I'm going home before Robert forgets he's got a mum.'

'Call me if anything comes up,' he said, then lifted a file of printouts from Jackie's desk and slipped it under his arm.

He entered The Central Bar from College Street. It seemed quiet for a Tuesday night. Not that he was in most Tuesday nights, just that there seemed to be more seats available than normal. At the bar, he asked for a Claverhouse and ordered a chicken burger with chips. Then he found a seat in a booth in the corner while he waited for his food.

He opened the file and started to read. But his mobile beeped, and he dug it from his pocket, half hoping, half dreading it would be Jack. But it was a text from Dick, confirming he would drop off Tosh's CD tomorrow morning.

On impulse, he dialled Cooper's number, and was about to

135

hang up before being dumped into voicemail, when she answered the call.

'Hello.'

Not a question. But he sensed sadness in her voice. 'Are you all right?'

'How do you define all right?'

He pushed himself to his feet, now wishing he'd waited until he returned home before calling. He swerved her question with, 'Can I help in any way?'

'No.'

He pushed through the swing doors into the evening din of Market Street, strode off the pavement on to the cobbled street. Overhead, night was trying to cover the sky with an indigo cloak. 'Where are you?'

'Why?'

With Cooper, it had never been straightforward. For one crazy moment he thought of wishing her the best and just hanging up. But doing so could hurt her, and hurting Cooper had never been on his agenda. Having decided to go through with her pregnancy, only to miscarry three months in, was pain enough for any woman.

And she didn't need him to add to her misery.

So he said, 'I'd like to talk to you.'

'I'm not up for this, Andy.'

He could tell from her tone that she was about to hang up, when he caught the deep echo of a man's voice in the background. His first thought was to ask who she was with, and his second that she could be in a public area, and not at home with a man-friend. As he forced these thoughts away, he said, 'Would you like me to call back?'

'What's the point?'

He had witnessed Cooper's sub-zero coldness before, seen it directed at her yet-to-be-*ex*-husband, Max, but had never felt the full effect of its ice-like chill until that moment. 'The point is that I care for you, Becky, and I don't want to lose you.' The words were out before he could stop them. The ensuing silence had him pressing his phone to his ear in an effort to catch her response.

But he needn't have bothered.

The line died with the hard click of a lost connection.

He faced The Central. Through the window he watched a tray of food being delivered to his table in the corner, and realised with a spurt of annoyance that he'd left an open police file on the table.

Back inside, he returned to his seat, relieved to see his file lying untouched. A couple of students at the adjacent table were too wrapped up in their mobiles to notice each other, let alone some-one else's belongings. He stared at the file, tried to refocus his thoughts. He had a case to solve. A child had been abducted, and was out there in the open world. Was she alive or dead? But try as he might, he could not shift the feeling that they would never find Katie, that she was already dead.

He had just taken a bite of his burger when his mobile rang. He checked the screen – ID Baxter – and felt something heavy slap over in his stomach. He took the call with a curt, 'Gilchrist.'

'I'm sorry to call at this hour, sir, but it's about your son, Jack.'

Gilchrist swallowed a lump that threatened to choke his throat. 'Okay,' he said.

'I'm sorry to tell you, sir, but I've had to arrest him on suspi-cion of possession and distribution of class A drugs.'

'Suspicion?' Gilchrist heard himself say.

'Yes, sir. His name and number were found in Samuel Bell's laptop, along with a number of other known drug dealers.'

He couldn't tell Baxter that he'd asked Jessie to talk to Jack earlier. Instead, he said, '*Other* known drug dealers would suggest that Jack is *also* a drug dealer.'

'We have to treat him with suspicion, sir.'

'What's Jack saying?'

'He denies it, of course.'

He waited a couple of beats. But Baxter seemed unwilling to offer more, so he said, 'Where is he now?'

'On his way to Glenrothes, sir.'

Which meant Jack was about to spend the night in jail. Gilchrist could do nothing about that. Nor did he feel inclined to. If Jack was innocent, which he now had doubts about, a night in custody might be the kick up the arse to get him off drugs once and for all. But if he were guilty, then jail was where he should be, and where he would likely spend the next ten years of his life.

All of a sudden the bar felt stuffy, the air too humid.

He tugged his tie, worked it loose, took a mouthful of Claverhouse. 'What's your gut feeling?' he asked Baxter.

'The truth, sir?'

Christ in a basket. Baxter's question gave him his answer. He pressed the flat of his hand against his forehead, felt the cold dampness of sweat. 'The truth,' he agreed.

'I think he's guilty.'

'Why?' It was all he had the strength to ask.

'We could smell it, sir. In his flat.'

Gilchrist felt a sliver of hope struggle to free itself and soar.

Jack was not stupid enough to smoke dope in his flat. He knew his father dropped by from time to time. He would never risk being caught by the drug's aroma, no matter how many windows he opened to create a draught, Gilchrist was sure of that.

'What about his girlfriend?' he asked. 'Tess.'

'Her name's Theresa McKenzie,' Baxter said. 'She's known to the Anstruther Office, and has a number of drug-related convictions. Been in and out of juvenile detention since the age of twelve.'

Something faltered in Gilchrist's chest. 'How old is she now?'

'Fifteen.'

Gilchrist groaned. 'Don't tell me . . . '

'He's denied that, too, sir, of course.'

'Of course.'

Gilchrist ended the call and hung his head in his hands. He'd suspected Jack was back on drugs, but he'd never known for sure. But if you threw in underage sex on top of it, Jack could be facing a lengthy custodial sentence.

Which he knew his gentle son could not survive.

He cursed under his breath. He would need to talk to Baxter again, persuade him to let him speak to Jack. It was against protocol, he knew.

But what else could he do?

CHAPTER 18

Jack entered Interview Room 2 in handcuffs.

Despite his paintings now selling for considerable sums, or so Gilchrist was led to believe, a threadbare sweater and jeans that had not seen the inside of a washing machine for weeks, maybe months, gave the impression of a struggling artist who'd never owned two coins to rub together.

He sat opposite Gilchrist, unable, or more likely unwilling, to look him in the eye.

'Take the cuffs off him,' Gilchrist said, and waited while the officer obliged.

When the door clicked to a close, he waited for Jack to lift his head.

'I'm innocent,' Jack said. His voice sounded strong, despite a defeated look.

Gilchrist let a couple of beats pass. 'Should I believe you?'

Jack jerked a look at him. 'I don't do drugs any more. I told you that. I've been off them for years, man . . . What . . .? What is it . . .? Why're you looking at me like that?'

'Have you had sex with Tess?'

'Well . . . yeah . . . I mean . . . ' He shrugged. 'Who wouldn't?'

'She's underage.'

'No she's not.'

'She is, Jack.'

'No she's fucking not, man. She told me she's twenty-two. I mean, you wouldn't say you're twenty-two if you were underage and in a bar. You'd say you'd just turned eighteen or something.' His voice had risen, and he sat back, pushed his hands through his hair as if that would help him breathe. Then he stilled. 'No way, man. No *fucking* way.' Panic swept over his face in a wave of incredulity. 'She's never underage, man. No *way*. Have you seen her?'

'I was told you denied having sex with her.'

'Yeah, well—'

'So you lied to a police officer—'

'It's none of their business, man. My sex life's mine. It's personal.'

'Except when it isn't.'

Silent, Jack returned Gilchrist's look with what he must have thought was a hardened look of his own. But it was more caught-in-the-headlights than assertive.

'How long have you been going out with her?' Gilchrist asked.

'Going out with her?' Jack's mouth twisted with disgust. 'I'm not going out with her. I'd never even seen her before until last week.'

'So what was she doing in your flat?'

'I picked her up last night.'

'Anyone with her?'

'She was by herself, I think. No, maybe with a friend. I don't know.' Then he stared at Gilchrist, and said, 'Don't look at me like that.'

Gilchrist thought for one troubling moment that his 24-year-old son was about to cry. But the moment passed, and Gilchrist pressed closer to the table, placed his hands flat on the surface. 'You're in trouble, Jack. You know that, don't you?'

Jack flicked him an angry look, then lowered his head as if beaten.

'I can't help you,' Gilchrist said.

Jack shook his head at the floor. 'I didn't know she was under-age. I didn't know she was smoking. I'd seen her around a couple of times, chatted her up, bought her a drink.' He looked up at Gilchrist, eyes wide with surprise. 'I mean, you meet a bird in a bar, and she's throwing back shooters like there's no tomorrow, and what? You're supposed to ask her how old she is? I mean . . . *Jesus fuck.*'

Gilchrist's heart could have burst for his son. How many children – because that's all they were – had he sent home to their parents, screaming and scratching and swearing their hearts out, after having been extracted from a pub? Maybe he should have arrested more of them, rather than only giving them a verbal warning.

'Tell me what happened.'

'She came on to me, man, last night. What am I supposed to do? I mean, she's all over me, begging for it. So I took her to my flat, and once we're inside, she lights up, and I'm like, put that out, I don't do that any more. But she's standing there in the scud, with a smile on her face, and I'm thinking like, well, what the hell.' His eyes widen. 'But I didn't take anything. I swear. I just let her get on with it, and then . . . you know . . . next thing we're in bed and . . . ' He shook his head, and grumbled, 'She was no virgin either, that's for sure—'

'And Sammie Bell?' Gilchrist said.

The snap in his voice startled Jack. He shook his head. 'Never heard of him.'

'The problem is, Jack, that he's heard of you.'

'Who is he? What does he do?'

'He's a registered sex offender. And drug dealer.'

'And he knows *me?*' Jack gasped. 'How?'

'That's the question.'

'I don't know how he would know me,' Jack said, and his eyes went small as his mind focused on something in the past. Then they widened. 'That wee bitch.'

Gilchrist almost smiled. He thought he knew Jack well enough to know he was telling the truth. When pinned against a wall, he would always fight back. But never to the detriment of others. If he thought someone else was going to be blamed for something he'd done, he would take it on the chin, without blinking. But if he thought he was being set up, he would cough the lot. And in Jack, Gilchrist knew he had a perfect witness to a drug entrapment scam.

He pushed his chair back, and panic fluttered over Jack's face.

'You'll have to spend the night in custody,' Gilchrist said. 'I can't do anything about that. But I'll talk to DS Baxter, the person who interviewed you—'

'Interrogated, more like.'

'It's what we're good at.' Gilchrist rose to his feet.

Jack did likewise. 'I'm sorry, Andy,' he said. 'But I didn't do anything illegal.'

'If you don't count underage sex.' Jack's face slumped, and Gilchrist had to fight off the urge to walk around the table and give him a hug. But Jack had never been the touchy-feely type, more the drinking and back-slapping and general bonhomie kind of a guy.

Gilchrist gave him a quick smile. 'See you later?'

Jack tried a tough-man grin, but failed. 'I'm not going anywhere.'

Gilchrist walked to the door, conscious of Jack's eyes on him all the way.

In the hallway, he phoned DS Baxter and found him in his office.

'How is he?' Baxter said.

Gilchrist had managed to persuade Baxter to let him talk to Jack – a violation of protocol, so it was better that they not discuss the meeting openly. But Tess was a different matter. He wobbled his head in a so-so gesture, then said, 'You spoken to Tess?'

Baxter handed Gilchrist a closed file. 'That's her statement. She denies everything.'

Gilchrist opened the report, scanned through it. But it told him nothing, and he handed it back. 'I'd like to talk to her, with you as a silent witness, and not a word.'

The room seemed more spartan now that Jack had gone, as if by his absence he had stripped it clean. The door clicked, and DS Baxter entered, followed by a young woman and the same officer who had escorted Jack.

At around six feet tall, with a pair of breasts that threatened to burst the buttons of her black blouse, and jeans tight enough to leave little to the imagination, Tess looked every bit the twenty-two years she'd told Jack she was, and then some. Jet-black hair in an overgrown crew-cut style – Rod Stewart dipped in ink, sprang to his mind – did what it could to hide a ceramic-white face. Purple eye shadow plastered eyes that had seen more of life than

144

most people in their thirties. As she crossed the floor, she glanced at Gilchrist for the briefest of moments. Two metal rings defined the end of each eyebrow. And not a tattoo in sight.

Well, that was something, he supposed.

The officer said, 'Sit.'

She sat, and the officer retreated to the door.

Gilchrist slid his business card across the table, as Baxter took the seat next to him.

'I'm Jack's father,' he said to Tess.

Silence.

Gilchrist explained her rights to her, then said, 'You also have the right to have a solicitor present, which you can waive if you choose. But I really only want to ask you a couple of questions which could help me on another matter, then I'm out of here.'

She refused to engage his look, just stared at her hands on the table. Fingernails that had been bitten to the quick were painted a purple that almost matched her eye shadow.

Gilchrist reached forward, switched off the recorder. 'To prove I'm asking for your help,' he said, 'this is off the record. Okay?'

She eyed the tape recorder, but said nothing.

'Do you know Sammie Bell?' he asked.

Her eyes flickered and flared, then died with a shrug of her shoulders.

'I take it that's a yes.'

Another shrug.

'That's what you do, isn't it? Pick up young men, offer them sex and a free reefer, then it's on to the harder stuff, and within the week you've got another name to add to Bell's ever-growing list for his supply-and-demand chain.' He pressed closer. 'But it

145

can't be much fun for you,' he said. 'What do you get out of it? Free drugs? Good sex? Not a lot of money, I bet.'

Silence. Only a dead stare at her hands.

'But you can never have a normal relationship with anyone, can you? You don't have a boyfriend, only a driver, Sammie Bell. And you can never be free from him, because he's got you addicted, too.' He sat back. 'But what if I told you I could get you away from him?' He caught a tensing in her fingers, and knew he had her attention. 'Do you know Sammie Bell's dead?'

Her lips parted, and she gave the tiniest of gasps.

'That's right, Tess. Sammie Bell is dead. We don't know why yet, although we have our suspicions. But I'll tell you what, Tess, I think you lucked out.'

She looked at him then, her question in her eyes.

'How old are you?' he asked. 'And don't even think about lying.'

She searched for her hands again, twisted her fingers. 'Nearly sixteen.'

'When did you last see your parents?'

She shrugged.

'I can help you,' he said.

Fire danced in her eyes. 'No you can't. He has a team.'

'Who has?'

'Sammie,' she whispered. 'I've tried before.'

'You have?'

She unbuttoned the sleeve of her blouse, pushed it up to reveal half a dozen raised and reddened welts, each the size of a five-pence piece. Gilchrist eyed the burn-marks, and made a mental promise to himself to do what he could to help her.

'Can you give a description of his team?' he asked. 'Any of them?'

'You're kidding, yeah? They'll have me for grassing on them.'

'They'll never find out.'

Her eyes blazed with the fire of an anger he could only imagine. Here was a young woman, a teenager, little more than a child, who had seen and done things that many women twice her age had never experienced. As he returned her gaze, watched her eyes moisten and tears swell until they spilled down her cheeks, a wild thought came to him, a possibility that might just win her over – a long shot, he knew. Maybe too long.

'There are three in his team, right?'

She jerked in surprise, then sniffed and ran the back of her hand under her nose.

'I've seen them,' he said, pressing on. 'I need you to help us ID them.'

She wrapped her arms around herself, as if to fend off a chill.

'Are you willing to do that?'

She pulled her arms tighter, pressed her lips into a tight line as tears swelled from her eyes, and Gilchrist found himself pushing to his feet and walking around the table to knead her shoulder. As his fingers squeezed, and the tears flowed, he caught Baxter's eye, his brow furrowed with concern. Baxter had a ten-year-old daughter, Gilchrist knew. And from the strain on the man's face he was asking himself – how would he feel if this were his own daughter in a few years?

Tess sniffed again, and Gilchrist sensed the tensing in her muscles.

He released his grip as she shrugged his hand free with an irritated, 'Get off.'

He retreated to his side of the desk, expecting to be glared at in anger all the way. But Tess's eyes were lowered, and back to staring at her fingers; for one unsettling moment, from the petted lip and smouldering scowl, she could have been his own daughter, Maureen, after he'd given her a telling off. And experience told him that trying to engage her in any meaningful discussion was beyond Baxter and him at the moment, that it would be better to have someone talk to her again first thing in the morning.

He signalled for the officer to take Tess back to her cell, and waited while she rose to her feet and shuffled from the room without a backward glance.

When the door closed, Baxter said, 'What d'you think?'

'That she could help us. If we help her.'

'She needs a right good clout around the back of the head, is what she needs.'

'I'm sure she does, but that's only going to alienate her.' Gilchrist moved towards the door. 'Try softly softly,' he said. 'You'd be surprised how well that works.' He was about to step into the corridor when he paused and said, 'She's the key.'

Baxter narrowed his eyes, but said nothing.

'Find out what she knows, and she'll lead you to Bell's killer.'

'You think?'

'It'll also help Jack. And if you haven't already done so, I want you to take a blood sample from him,' he added. 'So you'll find he's drug-clean.' He hoped to God he was right. He didn't wait to hear Baxter's ridicule. The surprised smile on the man's face was enough to tell him that he thought Jack was in it up to his drug-laden armpits.

Gilchrist closed the door and left the building, striding across the car park.

In his car, he stabbed the key into the ignition and jerked the engine to life. It always amazed him how the mind worked, how it pecked away in the subconscious, nibbling at ideas that shimmied and shifted in neural shadows, until it came up with what seemed like a lateral step in thinking.

Just as an outsider, Tess McKenzie, could be the key to solving Bell's murder – or so Gilchrist's gut was telling him – so, too, was Rachel Novo the key in the abduction of Katie Davis. It had been Novo's surname that triggered it for him; not Italian, as he'd first thought, but Russian, which he'd stumbled across while looking through Jackie's files in The Central.

He'd taken no notice of it at the time, just skimmed over the name without giving any thought as to why she'd shortened Novokoff to the more romantic sounding Novo, after her divorce – no divorce papers attached. Her marriage had lasted eighteen months, according to Jackie's research. So what better way to get beyond the past, than to redefine yourself by changing your name?

Of course, the same could be said for reverting to her original birth-name, Davis. But for Rachel Novo, the visceral hatred she felt for her father, Dougal, and the memory of abuse at his hands, would ensure she would never carry his name through any part of her life.

But was there another reason for her to change her name?

He eased into Napier Road and depressed the accelerator.

Tomorrow, after he'd slept on it, he might have a better idea.

149

CHAPTER 19

Wednesday morning

Gilchrist checked the time on his mobile – 04.42 – and groaned.

He lay there in the warmth of a debilitating need to sleep. Usually he slept straight through until his mobile woke him, but he'd had a fitful night. As he eased back the quilt, and set his feet on the floor, the ghostly remnants of a disturbing dream clung to his mind with the persistence of a spider's web.

Jack had featured in his dream, he was sure of that. And Maureen, too. But the what and the why remained as elusive as smoke in fog. Perhaps he'd been troubled by the thought of Jack spending a night in custody. Or Maureen's cutting remark about Cooper – *Please don't tell me you're going to get married, Dad. Not to that bitch* – had maybe nibbled away at his subconscious. But a piping hot shower did nothing to recover the memory, and by the time he'd dressed, the dream had all but faded to oblivion.

In the kitchen, he opened a packet of Gourmet Perle Ocean Delicacies and selected a pouch of Salmon and Whole Shrimps. Then he eased himself out the back door as quietly as he could and crept along the slabbed footpath, his breath fogging thickly in the early morning chill.

Movement at the hut door pulled him to a halt.

The cat looked at him, wide-eyed, body low and almost hugging the ground, as if undecided whether or not to make a run for it.

As slowly as he could, Gilchrist squatted. 'I'm not going to hurt you, puss,' he said, and gave the pouch a gentle shake. But the cat gave a slow blink, then slid from the hut and slunk around the door in a fluid movement as smooth as oil.

By the time he reached the hut, she was nowhere to be seen. But it pleased him to see that both bowls were empty, which he cleaned using the garden hose and his fingers. Then he filled one with water, and emptied the pouch into the other.

Back in the kitchen, he halved and sliced a grapefruit and mango, added strawberries, and peeled a banana, then carried the plate to the table. He powered up his tower computer, an ageing Dell connected to an overloaded double socket, with wires that spilled across the carpet like a nest of snakes. Maureen had been on at him to bin the Dell and purchase a new laptop, Wi-Fi compatible, which he could take to the office. But he'd decided years ago that computers were for the youngsters with gelled hair and fresh faces. As long as he could access the Internet, he was happy to let others keep abreast of the technical side of it all.

He opened Jackie's file, and found where he had left off.

Rachel Novo's ex-husband, Dimitri Novokoff – born in Dorking, Surrey, to a Russian diplomat – graduated from the University of London with a second class in Economics. His early years as a financial consultant took him to the Far East, after which he returned to the UK for two years to marry and divorce Rachel Davis – still no sight of the divorce papers. Dimitri had since left the UK to live in Maroochydore on Australia's Sunshine Coast, where he was allegedly a partner in a newly launched microbrewery. But a search for the brewery on the Internet left Gilchrist none the wiser.

Rachel Novo's life appeared more normal – if you didn't include her short marriage to Novokoff. She'd left school at sixteen with sufficient Highers to study Economics and Finance at the University of York, from which she graduated with a first-class honours. Super-intelligent, and mature beyond her years, she landed a job with Lloyd's where she'd been employed ever since, working her way into the upper echelons of a global company—

Gilchrist jerked at the sound of his mobile.

He picked it up – ID Baxter – and took the call with, 'You're up early.'

'Haven't been to bed yet.'

Gilchrist felt his throat constrict. Something had happened to Jack. He held his breath, swallowed the lump in his throat. 'I'm listening.'

'Got a call from the Anstruther Office last night, sir, the other side of midnight. A man's body was found floating in Cellardyke harbour.'

Despite the grim news, relief flooded Gilchrist. 'ID?' he said.

'Not on the body, sir, but I was intrigued by your interview of Theresa McKenzie last night. So I showed her a photograph.' Baxter cleared his throat. 'And bingo. She recognised him straight away. Stevie Graham. Twenty-two. From Edinburgh. Last known address, Perth. Been in and out of juvenile detention centres like a yoyo, but managed to avoid being found guilty of anything since he turned seventeen.'

'Was he one of Sammie Bell's team?' Gilchrist asked.

'No doubt about it. And get this.' Baxter's voice rang with victory. 'She also coughed up the names of his two mates. Pete Sweeney, a tosser from Glasgow, and Mac Binnie from Dundee. Last known address of both of them, the same as Stevie Graham's.'

Gilchrist's mind fired in staccato bursts. 'Have you found Sweeney and Binnie?'

'Not yet, sir. But I've put out an alert through all airwave channels, and a request through the PNC.'

'Do they have any previous?'

'Sweeney's been in court on four occasions for possession, but he's got off each time, not proven. And Binnie's had no drug-related charges, but two for alleged rape—'

'Of children?'

'No, sir. In both cases the women were in their twenties.'

'Did he get off with these, too?'

'He did indeed, sir.'

Gilchrist felt oddly deflated by Baxter's response, as if he could still somehow tie Bell to Katie Davis's abduction. So he went for the outrageous, and said, 'Was their solicitor Hughes Copestake?'

'Hang on,' Baxter said, then told him – some Glasgow firm he'd never heard of.

Well, it was worth a try. He pressed on. 'We need to check CCTV—'

'Already on it, sir. I've put out a request for footage in and around Cellardyke and Anstruther, sir, so I'm hopeful it won't be long until we pull them in.'

Gilchrist grimaced at Baxter's optimism. With a bit of care, and a little know-how, any pair of hoodlums could make their way to England via Scotland's network of country roads without ever coming across a CCTV camera. Still, Baxter was doing what he could.

'Did you find anything on Stevie Graham's body?' he asked Baxter.

'Pockets were emptied.'

'*Emptied*? As opposed to being empty?'

'Correct, sir. Turned inside out.'

'How was he killed?'

'We don't know it's murder yet, sir, although it's looking that way. But we haven't found any physical injuries. The PF instructed the body to be transferred to Dundee in the early hours, so we should know later this morning, sir. I'd be willing to put money on a drug overdose.'

Gilchrist nodded at Baxter's words. Bell had overdosed, so it was likely that Stevie Graham had done the same. But why? First Bell? Then Graham? And what about his own killer's signature theory? Bell and Graham might both have overdosed, but their deaths – joint murders? – could not have been more different.

Gilchrist had witnessed Bell's strength and muscled physique, so it was unlikely that three lightweight youths could have taken him on and killed him, unless they used their guile to overdose him first, then batter him to death. But his killer's signature theory persuaded him that the youths had not killed Bell. He thought back to that fleeting sighting in the Golf Hotel, the too-thin faces, bodies undernourished and underfed, a sign of drug abuse if ever there was. Had Sweeney and Binnie watched Stevie Graham take an overdose, then held his head under water until he drowned?

But if so, why? And if not, then who—?

'I'll call the forensic pathologist,' Baxter said, 'and tell her we need confirmation on Graham's death as soon as.'

'What about fingerprints?' Gilchrist asked.

'Haven't done anything with these yet—'

'Check Graham's prints against those on the hammer found next to Bell's body. I'm willing to bet his prints are on it. Maybe Sweeney and Binnie got rid of Graham to make it look like a one-man hit, excuse the pun.' And even as he spoke, his mind was reminding him of some recent memory, something he'd seen or heard or . . .

Then he had it.

'This common address in Perth,' he asked Baxter. 'Do you have it?'

Baxter had, and read it out – an address in Scott Street.

Gilchrist scribbled it down. 'That's not where Tess McKenzie lives, is it?'

'Not her registered address, sir. That would be her parents' home. I've already sent a uniform to check that out.'

'Get back to me when you bring in Sweeney and Binnie. And be careful how you handle it. Something tells me they've got good legal representation.'

'Will do, sir.'

Gilchrist ended the call, then picked up Jackie's file. He flipped his way through the loose-leaf pages, searching for what he thought he had read – one statement of many in the passing, nothing that jumped out at him, just a note that scratched his curiosity and had him wondering if the connection were possible.

It had to do with Sandy Rutherford, and how he earned a living. Vera Davis and he lived in an immaculate mansion in Perth, in a lifestyle that dripped with money – Bentley in the driveway, Range Rover in the garage; tiled conservatory; expensive furniture throughout; landscaped gardens.

He flipped over the pages, but still couldn't find it.

Three minutes later, he came across it.

He read Jackie's notes.

Alexander Rutherford is sole owner of a property management company based in Perth – A. J. Rutherford Properties Ltd – which he started after serving two years of a four-year sentence in HMP Shotts for aggravated assault. He was charged and imprisoned under his christened name, Alex Rumford, which he changed by deed poll prior to registering his company . . .

Well, well, well, Gilchrist thought. Out of nothing comes something.

First Rumford changes his name, then Novokoff.

He read on, flipping through the pages, until he found a list of properties managed by A. J. Rutherford Properties Ltd, as at the end of last year. He scanned the addresses, looking for one in particular, and caught his breath when he found it – Scott Street in Perth city centre; a four-storey sandstone tenement block, with shops rented out at street level, three storeys of residential flats above, every single unit managed by Rutherford's company.

Gilchrist checked the address against that given to him by Baxter.

He read it again, checking flat number and floor level, just to be sure.

But he was not mistaken. The ex-con Sandy – Alex Rumford – Rutherford's limited company managed the property rented to the three youths, one of whom had been found floating in Cellardyke harbour. Was that just coincidence?

But Gilchrist did not believe in coincidence.

He picked up his mobile and called Jessie.

CHAPTER 20

A stiffening wind, cold enough to have blown in from the wrong season, had Gilchrist puffing into his hands. He tugged up his collar and strode up Rose Wynd, the breeze at his back giving some respite from the cold. He entered Castle Street, beeped his remote fob, then stopped dead.

He eyed the length of the street, but the culprits were long gone.

He slipped his mobile from his pocket and called Jessie.

'Two calls in fifteen minutes?' she said. 'What is it? My birthday?'

'Your turn to drive.'

'What, you're over the limit all of a sudden?'

He walked towards his BMW, eyeing the damage. 'Four flat tyres,' he said, bending down to inspect the front nearside tyre. The sidewall grinned at him. 'Looks like someone's taken a knife to this one.' He glanced at the rear tyre. 'To all of them.'

'You need to be parking these flashy cars of yours overnight in a garage.'

'Easier said than done.' He breathed in an iced wind. 'How soon can you get here?'

'I've not got my face on yet.'

'I'll wait for you.' He killed the call, then walked the length of his car, examining the paintwork for any scratches, signs of damage. But, as far as he could see, they – whoever *they* were – had limited the damage to the tyres only.

Gilchrist had purchased his cottage on Rose Wynd after his divorce, moving from St Andrews to the fishing village of Crail. Over the years, he had modernised his home – central heating, double glazing, skylights, new kitchen – but its location in a cobbled street restricted to pedestrian traffic obliged him to park whichever car he owned in Castle Street. Every now and then he suffered the occasional act of vandalism – snapped windscreen wiper, fish supper spilled over bonnet, that sort of thing – but four tyres slashed beyond repair was a first.

He kneeled and, with his mobile phone, photographed the cut – a slice in the sidewall, about three to four inches long. It would take a sharp knife and a vicious blow to cut through a modern-day tyre. Each of the valves had been torn off by the culprit, presumably to deflate the tyres before slashing them, to avoid injury from an explosive release of air.

He checked the time – 06.23 – and pushed himself upright.

No shops were open that early. So, rather than return home, he walked down Castle Street towards the harbour, and chanced an early morning phone call.

Cooper answered on the fifth ring with a tired, 'What time is it?'

'Before seven.'

A pause, then, 'You'll have my report mid-morning.'

'That's not why I'm calling,' he said. 'I missed a number of late calls from you the other night, and I wanted to explain what—'

'You don't have to explain anything, Andy. It doesn't really matter.'

He found himself trying to read into the tone of her voice, then said, 'No, I suppose it doesn't.'

She exhaled, not quite a full yawn, and he imagined her stretching in that cat-like way of hers, shovelling her hair over her shoulders, shampoo fresh, breathing it in as it brushed over his face—

'Not now,' she said. 'I'm getting up.'

For a moment, Gilchrist felt confused, thought he had misheard, then realised with a stab of hurt that she was talking to someone else. 'Have I caught you at a bad time?' he said, and listened to her rush of breath as she walked from the bedroom – or whatever room she . . . or they, were in – then closed a door with a hard clatter.

'I have a friend staying over,' she said. 'It's no one you know.'

Was that supposed to make him feel better?

He stepped into Shoregate, faced the wind, its chilled breath squeezing tears from his eyes. He'd never understood the power of jealousy, knew only that it could turn warriors into weaklings, sane men into lunatics. Reason and rationale could be unreachable dreams—

'Don't go quiet on me,' she said. 'It doesn't suit you.'

'There's another body on its way to you,' he replied. 'A young man found floating in Cellardyke harbour in the early hours of the morning. We think he's associated with Bell in some way. But we need cause of death soonest. We suspect drug overdose—'

'We?'

'Fife Constabulary.'

'Ah,' she said, dragging the word out. 'That we.'

'DS Baxter's leading the investigation—'

'Oh, for God's sake.'

Gilchrist stopped, stared the length of the wall-lined street. 'Excuse me?'

'Don't tell me you're in the bloody huff, Andy. I don't need this. Not now.'

'What do you need, then?' He hated himself for snapping, but she was pressing his buttons.

'Some space.'

Well, there he had it. He thought of acting the fool, asking just how much space she needed, but he feared her answer – lots of it, maybe even the other side of the planet. He let out his breath, tilted his head. Clouds blustered across an ice-blue sky. In the distance, gulls shrieked. From the direction of the harbour, he thought he heard the clanking of chains, the bustling and bumping of moored boats.

'I need time by myself, Andy.'

He thought of pointing out that a friend staying over did not exactly meet the terms of 'by myself', but instead said, 'Take all the time you need, Becky. I'm here if you need me.'

He waited for her to say something, but after several seconds of silence, he hung up.

He took a deep breath, held it in puffed cheeks, then let it out. He stuffed his hands into his pockets and stood there, in the middle of the street. He looked left, right, then turned around, like a slow-spinning top undecided whether to keep turning or give up and fall.

Then he lowered his head and set off for home.

He had gone only twenty yards when his mobile rang – ID Jessie.

'On my way,' she said. 'Where are you?'

'I'll be at home. Calling garages and insurance companies.'

'Put on the kettle. Mine's a coffee, with lots of milk.'

'Door'll be unlocked. I'll be in the kitchen.'

He slipped his phone into his pocket, annoyed now at having called Cooper. *I have a friend staying over. It's no one you know.* He cursed under his breath, and pressed on, his heart heavy with hurt. He saw Cooper differently now, as if with professional detachment. *Cold, heartless, calculating* were words that slithered into his mind. *Untrustworthy* another. *Two-timing bitch* brought an, 'Ah, fuck it,' to his lips, and sent him trudging up the road, eyes to the ground.

Jessie knocked on his door at 07.11 and let herself in.

'Bloody hell,' she said, when she walked into the kitchen. 'Did somebody die?'

Gilchrist poured her a mug of coffee, topping it up with a good helping of milk. 'Bit of a frustrating start to the day, you might say,' he said, and handed it to her.

Jessie cupped the mug in her hands and took a sip. 'Just what I needed.' She nodded to his paperwork scattered over the table. 'Trying to contact your insurance company?'

'Trying being the operative word.'

'Last time I phoned my insurance company before ten o'clock, it was a waste of time. I don't think the wankers get out of their beds before midday. Talking of which, it'll be midday by the time we drive to Perth in that Batmobile of mine. So, what have you got?'

Gilchrist explained his thoughts, then handed her Jackie's printout, the address in Scott Street highlighted. 'Coincidence?' he asked.

She scanned the documents, her mouth forming an O for a whistle. 'Does that old git own all of these?'

161

'Manages most of them. The asterisked ones he owns – or, I should say, his limited company owns.'

'Must be worth a few bob. And then some.'

Gilchrist's mind pulled up an image of a gleaming Bentley parked on a weed-free driveway, and the glint of a Range Rover in the garage. For some reason, his mind held on to that image, as if it was having difficulty computing the cost of running two vehicles like that.

He shook the image free.

'I've made some toast,' he said, and removed two slices from the toaster. 'Gone a bit cold and crispy, sorry. Want me to put in another couple?'

'Nah. Butter'll melt if they're hot.'

'In the fridge. Help yourself.'

'You sure?'

'When were you ever shy?'

Jessie opened the fridge and scowled at it. 'What is it with men and fridges? It's like they're afraid to put anything in them.' She removed a tub of butter and a jar of marmalade, then nudged the fridge door closed with a swing of her hips. 'Fridges preserve food. You're supposed to fill them up.'

He handed her a knife. 'Bread board's by the wall.'

'Got it.' She laid the board on the tiled surface. 'So we drive to Perth today, and ask this Rutherford-Rumford punter if he knows this harbour floater whatsisname—'

'Stevie Graham.'

'Stevie. That's it. And he either says he does or he doesn't?' She took a bite of toast. 'This marmalade's good. Home-made, is it?'

'Granny McPherson's.'

'And?'

'And she lives two doors down.'

162

'And?'

He frowned at her for a moment, then said, 'And I'll ask her for an extra jar for you.'

'Well done.' She closed her eyes. 'This is really good. Can you make it two jars?'

'If you insist.'

'I do,' she said, and picked up the second slice of toast. 'But what's troubling me is that the media's crawling all over us, and we're no closer to finding Katie than we were on Monday morning. The CS is foaming at the mouth, not to mention the Chief. And we're going to ask this Rutherford-Rumford punter what . . .? How much he's getting for rent?'

'Not quite,' Gilchrist said, although Jessie's words were hitting home. But he never could explain his gut instinct, that sixth sense of his that poked and prodded away in the depths of his mind, until all he was capable of doing was following it.

'I don't believe in coincidence,' he said. 'So I'm thinking, why does Rutherford just happen to rent property to someone who's turned up dead? And we now have one murder, one suspicious death, and one missing child.'

'It's a stretch.'

'I didn't say it wasn't.' He nodded to her toast. 'You look as if you could eat another couple of slices.'

'Skipped breakfast.'

'Isn't that what you're having?'

She stopped mid-crunch, then gawked at him. 'You called at oh-dark-hundred in a tizzy, so I held on to my knickers and dropped everything else, and drove like a nutter all the way to Crail, to find you sitting with your feet up. Better weather and you'd've been out the back on a sun lounger.'

'Finished?'

'Nearly.' She took another bite that left not much more than the crust.

'Let's go,' he said, and gathered Jackie's report. 'I need to drop off the car keys at the local garage.'

'Four tyres, you say?'

'All of them.'

'At least you're covered by insurance. If you ever get through to them. What? What's that look for?'

'You know how much the excess is?'

'A lot less than four tyres.'

He grimaced as he followed her along the hallway, and stepped into a wind that felt as if it had picked up ice from the Arctic. As he pulled his front door shut, and turned the key, his gaze slid left and right, checking out the length of the Wynd.

Even though the street was deserted, he could not rid himself of the feeling that someone was watching.

CHAPTER 21

They arrived in Perth at 9.14 a.m., their journey delayed by a toilet stop for Jessie – *Don't know what it is about coffee. Goes straight through me. Should just pour it down the toilet and cut out the middle bit.* Another stop for petrol, with Jessie's credit card not being accepted – *Remember when we used to use notes, or in your case pounds and shillings?* It ended up with Gilchrist having to use his debit card, and cursing at the machine for being out of order, and not printing a receipt – *Cheer up. I'll buy you a pint later.*

Jessie pulled her Fiat through the stone gateway, on to the paved driveway, and parked behind the Bentley, which looked as if it had not moved an inch since their last visit. Gilchrist stepped out, surprised to feel the air warmer, the wind died, and warmth spreading over his face from a sun that was already high in a cloudless sky.

He was about to ring the doorbell when a man's voice said, 'Can I help you?'

They turned together, like some choreographed act, and faced Sandy Rutherford.

The first thing that struck Gilchrist was how tanned Rutherford looked, stripped to the waist, denim shorts, and bare feet, as if he'd been sunbathing out the back. The second was his muscled physique and scowl on his face. He could have just interrupted two burglars and be working out how to go about tearing them apart, limb from limb. The third was how he would have to reassess first impressions, now seeing the strength in a body used to physical work, the words 'ex-SAS' springing to mind.

Gilchrist held out his warrant card. 'We spoke on Monday.'

Sweat dotted Rutherford's brow like raindrops. 'I haven't forgotten.'

Gilchrist was fascinated by Rutherford's eyes, a cold white-blue that reflected the sky, and returned his gaze in a hard, unforgiving stare. As he walked towards him, he caught the telltale pink line of a scar high up on his chest, three inches or so above his left nipple, the pectoral muscle tightening and relaxing, as if shivering with anticipation.

Jessie said, 'You never told us.'

Rutherford turned his laser-gaze on her. 'Told you what?'

'That you'd spent time at Her Majesty's pleasure.'

'Thought you were looking for our missing granddaughter,' he said. 'Didn't think you needed to know anything about me.'

'That was why we came,' Gilchrist said. 'To ask questions, and find out—'

'Find out *what?*' he snarled. 'Stuff from the past? Anything you could lay your hands on and try to pin on me? I've seen how you lot work. I've been at the wrong end of the stick before with you lot. Fucking stitched me up last time, so I'll be fucking sure you don't stitch me up this time.'

Spittle frothed at the corner of his lips; when he blinked, Gilchrist thought he understood the problem, or at least part of it. He'd been drinking. Not yet ten in the morning, and he was already flying high, maybe shooting for the sun.

'We're not here to talk about Katie,' Gilchrist said, and puzzled at the sudden change in Rutherford, as if some lever had been pulled and the electricity rushing through his system in a raging current was powered down in an instant to a mere trickle.

Rutherford smiled, as if in relief. 'I'm working out the back,' he said. 'Vera's still in bed.' Then he turned, leaving Gilchrist and Jessie to trail after him.

The back garden appeared to exaggerate the size of the residential structure. Its stone walls reared two storeys high to the side of them, with four small windows, and a large one, six foot high, as best Gilchrist could tell, with stained-glass panels, which from memory was at the half-landing. A threepenny-shaped conservatory nestled in the corner of the building, giving the impression of pinching it to the side and the rear.

In the corner, the grass was covered in wood chips. Gilchrist followed Rutherford across a lawn as smooth and level as a bowling green, and drew to a halt when he leaned down and retrieved an axe from the stump of a tree almost flush with the grass.

'Been meaning to uproot this bloody thing for years,' Rutherford said, and nodded to the lawn at his side. 'Roots are still growing. Buggering up the lawn.'

Gilchrist eyed the grass, its surface perfect as best he could tell.

All of a sudden, Rutherford lifted the axe, swung it in one smooth movement up and over his head, like an extension to his arm, and thudded it into the middle of the stump. Then he rubbed his hands, his shoulders and biceps flexing. 'So what did you want to ask me?'

Once again, Gilchrist was struck by the change in the man. The display with the axe was a show, he was sure of that, like some warning that, if they wanted to take him on, they'd better be ready for a fight.

'Is it wise to be wielding an axe like that when you've had a few?' Gilchrist said.

Rutherford wiped his lips, glanced at the conservatory, as if to make sure Vera was still asleep, or out of earshot. 'It's a good way to start the day, get the old engine going.'

Jessie said, 'So now we've got the testosterone issues resolved, maybe you can tell us why you think you were stitched up. You got four years for aggravated assault.'

Rutherford's eyes seemed to shrink as he stared at Jessie. Then he clenched both fists and held them up. 'I've never hit anyone with anything other than these,' he said to her. 'But some smart-arsed high-flier of a fucking solicitor picked up that I used to box as a junior. A junior, for fuck's sake. I was only twelve when I stopped boxing.' Rutherford shook his fists and his face reddened. 'So he turned these into weapons.'

'So who did you hit?' Gilchrist said, just to shift the anger away from Jessie.

'A bouncer.'

'Causing trouble were you?' Jessie again.

'He tried to take my watch off me.'

'The bouncer?' She seemed surprised.

'It's what they did back then. A scam. Throw you out and tear your watch off your wrist in the process. When you complain, they say it must have fallen off in the scuffle. I was having none of it. So I let him have it.'

'You hit him?'

'Aye. With these.' Rutherford sniffed, lowered his fists, pressed the flat of his hands to his thighs. 'But he'd got contacts. Turned out his old man was a cop. Next thing, I've got witnesses popping up all over the place, and before you can say Desperate Dan, I'm locked up and serving four years.'

'Is that why you changed your name?'

'I'd heard he was going to come after me when I got out, the guy I hit. I wanted nothing to do with it, so I changed my name and moved out of Glasgow. Came to Perth. That's when I met Vera.' He stared at the grass at Gilchrist's feet, and when he raised his eyes, the meek and mild-mannered Sandy Rutherford of yesterday stood before them. 'It all happened years ago. Vera knows all about my past. She forgave me.'

'What about Sammie Bell?' Jessie asked.

Rutherford shook his head, but Gilchrist thought his eyes gave it away. 'Don't think I know him,' he said. 'But these days my memory's not what it used to be.'

'Samuel Johnson Bell?' Gilchrist emphasised, just in case he was confused.

'No.'

'Stevie Graham?'

Another shake of the head.

'Pete Sweeney? Mac Binnie?' Gilchrist tried.

Rutherford frowned. 'Look, what is this?'

'Is that a No?' Jessie said.

'It's a No. I've never heard of any of them.'

'How about the flat in Scott Street?'

Something seemed to dawn on Rutherford then, and he smiled. 'They must rent from my company. Is that it?'

Silent, Gilchrist returned his gaze, pleased that Jessie was doing

169

likewise. Sometimes the way to get answers was not to ask questions. And Rutherford obliged.

'You'd need to talk to Shari about that,' he said. 'She runs the Perth office. I've been semi-retired from the business now for a year or more.'

'We will.' Gilchrist held out his hand. 'Thanks for your assistance.'

Rutherford's grip crushed it, as if to remind Gilchrist never to mess with him.

Jessie turned and walked away.

Gilchrist watched her go, and said, 'That Range Rover of yours.'

'What about it?'

'Ever take it off-road?'

'Not if I can help it.'

'When was the last time you did that? Take it off-road.'

Rutherford screwed his face, giving some thought to the question, and Gilchrist knew that the next words out of his mouth would be a lie. 'Couple of weeks ago, maybe. I can't remember.'

'Short-term memory gone?'

'That's what goes first, so they say.' Rutherford placed a friendly hand on Gilchrist's shoulder, and started walking towards the front of the house and the driveway where the Fiat sat behind the Bentley.

'You keep the place spotless,' Gilchrist said.

'Vera's a tough taskmaster.'

'I'll bet she is,' he said, and gave a short chuckle. 'The cars are immaculate, too. All done by hand. Not run through the car wash, like I do. You clean them yourself?'

'I do, yes.'

They stepped on to the driveway, and Rutherford's hand slipped from Gilchrist's shoulder. Gilchrist lifted his chin to the Bentley. 'All polished,' he said. 'She's a beauty. Spick and span. Does Vera insist you clean them once a week?'

'At least.'

Jessie opened her Fiat's door, and Rutherford took a step back, as if to give her room to reverse.

'You mind if I have a look at the Range Rover?' Gilchrist asked.

'Why?' Rutherford said.

'I've been thinking of trading in the BMW,' Gilchrist said, and caught Rutherford glancing at the Fiat. 'It's in the garage this morning. Four tyres slashed. You wouldn't know anything about that, would you?'

Rutherford bristled. 'Why would I?'

'I thought not.' They stood facing each other, as if waiting to see who would blink first. Then Gilchrist nodded to the garage. 'Do you mind?'

Rutherford came to with a jolt. 'Of course not. It's unlocked. Help yourself.'

Gilchrist walked towards the garage, conscious of Rutherford's eyes on him, Jessie's too. He leaned down, gripped the handle and twisted. He pulled the door towards him, and it lifted up and over to slide under the ceiling on well-oiled wheels.

The Range Rover was top of the range and, as Gilchrist suspected, polished to within an inch of its life. To keep up the pretence, he entered the garage, rubbing his hands over the paint-work, finding himself automatically searching for dings and scratches, but finding none. He opened the driver's door to an immaculate interior, rich with the heady fragrance of new leather. The door closed with a solid click. Round the front to eye the extra fog lamps, then along the passenger side, with a quick dip to run a hand under the wheel arch.

Not a speck of dirt.

He eyed the DIY tools that stood on the concrete floor and lined the garage wall. The power-washer sat with its pressure hoses tidily wrapped around it, between a petrol-driven lawn-mower – for perfect stripes on the lawn – and some scarifying contraption.

Then he was outside again, into the fresh air.

The garage door slid back down with barely a squeak, and a quick twist of the handle secured it. He walked up to Rutherford, watched suspicion flicker over the man's face. Even though he was a good two inches shorter than Gilchrist's six-foot-one, they stared at each other eye to eye.

'A couple of weeks ago?' Gilchrist said.

Rutherford's eyes narrowed, and he nodded in puzzlement. 'About that, aye.'

'You couldn't be mistaken, could you?'

Rutherford's eyes creased with amusement. 'I could be. But as I said, short-term memory's shot these days.'

Gilchrist returned Rutherford's hard look with one of his own, but it was a bit like trying to light a fire with willpower. The man neither moved nor blinked; just stood there, steady as a rock, jaw set, lips tight. The stalemate lasted all of five seconds, but could have been five minutes, in which Gilchrist had seen into the man's soul, a heartless pit from which compassion could never surface.

'We spoke with Rachel Novo,' Gilchrist said.

'Not interested.'

'You? Or Vera?'

'Both.'

172

'Andrea called her yesterday morning.'

'As sisters do.'

'But Andrea lied about it.'

'As women do.'

'Do you not find that strange?' Gilchrist said. 'That she spends twenty minutes on the phone with her sister, before calling 999?'

'We all act differently when panic sets in.'

'What do you think they were talking about?'

'I thought you spoke to Rachel.'

'She lies, too.'

Rutherford's eyes creased in amusement. 'Now there's a surprise.'

Some movement caught the periphery of Gilchrist's view, and he shifted his gaze over Rutherford's shoulder, caught a glimpse through the lounge window of Vera before she slid from sight into the dark interior. 'Quite the dysfunctional family you have here.'

Rutherford grinned. 'There's nought wrong with this side of the family, Mr Gilchrist. Nought at all. But if you don't mind me saying, you're looking in the wrong place. Vera's well rid of that bastard, Dougal. That's where you should be looking.' He eyed the grounds around him – trimmed hedges, manicured lawns, weed-free driveway. 'We've worked hard to turn this into a home,' he said. 'And it's taken years for Vera to get over her nightmare with that bastard.' He fixed Gilchrist with an ice-cold stare that burned straight through him. 'So I don't take kindly to you lot coming into our lives again.'

Gilchrist resisted the urge to swallow a lump in his throat, and said, 'There was mud on your Range Rover's wheels on Monday, and there's no mud on them today.'

'As you said, I keep the place spotless.'

'You last drove it off-road a couple of weeks ago. Your words.'

'Must have driven through a muddy patch in Perth since then,' he said. 'You wouldn't believe the state of the roads here.'

Gilchrist shuffled a step closer so that his face was only inches from Rutherford's. The ripe smell of alcohol and manly sweat swamped his senses. 'You're not telling me everything,' he said. 'But I'll find out what it is. I always do.'

Rutherford jerked his head to the side, hawked up a gob of sputum that stained his spotless driveway. Then he levelled his eyes at Gilchrist. 'When you do, let me know.'

Gilchrist nodded, then stepped around Rutherford and slid into the Fiat.

His parting image of Rutherford was of him standing there, staring at him in that cold-eyed way of his, as Jessie worked a three-point turn and exited through the stone-walled entrance.

CHAPTER 22

A short visit to Shari of Rutherford's property management company turned up nothing of note. The three youths had rented a two-bedroom flat in Scott Street for only six months, but moved out two weeks ago.

'The place had to be redecorated,' Shari assured them. 'They lost their deposit. But it didn't even touch the subbies' costs.'

'Did they leave any evidence of drugs – needles, empty packages?' Gilchrist asked her. 'Anything at all?'

'Does shit in the bath count?'

'Don't tell me,' Jessie said.

Shari screwed up her face. 'It's disgusting what some tenants get up to.'

On the return journey, neither of them spoke until Jessie was driving across South Street bridge. 'What was all that with Rutherford?' she asked. 'High noon in Perth?'

Gilchrist stared off over the slow-moving waters of the River Tay, the surface smooth enough to glimmer blue in a mirror to the clouds. 'Not sure what to make of him,' he said.

Jessie snorted. 'The other day he was wearing an old man's cardigan, a pipe-and-slippers job. And today he's an ageing Rambo. What age is he, anyway?'

'Sixty-eight.'

'Whatever diet he's on, I want it.' She turned right on to Dundee Road, then let out a short laugh. 'Just imagining the two of them in bed,' she said. 'Compared to Rambo, Vera's got to be like a granny.'

'I didn't think she looked too bad.'

'If you cover up the chicken wattle for a neck and put a paper bag over your head. But it makes you wonder what he sees in her.'

'Money?'

Jessie wobbled her head. 'Maybe that's how he got started in his property business. Gets out of prison, moves to Perth, meets Vera. She's got some money, maybe owns another property, I don't know. Invests in his company, and he takes it from there. That house must be worth a tidy sum.' She indicated to overtake, then changed her mind and slipped back in behind an articulated lorry. 'My hairdryer's got more power than this thing,' she grumbled.

'We're not in any hurry.'

'Coming from Coulthard the Second, that's saying something.'

Gilchrist breathed a silent sigh of relief as Jessie let the gap widen between her Fiat and the lorry ahead.

'And why would he move to Perth in the first place?' Jessie said. 'He looked like he could take care of himself. Do you believe that story about the fists?'

'If he'd been set up like he said he had, then it was a good move leaving Glasgow. He would only have found himself set up again, and probably after a good beating.' He glanced at her, gave a quick smile. 'But I'll have Jackie check it out.'

Jessie kept her eyes on the road. 'But none of this answers why Andrea called Novo that morning? Why not call 999 first? Why speak to her before reporting Katie missing? Her house had been broken into. For all she knew, her own life could have been in danger.'

Gilchrist ran the logic through his mind. Any mother would have been distraught at the discovery of her child being kidnapped. Yet Andrea Davis had wasted arguably the most important minutes in any investigation, by delaying the 999 call—

'And where is Dougal Davis in all of this?' Jessie asked. 'According to Novo, he abused her before she was in her teens, but denies he ever tried anything on with Andrea. You ever wonder why?'

'They're lying, I'd say. Hiding something. But if Andrea was molested as a child, it could explain why she's so . . . ' He nearly said fucked up, but instead chose, 'confused'.

'Do you think Dougal Davis is at the root of it all? Even Rutherford said we should be looking at him. Or maybe we should arrest Andrea, and take her to the Station and keep her there until she decides to cough up the truth.'

Gilchrist said nothing. The thought that McVicar was keeping a close eye on the case stifled all thoughts of arresting Andrea. He could try talking to her at home again, but where would that get him? Thrown out a third time? Maybe Jessie was correct. Maybe Dougal was the better bet. But the memory of Simon Copestake in Davis's office in Edinburgh dampened his enthusiasm. Or had this morning's face-to-face with Rutherford put him off the idea of further confrontation?

.He spent the remainder of the return journey to St Andrews on his mobile catching up with other members of his team, fighting off that sickening feeling that Katie's abduction was becoming more permanent with every passing minute, that his investigation was going nowhere, on the verge of stalling.

Back in his North Street Office, he found a message on his desk from CS Greaves – *CALL*. Not that Greaves meant Gilchrist to phone him, he thought he understood that much. No, the note was an instruction for Gilchrist to talk to Greaves in person.

So he set Greaves's note aside and checked his emails.

One from Jackie grabbed his interest, which stated that a DCI Brent Travis from the Greater Manchester Police had been the SIO in the investigation of a triple murder two years earlier, with a similar MO to that of Sammie Bell's. He opened the attachments – excerpt clippings from local newspapers, and a reference number on the PNC – which confirmed that no charges had ever been brought, and that the case was in effect still open.

He dialled the number hand-printed by Jackie, and his call was picked up on the first ring with, 'DCI Travis. Make it quick.'

Although the voice came across as commanding, cross-me-at-your-peril, Gilchrist had the strangest feeling that Travis was trying to project himself as someone more experienced and case-worn than he really was. Gilchrist formally introduced himself and said, 'We're investigating a murder that took place yesterday, which you might be able to help us with.'

'Hit me.'

'A local paedo, Sammie Bell, had his face hammered beyond all recognition.'

'One-piece metal hammer?'

'Yes.'

'Left close by?'

'Yes.'

'No other weapon?'

'No.'

'Nude?'

Gilchrist stumbled at that question, then said: 'It looks like they used his shirt to smother the blood-spatter–'

'They?'

'Figure of speech.' Gilchrist held on, expecting another snap question, but when the line remained silent, he said, 'Any suggestions?'

'Plenty. But I can't speak at the moment. Send me what you've got. Photos. Reports. Anything and everything. I'll have someone get back to you within twenty-four hours.'

The line died, leaving Gilchrist to replace his handset. He responded to Jackie's email, instructing her to send crime-scene photos to Travis, then dialled Greaves's extension.

'You asked me to call, sir.'

'Yes, Andy. Where are you?'

'At my desk.'

Greaves tutted, then growled, 'Come to my bloody office right now.'

Gilchrist replaced the phone, accessed his computer, and checked flight and train times to London. He then phoned Lloyd's and asked for Rachel Novo's office.

When the call was answered, he said, 'Is Ms Novo in any meetings today?'

'Can I tell her who's calling?'

'No need to disturb her,' he said. 'Can you tell me if she's free this afternoon, or tied up in meetings? I may have to call later and ask her a few questions.'

'Perhaps someone else could help?'

'Just tell Ms Novo that Detective Chief Inspector Gilchrist of Fife Constabulary may try to contact her later today.'

His formal approach worked, for she said, 'Yes, sir, let me check her diary.' Some clicking in the background told him she was checking her computer – whatever happened to handwritten diaries? 'She has a staff meeting at two p.m., sir, which are usually done within an hour; so if you phone, say, between three and six, I would expect her to be available.'

Gilchrist thanked her and hung up, then left his office.

He knocked on Greaves's door and eased it open.

Greaves eyed him from behind his desk. 'What is it about *right now* that you never seem to understand, Andy?'

'Toilet call takes precedence, sir.'

Greaves let out a heavy sigh. 'Come in, for goodness' sake.'

Gilchrist closed the door. He had always thought Greaves would have been a terrific headmaster – not terrific in the sense of greatness, rather in the sense of terrifying. His tight eyes, fearsome growl, and a mouth that turned down at the corners in a perpetual scowl would have been frightening to any child.

Greaves pressed both hands flat on the table. 'I've heard from the Chief Constable,' he said. 'He's had a verbal complaint from Hughes Copestake Solicitors on behalf of Dougal Davis. Does that surprise you?'

Gilchrist thought silence his best option.

'No, I thought not,' Greaves said. 'A written complaint is expected shortly about the disrespectful manner in which you allegedly conducted an impromptu visit to his offices in Edinburgh yesterday.' He lowered his head, glared at Gilchrist. 'Are you going to deny it?'

'That I was there? Or that it was impromptu? Or that I was disrespectful?'

Greaves exhaled in silence. 'What is it about authority that riles you, Andy?'

'I didn't know it did.'

'Apparently you also spoke to Dougal Davis's other daughter, a Ms Rachel Novo, by phone.' Greaves's eyes shrank.

Gilchrist tried to hide his surprise, but didn't think he pulled it off. Had Novo been in contact with her father? From what little he knew of her, he thought there would be more chance of the Pope changing religion than Novo doing that. 'I did,' he said. 'Yes.'

'Why?'

'Because she's involved.'

Greaves pushed back in his chair and stared in disbelief. 'Did I hear you correctly?'

'I said that Dougal Davis's other daughter, Ms Rachel Novo, is involved *somehow* in Katie's abduction.' And as he said the names out loud, another thought flickered alive . . .

Katie instead of Katarina. Novo shortened from Novokoff.

Russian father? Russian name for his daughter?

Had Dimitri and Andrea had an affair?

Now that might be good enough cause for Novo to divorce—

'Somehow?' Greaves spluttered. 'Is that it? She's *somehow* involved?' He gripped the edge of his desk as if toying with the idea of throwing it across the room. 'Please tell me you have more evidence than just another one of your hunches.'

181

Gilchrist cocked his head. 'I might like to interview Dougal Davis again,' he said. 'He needs to be careful in his answers.'

Greaves stilled, as if the air around him had locked him in place and time. Then the frame rebooted, and he said, 'I don't think you've been listening, Andy. Dougal Davis is off limits. How much clearer can I make it? His first wife went to school with the Chief, who has already expressed his deepest concern to me that your investigation is dying. Foaming at the mouth, might be an appropriate description of how the Chief is feeling at the moment. So if anyone needs to be careful in his answers, Andy, I would point the finger at you.' His lips tightened to a white scar. 'Do you understand?'

'I do, sir. But I don't agree.'

Gilchrist thought it sad the way Greaves's face shifted from determination, through puzzlement, then on to anger. They'd once had a strong professional relationship, which had soured to the point of enmity after Greaves came to realise that Chief Superintendent was as far up the police tree as he was ever going to make it. His application to fill McVicar's ACC shoes after his recent promotion to Chief Constable never made it off the launch pad, or so the rumours went.

'If I could explain, sir.'

'Yes. Please do.' Greaves sat back, fingertips pressed together, held to his lips.

'Rachel Novo has confessed to having been molested by her father at a young age—'

'About which she's done nothing.'

Greaves's snap response told Gilchrist that Greaves must have known about Dougal Davis's sexual advances on his daughter. But more troubling was the inference that he'd been told by none

182

other than Chief Constable McVicar. Rather than tackle Greaves on his source, Gilchrist said, 'We're looking into the likelihood that Andrea Davis was molested, too.'

'Conjecture, or fact?'

'At the moment, conjecture, sir.'

'Leave it at that.'

'Sir?'

'Don't dig any deeper. That's an order. You're primary remit is to find the missing granddaughter first and foremost. *Not* to air dirty laundry.' Greaves lowered his head, as if eyeing Gilchrist over imaginary specs. 'Do. You. Under. Stand?'

He thought it revealing that Greaves had used the phrase miss-ing *grand*daughter, not *daughter*, which told him that his investiga-tion was being manipulated by Dougal Davis, or at least its progress monitored in deference to his presence. But just how close was McVicar to the patriarch of the Davis family? Maybe it was time to find out . . .

'I'm waiting,' Greaves said.

'Yes, sir, I hear you.'

'I'm not asking if you hear me or not. I'm asking if you understand.'

'I understand, yes, sir. Anything else?'

Greaves's eyes almost hinted of a smile. 'Just the one,' he said, then scanned his desk, as if searching for something on which to write. 'How do I put this?'

'Any way you like, sir.'

Greaves's lips parted to reveal front teeth blackened from years of biting into a pipe stem. 'I've done what I can to stand up for you,' he said. 'Reminded the Chief Constable of your excellent record, albeit on the maverick side of the equation.' He screwed

183

up his face, as if the very mention of Gilchrist's record had fouled the air. 'But Archie's a difficult man to appease when he's got the bit between his teeth.'

Gilchrist thought an agreeable nod as good a response as any.

'So. Bottom line. If you haven't found Katie by close of business Thursday, you're being pulled off the case.'

'Thursday's tomorrow,' Gilchrist said.

'Clever you.'

Well, there he had it. Shot at by his own side, and shat upon from above. He doubted Greaves would have put up any meaningful resistance to McVicar – more than likely simply acceded to his demands; maybe even encouraged setting a deadline.

The shorter the better.

Tomorrow gave him no time at all. But it did give him clarity of thought.

Katarina was a Russian name. And Dimitri Novokoff was a Russian man.

Which opened up another set of possibilities if you thought about it.

He turned on his heel, and left Greaves's office without a word.

CHAPTER 23

Leuchars Station

Jessie screeched her Fiat to a halt. 'Bloody hell,' she said. 'I think this hairdryer's just blown a gasket.'

Gilchrist opened the door. 'I'll buy you a new one.'

'Hairdryer or gasket?'

He gave a toodle-oo wave as he ran to the platform, and managed to board the train with seconds to spare. He found a seat in a relatively quiet compartment – two elderly women chattering about their purchases from a St Andrews charity shop; a teenager with a stud in his eyebrow and an acned face that must surely hurt, on his mobile, oblivious to everything around him; a scruffy gentleman with the rubicund cheeks of a farmer and the rheumy eyes of a drunk, deep into the *Daily Mail* sudoku puzzles.

Gilchrist laid his office laptop on the table. He'd almost forgotten to take it with him – a last-second reminder in the car park by Jessie had him scrambling back to the Office. He tried to connect to the train's Wi-Fi system, which only reminded him that when

185

it came to IT literacy, he was bottom of the class. It took him some time – between Cupar and Springfield – before he managed to access the Internet and work his way back into his email account.

He opened his copy of Jackie's email to DCI Travis – she'd attached everything he'd asked her to forward – and read Travis's response, which included the names of a couple of suspects who meant nothing to him: Stuart Hyde and Malkie Forester. So he prepared a short message to Baxter, and sent the email string to him. Next, he searched his inbox for messages from Cooper, but found none – surprised to feel the bitter nip of disappointment; then sent her an email, professional and to the point, instructing her to copy in DCI Travis on Stevie Graham's post-mortem, then powered down his laptop.

He checked his mobile for any last-minute messages, then switched it off, intending to catch up on some lost sleep on the remainder of the journey to Edinburgh's Waverley Station and the connection to London. But the echo of Greaves passing on McVicar's threat to toss him off the case reverberated in his mind and, as he shuffled around in his seat, and gazed out the window at the worsening weather, the skies seemed to darken in tune with his mood.

Four hours later
Late Wednesday afternoon

Jessie slowed down as she neared Grange Mansion, struck by how quiet the area was. Even though the investigation was still wide open, the packs of journalists and TV crews that had choked the entrance for the past couple of days appeared to have fled the scene. If it hadn't been so odd, it would have been pleasing. But she sensed that the lack of reporters was the quiet before the storm.

She drove through the entrance and eased her way along the potholed track. She felt the front wheel dip into the worst of the hollows, heard the splash of mud on her axle and door panel, and an image of Gilchrist challenging Rutherford flashed into her mind with a surge of irritation. Why had she not noticed the tell-tale splashes of mud on paintwork?

Rather than park next to the vehicles that surrounded the Mobile Incident Room, she veered to the left and pulled up behind the white Lexus – did Andrea Davis ever drive it? As if on cue, Mhairi stepped from the Incident Room and walked towards her.

'Any change?' Jessie asked her, and nodded to the mansion.

'She hasn't put a foot outside since her daughter's disappearance.'

Jessie felt her gaze being pulled to the Lexus. Could be worth making an offer for it – one woman owner, hardly used – but she could not afford to upgrade at the moment, let alone bear the brunt of the additional road tax and petrol costs.

She closed her Fiat's door and together she and Mhairi walked to the front door.

When Andrea answered, Jessie thought she looked tired, as if lying on the sofa all day long, watching TV and doing bugger-all in general was exhausting work. Jessie held out her warrant card. 'We'd like to ask you some more questions.'

'Not again.'

'Can we come in?'

Andrea sighed, turned and walked along the hallway.

Jessie waited while Mhairi closed the door behind them, then let her lead the way past the staircase and into the welcoming warmth of the kitchen.

Chivas was asleep on the rug by the cast-iron range cooker, and paid no attention to them as Andrea dragged a wooden chair from the side of the table with a loud screech on the tiled flooring.

The kitchen felt warm, almost stuffy, as if that room was the heart and soul of the house. Jessie resisted the urge to quip about hot flushes, and removed her rainproof anorak and hung it over the back of her chair.

She took her seat opposite Andrea, who had lit a cigarette and was dragging on it as if trying to kill it in one breathless hit. Jessie had to look away as she exhaled, resisting the urge to breathe in secondhand smoke. She'd not had a cigarette for three years now and, just like Gilchrist, had to fight off that often inexplicable need to light up.

Andrea said, 'Tell me you're not going to ask me about my sister or father.'

Jessie rested her elbows on the table. 'We're not going to ask you about your sister or your father.'

Andrea scowled at her. 'I don't much care for your attitude,' she said.

'We could arrest you and take you down to the North Street Office. That would do wonders for my attitude. On the other hand, you could put out your cigarette and show some respect.'

Andrea risked a glance at Mhairi, took another draw, then exhaled at Jessie, smirking at her through a blue haze. 'Looks like you've grown a pair of balls now they've let you out on your own.'

'Balls are delicate and sensitive,' Jessie said. 'Pussies are tougher. They take a lot of pounding.'

Andrea snorted. 'I'm sure they do in your case.'

'That sounds like the pot calling the kettle black.'

Andrea ground out her cigarette with a force that should have screwed it through the table. Then her eyes burned. 'Get out,' she said, and snapped a look at Mhairi. 'Both of you.'

Mhairi shifted in her seat, as if to stand, but Jessie said, 'It's not going to work this time. I've had enough of you ruling the roost. If we go, you're coming with us.'

'What right do you have to—'

'*Every* right,' Jessie snapped. 'We're trying to find your missing daughter, and you're trying to pap us off at every turn. Either you tell us what's going on, or I'm going to arrest you here and now and take you down to the Station.'

'On what grounds?'

'On any grounds I can make up.' Anger rushed through Jessie like a burst of flame. Her breath pumped hard. But it felt good watching doubt cross the woman's face. 'Call your solicitor, and tell him to meet us at North Street. We can take it from there.'

Andrea tugged her mobile from her pocket and poked a finger at the screen.

'Not that one,' Jessie said.

Andrea frowned at her, finger hovering over the pad.

'Your other mobile. The one you used to call your sister, Rachel.' Jessie opened her own mobile, dialled a stored number, then stared at Andrea.

Mhairi heard it first, a melodic tone that could have been a distant doorbell.

'That one,' Jessie said. 'Aren't you going to answer it?'

189

Andrea's lips pressed white, but she made no attempt to move.

Jessie nodded to Mhairi, who pushed to her feet and left the room.

Within thirty seconds the ringing ended, and Mhairi returned with another phone in her hand. 'We'll be taking that,' Jessie said to Andrea.

'You have no right.'

'Here we go again. Call your solicitor.'

Jessie placed the other mobile on the table between them, a reminder to Andrea that she'd been lying to them. And it struck her that it always seemed to be the well-to-do people from upper-class families – with old money behind them or new money in the bank – who acted as if the law applied only to others less privileged, and how dare you bother us with your impertinent questions and your irritating presence.

Having come from a rough upbringing of her own, Jessie felt an infuriating sense of injustice fire through her system now, filling her with an almost overwhelming desire to slap the condescending look off Andrea's face. But she forced it behind her, and said, 'Mark Davidson. Remember him?'

'Should I?'

'You've been shagging him often enough. I'd be surprised if you didn't.'

'How dare you,' Andrea snapped.

'You deny it?'

'No comment.'

'Hello? Earth to Andrea. Anybody home?' Jessie rapped her knuckles on the table. 'There you go again. We're trying to find your missing daughter—'

'Hah,' she said. 'That's a laugh.'

'Was Mark Davidson with you the morning you discovered Katie was missing?'

'Don't be ridiculous.'

'Was he with you the night before?'

She tutted.

'I take it that's a Yes.'

'That's a No. No, he wasn't *with* me, as you so ridiculously put it.'

'Oh, I see – should I be asking has Mark Davidson shagged you any time within the past week? And I'd be careful how you answer that, as we've already spoken to him.'

Andrea removed her hands from the table, wrapped them around her middle, as if to fend off a cold wind. 'This is ridiculous,' she said. '*Utterly* ridiculous. I don't see what any of this has to do with Katie's disappearance.'

'Could Mark have taken her?'

'Don't be ridiculous.'

'Why is that ridiculous?'

'Mark would never harm Katie.'

'I thought you didn't know him.'

'I know him well enough to know he wouldn't harm a child.'

'He's not into children then?' Jessie said. 'More into older women?'

Andrea tightened her embrace, then seemed to find interest in something on her lap.

Jessie pressed on. 'Anybody else you're not telling us about? Anybody else that you know well enough? How about Sammie Bell?'

Another tut. 'Never heard of him.'

'Sammie Bell's into children. He's a registered sex offender.'

Andrea lifted her eyes as if to ask a question. But the moment passed, and she tutted again and returned her attention to her lap.

'Sandy Rutherford knows Sammie Bell,' Jessie said, just throwing it in there to search for a reaction, and thought she caught a flutter of panic behind Andrea's eyes. 'Indirectly, of course,' she added.

'Sandy would have nothing to do with any registered sex offender,' Andrea blurted.

'Sandy's an ex-con,' Jessie said.

'He's a *what?*'

'Didn't you know that?'

Something like distress creased her features, and for a moment Jessie thought she was going to reach across the table and punch her. 'I don't believe you,' she screamed, then lifted her hands to her face, and sobbed in dry heaves that shuddered her shoulders and had Chivas looking up, wagging his tail. 'Will you leave?' she gasped. 'I'm begging you. Please leave. Now. All I want is to find Katie again. Please leave.'

Mhairi looked as if she was about to reach over and take Andrea in her arms. But Jessie caught her eye, shook her head, then pushed herself to her feet. All of a sudden, she was aware of what Andy had told her: that Andrea's mother and Chief Constable McVicar knew each other. A complaint to the Constabulary would likely be filed, and an unsettling sense of worry, along with a rush of doubt that she had pushed too hard, swept through her.

'Because you lied about talking to your sister,' Jessie said, 'and denied having another phone, I'm taking this for further investigation.' She handed the mobile to Mhairi. 'Next time we meet, I'll be expecting honest answers to some straight questions. And

192

I would advise you to contact your solicitor, if you've not already done so.' She turned and walked from the kitchen, leaving Andrea sobbing behind her.

But as she walked into the hallway and past the staircase, she had the oddest feeling of having just been duped.

CHAPTER 24

Gilchrist surfaced from Aldgate Underground into the city-centre heat of a rush-hour London evening. Fellow travellers bustled around, swarming up and down the Underground stair-case like bees raiding an infested hive. Traffic rushed along the street with noisy purpose, plugs of metal that shunted in stop-start bursts between traffic lights. Glass walls towered by his side, reflecting the heat and noise and the discordant march of a thousand feet.

Compared with the quiet of the Fife countryside, he could be in a foreign country.

He took several seconds to get his bearings, then removed his mobile and dialled Lloyd's. He'd called Novo's office earlier – at 1 p.m. and 3.30 p.m. – to make sure she hadn't left the building on some impromptu overseas jaunt. But he needn't have worried. She'd been tied up in meetings on both occasions.

This time he asked to speak to her in person.

He walked along Aldgate High Street while he waited for the connection to be made, and had to press a hand to his ear to block out a burst of traffic noise.

'She says she doesn't want to speak to you.'

'Tell her she has no choice. She needs to speak to me as a matter of urgency.'

'She says she's adamant, sir.'

'Tell her.'

'One moment.'

When Novo eventually came to the phone, she said, 'I have nothing to say.'

'We interviewed your sister, Andrea, this afternoon, and we have her other mobile, the one she took out under the name of Katarina Davis.'

'Is that supposed to mean something to me?'

'Don't you think it odd?'

'Is this the urgent matter? To ask if I think it odd that my sister has two phones?' She snorted a derisive laugh. 'Goodbye, eh . . . who did you say you were again?'

Gilchrist smiled at her attempt to minimise him, then said, 'You continue to avoid—'

But the connection was already dead.

He slipped his mobile into his pocket and eyed the street for a taxi. He saw one, tried to flag it down, but the driver appeared to ignore him, as if he'd been warned not to pick up irritated Scotsmen wearing leather jackets on a warm April evening.

He slipped off his jacket, undid his tie, and carried on walking.

When he arrived at Lloyd's office in Lime Street, he checked the time – not yet 5.30 – and entered the steel and glass building, trying to calculate how much it cost to build such a glittering monstrosity, but coming up blank. The air-conditioning had him slipping on his jacket again. He studied the address board on the wall, but could not identify Novo's office with any certainty, so he pulled out his mobile and dialled her office.

He recognised the receptionist's voice. 'This is DCI Gilchrist,' he said, 'and I would remind you that I'm a detective with Fife Constabulary.

A pause, then, 'Yes, sir. How can I help you?'

'Can you tell me what time Ms Novo will be leaving the office this evening? As she refuses to take my call at work, I thought I might try her at home.'

'She's actually just about to leave, sir.'

'Going straight home, you think?'

'I don't know, sir.'

He thought it best not to bring attention to himself, so he thanked her and ended the call. Then he strolled to a spot in the entrance foyer, and stood with his back to the wall with an unrestricted view of the lifts and door.

It did not take long – five minutes – before he recognised Novo from one of Jackie's downloads. She looked older in real life, as if the daily pressure of working in the country's nerve-centre had aged her. And not as slim as he'd imagined, either. Where her sister, Andrea, was thin – not skeletal, more undernourished and uncared for – Novo's white silk blouse and navy-blue jacket looked business expensive but one size too tight. A matching skirt hugged tanned thighs, and her high heels gave a solid definition to a pair of well-shaped legs.

Her hair was much blonder than Andrea's, and in better condition, tied back in a loose bun that exposed wisps of dark hair and a freckled neck still ruddy from a recent visit to some place in the sun. She was accompanied by two men in ubiquitous dark business suits, who spoke far too loudly for their surroundings, their harsh voices echoing as they joked and laughed, as if willing their female associate – or, maybe, boss – to join in the fun.

But Novo's bitter lips told Gilchrist that she was having none of it.

He followed them out of the building and down the entrance steps, keeping a good distance back, blending in with others leaving the office, just one more employee in a field of employees at the end of a working day. As they neared the junction at Leadenhall Street, he worried that they might hail a taxi. He could hail one himself, even call Novo on her mobile if he had to – number courtesy of Jackie, the best researcher in the world – but if Novo got wind that he was anywhere near London, she would kill the call.

Still, it was an option.

As the trio crossed the street, one of the men, the taller and older of the two, bumped his thigh against Novo's once, twice – deliberately, Gilchrist thought – but when he tried a third time, she sidestepped him with practised ease, and turned her head to talk to her other companion.

Gilchrist followed them – now a party of two and straggler of one – as they crossed Leadenhall Street and entered Creechurch Lane, a narrow one-way street that seemed more road than lane. When they paused at the window of a restaurant, Gilchrist walked on, mobile to his ear, just another one of London's eight million souls making a call home. The younger of the two men held the restaurant door open, and had more than a casual glance at Novo's rump and legs as she entered.

The older man followed her inside, and something passed between the two men – a subtle smirk, a secret shared, an evening to look forward to?

Gilchrist walked on, and caught them moving towards a seat by the window. Novo squeezed in beside her door-opener, both facing their lonely associate opposite, who seemed resigned to his position as an outsider – although the memory of that passing smirk suggested his loneliness might be only temporary.

Gilchrist reached the end of Creechurch Lane, then called Jessie.

'You spoken to her yet?' Jessie asked him.

'Just about to.' Gilchrist eyed the lane. Despite the short walk, sweat dampened his shirt, and he edged into the cooler shadows. Groups of threes and fours sidled along the road, as if intent on slaking their thirst in the nearest bar. 'Anything on that other mobile?' he said.

'Our IT guys are checking it out, but they're telling me it looks like it's hardly been used at all. The only number it's ever dialled is Novo's. Strange, don't you think?'

'What did she say about Mark Davidson staying over?'

'Another denial. What else? But she kind of semi-caved in the end.'

'Not an open admission, you mean?'

'Precisely. But I'd love to be a fly on your wall tonight.'

'Let me get back to you,' he said, and strode back along the lane.

Through the window, Novo and her male companions were deep in conversation, heads huddled over the table. Both men had clouded schooners of beer as light as lager, while Novo was stirring a straw in a tall glass topped with ice and rimmed with a pink umbrella, a slice of lime and another of orange.

Inside, the restaurant was redolent of curry spice, and echoed with the ring of cutlery and glassware chinking. Several customers sat at a long bar that fronted a shelved gantry filled to the brim, behind which an ethnic barman in a white shirt polished glasses.

Gilchrist approached Novo from behind, swung in, and sat opposite her.

The older companion flashed a panicked glance at the strange man by his side, and said, 'That seat is taken, if you don't mind,' voice purring with public school eloquence.

'I do mind,' Gilchrist said, and showed him his warrant card.

'I don't believe this,' Novo gasped, and reached for her handbag as she slid from her seat, the younger of her associates scrambling after her.

'You can leave if you like,' Gilchrist said as she pushed to her feet, 'but I don't think you would like either of your companions to hear what I have to say.'

'Would you like me to get rid of him for you, Rachel?' the younger man said. He was standing by her side, eyes glowing with a strange light, as if anger was burning within him.

Gilchrist grinned up at him. 'This'll be interesting.'

The younger man slipped his mobile into his hand, and swiped the screen.

Gilchrist turned to the man by his side. 'I'm a Detective Chief Inspector with Fife Constabulary in Scotland and I'm investigating—'

'How *dare* you.' Novo's voice was loud enough to have a couple seated at the bar turn and stare at her.

Her young associate froze, mobile in hand, mouth opened in a silent: *What?*

'How dare I what?' Gilchrist said. 'Explain my presence?'

'You have no jurisdictional right in London—'

199

'I have every right to investigate a missing—'

'Will you excuse us?' Novo snapped to her companions.

The younger man held out his mobile, as if to let her see it. 'I can call the police.'

'He *is* the police, you idiot.'

Gilchrist slid from his seat to let the older man push past.

'Call later, Rachel, darling,' he said, thumb and little finger at his ear.

And with that parting comment, Gilchrist found himself alone with Novo.

He took his seat, and watched the two men spill on to Creechurch Lane, mobiles in their hands, and stride towards Leadenhall Street like two strangers.

Novo seemed in two minds whether to stay or not, until Gilchrist held out his open palm, a silent invitation for her to join him. She jostled into her seat, thumping her bag down beside her, then lifted her glass. 'I've a good mind to throw this over your face.'

'It'd be a waste of an expensive drink.'

She eyed him over the rim of her glass, with a laser look that could have cut through steel. Then she took an angry mouthful, almost finished it, and returned the glass to the table with a hard thud that should have cracked it. 'I resent your interrupting my evening, and I resent your trying to embarrass me in front of—'

'Cut the cackle,' Gilchrist snapped. 'I've had enough of listening to you and other members of your family trying to fob me off. We can do this the easy way or the hard way. It makes no difference to me. But what I will say is, you and me are going to have a heart-to-heart.' He leaned forward, close enough to see hairs on her upper lip, blackheads on a fine nose, flakes of mascara on caked eyelashes.

'I'm the Senior Investigating Officer in the search for a missing child, Katarina Davis, your twin sister's daughter, your niece, and not once have you asked how that investigation is coming along.'

From her burning glare, he had her attention, all of it.

'And I'm here to find out why.'

CHAPTER 25

Novo held Gilchrist's look as long and as hard as she could, until a tremor tugged at the corners of her mouth and she reached for her glass and pressed it to her lips. 'You don't understand,' she said, then drained her drink, and flashed a look at the bar.

Silent, Gilchrist watched while a waiter appeared at the table.

'Same again,' she snarled at him.

Gilchrist's thirst obliged him to grab the opportunity; he asked for a bottle of Sam Adams, but had to settle for a Cobra. 'Large one,' he agreed.

'Perhaps I should phone my solicitor,' she said.

'That's your prerogative, of course. But I don't believe you're involved in Katarina's abduction,' he said, just to settle her down. He gave her a short smile, but it was only one-way. 'Why don't you start by telling me about Dimitri?'

'What's there to tell?' she said. 'I fled Scotland to get away from one abuser, only to end up with another.' She opened her handbag and scrabbled through it, then snapped it shut, as if remembering that the restaurant was non-smoking.

'Did Dimitri know Andrea?' Gilchrist tried.

Her lips pursed.

'I think he did,' he suggested. 'And I think they met.'

'Why would you think that?'

'Why would she give her daughter a Russian name?'

Novo narrowed her eyes, as if seeing him from another angle. 'Maybe she likes Russian names. How would I know? I never see her.'

'But you talk to her.' He studied her through the movement of her eyes, and came to see that here was a woman who thought quickly on her feet, who would manipulate the truth, who could never be trusted, who would seduce you as soon as ditch you, just to get what she wanted.

'So what are you saying?' she said.

'I'm asking you about Dimitri.'

'If he met Andrea?'

'More than that.'

'More than what?'

'How close was he to Andrea?'

'Do I have to spell it out?' she said, then tightened her lips as her eyes searched for the waiter again.

He tried to keep his surprise hidden. Had she just confirmed his suspicions?

'When we first spoke,' he said, 'you came across as someone in control. And when I saw you in the office lobby this evening, I thought that too. But now . . . ' He let his comment hang between them. 'Now I see I was wrong.'

The waiter returned, placed another highball tumbler before her, then poured Gilchrist's Cobra into a fluted glass, as if it were vintage champagne.

When the waiter left, Gilchrist said, 'So Andrea and Dimitri were . . . for want of a better word . . . *close?*' He paused for a few beats, but she was giving nothing away. 'Was that why you divorced him?'

She frowned for a moment, as if caught off-guard, or appalled by the question. Then she seemed to recover, and said, 'One of the reasons.'

He decided to go straight to the heart. 'Does he know Katarina is his?'

Her eyes flashed at him. 'You don't expect me to answer that, do you?'

'I wouldn't have asked if I hadn't.'

'What do you think?'

If this evening was anything to go by, he thought, possibly not. But he said, 'Dimitri fathered Katarina, I think.' The Russian name had been the inescapable clue, but it seemed odd to him that her eyes softened at his comment, and she eased her glass to her lips and took a ladylike sip.

He took a mouthful of beer, too, conscious of having to pace himself, or he'd be on his second glass in no time. He watched Novo's gaze dance around the restaurant, and could not help but feel that he was missing something, some major part of the story without which nothing made sense. He waited until her gaze returned, then said: 'Tell me about Andrea.'

'What about her?'

'Do you miss her?'

'Not at all.'

'And your mother?'

'Slut,' she hissed.

'That sounds heartless.'

'Being brought up in a heartless environment called home made me cold-hearted, too. Just like my mother.'

Well, he couldn't disagree with that. 'If Andrea had Dimitri's child,' he pried, 'why do you keep in touch with her?'

It was such a simple question, but one that seemed to carry a load. Novo grimaced as if crushed by a ton weight. Then she unclipped her handbag, removed a packet of tissues, and ripped one free. She folded it around her finger and dabbed the corners of her eyes. Then she sniffed, and crumpled the tissue in her hand.

'Andrea has no one to talk to,' she said.

Gilchrist returned her gaze, surprised by the ease with which tears appeared. 'So she calls you on the morning her daughter disappears, for what? To have a chat?'

'She was upset.'

'Not when she dialled 999 she wasn't. I've listened to that recording.'

'It's how she handles difficult moments,' Novo said. 'The Davis way of showing pain to the public. They don't.' She reached for her drink, gulped more than a sip. 'God help you if you show any weakness. No Davis can ever do that.'

'Except that you're doing that right now.'

'I'm no longer a Davis,' she snapped. 'I got out of that family before I lost my sanity.'

'And Andrea didn't.'

'Precisely.' Something settled behind Novo's eyes, as if she'd remembered some long-forgotten incident. Then she returned her glass to the table, and stared at it. 'She's not a well woman, Mr Gilchrist. My sister is the weaker of the two of us. She always was. Growing up, we were as close as . . . ' She gave a flicker of a smile. ' . . . Twins, I suppose. Two peas in a pod. We even had the same thoughts at the very same moment, as if our brains were linked in some way.'

'Not a well woman,' he said, trying to nudge her back on track.

'No, she's not. Psychologically she's . . .' Novo shook her head. 'Damaged.'

Gilchrist waited for more to follow, but Novo looked spent, as if the thought of her sister being damaged was now affecting her. 'But *you're* not,' he said. 'You're strong. And you're strong for Andrea. Is that why she called that morning?'

'She was upset. She didn't know what to do. She was in tears. I told her to call 999 and report Katie missing.'

Katie. No longer Katarina. He sipped his beer while he worked through the rationale. When he returned the glass to the table, he said, 'So how do you think having her only child abducted will affect Andrea?'

'If she loses Katie, she'll probably commit suicide.'

Gilchrist stilled as cold fingers brushed his neck. If he had any doubts about Novo's cold-heartedness, they were dispelled there and then. Committing suicide was as ordinary as ordering a pizza. Over the years, he'd come up against many a chilling individual, but Novo was striving to set herself apart.

He decided to change tack. 'The day you left home to go to university, you were what . . .? Seventeen?'

She nodded.

'But you were leaving Andrea. How did that make you feel?'

She shrugged. 'I had to leave. She knew that.'

'And when you last saw your father, can you remember what he said?'

'He said nothing. I slapped his face as hard as I could.'

'Because he'd molested you?'

'Yes.'

'But not Andrea.' His statement seemed to confuse her. 'He never molested Andrea?'

'No.'

The answer seemed too quick, too assertive. 'It doesn't fit,' he said. 'I think he did.'

'Think what you like. I can assure you he never did.'

'Why?' he asked.

Novo frowned. 'Why what?'

'Why did you not report your father to the police? Despite this hatred that you carry around for him still, you never reported him. You should have.' He leaned closer. 'Are you protecting him?'

She pressed her glass to her lips, as if hiding behind it. 'I told him never to contact me again. And he never has. He's boxed. So there's no need to report him.'

'And what about your mother in all of this? The slut, as you put it. You seem to hate her as much as you hate your father. What did she do? Or perhaps I should be asking, What *didn't* she do?' He studied her eyes, thought he caught a flicker of uncertainty, then came to see that his words had frightened her in some way.

'You're not protecting your father,' he said. 'Or your mother.'

She sipped her drink, unwilling to meet his eyes.

'You're protecting Andrea.'

He watched her cup her glass in both hands again, as if to steady a tremor that shook her fingers. Then she closed her eyes, and tears squeezed from between mascaraed eyelashes to run in black streaks that converged on her chin.

'He molested Andrea, too,' he said.

She tightened her lips, trying not to admit it.

'Did he have sexual intercourse with her?'

She lowered her head.

'And he raped you, too.'

She gave out a tiny gasp of breath that caused tears to slide from her chin and drop to the table.

'Which your mother knew about. But did nothing.'

She gave a shiver for a nod.

'Does Sandy know?'

His words had the effect of restarting a frozen scene. Novo raised her head, opened her eyes. Anger verging on panic flamed within them. 'No one must know,' she said. 'That's what this is about. I've never accused the mighty Dougal Davis of incest because it would destroy Andrea. She's not strong. She would never be able to stand up in court to testify against him. Her mental state is too fragile. You must leave her alone.'

'But your mother knew?' he said, just to make sure he was not missing anything.

Anger carved her face with lines of hatred. 'Of course she knew. When he was having it off with us, he would leave her alone.' She glared over his shoulder, set her eyes on some distant memory. 'It was always the same the next morning, after he'd . . .' Her eyes closed, then opened in a long, slow blink. 'She was nice to us. Making us breakfast, fussing over us. When we were young we were just thankful for some kindness in our lives. It wasn't until I was older, in my mid-teens, that I put two and two together and realised she'd known all along.'

'Did you confront her?'

'Once, but she denied it.'

'And what about Sandy?' he tried again. 'Does he know?'

'No.' Her answer was too quick.

He was undecided how much of her confession to believe, because that's what it was, a confession. All these years, and she'd kept her incestuous affair secret to protect her weaker twin sister and, perhaps arguably, her mother. But just how weak was Andrea? She'd ordered both Gilchrist and Jessie from her house, not once, but on two separate occasions – hardly the action of a woman too weak to stand up for herself. He needed to push harder, take Novo to the edge, and only then decide whether to believe her or not.

'You realise I can't let this lie,' he said.

Her gaze snapped back, eyes locked on his. 'I won't testify. And neither will Andrea. I'll make sure of that.'

'And your mother?'

'Drag her good name through the mud?' she scoffed. 'That'll be the day.'

'She won't necessarily have any say in the matter.'

Novo smiled at him then, as if she were about to spoil the ending of some dirty joke. 'For someone as intelligent as you are, Mr Gilchrist, you're being remarkably obtuse.'

Silent, he returned her stare.

'My mother won't testify against my father. You should understand that. No matter what evidence you come up with, it isn't going to happen.'

'Even though he's clearly hated so deeply.'

'My father has a reach far greater than you can imagine,' she said. 'But with my mother, he'll never need to use it.'

'Why?' It was all he could think to ask.

'Because he scares her.'

Dougal Davis was an ex-MSP. That position would have helped him build a network of powerful associates the length and breadth of the nation. Despite being expelled from the party for alleged wife abuse, with a silver tongue he could allay concerns with any number of mistruths – nothing more than fabricated lies by enemies with political grudges, for example. But if he were accused of incest and rape by his daughters, his network of associates would vanish like haar in a heatwave.

The possibility of building a case against Dougal Davis was all good and well, but it was not helping Gilchrist find Katie. He drained his beer, pushed the glass to the side to clear a space between them. 'You abandoned your family to protect your sanity,' he said.

'Is that a question?'

'And you don't miss them at all?'

'No.'

Gilchrist held her cold eyes, beginning to see in them what he'd suspected before his trip to London. Novo might come across as the ice-maiden, but for just that moment, when pressed about her twin sister, she'd almost broken down.

So how did compassion fit into the profile of frozen steel?

He thought he knew the answer. All he had to do was gauge her reaction.

'The burning question still remains,' he said, and leaned forward, his eyes settling on hers. 'Why haven't you asked how my investigation into Katie's abduction is coming along?'

She snorted, gave a tiny shake of her head. 'You've not been listening.'

'Oh I have,' he said. 'I've been taking it all in. Every single word you said. And what you said fits. Up to a point.'

'Which is?'

'The point where you show no concern over your niece's welfare, as if you couldn't care less whether she's alive or dead.'

He caught the bobbing of her Adam's apple, the flicker of a glance to the side. 'And I know why.'

She pressed her glass to her lips, but it was empty. She put it down.

He sat back, and smiled. It was the only logical explanation he could think of.

'You know where Katie is,' he said.

CHAPTER 26

Novo glared at him with a cold look that could weld rebar, and from that point on she reverted to the ice-maiden Gilchrist had first met. Despite his prying and prodding, twisting and turning the questions, she denied everything, replying with a glacial coldness that defied emotion. Gone were the tears. Gone was the concern for her twin sister. Instead, Novo spoke with a quick-thinking sharpness that reminded Gilchrist of some German actor whose name eluded him, playing the role of a psychopathic solicitor.

By 6.30 p.m. he had done all he could, exhausted all attempts to coerce any confession, or uncover some secondary titbit that would help his investigation. Instead of loosening Novo's tongue, it seemed he had managed to staple it down.

He slid from the booth with a suddenness that startled her.

'Aren't you going to arrest me?' she smirked.

He pushed to his feet, and grimaced. 'To achieve what? Establish the truth?' He shook his head. 'I don't think so. I would only be wasting my time sitting in an interview room in London listening to you lying with your solicitor present—'

'I'm not lying. You've accused me of somehow being involved in the abduction of my sister's daughter. The whole thing's so preposterous,' she said, 'that I'm speechless.'

'But you're not.'

'What do you expect me to say?'

'I *expect* nothing,' he said, and held out a business card. 'I was hoping you might be more truthful—'

'You're still not listening. I'm telling the truth. I can't be held accountable for your wanting to cling on to some ridiculous theory that has no substance whatsoever.'

She ignored his business card, but he placed it on the table.

'I'll sort the bill,' he said, then turned away and walked to the bar.

In the mirror, he watched her pick up the menu and flip it over, then back to the front; a telling action he thought, not what he expected. She should have used her mobile – to call her solicitor, arrange a meeting; phone her associates to resurrect their shortened evening: come back to the restaurant, the lunatic from Scotland has been chased away with his tail between his legs; phone for a taxi; phone someone, anyone.

But she did none of that.

Instead, she kept her gaze drilled on the menu, her mobile secure in her handbag.

Gilchrist paid the bill, slipped the receipt into his wallet.

In Creechurch Lane the temperature felt as if it could be in the 90s, so different from the dreich Fife coast weather with its perpetual chill from the sea, and a cold haar that could suck the warmth from any sun. The city seemed to hum with a basal noise that touched the senses. For a moment he thought of stepping into the shadows like some third-rate spy, waiting to see when

– not if – Novo used her mobile. But doing so could draw attention to himself, and if Novo had any inkling that her stonewalling had not hounded him from the city to follow leads anew in the north, she would not make any call.

Of course, he could be wrong. He could be so far off track that he could be outside looking in. But he strode into the evening warmth without a backward glance, heading for Leadenhall Street and the first pub that sold a pint of real ale – Caledonian, if they had it.

He powered his mobile up, and saw he had one missed call and three texts – two from DS Baxter confirming that Stevie Graham's DNA and fingerprint results were back, and that the body in Cellardyke harbour was definitely his, and that Jack had now been released from custody without bail. And one from Cooper asking him to call, signed off with *sorry b xx*.

Well, an apology was a start, he supposed.

Or was it an ending?

He resisted the urge to delete Cooper's message, remembering that he'd asked her to call him any time. But the echo of her voice whispered in his mind – *I have a friend staying over. It's no one you know* – and he knew she wouldn't tell him who, and wondered how they would talk their way around this blip in their relationship – *none of your bloody business*, sprang to mind – if they still indeed had a relationship.

The missed call was from Jessie.

'Any luck?' she asked him.

'Dimitri Novokoff is Katie Davis's father.'

'Holy shit,' Jessie said. 'Didn't expect that one.' She whistled a surprised gasp, and said, 'Where is he? We need to question him. He could be behind the kidnapping.'

'According to Novo, he doesn't know anything about the child.'

'That's what they all say. Do you believe her?'

'To a point,' he said. 'I think she still knows more than she's letting on, but it's too soon to say,' he added, not wanting to hint that Novo might be party to the abduction and know where Katie was – a sixth-sense hunch as far-fetched as he'd ever had. He moved off the subject with, 'Get Jackie to find out Dimitri's contact details, and let's see if we can talk to him at least.'

'Already on it.'

'So what did you find out?' he asked her.

'According to Lady Cooper,' she said, 'Stevie Graham didn't drown. He OD'd on crack cocaine. His fingerprints match those on the hammer, so we're thinking he's been set up by his two mates.'

'Who've gone into hiding, no doubt.'

'Looks that way. And we've had no luck with that other mobile we found in Grange Mansion. Outgoing calls only. And all to Novo. I don't get it. Why take a phone contract out in her daughter's name? Why all the undercover stuff?'

'She doesn't want anyone to know she's still in contact with her sister.'

'But why? Who's going to bother?'

Jessie's question worked through his system, and he realised he should have asked Novo one more question. But he couldn't go back now. 'Just because the contract was taken out in Katarina's name,' he said, 'doesn't necessarily mean it was Andrea who took it out, does it?'

'So you're thinking . . . who? Novo?'

'Not sure,' he said. 'Why don't you check with Andrea?'

She cackled a laugh. 'She ordered Mhairi and me from her home this afternoon.'

'Becoming a habit of hers.'

'Told her I was having none of it this time.'

'So you don't want to talk to her again?'

'Waste of time, I'd say. I'm not likely to be told the truth.'

'Are we ever?' he said.

'Touché. We can always challenge her later if we uncover anything more.'

'Any news on Katie?'

'No further forward,' she said. 'We're coming up empty-handed. Greaves is not long off the phone, demanding answers and looking for you. I told him you'd get back to him at the first opportunity, and he hung up. Why would he do that?'

'He thinks you're full of crap.'

'Well, you will get back to him, won't you?'

'Of course not.'

Jessie chuckled, a throaty roll that sounded – dare he say it? – sexy. 'How to make friends and influence people, right enough,' she said, then added, 'Anything from Tosh?'

'Not yet,' he lied, not wanting to get into it with her. 'But it's only a matter of time until he tries something.'

'Want me to talk to someone?' Jessie said.

Gilchrist pressed his mobile to his ear, not sure what she was implying. 'Like who?'

'I've got friends in Glasgow,' she went on, 'who owe me one. Leave it with me—'

'Jessie,' he snapped. 'Forget it. I'll take care of it.'

A pause, then, 'If you ever—'

'I hear you,' he said. 'But don't get yourself involved with Tosh. Not for me. Okay?'

She took a few beats to respond. 'Okay.'

'I'll talk to you later about it,' he said, then killed the call. Jessie's mention of Tosh made him realise that he still needed to call Strathclyde HQ and talk to Dainty. But Dainty was on one of his rare days off, and Gilchrist managed to track him down on his home landline.

'You're not trying to sell me anything, are you?' Dainty joked. 'Fucking bombarded with punters selling solar panels, or insulation, or God knows what. Should switch the fucker off at night.'

'What have you got on Tosh?' Gilchrist said.

'That bastard?'

'The one and only.'

'You need to be careful. Tosh has got some contacts. He's tight with CS Maxwell.'

'Never heard of him.'

'And you're all the better for it,' Dainty said. 'Chief Super Victor Maxwell heads up the BAD Squad—'

'*Bad* Squad?'

'Used to be a branch of the Drugs Squad until Maxwell was called in to take over, then renamed it Battle Against Drugs – BAD. And I tell you: bad by name, bad by nature. He's been pulled in a couple of times over some questionable interviewing techniques, but he's more slippery than an eel in an oil slick.'

'Sounds like Tosh is in good company.'

'You don't want to mess with these guys, Andy. You'd have to watch your fucking back if you foul them.' The phone rustled, and Dainty said in an off-stage voice, 'With you in a minute, sugar,' then came back with, 'Got the call from the wife. I'll get back to you if I come up with anything.'

The connection died.

Gilchrist wiped sweat from his lips. He didn't like the sound of Tosh teaming up with Maxwell – *bad by name, bad by nature* – but he forced his thoughts back to the present, and glanced at his watch. Ten minutes had passed since he'd left Novo, which was enough time for her to make a call. But he chose to give her another couple of minutes, and called Jack on his mobile.

'I heard they released you without charge,' Gilchrist said. 'How'd you get home?'

'Taxi.'

Gilchrist cringed. A taxi from Glenrothes to St Andrews could run the best part of thirty quid. But maybe this was a way for Jack to be taught a lesson—

'I'm really pissed off, man—'

'I know you are—'

'No you don't. You don't know how fucking really pissed off I am. You hear about fuck-ups like this, about innocent guys being found guilty for some shit they didn't do. Well, I did nothing wrong. *Nothing*, man. Straight up. And that Baxter kept hammering on about Sammie Bell this, Sammie Bell that, as if he's my best mate or something. Fuck sake, man.' A pause, then, 'I mean, for *fuck's sake*.'

It took Gilchrist several seconds to realise that Jack had hung up. He redialled his number, then cut it off before the connection was made. The more he thought about it, the more he could believe Jack was innocent; that he didn't know Bell, but had been led into some entrapment scheme through the over-mature Tess.

Which opened up another possibility.

Having seen Tess, it would be difficult for anyone to believe she was younger than sixteen, and he now wondered if he could work that to his advantage. Jack had inadvertently confessed to having had underage sex, and was in trouble. Could he use that to bring down the drug syndicate that Bell had been setting up? With that thought, he made a mental note to contact Baxter and discuss the possibilities.

He checked the time again, decided Novo'd had long enough, and phoned Dick.

'Anything from six-thirty onwards?' Gilchrist asked.

'Recording her right now,' Dick said. 'She's hardly been off the phone. So far she's made nine calls since six-thirty. Most of them boring stuff about insurance contracts and meetings and stuff. And a few where she's let off steam about some Detective Chief Inspector giving her a hard time.' He chuckled. 'I take it that was you?'

'And . . .?' Gilchrist asked, failing to hide his impatience.

'And one of them was odd.'

'Was that the first one she called after I left?'

'It was, yes.'

Gilchrist pressed his mobile to his ear as the sound of laughter and chinking of glasses had him glancing along a side street, and changing course towards the entrance to some pub tucked into the side of a pedestrian lane.

'It was odd you said. In what way?' Gilchrist asked.

'Short and meaningless. Here, let me play it back for you.'

Four young men with shorn heads and tattooed arms stood outside the entrance to the pub, each with a pint of lager in one hand and a cigarette in the other, too loud for their own good, he thought. But he nodded a smile to them as he walked past and found a spot about ten yards farther on, which gave him a level of privacy. He faced the pub and read the blackboard outside, trying to work up an appetite while he waited for Dick.

'Here we are,' Dick said. 'You still there?'

'Go ahead.'

A click, then the double burring of an old-fashioned British landline that cast up an image of his parents' house, and him as a young boy answering the phone in the freezing chill of the entrance hallway.

The connection was made, and a man's voice said, *Hello?*

That weekend away you were thinking of having? He recognised Novo's voice. *Take it this weekend.*

Silence for two beats, then, *Why?*

Trust me.

The line clicked.

'That's it,' Dick said. 'Mean anything to you?'

Other than the fact that Novo was passing on some semi-cryptic message, it made no sense. 'No,' he said, 'but can you find out the number of who she was calling?'

'Already done that. It's a mobile registered in the name of Kevin Kirkwood.'

The name meant nothing to Gilchrist. 'You got an address?'

'I do,' Dick said, and rattled it off: a street in Dumfries, which again meant nothing.

But he thanked Dick, told him to look into Novo's mobile records for non-business-related calls she'd made in the past week or so, and get back to him if he found anything. He was about to end the call when Dick said, 'Did you look at the CD I dropped off at your cottage?'

'Haven't had a chance,' Gilchrist said.

'You'll find it interesting.'

When the call ended, Gilchrist called Jackie's direct line in the North Street Office and left a message on her voicemail, giving

Kirkwood's name, address and phone number. 'And see if you can find any connection between him and Rachel Novo, now divorced from a Dimitri Novokoff,' and added, 'Formerly Rachel Davis. And while you're at it, how about getting me a copy of the Novokoffs' divorce papers.'

He slipped his mobile into his pocket and was about to enter the pub when one of the four youths turned to snuff out a cigarette dout with his boot and bumped his arm against his.

'Careful there,' Gilchrist said, then sidestepped him.

'What you on about?' the youth said.

Gilchrist was about to step inside, when a hand grabbed him by the shoulder.

'You spilled my beer, you fucking sweaty sock.'

'I think you spilled it yourself,' Gilchrist said.

'Cheeky bastard,' one of his mates chipped in. 'Go on, Bev, fucking have him.'

Gilchrist slipped out his warrant card. 'Don't get yourselves into trouble, boys.'

'Do what?' the mate said.

Gilchrist eyed the group. Bev was having second thoughts. He released his grip on Gilchrist's shoulder and said, 'Leave off, Gus,' then turned away and gulped at his beer.

'So who the fuck is this then?' Gus said. 'The flying fucking Scotsman?'

Gus seemed to be the leader, and the most drunk. His pained face grimaced red-eyed, as if he'd not slept for a week, maybe longer. He approached Gilchrist, fists clenched, face tight with drunken rage.

When the punch came, Gilchrist was ready for it.

He grabbed the arm as it swung at his face, used the blow's momentum to topple the man to the ground before his stunned

221

brain had time to tell him he was no longer standing. A tug and a twist of the arm had Gus on to his stomach, and a curse from Gilchrist as he jerked the arm up the back had Gus squealing like a scorched pig.

Gilchrist held his hand out to the others like a warden stopping traffic.

'That's enough, boys,' he said, to keep them at bay.

'*Fucking arm you cunt—*'

One more jerk pulled another squeal from Gus's mouth, and put an end to matters as Gilchrist felt the fight go out of the guy. Just to be sure, he kept the pressure on, and leaned forward so his mouth was inches from Gus's ear. 'I can arrest you for assault,' he said, loud enough for the others to hear. 'Or I can have a pint on my own, in some peace and quiet.'

Gus's mouth spluttered with fury as he tried to resist. But with Gilchrist's knee on his back, squeezing the air from his lungs, he was in no fit state.

Gilchrist looked up at the others, but they were backing off, not wanting to risk being arrested as accomplices. 'What do you say, boys? Should I arrest him? Or can I have a quiet pint on my own?' He rose to his feet with a parting jerk that released a gasping grunt.

Silent, Gilchrist faced the group for a couple of seconds, then turned and entered the bar.

He showed his warrant card to a wide-eyed barman with a mobile to his ear. 'I'm with Fife Constabulary,' he said. 'So no need to call the police. I won't be pressing charges,' and waited while the barman slipped his mobile back into his pocket. Then he nodded to the beer taps. 'But I'll try a Sambrook's Junction when you've got a moment.'

In the mirror, he kept an eye on the group outside. Gus had been pulled to his feet, and stood, red-faced, grimacing in agony, holding his right arm as if in a sling. He shifted his stance and stared at Gilchrist's back, and for one uncertain moment Gilchrist feared the man was drunk enough to continue the fight inside. Then one of the others grabbed Gus by his good arm and hustled him away.

When his pint arrived, Gilchrist waited for its creamy head to settle before taking that first glorious sip, so silky and smooth that he had to ease the glass from his lips at the halfway mark.

Then he pulled out his mobile and called Cooper.

KILKENNY COUNTY LIBRARY

CHAPTER 27

On the third ring, Cooper answered with, 'I thought you might not call back.'

'I got your message,' Gilchrist said.

'Where are you?'

'In a bar.'

'I gathered that much,' she said. 'Would you mind if I joined you?'

He caught the uncertainty in her voice, the worry that perhaps she had pushed him too far this time, that she was no longer in control of their relationship, that whatever she thought they once had might have been lost for good. But he said, 'I wouldn't mind,' then added, 'although I'm sorry to tell you I'm in London.'

She waited a beat, then said, 'I suppose that means I can't see you tonight.'

'Unless you can beam me up.'

She laughed at that – a bit forced, he thought, and he wondered if she was worried that he might press for the name of the person who stayed over last night. Should he feel such a strong need to know? Did it really matter? But an echo of a man's whisper entered his mind with such clarity that he glanced to his side to make sure no one was talking to him. He thought he would have vanquished the memory of his ex-wife's infidelity by now, that the jealousy that smouldered in his heart would finally have burned out, but it was all he could do to cough and try to snap the image away.

'Are you okay?' she said.

'Something in my throat.'

Neither of them spoke for what seemed like five minutes, until Cooper said, 'I made a mistake, Andy. One that I deeply regret. And I'm truly sorry.'

He found himself struggling to translate her open-ended apology. Sorry she'd fallen pregnant by him? Sorry she'd had a miscarriage? Sorry she'd got herself involved with him in the first place? *Sorry for what?* he wanted to shout.

Instead, he said, 'We all make mistakes, Becky. But we have to live with them. What else can we do?'

'Move on,' she said without missing a beat.

His heart shivered, as if ice-chilled fingers had reached inside his chest and gripped it. 'Is that what you want to do?' he asked. 'Move on?'

Electronic silence filled the line for so long that Gilchrist thought the connection was lost. Then Cooper said, 'I'm confused, Andy. I'm sorry. I . . . when I first met Max, I thought I'd found the perfect man – handsome, intelligent, articulate, urbane, and madly in love with me, or so I believed. When we married, I wanted to start a family, we both did, but then . . . well . . . nothing happened. I thought the problem was me. I truly did. Max has two children by his first wife. Teenage boys. Did I tell you that?'

Gilchrist reached for his pint. 'You never did, no.'

'Well, everything pointed to the fault being with me.'

Gilchrist took a sip of beer, then realised she was waiting for him to speak. 'Did you seek medical advice?' he asked.

'No,' she said with a finality that warned him he was close to touching a nerve. 'That was my mistake. I should have. But I didn't. Max insisted that we make an appointment, but I refused. The more he persisted, the more I dug in my heels.' She let out a sigh. 'Am I holding you back?'

'I'm having a pint. I'm sure I can have another.'

She chuckled, and an image of her raking her strawberry-blonde hair pulled a smile to his lips. If he closed his eyes, he could almost feel the wind's breath, hear the waves rushing shoreward, ice-cold water licking their bare feet. They used to walk the beaches together, go for long walks at the end of the day, or whenever they had time, and no matter how long they spent, it always seemed too short for all they had to say to each other. He'd had a number of short-term affairs since Gail left him – was it really ten years ago? – but none had ever amounted to much. That is, until old Bert Mackie retired, and Dr Rebecca Cooper took over as Fife's forensic pathologist. In Cooper, he thought he'd found a like soul, someone who handled the professional side with a passion verging on the obsessive, and who'd also managed to free herself from a damaged marriage. They seemed the perfect couple, or so he'd once thought . . .

'You've gone all quiet on me,' she said.

He was on the verge of telling her that she might have that the other way around, but the last thing she needed from him was conflict. So he said, 'You were talking about digging in your heels.'

'Yes,' she said, as if trying to remember the gist of what she'd been saying.

He nudged her along with, 'You never sought medical advice.'

'No, I didn't. Which was the start of the demise of my marriage.'

They had both discussed the failings in their respective marriages, but he'd always thought that Cooper was holding something back, as if she were reluctant to hang her dirty washing out for Gilchrist to inspect. He'd thought her on-again-off-again downward spiral with Maxwell had been the reason for her reticence, that somewhere in the deepest part of her psyche she believed, maybe even hoped, they would survive and remain together. But only in the last several months had it become clear to both of them that Cooper's marriage was over for good. Of course, his own marriage was long gone.

He took another sip of beer, and only then realised that the muffled mewing on the line might be Cooper crying. 'Are you all right?' he asked.

'I'm hurting, Andy. I'm hurting in a way I've never felt before. It's . . . I'm sorry for troubling you—'

'You're not troubling me at all—'

'Truly I am, but I'm so sorry.' A pause, then, 'Max stayed over last night. I was going to tell you. He caught me in a moment of weakness. And I'd had too much to drink. I'm sorry that you had to find out the way you did.'

Well, alcohol was always a catalyst for trouble: he would be the first to agree.

'Becky,' he said, 'what you've been through is emotionally devastating. To want a child so much, then to . . . to . . . ' He struggled for the kindest word, but in the end said, 'To go through such a difficult time, it's bound to affect you. It would be unnatural if it hadn't.' He pressed his hand to his other ear to drown out a burst of laughter from the far end of the bar. 'You're still young enough,' he said. 'You're not too old to try again.'

She sniffed, and he sensed she was pulling herself together.

'Forget last night,' he said. 'And forget Max,' he added as a joke. 'I know I have.'

'Have you?'

'Of course I have,' he lied. Past experience told him that an image of Cooper being close to Max would creep its way into his thoughts with resolute frequency for years to come, maybe even in perpetuity. But he shoved it away as best he could, and said, 'I'll be back tomorrow morning. I can swing by Bell Street, and you can bring me up to speed with some blood work—'

'I'm taking the rest of the week off,' she said. 'Going to head off for a few days.'

He almost said *Alone?* but managed to bite his tongue. 'Give me a call when you get a chance. Or text. Who knows, if Greaves kicks me off the case, I could come and join you.' He sent a chuckle down the line, but from Cooper's silence it sounded out of place.

'I'll be in touch,' she said, and the line clicked dead.

He stared at his mobile, as if the disconnection had been a fault on the line. But she really had hung up. With Cooper, there never seemed to be any middle ground; no greys, just blacks or whites, like living in a binary world, he thought – either on or off, end of. Still, she had been in tears – a first, he'd have to say – but the manner of her parting seemed in conflict with that momentary loss of composure, and displayed a coldness that had to be unhealthy.

He slipped his mobile into his pocket, then picked up his pint.

It took another couple of Sambrook's Junctions and a Drambuie on the rocks before he decided to find a taxi and make his way to Euston and the sleeper to Edinburgh. Force of habit had him checking his mobile for text messages from Cooper, even though he knew there would be none.

He flagged down the first available taxi, irritated that Cooper seemed mentally more resilient than he ever was when it came to matters of the heart – always a failing of his. The taxi drew up to the kerb, and he found himself powering his mobile down before he opened the door, just to make sure he could not succumb to temptation.

Then he slid inside and slurred, 'Euston Station.'

The sleeper was nothing more than a reclining seat, which he pushed back as far as he could, not worried about cramping the space of the person behind – it was a sleeper, after all. The carriage was almost too warm for comfort, but the alcohol at the end of a tiring day was as good as any sleeping pill, and he was sound asleep before the train left the station.

He saw Katie on the beach, black rocks rising sixty feet by her side. He saw her little face looking at him, eyes open with childish surprise as a woman dressed from head to toe in a white medical smock lifted her. Then Jack took Katie and walked with her towards the sea. Watch out for the waves, he shouted, as they reached the water's edge. Jack flicked his reefer into the wind, and little Katie watched it spinning and tumbling over her head, sparks flying, until it turned into a cartwheel firework that broke loose from a pole and spun away like a comet into the night sky.

Cooper whispered something in Gilchrist's ear, in a foreign

language like Chinese. What had she said? When he next looked at Jack, he was stepping into the sea, Katie high on his shoulders. But with every step, the sea receded – twenty yards, thirty, fifty; and still it fell away, leaving fish flopping in shallow puddles. Tsunami, Gilchrist tried to warn them, but his voice was muffled, his arms and legs buried in sand as heavy as lead, and the woman in white turned to him and laughed. He could see her teeth, but not her face, and he shouted at her to run – Run. *Run*. Behind her rose a wall of water, a black mountain that swelled like an eruption and tumbled towards them—

'Hey, hey, hey there, hey . . . '

Gilchrist opened his eyes, jerked his head back from the woman's troubled face at his side. 'What . . .?'

'We cannae get any sleep here, with you roaring your head off.'

'Oh . . . sorry, I . . . I must've been dreaming.'

'Having a nightmare, more like.'

Gilchrist nodded. He swept his gaze around the carriage, but other than the woman at his side, everyone seemed asleep. 'Sorry,' he said.

'Aye, well,' she said, and pulled herself back into her seat across the aisle.

He glanced out the window, at a dark countryside that swept past in flickering blacks and greys. Overhead a starless sky hinted of the coming dawn. He glanced at his watch, but his eyesight was not what it used to be, and as best he could tell it was 2.25 a.m., or maybe 3.25 a.m.

Not that it mattered, he supposed.

His mouth felt dry, and he removed a plastic bottle of ginger ale from the back of the seat in front, pleased that he'd had the foresight to buy a couple of soft drinks before boarding the train.

230

His head swam from too much alcohol on an empty stomach, and he still felt tired enough to sleep in a heartbeat. But, once wakened, it seemed that he could never return to the land of nod. Besides, remnants of his most recent dream – call it nightmare – echoed in his mind, forcing him to question the deeper meaning, the twisted rationale. He necked another mouthful of ginger ale, then burped as discreetly as he could, only to have the woman across the aisle glare at him.

He smiled at her, and shrugged, then powered up his mobile.

It was the woman in white in his dream who troubled him the most. Who was she? Why did she turn to him and laugh as the tsunami reared up from the horizon behind her? His phone beeped to life, and he checked his messages to find only one – a text from Jackie.

Because of her cerebral palsy, Jackie was allowed to work from home, as long as she turned up at the Office at least three times each week, which meant she was cleared to access the main Constabulary server remotely to enable her to carry out her research work. Living alone, and with a disability that limited outdoor activities, Jackie spent more hours on the computer than many of her associates, and probably more hours than was good for her health. But working as a researcher made her feel like she was contributing as a normal member of society, and her job had become more to her than a way to earn a living; it was her passion.

Which explained why she'd worked on his query overnight.

He opened her text message.

Kevin kirkwood married annette martin 10 years ago. Rachel davis and annette on same course at york uni. Rd and am graduated with economic degrees in 95. Have emailed more details 2u cc ds janes.

Gilchrist reread the text message. This showed a link between Kevin Kirkwood and Rachel Novo. Well, of course there was a link. There had to be. Why else would Novo have phoned Kirkwood and left a semi-cryptic message?

That weekend away you were thinking of having?

Take it this weekend.

Trust me.

Why? Gilchrist thought. And, even in his still-over-the-limit hungover stupor, the outline of some scratchy thoughts material-ised into an image of a woman dressed in white being handed a young child, then turning and laughing at him, only to manifest into Novo's sister, Andrea, before evaporating into a blank face.

Which was the key.

Not Rachel. Not Andrea.

And definitely not handing over any child.

For the ploy to succeed, that would not work.

Trust me.

Oh, Kevin would trust Novo all right. Of course he would. Kevin's wife and Novo were university students together, on the same course together; they graduated together, maybe even lived in rented accommodation together. And, having shared all of that, what else might they have shared? Secrets from the past, no doubt.

Which led to secrets in the present?

Trust me.

Why would I trust you? Gilchrist thought. No phone calls from the restaurant until you were sure I was out of sight. That was the giveaway. That was your mistake. You'd just been interrogated by me, effectively harassed without legal representation. You should have picked up your mobile and called your solicitor as soon as I left, even insisted on filing a formal complaint. I know you should have, because that's what I would have done.

Instead, you waited until I paid the bill and left the restaurant before calling.

And not your solicitor, but Kevin, your friend Annette's husband.

To leave a cryptic message.

Trust me.

Oh, I trust you all right, Gilchrist heard his mind say.

I trust you as I trust a snake.

CHAPTER 28

7.26 a.m., Thursday morning
Waverley Station, Edinburgh

Jessie met Gilchrist as he strode through the ticket barriers.

'What did you find out?' he asked, stepping in beside her.

'I think we might be barking up the wrong tree. The Dumfries Office has already been in contact with Mr and Mrs Kirkwood, and they've nothing to report.'

Gilchrist felt a wave of nausea sweep through him at the ever-increasing likelihood he was wrong – *again*. The sound of a thousand shoes scraping the platform felt like gravel and cement mixing in his head. He adjusted his step to avoid a limping pigeon as it scavenged the concrete on stumps for feet, its claws burned off from roosting on electrical wires.

'Have they gone to their home like I asked?' he grumbled.

'A couple of uniforms dropped by about five-ish this morning. Reported both cars in the driveway, and curtains drawn.'

'And what did the Kirkwoods say?'

'They never knocked them up.'

'So they don't know if they're at home or not?'

'They believe they're at home.'

'Jesus Christ,' he said. 'You see the problem with that word *believe*? It means we don't bloody well know for sure. That's what believe means.' He bumped into Jessie as she veered to the right. 'Where're you parked?' he snapped.

'Got Mhairi with me,' she said. 'Couldn't find a parking spot, so she's still circling, looking for a place to land.' She slipped her mobile to her ear. 'We're on our way. Where are you?' Then she slapped it shut. 'Top of the ramp. Let's go.'

Sure enough, Mhairi had an unmarked police car – a black Vauxhall Vectra – parked on double yellow on Bridge Street.

Gilchrist held the rear passenger door open for Jessie.

'Am I in the back, then?' she said.

'You certainly are.'

'A gentleman to the last.'

Gilchrist closed the door behind her and took the front passenger seat. 'You know the way?' he asked Mhairi.

'I do, sir, yes,' she said, accelerating into traffic.

'How long will it take?'

'About two hours, sir. Depending on traffic.'

Jessie said, 'Would you like me to call the Dumfries Office and tell them to arrest the Kirkwoods?'

Gilchrist jerked a look at her. 'No. Don't,' he said, and hoped his tone had not come across as panicked as he'd felt. He was flying by the seat of his pants again, going with his gut instinct, that sixth sense of his which, even though it had worked for him over the years, was far from infallible, he knew. And oh, how he knew. 'Call them, and tell them to park outside the Kirkwoods' home. If the curtains are still drawn at eight o'clock, get them to check it out.'

Jessie dialled her mobile, and Gilchrist said, 'On speaker.'

She did, and within a minute was put through to a Detective Sergeant Chambers.

'We have two of our boys in blue already parked outside their house,' DS Chambers assured her. 'And the curtains are now opened, so we're happy to report that the Kirkwoods are still at home, safe and sound.'

Gilchrist half turned in his seat. 'This is DCI Gilchrist,' he said. 'I'm the SIO in the Katie Davis abduction case. I'd ask that you keep this super-low profile for the time being. We don't want the place flooded with media if any of it leaks. Can you do that?'

'Yes, sir.'

Jessie thanked DS Chambers and ended the call. 'Ever felt like a twerp?' she said.

Gilchrist said nothing, just stared at the road ahead, struggling to ignore a burning feeling that threatened to scorch his gut. Now he was sobering up, what had seemed so clear last night on the sleeper, so irrefutable in its step-by-step alcohol-induced logic, was now beginning to lose its lustre, the gold-plated prize looking more like rusted scrap.

Did he have it all wrong? Only time would tell.

'Want me to stop for coffee, sir?'

'Let's get there as fast as we can,' he said, and slumped into his seat, as miserable as he had ever felt.

The Kirkwoods lived in a detached red sandstone mansion on Edinburgh Road. A Mercedes ML350 SUV, and a dated Porsche with a black go-faster spoiler on the back stood bonnet to boot on a grey asphalt driveway that could do with being re-tarred.

Sure enough, the curtains were opened.

Gilchrist approached the unmarked police car parked some fifty yards farther along Edinburgh Road. He introduced himself, and asked to be updated, only to be told that neither Mr nor Mrs Kirkwood had made an appearance that morning.

Gilchrist checked the time on his mobile – 09.41. 'Do they not work?'

'Couldn't tell you, sir.'

He nodded to Mhairi. 'Find out where they work, and if they don't work from home, why they're not in the office.' Then he strode towards the entrance and eyed the mansion, wondering how much the Kirkwoods earned – more than he ever would, came the answer. He glanced at Mhairi, but she was still on the phone.

'Come on,' he said to Jessie. 'Let's get this over with.'

'You don't sound as confident as you did last night,' she said.

'I'm sober now.'

'Ah, the demon drink.'

'Indeed.'

Together they strode up the driveway. An expansive lawn spread off to the right. Its edges could do with a bit of a trimming – not Mr and Mrs Perfect – although the shining paint and glistening brightwork of the Mercedes and Porsche could have fooled many a man. Even the tyres' black sidewalls looked freshly dressed.

'Looks like they're not short of a bob or two,' Jessie said, as she stood on the tiled porch and eyed the plants – dwarf conifers, pansies, trailing ivy – in floral blue and white ceramic pots.

Gilchrist rang the doorbell, and ten seconds later the door cracked open to a dark-haired woman in her late thirties – same age as Novo, he guessed, but a few inches taller – who stared at him wide-eyed as he held out his warrant card.

Her gaze darted to Jessie, back to Gilchrist. 'Let me fetch my husband,' she said, and closed the door.

'Charming,' Jessie quipped.

Two minutes later, Gilchrist was on the verge of ringing the doorbell again, when Mhairi walked up the driveway towards them.

'What you got?' Jessie asked her.

'He runs his own chartered accountancy firm here in Dumfries – Kirkwood Associates – and she's the regional representative for an international clothes distributor, Maycom. Never heard of it. He's already called in this morning and told them he was off on holiday for a week.'

That weekend away you were thinking of having? Take it this weekend.

'Where to?' Gilchrist asked.

'Didn't say.'

'What about her?'

'Seems to be her own boss, keeps her own hours, so I don't know, sir.'

'Right.' Gilchrist rang the doorbell, kept his finger down to the count of five. A chime echoed back at him from somewhere deep in the hallway. He counted to twenty, and rang the doorbell again, and was about to give it one more shot when he caught movement through the frosted panels.

The door opened and a tall man – six-four, give or take an inch – wearing jeans and a white open-necked shirt looked down at them with a goofy smile more suited to a horse than a human. Sweat dotted his brow. A bead trickled down his cheek.

'Whatever you're selling, we're not interested,' he said.

Gilchrist held his warrant card out. 'Kevin Kirkwood?'

'Yes?'

'It may be better if we talked inside.'

'What's this about?'

'You're going on holiday?'

'Look, what's this about? We're busy packing.'

Gilchrist thought he heard a door slamming shut, maybe on the upper floors, but he couldn't be sure, then said, 'That's it,' and pushed past Kirkwood.

'Wait a bloody minute,' Kirkwood shouted after him.

But Gilchrist was striding down the hallway, galloping up the stairway.

He opened the first door on his left, guest bedroom, closed it, tried the next – another bedroom. From behind him, he heard the thud of feet reaching the top of the stairs.

'What the hell d'you think you're doing?' Kirkwood shouted after him.

Gilchrist took a chance and opened the door at the end of the hallway, and found what he was looking for – the master bedroom. The bed was not made. Pillows were scrunched to one side. A continental quilt lay crumpled at the foot of the bed. A counterpane had slipped off the end and fallen to the floor. A laptop sat opened on a chair in the corner. Imprints on the carpet told him the chair had been moved. Phone-charger cords coiled from wall sockets to mingle with nightclothes that lay where they'd been dropped – negligee and panties for her, pyjama bottoms and vest for him.

If they'd arrived an hour earlier, he might have caught them at it.

He was about to walk to the en-suite bathroom when a hand thudded on his shoulder and spun him around. 'You've absolutely no fucking right to come barging in here like—'

'You're packing,' Gilchrist said. 'Where are the suitcases?'

'What?'

'You heard.'

'And you hear this,' Kirkwood snarled as he turned from the bedroom, mobile pressed to his ear. 'I'm calling the police.'

'Would you like me to arrest you instead?'

'Do what the hell you like,' Kirkwood snapped. 'But you're out of order,' and strode along the hallway, heading for the stairs.

Gilchrist found himself chasing after him, annoyed that he'd been so easily fobbed off. He struggled to keep up as Kirkwood skittered down the stairs with his lanky legs and entered the second door off the entrance hallway.

Gilchrist followed him into a lounge decorated in creams and lilacs. Kirkwood's wife, Annette, stood with her back to the room, staring at a landscaped garden for which money seemed to be no object. Kirkwood stood beside her, facing Gilchrist as if to protect her from this strange lunatic. Jessie and Mhairi were nowhere in sight, although Gilchrist knew they would be searching the lower floor. Which brought its own set of problems. Any search was illegal, and evidence of the Kirkwoods' involvement with Katie Davis could be inadmissible in a court of law.

Still, finding Katie would be an answer in itself.

Kirkwood appeared to be having trouble getting through on his mobile, and stabbed at its screen in tight-lipped frustration.

'Put the phone down,' Gilchrist tried.

Kirkwood snatched a glance at him. 'I'm calling the police.'

'We *are* the police.'

240

'You have absolutely no right to enter our home in this manner, and to . . . to—'

'You know Rachel Novo,' Gilchrist interrupted. 'Formerly Rachel Davis.'

His words had the effect of stilling Kirkwood, but jump-starting his wife, who turned from the window and faced him. Her eyes brimmed with tears. A quiver jerked the edges of her lips. Then Kirkwood's arm was around her shoulder, hugging her to him. He twisted his body and kissed the top of her head.

'It's okay, it's okay,' he whispered. 'I'll take care of this.' Then he pulled himself upright to his full six-four, maybe -five, and said, 'We know Rachel. Yes.'

Gilchrist took the opportunity to advise them that he was with Fife Constabulary and the Senior Investigating Officer in the abduction of Rachel's niece, Katie Davis, and that they could call their solicitor to be interviewed at the local police station.

Something seemed to pass between Kirkwood and his wife then, and Kirkwood said, 'We have a plane to catch this evening.'

'Of course,' Gilchrist said.

Jessie and Mhairi entered the lounge; he knew from the look on Jessie's face that they'd found nothing, that he'd had it all wrong, that his blustering entrance was just the sort of thing that CS Greaves would use to get him booted out of the Constabulary once and for fucking all. Jesus Christ, if it wasn't so serious, it would be funny. But no matter how he tried, he could not pull a sliver of a smile to his face.

His only course of action was to press on.

'Rachel called you last night,' Gilchrist said, and noticed something close to panic sweep across Annette's eyes. Kirkwood, on the other hand, stood tight-lipped. 'We can check your phone records,' Gilchrist suggested, 'if that makes your decision on whether or not to be truthful any easier.'

'She called last night. Yes,' Kirkwood agreed.

Gilchrist knew he had to proceed with extreme caution. If he showed any knowledge of what had been said during that call, it could backfire; point them to Dick's illegal tapping of Novo's phone. Talk about wading deeper? It didn't bear thinking about.

'Why did she call?' he asked.

'To wish us a safe flight, and to enjoy our holiday.'

Lie number one. 'Why would she do that?'

'Why not? We're friends.'

'Where are you going?'

'Corfu. It's nice this time of year.'

'I'm sure it is.' Gilchrist managed a smile, but it was not reciprocated. 'Just the two of you, then?

'Yes,' Kirkwood snapped. 'Who would you think we were taking?'

'Other friends, maybe?'

Kirkwood's Adam's apple dunked. 'Oh. I see. No. Just the two of us.'

'Taking?'

'Excuse me?'

Gilchrist stepped closer. 'You asked me who I thought you were *taking*.'

'Yes?'

'Odd choice of word – *taking*.'

'In what way?'

'I would've thought *going with* would be more appropriate – who would I think you were *going with*? – if you were, well, going with some friends on holiday. Of course, if you were *taking* someone younger, *much* younger, then I could understand you saying *taking*, which would be more appropriate.' He searched Annette's gaze, but she seemed unable to return his look, and eyed the carpet. Kirkwood's hand squeezed her shoulder.

Jessie said, 'Can you show us the plane tickets?'

'I've only got the e-ticket printouts,' Kirkwood said.

'That'll do.'

'I haven't printed them out yet.'

'We'll wait,' Gilchrist said. 'Your laptop's in the bedroom. Where's the printer?'

Kirkwood seemed reluctant to leave his wife, who surprised Gilchrist by saying, 'I'll print them out from my computer in the study.' Then she squirmed free of her husband's grip and left the room. Gilchrist nodded for Mhairi to follow her.

Kirkwood raked his hair with long fingers. 'You know, we . . .' He showed his horse teeth. 'You make us feel like criminals. We've done nothing wrong.'

'Force of habit,' Gilchrist said, and tried a smile of reassurance – for Kirkwood, or for himself, he could not say. He felt so sick to the pit of his stomach that he could easily tilt his head and throw up all over their nicely vacuumed carpet. How had he managed to convince himself that Novo's call last night had been to warn the Kirkwoods to move, that the police were closing in? And now he was here – his gaze shifted around the room – he was closing in on what? The Kirkwoods were working professionals, with no family of their own. He eyed the room, tried to imagine a child in this house, but the image failed to compute.

As if sensing Gilchrist's weakness, Kirkwood said, 'We're happy to help, but we've got a lot to do before flying out this evening. So I . . . I . . . we'd like you to leave.'

243

Gilchrist would have liked to leave, too, the sooner the better. He glanced at the lounge door, hoping to see Mhairi return with the e-tickets, then he could make a quick exit, try to get over the utter fucking balls-up he was making of it all.

He eyed Kirkwood again. 'You said you were packing.'

Kirkwood gave a sheepish grin. 'I lied. I'm sorry. I hadn't started.'

'So what took you so long to come to the door?'

'I was in the toilet,' he said, and his eyes lit up with relief as his wife returned with several pages of printouts, which she handed to Gilchrist.

He stared at them. Two tickets: one in the name of Kevin James Kirkwood, and the other, Annette Kirkwood. It all seemed so clear to him now, the fatal flaw in his rationale, the error in his logic that two adults would try to leave the country with an abducted child whose photograph had fronted every national newspaper for the last several days, been highlighted on every news channel, been on the radar of every police force. As a family, the Kirkwoods would never get through Customs without being stopped. He had made such an error that all he wanted to do now was wish the Kirkwoods a safe flight, then shrink from view, and return home to crawl into bed and lick his wounds.

After being fired by Greaves, of course.

He handed the e-tickets to Jessie, and said to Kirkwood, 'If you could take a few minutes to give statements to DS Janes, we'll get out of your hair.'

Kirkwood struggled between smiling and grimacing. 'Of course.'

'In the meantime, do you mind if I look around?'

'Yes I bloody well mind,' Kirkwood snapped.

Gilchrist gave a wry grin, and a nod of his head.

It really had been stupid to ask, he supposed.

He turned and walked from the lounge.

CHAPTER 29

It took Jessie and Mhairi just over half an hour before they returned to the Vectra.

They slid into their seats in silence – Mhairi behind the wheel, Jessie the passenger – as if they didn't have it in their hearts to try to cheer up Gilchrist with the good news that the Kirkwoods had broken down and confessed.

Fat fucking chance.

Just that thought almost brought a groan to Gilchrist's lips. He sat alone in the back, dejected and miserable. He had tried to take his mind off his failing investigation by calling Jack. But the beeping tone told him that Jack had powered down his mobile, which was how he dealt with stuff – ignore the storm until the sun comes out. He'd been in no mood to call Maureen, either. Nor Cooper, for that matter. She was on holiday for the rest of the week, fuck it.

But his mind refused to let go.

No matter how much he chastised himself for screwing up, a child's life was still at stake. He had to get his investigation back on track – *somehow*. He needed to go through the files again, see what he had missed, because he was missing something. But more troubling was the fact that, as each hour passed, the chances of finding Katie shrank, and as Greaves's words came back to him, *If you haven't found Katie by close of business Thursday, you're being pulled off the case*, he realised he might already be out of time.

He shrunk deeper into his seat, and stared out the window.

No one spoke until Mhairi exited Dumfries town limits and accelerated towards the M74. Jessie shifted in her seat, looked over her shoulder. 'Want to talk about it?' she said.

'Not really.'

'It was a good theory. You almost had me convinced.'

He grimaced at the word *almost* and said, 'Until?'

'Until we couldn't find anything.' Jessie shook her head. 'When the wife answered the door with that look on her face, I'm thinking to myself, bloody hell, we're onto a winner here. We've nailed it. Game over.'

'But you found nothing,' he said, more comment than question.

'Not a thing, sir.' Mhairi touched the brakes as she approached a roundabout. 'But I don't know,' she said. 'Something about the whole thing didn't seem right.'

Gilchrist pulled himself upright, gripped the back of Mhairi's seat. 'In what way?'

'They both looked tense, sir. Unnaturally so.'

'What about you, Jessie?'

'You'd have to think they were hiding something. But whatever it was, it wasn't Katie Davis. Of course, bursting into their home the way we did wouldn't exactly settle nerves.'

'Do you think they'll make a formal complaint, sir?' Mhairi asked.

'I'd be surprised if they didn't,' he said. 'But you were following orders. Got that?'

'Yes, sir.'

'Jessie?'

'Whatever.'

Gilchrist slumped back into his seat. He had failed. He had made a fool of himself – *majestically*. He had taken the beast by the reins and gone straight in, full gallop, dragged Jessie and Mhairi with him, and failed as only *he* could. Kirkwood and his wife would file a complaint to the powers that be, and DCI Andy Gilchrist would be carpeted. Of that he had no doubt – none whatso-fucking-ever. Just how thick that carpeting would be was another matter. Kicked off the case? Suspended from the Force? Asked to resign?

Or just fired on the bloody spot?

Quite a few options, if you thought about it. But as his mind contemplated the end of his career, already working out how to come to terms with it, his subconscious niggled away at some deeper level. He had never understood how the mind worked, or more exactly, how *his* mind worked. Ideas popped in and out all the time, like insects through open windows.

Sometimes they flew in and stayed. Other times they flew off.

But the sweat on Kirkwood's face stayed. His excuse about packing stayed, too. And why lie? Because Kirkwood had thought Gilchrist was a salesman? Even after he flashed his warrant card to his wife? Her stare when she first opened the door: that stayed, too. And her trembling lips; her inability to look him in the eye.

These images did not fly from his thoughts. No, they stayed.

And the e-tickets had not been printed out, even though Kirkwood said they had. And why had his wife offered to print them out? Because she had not wanted Gilchrist to go back upstairs to the master bedroom, with all its personal and private clutter, and the carpet not vacuumed, with its electrical wires, its discarded clothes, and its imprints . . .

He caught his breath.

. . . its discarded clothes, and its . . .

. . . imprints.

He forced himself to think back to what he'd seen, but could not recall the details, only that the imprints on the carpet looked . . . what? Different? Wider than the chair legs?

Then he came to question what his eyes had seen but his mind failed to register, and he shook the back of Jessie's seat. 'What did you find downstairs?' he asked her.

'Nothing—'

'No. Were the rooms neat? Tidy? Hoovered? What?'

'Tidy. The whole place was immaculate.'

'Exactly,' he said. 'No mess anywhere. In any of the rooms. Right?'

Silent, Mhairi returned his gaze in the rear-view mirror.

Jessie turned to face him. 'Right,' she said.

'Except the master bedroom,' he said.

'I wouldn't know.'

'But I do.'

'So you're saying what?'

What indeed? If only he could still these ephemeral thoughts that flitted in and out of his mind like summer ghosts; clutch them, study them, work out what they meant. 'Kirkwood said he was packing,' he tried. 'Did either of you see any evidence of that? Any suitcases?'

'They weren't flying out until that evening, sir,' Mhairi reminded him.

And Jessie said, 'He hadn't started packing yet. He said that, too. Remember?'

'I do, yes. But he was sweating when he answered the door. So I'm asking – Why? What had he been doing to make him sweat?'

'Maybe he was nervous?' Mhairi ventured.

Gilchrist had seen criminals sweat from nerves. Kirkwood hadn't been sweating from nerves – not to begin with. He'd been sweating at having put in some effort. 'They'd moved quickly,' he said. 'They get a call last night. They book their flights. But they haven't packed yet. Why?'

'I'm not sure I follow, sir.'

'Because they had to do something else first,' he said, pressing forward between the front seats, so that he was almost in line with both of them. 'Let's say that they have Katie . . . I know, I know, no need to look at me like that, I know it's a stretch.' He waited until Jessie settled down. 'But for the sake of argument,' he went on, 'let's just say that they do in fact have her. What would they have to do first if they were flying out of the country?'

'As a family of three?'

'No. They would be risking it if they took Katie with them.'

'Then they'd need to arrange for someone to look after her,' Mhairi said.

Gilchrist smiled. His logic was getting there. But it was still too grey, not enough black and white. 'And who would that have to be?' he asked.

'Someone they trusted?'

'Or someone who was in it with them,' Jessie added.

'Maybe,' Gilchrist said. 'But for the sake of argument, I'm thinking that the fewer people who knew, the better it would be—'

'The fewer who knew?' Jessie snorted. 'Everybody knows Katie's been abducted. It's in all the news—'

'I know, I know, but think about it. If someone didn't know, who would that someone have to be?'

'Someone who wouldn't be up to speed with the news?'

'Yes,' he said.

'And maybe someone old, or older, sir.'

Jessie blew out her cheeks. 'One of their mothers?'

Gilchrist reclined back into his seat, mobile in his hand. 'You got Kevin Kirkwood's mobile number?'

Jessie accessed her records, then read it out to him. 'You going to phone him up and ask?' she said.

He shook his head. 'I've got a friend who owes me a favour,' he said, not wanting to mention Dick by name. The trouble with Dick was that he had no qualms about crossing legal boundaries for a fee, a fact Gilchrist kept to himself and remote from his colleagues. 'Text Jackie,' he said to Jessie, 'and get her to find out where their parents live.'

'Would you like me to head back to Dumfries, sir?' Mhairi asked.

'Not yet,' he said. 'Take the next exit, and see if we can find a coffee shop. My mouth feels like the bottom of a parrot's cage.'

By the time they drove into the tiny village of Crawford, Jessie had heard back from Jackie, who'd texted with confirmation that Annette Kirkwood's parents had retired to Bude in Devon – too remote to fit in with Gilchrist's thoughts. But Kevin Kirkwood's father had passed away ten years ago, and his mother, now in her seventies, lived alone in a bungalow in Queen Elizabeth Drive in Castle Douglas, less than twenty miles south-west of Dumfries.

251

Which gave Gilchrist food for his theory.

He'd already passed Kirkwood's mother's details to Dick, but after his earlier fiasco that morning, he'd be damned if he was going to take further action without first hearing back from him.

Mhairi pulled to a halt in front of an old stone building that doubled as a post office and licensed grocer's. The air smelled fresh and clean, and a cool Scottish breeze that kept the temperature in the fifties ruffled Gilchrist's hair as he stepped from the car. The endless rush of motorway traffic droned in the background.

'Anyone like a bite?' he asked.

'Watching my weight,' Jessie said.

'Still?'

'Bugger off.'

Mhairi shook her head. 'Coffee only, sir.'

Inside, Gilchrist placed the order, then retrieved his mobile. If his gut was correct, he expected Dick to confirm that Kirkwood had phoned his mother shortly after Novo's cryptic call to him.

Dick picked up on the second ring. 'Can't find anything, Andy.'

A buffalo hoof kicked the air from Gilchrist's lungs. 'Tell me you're joking.'

'No joke.'

Bloody hell. How many times could he be wrong in the one fucking day? He thought he'd worked it all out. But no, he was wrong. How could that be? He was missing something. He just *had* to be. But what? The answer was there, before him. All he had to do was find it.

'When was the last call made?' he tried.

'There've been no calls out from that number since late yesterday afternoon.'

'Could he have lost his phone?'

'He could've,' Dick said. 'But I've just been checking that Castle Douglas number you gave me. It's taken three calls in the last twenty-four hours. All from the same incoming number. One last night, two this morning. I was about to work on that when you called.'

'Give me that incoming number,' Gilchrist said and, once he had it, said, 'Let me get back to you.' He ended the call, tapped in the code to withhold his own number, then dialled the number Dick gave him. He covered the mouthpiece as the connection was made, held his breath as it rang once, twice, then was picked up on the third ring.

'Hello?' a woman's voice said.

Gilchrist killed the call.

The pieces slipped into place. He recognised the high-pitched tone, the almost whine-like voice, and felt a spurt of irritation at his limited thinking. Why had he thought that only Kevin Kirkwood would have called his elderly mother, and not her daughter-in-law—?

'There you are, mister.'

Gilchrist faced the counter as the till was ringing up, pulled out a tenner and handed it over. Then he grabbed the three coffees with two hands, and backed out of the door without spilling a drop.

Mhairi was seated in the Vectra, on her mobile, while Jessie strode down the gravel side road, talking into hers. She looked up as Gilchrist walked to the car, and she nodded to him, then rushed to finish her call.

'What kept you?' she said, popping the top off and taking a sip.

'Had to take a call,' Gilchrist said. 'Let's get back on the road while I run some thoughts past the two of you.'

Mhairi fired up the ignition, reversed from her parking spot. 'Where to, sir?'

'Back to Dumfries,' he said.

Jessie looked at him, incredulous. 'About to make an arrest, are we?'

'Not yet. But we're getting there.'

CHAPTER 30

By the time Mhairi worked her way back on to the M74, Gilchrist had run his thoughts past her and Jessie. 'So, what do you think?' he said.

'That it makes sense,' Jessie said.

'It does, doesn't it?'

'But so did your last theory, and look where that got us.'

'Sir, would you like me to call DS Chambers,' Mhairi said, 'and arrange for some local support again?'

Time was critical, he knew. Chambers had jumped when asked earlier, but it would be too much to expect him to jump a second time after his earlier fuck-up. 'Let's test the waters first, before we go diving in again,' he said.

'Oh, I like that,' Jessie said. 'The royal *We*. Excuse me, but speaking for myself, *I* was diving in the first time following orders. Specifically *yours*.'

With Jessie, Gilchrist was never sure if she was being tongue-in-cheek, or downright serious. But no matter how he looked at it, she was correct. 'Noted,' he grumbled, and was about to slump back into his seat when his mobile rang – ID Greaves. 'Bugger it,' he said, and took the call.

'Where are you?' CS Greaves started, without introduction.

'Following a lead, sir.'

'Well, I need you in my office no later than midday, Andy. I've had the Chief on the line, and he's hopping mad. Never heard him so frustrated. Nearly blew my eardrum out.'

A clamp tightened around Gilchrist's chest. Kirkwood had moved quicker than he'd anticipated. 'Anything in particular upsetting him?' he tried.

Greaves held his chuckle so long that Gilchrist thought he was listening to a recording that had stuck. Then his voice broke in with, 'I think this day's been coming for a long time, Andy. Although it won't be pleasant watching big Archie chew you down to size and spit you out, I think it's well deserved.'

'I'm sorry to hear that, sir.'

'Me, too, Andy. But you really can be the cheeky bastard.'

'Yes, I can, sir.'

'Midday. My office. And best to bring a box, a big one.'

The connection died.

Gilchrist laid his mobile on his lap and stared out the window. If he'd had any doubts that Greaves had it in for him, they were quashed right there. Even though Gilchrist had been McVicar's blue-eyed boy over the years, this case was personal to him, through his friendship with Vera Davis, or perhaps through the political weight of her ex-husband, Dougal. Even though Dougal was a disgraced ex-MSP, he still had political clout, of that Gilchrist had no doubt. And chief constables never liked to be in any politician's bad books, disgraced or otherwise—

'That sounded like it went well,' Jessie said. 'Let me guess. The Chief Super?'

'Got it in one.'

'How long now before you get kicked off the case?' she quipped.

'I wish,' he said, conscious of the sudden silence in the car while Jessie shifted in her seat so that she faced him. Mhairi's eyes held his in the rear-view mirror.

'Don't tell me,' Jessie said.

'Afraid so.'

'You're kidding me. He hasn't fired you, has he?'

'He's leaving that for McVicar. If where we're heading turns into another balls-up, I'll be walking the West Sands tomorrow morning looking for seashells.'

Jessie held his gaze for several silent seconds, then turned to stare out the windscreen, nudging Mhairi as she did so. Without a word, Mhairi pulled the Vectra into the fast lane and eased the speed upwards.

Pine-covered hills flashed past in a green blur. Across the M74, fields rose like swelling waves to the ugly sight of electricity pylons. Overhead cables streaked the sky like string. He glanced at the speedometer, watched the needle touch the ton, and creep beyond it – 105, 110. He thought of telling Mhairi to slow down, but it really didn't matter. The sooner they got to Castle Douglas and established that his convoluted theory was just that, a theory, the sooner they could all head back to St Andrews and his personal sacking.

He almost smiled at the thought.

Big Archie was a fair man, who had often stood up for Gilchrist when others would have dropped him like a hot rock. It would give McVicar no great pleasure, he knew, but you did not become Chief Constable by pussyfooting around. You had to be tough, and McVicar could be tough when called upon. He would do the

257

necessary – oh, he would be diplomatic about it, of course he would; probably make Gilchrist feel as if he were doing him a favour in the end – then he would move on with business. And Gilchrist's career – the long days, the late nights, the missed week-ends, the stress and the heartbreak, the relief and the laughs – would be nothing more than a mention in case records and a closed personnel file.

The Vectra ate up the miles, Mhairi resolute in her determination to make it to Castle Douglas in as short a time as possible. Only once on the M74 did she let the speed drop below the ton, and when she slipped off the motorway she held it a steady sixty.

Trees, hedges, bushes flashed past in a silence broken once by Jessie saying, 'I think we should alert the local Office.'

'And get the pair of you dragged into my mess?' Gilchrist said.

'But we—'

'Not this time,' he said. 'This is all on me.'

Not another word was spoken until they reached the exit for Dumfries.

'Should we drive by and pick up Mr and Mrs Kirkwood, sir?' Mhairi asked.

'Keep going,' Gilchrist said. 'With a bit of luck, we can do that later.'

Gilchrist sank into his seat, shrinking so that his head was below sill level, as if for fear of the local police seeing him – there goes that mad DCI from Fife. He could hear their voices now, see them chuckling, shaking their heads, his name the topic of jocular pub talk from now until Christmas – maybe into the New Year and beyond. He could be a cult legend or a laughing stock. Who knew? For the hundredth time, it seemed, his mind worked through the rationale, and for the hundredth time came up with the same answer – Katie was with Kirkwood's mother.

She just *had* to be.

And no one spoke as the miles clicked by on the A75.

Mhairi paid attention to the change in speed limit, slowing down in advance of the thirty miles an hour limit as they approached the next small town. It seemed to Gilchrist that she, too, was dreading what they would find. They drove through the occasional village; nothing more than rows of houses, the odd shop and pub on either side of the road. In one village, whose name he failed to catch, bunting stretched from lamp pole to lamp pole. He thought he caught the twisted wires of fairy lights entangled among the flags – either put up too early for this Christmas, or not taken down from last.

The occasional farmhouse, cottage and B&B flickered past. But mostly the scenery was one of bucolic tranquillity – open fields, rows of trees, bushes, lines of fence posts, and untrimmed hawthorn hedges that bordered roadside ditches. Overhead, a blue sky could trick you into thinking summer had at last arrived. The temperature gauge on the dashboard, 15°C, which required a quick mental calculation to convert it into old money – 59°F – confirmed otherwise.

Gilchrist pulled himself upright as they passed the brown road sign for local services at Castle Douglas. Mhairi indicated left as she slowed for the approaching roundabout and, five minutes later, they were cruising along King Street, the main road that ran through the heart of the old Scottish town.

Old sandstone buildings, with their lower levels converted to banks and shops, slipped past on either side. The sat-nav directed Mhairi to turn left, and she did so at Academy Street, following directions until she eased into Queen Elizabeth Drive, an eighties-styled residential area of mostly bungalows that seemed to spill down a shallow incline.

Farther along the drive, lawns became sparser, their front gardens consisting of brick paving or gravel yards, which doubled for parking space, mostly deserted. They found the elderly Mrs Kirkwood's address before the end of the drive, a tidy bungalow with a grass lawn that looked small enough to lift and lay. Rose bushes, pruned to their core, spiked a strip of soil on the other side of a low garden wall.

Mhairi pulled up to the kerb, and switched off the engine.

Jessie peered through the side window. 'What d'you think? No car in the drive. Is she at home?'

Gilchrist had the door open and his feet on the ground, strangely eager to get on with it, like a condemned prisoner's moment of relief when the priest enters his cell at long last. The air felt cool, clear, Scottish-fresh. He caught the faintest smell of manure on the wind and tilted his head to it. Then he eyed the bungalow as first Jessie's door, then Mhairi's, slammed shut.

'I don't think she's in,' Jessie said.

'Which doesn't bode well,' he added. 'Can't imagine a seventy-year-old pushing a pram, can you?'

'Seeing as how you put it like that, no, neither can I. Maybe she's got a babysitter.'

'She *is* the babysitter,' he corrected her.

'Oh, right, of course,' she said. 'Let's go.'

Together, they strode up the garden path to a door that fronted a vestibule.

Gilchrist rang the doorbell, heard it echo from within. Then he stepped back and eyed the windows. The curtains were drawn back, the blinds open, so things looked hopeful – in a dark meaning of the word. He was about to ring the bell again, when the inner door opened, and an elderly lady with a mop of white hair and knuckled hands clutching a walking stick waved at them to come in.

'It's not locked,' she shouted.

Gilchrist tried the handle and, sure enough, the door opened.

'Mrs Kirkwood?'

'Yes?'

'We're with Fife Constabulary,' Gilchrist said, holding out his warrant card. 'Can you spare a few minutes to talk to us?'

'Fife, you say?'

'Yes.'

'It's been a while since I was in Fife. Michael spent his childhood in Lower Largo,' she said, as if everyone was expected to know who Michael was – her late husband, Gilchrist was willing to bet. 'He was born there. But I haven't been back for . . . oh, I don't know how many years now.' Then she looked at him, as if expecting him to tell her when and where she'd last been in Fife.

'May we come in?' Gilchrist asked.

She gave him a narrow-eyed look, shifted her gaze to take in Jessie and Mhairi then, seemingly satisfied, said, 'I was just about to put the kettle on. Would you like a cup of tea?'

'That would be very kind of you, Mrs Kirkwood,' he said, just to keep up his side of the conversation.

Gilchrist went first, not for the purpose of being discourteous, but so he could assess the situation quickly, tell the others to backtrack if they had to, just leave the place, he'd got it oh-so-fucking wrong again, and let's head back to St Andrews for the sacking.

261

He followed the elderly woman along a short hallway and into a cosy lounge that overlooked a tidy back garden, again spiked with rose bushes so severely pruned that they looked like whittled sticks that had no chance of flowering that summer, maybe even the next. But as Gilchrist walked to the window, taking in the details – boxes of pills dotted the mantelpiece, the *People's Friend* open-flapped on the arm of a well-worn chair, specs, magnifying glass, dog-eared romance novels stuffed in an overflowing magazine rack by the hearth, five or six library books with jackets covered in clear plastic piled on the floor, a well-thumbed Bible, all within easy reach of a seated pensioner – he saw no sign of any toys, or children. The house had an empty feel about it – walls bare of pictures, flat and polished surfaces devoid of photographs; not even any of her own son, Kevin. And Michael might have spent his childhood in Lower Largo, but whoever he happened to be, he was all but forgotten in Castle Douglas.

A television sat in the corner, its screen black – no sign of the remote.

Rather than backtrack out of the place, Gilchrist said, 'Do you watch TV?'

'Hardly at all,' she said. 'I much prefer to read.'

Gilchrist stood with his back to the window, while Mrs Kirkwood fussed and faffed around Jessie and Mhairi, fluffing up cushions, instructing them to take a seat while she went to the kitchen to get the tea ready. Gilchrist caught Jessie's eye, and nodded.

'I'll give you a hand to make the tea, Mrs Kirkwood,' Jessie said.

'Would you, dear? That would be so kind of you.'

Silent, Gilchrist felt the heavy weight of defeat settle over him, pulling him down as he eyed the doors off the hallway – one to the front bedroom, no doubt, another to the back bedroom, or maybe the main bathroom. From the kitchen he heard the clatter of dishes, the melancholy mumble of voices. He caught Mhairi's despairing look, her silent question – do you want me to poke around? – and shook his head.

'We'll have a polite cup of tea,' he said, 'then head off.'

Mhairi returned his gaze, tight-lipped.

He could almost feel her disappointment. He'd let her down; let them all down. His gut instinct was no longer the force it had once been. He'd got it wrong. He'd had them drive here on the back of the slimmest of slim hunches. There was no evidence of any child being here. On top of that, Mrs Kirkwood seemed too old to look after a young child.

Mhairi turned her head to the kitchen door, as if she'd heard something.

Before Gilchrist could move, Mrs Kirkwood walked from the kitchen.

Jessie followed, giving a fleeting wide-eyed stare at Gilchrist – can you believe this? – as the elderly lady reached for a door handle and eased the door open with barely a creak.

From where Gilchrist was standing, the room stood in shadow as the missing jigsaw pieces flipped over and clicked into place. He found himself pushing Jessie aside, squeezing past her to make his way into the room.

'Sshh,' Mrs Kirkwood admonished.

But he moved forward in the semi-darkness towards the cot, its four legs as wide apart as the imprints on the Kirkwoods' bedroom carpet. Even in the dim light, he could make out the shape of a sleeping child, although the unhealthy silence had his heart racing.

'Light switch,' he said.

'She's asleep.'

'I know she is,' he said to Mrs Kirkwood. 'But I need to know she's okay.'

'Of course she's okay, dear. Why wouldn't she be?'

The room burst into brightness as Jessie clicked the switch.

Gilchrist leaned into the cot, his heart pumping in his mouth at the uncanny stillness, the deathly silence that told him what he dreaded. Despair swept through him in a debilitating spasm as he reached out and took hold of the small, silent bundle, a woollen Chivas falling off to the side.

They had arrived too late, all their efforts in vain.

'Dear God, no,' he gasped.

He eased the lifeless body from the cot, pulled the child to him . . .

As she let out a hearty cry that almost took his eardrum with it.

CHAPTER 31

'You've woken her up,' Mrs Kirkwood complained.

Gilchrist laughed as he stared into the child's eyes. Even through her swelling tears he could not be mistaken. 'I have indeed,' he agreed, and hugged her to him. He pressed his lips to her little face, feeling warmth that he'd failed to register in his earlier panic, and rocked her in his arms to settle her.

But she was not for giving up.

'What's her name?' he asked above the din.

'Michelle,' she said. 'After my late husband, Michael.'

Although he was confident he knew the answer, he needed to ask the question. 'Who are Michelle's parents?'

'Kevin and Annette,' she said, as if that explained all.

Well, there he had it. But he needed more, so he chanced it with, 'I was told they couldn't have children.'

'They've been trying for years,' she said, not put off by his piercing comment. 'But they've been blessed with this child now.' She reached out to take Michelle from him.

But Gilchrist wanted to cherish the moment. 'I'll carry her through to the lounge for you,' he offered, 'and you can sit with her there.' He blew warm breath on the child's neck, whispered sweet nothings, the way he used to with his own children, surprised to find that it still worked. Her hard cries softened, and by the time they stood in the lounge, she was looking around her. He blew on her neck and cheek again, her eyelashes fluttering with surprise. 'There you go, my little princess.'

Mrs Kirkwood eased herself into her fireside chair. Gilchrist leaned forward, handed the bundled child to her, which she slipped on to her lap with a confidence that defied her years.

'I'll get the tea,' he said, then strode towards the kitchen, followed by Jessie.

In the kitchen, two hefty cardboard boxes filled with assorted baby foods and toys sat on the floor in the corner, presumably where they'd been left the previous night by her son.

'How do you want to handle this?' Jessie asked him.

He had his mobile out, was already auto-dialling Chambers. 'Arrest and charge the Kirkwoods for starters,' he said. He wanted to make the arrest himself, but needed to move quickly, no matter what. When he got through to Chambers, he said, 'How soon can you bring in Kevin and Annette Kirkwood?'

Chambers didn't remind him of his earlier fiasco, but said, 'What've you got, sir?'

'Katie Davis. She's with Kevin Kirkwood's mother in Castle Douglas.'

A pause, then Chambers was back, all business. 'I'll get on to it myself, sir.'

'Keep the press out of this,' Gilchrist said, 'at least until the Kirkwoods are in your custody. And send a medical team to . . .' He rattled off the address in Queen Elizabeth Drive. 'Katie appears to be unharmed, but I don't want to take any chances.'

'Will do, sir.'

He ended the call, then faced Jessie. 'Get the car keys off Mhairi, and tell her to stay here and keep an eye on them. You and me, we're heading back to Dumfries.'

Before leaving, he checked on Katie. She had fallen back to sleep, snuggled into old Mrs Kirkwood who looked ready to nod off, too. He leaned down, and spoke quietly so as not to waken Katie.

'We've got to step out,' he said. 'DC McBride will make you that cup of tea.'

'All right, dear,' she said, but by the time Gilchrist and Jessie left, the old lady's head was already nodding.

In the Vectra, Gilchrist stabbed the key into the ignition and floored the pedal, the tyres spinning for grip on the asphalt.

'Steady on,' Jessie said. 'I've not brought a spare pair of knickers.'

Gilchrist eyed the dash, forced himself to stay at a calm thirty-five as he worked his way through the housing estate towards the main road. But his mind remained on overdrive. He had been right about Novo. Her lack of interest in her niece's abduction had not just spoken volumes, but *yelled*. She had known Katie was safe and not murdered and buried in an unmarked grave in some desolate Scottish wasteland.

She had known, because she had instigated it. She *must* have . . .

'You're gritting your teeth,' Jessie said.

He jerked a look at her. 'Force of habit.'

'Anger, I'd say. What're you thinking?'

What indeed? Should he arrest Novo? Had she organised the whole thing? But, if so, why kidnap her sister's daughter? It made no sense. As he tried to work through the logic, he came to understand that to determine the extent of Novo's involvement, they needed to work backwards – back from the person who'd removed Katie from her home? Or back from the person who'd received her?

Or were they one and the same person?

The obvious candidate was Kirkwood. If he'd taken Katie from St Andrews, they would find footage on CCTV and the ANPR – automatic number-plate recognition system. If Novo had not participated in person, had she been responsible for organising the abduction? He thought back to that first call to her office. She'd just returned from a trip to China. Had she flown in from Scotland instead? When her twin sister, Andrea, called her that morning on her second mobile, where had Novo been?

In bed in London? On the road to Castle Douglas?

Or had Kevin and Annette Kirkwood abducted Katie?

But if not them, then who?

His head was spinning from too many questions, and he felt an overwhelming need to put a lid on it for the time being. 'Get on to Chambers again,' he said to Jessie. 'We're about to make another arrest and, until we do, he can't tell the media a thing. Not a bloody thing. You got that?'

'Let me guess. Novo?'

Gilchrist wanted to agree, but he wasn't sure. He could ask the Met to detain Novo, but if she found out that Katie had been found, how would she react? And it struck him that he might have more to gain by not arresting Novo, but by watching her instead. Decision made, he said, 'And get on to the Met, too, and see if they'll tail Novo for us. But they're not to detain her unless she's about to leave the country.' He eased his speed up to fifty as he left the town's limits.

'And what about your midday sacking?' Jessie said.

Despite having found Katie, Gilchrist knew his job was not yet secure. Not by a long shot. If anyone found out how he'd managed to track Katie to Kevin Kirkwood's mother, he could still be walking the West Sands in the morning, searching for seashells.

'Leave Greaves and McVicar to me,' he said.

He powered through the roundabout, floored it on to the A75 as he listened to Jessie instruct Chambers to put a lid on the media.

'I know you heard that from DCI Gilchrist first time, sir. I'm not disputing that. No, sir, yes, yes . . . but DCI Gilchrist intends to question another suspect. If we let slip that Katie Davis has been found, he would lose . . . yes, I know . . . ' She held on to her mobile for several seconds, then slapped it shut. 'Jesus,' she hissed. 'What is it about men taking orders from a woman? You'd think I was going to crush his balls.'

'That might come later.'

'I can't wait.'

By the time Gilchrist pulled into Loreburn Street and parked opposite the police station, Jessie had arranged for the Met to tail Novo.

Dumfries Police Station is a modern-looking brick building that echoes when you push through the main door. He and Jessie were led to DS Chambers's office. A quick shake of the hands, with Gilchrist reiterating Jessie's phone request to keep the media out of it, and Chambers confirming that Kevin Kirkwood was in Interview Room 1, his wife Annette in Room 2.

'They've requested their family solicitor,' Chambers said.

'Do they know we've found Katie?' Gilchrist asked.

'No chance.'

269

'Let's keep it that way,' he said. 'What about their solicitor?'

'She's already here. Her office is just along the road.'

'Good,' Jessie said. 'Let's tackle the wife first.'

Interview Room 2 was nothing more than a windowless room with a table and two chairs either side. Annette Kirkwood's eyes were swollen from crying and she tried to give Gilchrist her best angry glare as he entered. But it fell short. Her solicitor sat by her side, a plain-looking woman – Gilchrist put her in her mid-forties – with salt and pepper hair that looked like scouring wire scraped straight, and a black jacket that was far too tight, testing the stitching around the buttons.

Jessie walked to the end of the table and switched on the recorder. She took a seat and introduced herself and Gilchrist, stating the time and date. Gilchrist slid a business card across the table, in exchange for one from Kirkwood's solicitor, and stated that Mrs Annette Kirkwood was being detained under Section 14 of the Criminal Procedure Scotland Act 1995 on suspicion of the abduction of Katie Davis from her home in St Andrews, and that she was being represented by her solicitor, Jane Whetlow of Whetlow and Associates LLP.

Whetlow began with, 'I've been advised that you forced entry into my client's home earlier this morning.'

Gilchrist returned Whetlow's cold stare. 'Forced entry?'

'Were you invited in?'

'When a child's life is at stake, we have to move quickly.'

'Nonsense. I want my client's complaint formally acknowledged.'

'Noted,' said Gilchrist, and turned to Annette. He waited until he established eye contact, then said, 'Do you have anything you'd like to tell me?'

She shook her head.

'Speak for the record,' Jessie reminded her.

She cleared her throat. 'I don't have anything to tell you.'

'Are you sure?' Gilchrist pried.

'Yes.'

'How well do you know Rachel Novo?' he asked.

Annette blinked with surprise, then recovered with a shrug. 'Not very well.'

'But well enough to know she shortened her surname from Novokoff to Novo.'

Her face flushed at being caught out so easily. 'Someone must have told me.'

'Who?'

'Probably Kevin. But I can't remember.'

Gilchrist waited a couple of beats, then said, 'When did you first meet Rachel?'

'In primary school.'

'You must know Andrea, too, then?'

'Yes, but not as well as Rachel.'

'I thought you didn't know Rachel very well.'

'I . . . I meant that I knew Rachel better than I knew Andrea. Rachel invited me to her tenth birthday party. That's when we first became close, if you could call it that.'

'Being twins, it must have been Andrea's birthday party, too.'

'But Rachel invited me, not Andrea.'

'Who did Andrea invite?'

'No one. It was just the three of us.'

'At the birthday party?'

Annette nodded. 'Her mother was very strict.'

'And her father?'

'I never saw him. He was at work, or away on business. I never asked.'

'And you kept your friendship with Rachel through primary and secondary school?' Gilchrist said, trying to edge the interview towards the present day.

'Yes. But we were never really close.'

Gilchrist had a sense of Annette trying to distance herself from Novo, so he said, 'But you were close enough to go to university together.'

She nodded. 'I suppose so.'

'York University?'

'Yes.'

'Did you live together?'

She frowned for a moment, then glanced at her solicitor.

'We can confirm that easily enough,' Gilchrist said. 'And I would remind you that this interview is being taped for the record.'

She lowered her eyes, and said, 'We shared a flat.'

'So, after graduating from York University, you kept in touch over the years?'

'Not really.'

'But you have been in contact with each other, am I right?'

'Yes.'

'When did you last talk to her?'

She shook her head. 'Years ago, I think.'

'Before she became Rachel Novo?'

Her eyes danced, then stilled. 'It must've been after that, but I can't remember when.'

The problem Gilchrist faced was that he'd found the Kirkwoods by Dick listening in on Novo's calls – which was illegal as hell, and could have him pensioned off in a heartbeat. It wouldn't matter that doing so had helped recover a missing child. It mattered only that he'd broken the law. So he thought it best to distance himself from that line of enquiry, and focus more on how desperate the Kirkwoods must have been to have a child.

But Whetlow advised Annette not to answer any questions of a personal medical nature and, five minutes later, Gilchrist decided to cut his frustration short by bringing the matter to a head.

'So what can you tell me about Michelle?' he asked.

Annette jerked a gasp, clasped her hand to her mouth, and shut her eyes tight. Tears squeezed from under her lids and slid like raindrops down her cheeks.

Whetlow glared at Gilchrist. 'Michelle? Who's Michelle?'

'Katarina Davis,' Gilchrist said, wondering if the Russian name would light a spark.

But Whetlow's wild look evaporated, and she mouthed a silent *What?* then turned to Annette. 'We need to talk,' she said to her.

Jessie said, 'I'd like to—'

'*In private.*' Whetlow turned on Jessie, eyes blazing. 'I'm instructing my client to make no further comment.'

'You're doing your client no favours,' Jessie said.

'I'll be the judge of that.'

Gilchrist leaned closer. 'Who put you up to it, Annette?'

'No comment,' snapped Whetlow.

'We're asking your client, not you,' Jessie snapped.

'Annette?' Gilchrist urged.

She lowered her head and, in a barely audible voice, said, 'No comment.'

'Did you and Kevin both drive to St Andrews?'

A frown creased her forehead, and her eyes flickered a puzzled glance, as if she was struggling to understand what was going on. Then she focused on her hands once more, and said, 'No comment.'

'Or was it only Kevin?' he asked.

'No comment.'

'I think it was Kevin.'

'No comment.'

'That wasn't a question,' Jessie said.

Whetlow glared at Jessie, her lips white with anger. But rather than persist with the petty needling, Gilchrist pushed his chair back. 'DCI Gilchrist leaving the interview at . . . ' He glanced at the recorder. ' . . . 12.44,' then said to Jessie. 'I'm taking a ten-minute break. Once you've done the necessary, give me a call.'

He walked to the door, Jessie's voice trailing after him.

'Annette Kirkwood, I am arresting you for the wilful abduction of Katie Davis and . . . '

Outside, the sky had dulled, an uncanny reflection of his mood. Despite the fact that they'd found Katie alive and unharmed, he felt oddly deflated. It had been Annette's eyes that had him doubting his rationale. When he'd mentioned driving to St Andrews, he thought he caught her momentary confusion, making him see the possibility that the *adoption* – and most probably the truth – had been kept from her. After all, Novo had phoned Kevin, not Annette.

But just how deep was Novo's involvement?

Could she have removed Katie from her sister's house that morning? But for the life of him, he could not see her motive, even if she'd had the opportunity. Had her business trip to China been nothing more than a front, an excuse to fly out of London?

Lloyd's was a global company, so it would be simple enough to establish if her Chinese trip was fabricated.

But perhaps her mobile-phone records could reveal more.

On the off-chance, he called Dick again.

'You find anything interesting on Novo's mobile records?' he asked.

'Got a list of numbers she called last week,' Dick said. 'Some of them from overseas – China, as best I can tell. Not too many. I cross-referenced them to the names on the registered phone accounts. There's only a dozen or so but, if you've got a minute, I can rattle them off for you.'

Gilchrist agreed, and waited while Dick retrieved his file.

'Here we go,' Dick said, and recited a list of names, none of which meant anything, until one jerked his senses alive – Rumford.

'Wait,' Gilchrist said. 'Say that last one again.'

Dick did. 'Does it mean anything to you?'

Alex Rumford had been Sandy Rutherford's name before he changed it. Coincidence? Or not? But if you believed there was no such thing as coincidence, you would be surprised at what you could uncover.

'That's not a mobile number, is it?'

'Landline.'

'Do you have an address for it?'

'I do,' he said, and read it off – an address in Blackford.

'Where's that?' Gilchrist asked.

'Close to Gleneagles Golf Course, I think.'

Somehow, hearing that deflated Gilchrist. The Blackford property could be one of several owned by Rutherford's management company, leased out to golfing parties. And the landline could have been registered in Rumford's name before he changed it to Rutherford all these years ago. And Novo's call could be completely and utterly coincidental.

And in a perfect world, pigs could fly.

He thanked Dick and killed the call.

The Met should have someone tailing Novo by now, so he phoned her mobile.

She answered on the third ring with, 'This is becoming tedious.'

'Does the name Alex Rumford mean anything to you?'

The line went quiet for a couple of beats, until she said, 'If you want to talk to me again, you speak to me through my solicitor.'

The connection died.

Gilchrist held on to his mobile for a few seconds longer before closing the screen.

His call to Novo had hit a nerve, smack dab in the centre, but given him no answers. He was still not seeing the whole picture. Which had him thinking that talking to Rutherford – or was it Rumford? – before flying to London to interrogate Novo would be worthwhile.

For someone who claimed never to talk to her family, Novo was turning out to be a persistent fibber – one sure way to grab his attention. But his head was spinning, his thoughts confused, and it really was time to bring CS Greaves up to speed.

He dialled his number.

'Good afternoon, DCI Gilchrist,' Greaves said, his formal address warning Gilchrist that McVicar was close by. 'It's good of you to call. We had a meeting scheduled for over an hour ago. Are you calling to confirm that you're running late?'

'Sorry, sir, I got held up.'

'I have the Chief Constable with me. He'd like a word with you.'

'Can you put him on speaker phone?'

'I don't see any need for—'

'On speaker, sir, please, if you don't mind.'

The line clicked a number of times, went dead for a few seconds, then came alive again with, 'Can you hear me, Andy?'

Gilchrist recognised the authoritative voice of Chief Constable Archie McVicar. 'I can indeed, sir, yes.'

'Good, well, I won't beat about the bush, Andy. This to-do with the missing child.' A pause, then, 'I have to tell you that it's turning into a bit of a mess. So, I'm going to—'

'I can update you—'

'Let me finish, Andy. This isn't pleasant for any of us—'

'We have her,' he said. 'We've located Katie Davis.'

It took two beats for McVicar to say, 'Good Lord, is she . . .?'

'She appears to be in good health, sir. But I've arranged for a medical—'

'DCI Gilchrist,' Greaves cut in. 'How quickly can you get here? We need to set up a press conference, and—'

'No we don't,' Gilchrist snapped. 'We can't afford to let this out yet. *Sir.*'

'Andy? Is there a problem you're not telling us about?'

Overhead, blue patches punched holes in a slate-coloured sky. Yes, there's a problem, he wanted to say. I don't know who abducted her. I don't know why Novo's involved. I don't think this case is as simple as it seems. We might have Katie safe, but—

'Andy?'

'DCI Gilchrist. I am instructing you to—'

'Listen to me,' Gilchrist said. 'And listen carefully. I am about to make another arrest. But if word gets out that we have the child, I could lose any leverage I might have. It's vital that we keep this quiet for the time being. I'll be in a better position to advise you later. Do you understand, sir?'

'What time will you know, Andy?'

'I can't say, sir.'

'How about the child's mother? Does she know yet?'

This was the worry for Gilchrist, that the press could pick up on this point later, blast it back at the constabulary in a journalistic fusillade. Surely any mother has a need to know that her daughter is safe. What right does anyone have to withhold such vital information, particularly when the mother is devastated? – or so the media would have you believe.

'We might be in a position to tell her later tonight,' he said. 'But if I'm being honest, sir, it'll more than likely be tomorrow morning, and probably later.'

Another pause, then, 'Very well, Andy. Tomorrow it is.'

Gilchrist killed the call, and powered down his mobile.

He needed to get back to the local Office and interrogate Kevin Kirkwood. After that, they had reports to complete, forms to fill out, before the drive back to Fife. But now the Met were tailing Novo, he could tackle Rutherford first thing in the morning.

CHAPTER 32

Friday morning, Perth

Gilchrist arrived in Perth after 6. a.m., driving his BMW with four new tyres – the garage had returned it to its spot on Castle Street on Wednesday afternoon. He'd also picked up Tosh's CD, lying on the hallway floor where Dick had slipped it through his letterbox. But, after giving it a quick review, he realised it was too late in the night to have it out with Tosh. Instead he sent him a text.

We need to talk. Call me tomorrow.

After that, he had slept fitfully, his mind firing questions all night long.

It had been that tenth birthday party, when the Davis twins had been allowed for the first time to bring only one friend to their home – Annette Kirkwood – which had sealed it for Gilchrist. Dougal Davis had not been there, which told him that Vera had not dared risk the welfare of any children in his presence. So she must have known, and must have lived with the secret of Dougal's incestuous abuse, rather than report him – she *must* have.

Unable to sleep, Gilchrist had risen from bed close to four o'clock.

Now, despite his urge to get on with it, his stomach was grumbling. He slowed down as he neared the Rutherfords' home. The garage door was closed – Range Rover tucked away securely, no doubt, and Bentley parked alone on the driveway. Again, it struck him as odd that such a majestic car would be exposed overnight to the elements, while a common-or-garden Range Rover was garaged.

He lowered the window, breathed in the morning air, a hint of a chill on its breath. The lawn glistened with a light covering of dew. Flowers bowed their heads with the weight of it all, as if praying for the sun to touch them. The brick paving was dotted with tiny clumps of sand pushed to the surface from ants nesting beneath the driveway.

Not like Rutherford, he thought, to put up with such infestation.

Curtains on the upper floors were open, but a pair of windows that overlooked the glass conservatory and the rear lawn had the curtains drawn – the master bedroom, if he was a betting man. Through one of the lower windows, he thought he caught movement deep inside the house, but could not be sure.

The clock on the dash read 06.37. He accelerated away.

He drove around the town centre before finding a Costa Coffee at the corner of Scott and High Street, and ordered a tall latte and a blueberry muffin. He took a seat by the window and powered up his mobile – seven missed calls and five text messages. He should power his mobile down more often, be less of a slave to his phone, make it harder for demented chief superintendents and insane Toshes to track him down.

Only one call was not business related, from his daughter, Maureen; nothing from Jack. He took a sip of coffee and dialled her number.

'Jeezo, Dad,' she grumbled. 'What is it with you and mornings?'

Just the husky sound of her sleepy voice pulled him close to her. If he shut his eyes he could be holding her, pressing his lips to her head, telling her it'll all be all right, it'll be okay, don't worry, he would always be there for her, always – well, except when he wasn't.

'I'm returning your call, princess.'

'Oh, that, I . . . eh . . . I was calling to tell you that I got a message last night. A kind of a strange message—'

'Who from?'

'That's the thing, she didn't say. It sounded like Rebecca, but I'm not a hundred per cent sure. I tried calling back, but the line was disconnected or something.'

'What did she say?'

'She just said – take care of your father.'

Gilchrist felt his blood turn to ice, the power in his legs leave him. He slid back on to his stool. *Take care of your father.* If the call was from Cooper, it could mean one of only a few things, none of which he would have thought possible a day or so ago: she was leaving the area; she was leaving him; she was going back to her husband – or, more worrying, was the possibility of her harming herself, something Gilchrist refused to accept and forced out of his mind. But why leave a message on Mo's phone? It made no sense, except in a roundabout kind of a way it did – his mobile had been powered down last night.

'When did she leave the message?' he asked.

'Just before midnight.'

'You still got it?'

'Yes.'

'Can you read out the number?' he asked, which she did. 'Don't delete that message. I'll get back to you.' He ended the call and accessed Cooper's contact details. He had a good memory for numbers, and he confirmed that the number recited to him by Maureen was the same as the one he'd saved in his mobile's system under *Becky*.

So, Cooper had left a message on Mo's phone? Which meant what, exactly?

He hit Cooper's number, and on the first ring got through to the automatic voice recording – *the subscriber you are trying to reach is not available at this time. Please check the number and try again.*

He tried again. Same result.

He hung up.

Outside, pedestrians walked past, some on phones, others grim-faced with audio leads plugged in their ears, as if the music they were listening to was intended to put them in a foul mood. For one insane moment he thought of phoning Cooper's landline and speaking to her husband, or soon-to-be-ex-husband, or whatever the hell Cooper had deigned him to be. But, thankfully, sanity prevailed.

Instead, he called the Force Contact Centre in Glenrothes, and gave the controller the registration number of Cooper's Range Rover. He asked her to run it through the ANPR – which could track vehicles in real time – and let him know if she received any hits.

'Are we looking to apprehend the driver, sir?'

'No,' he said. 'Just trying to establish where the car is, and where it might be going.'

'One minute.'

Gilchrist sipped his latte as he listened to the clatter of a computer keyboard. In the background, he caught the discordant drone of others speaking. He tore off a piece of muffin, tried a nibble, but his appetite had deserted him. As if to confirm his mood, the morning sky had lost its blue sharpness, already fading to a lacklustre white-grey. For all anyone knew in Scotland, it could be snowing by the afternoon—

'We have it located in Glasgow International Airport,' the controller said. 'Picked up entering satellite parking at 23.17 last night, sir.'

'Is it still there?'

'It appears to be, sir, yes.'

Gilchrist thanked her and hung up.

The timing of Cooper driving into satellite parking, then calling Maureen, made some sense. She had parked, made her way to the airport terminal and phoned Maureen from there, before powering down her mobile then boarding a flight to God-only-knew where.

Well, at least she was safe. Although her cryptic message puzzled him.

He checked the time, and realised he needed to get moving.

Coffee finished and muffin binned, he returned to his car.

He parked short of the Rutherfords' paved driveway, but when he walked through the entrance gateway, the first thing he noticed was the garage door open, and the Range Rover missing. He cursed under his breath. He should have been patient, sat in his car, waited until one of them made an exit. Or, more sensible still, gone to the door and held his finger to the bell until one of them answered.

He eyed the driveway, noted the telltale tracks on the fading dew – the Range Rover reversed from the garage, into a two-point turn, then drove through the gate on to the road. A matching pair of short skid-marks hinted that Rutherford might be an impatient driver.

Gilchrist walked past the Bentley, unable to resist running his hand along the polished paintwork, leaving a smear-line across the bonnet. On the top step, he rang the doorbell, now hoping that Rutherford and Vera had not driven off together. But, within seconds, he caught a shimmer of movement through the frosted glass door, which manifested into the body of a woman wearing a full-length dressing gown.

The lock clinked with the effort of a key turning, then the door opened to a frowning Vera Davis, who stared at him in silent amazement.

'May I come in?' Gilchrist said.

'Why?'

'To talk.'

'About what?'

'Katarina.'

At the mention of the Russian name, suspicion shifted across her face like a fleeting shadow. Her eyes narrowed, as if she were trying to work out why he had come. 'Can't it wait until Sandy returns?'

'No.'

She tutted. 'Very well then,' she said, and turned and walked along the hallway, leaving Gilchrist to close the door and traipse after her.

She seemed remarkably sprightly for her age – which he'd worked out at sixty-four – and showed no signs of any ageing aches or pains, as if her limbs and joints were well oiled. He caught a glimpse of bare ankles, surprised to see the skin tanned and tight, nothing like an elderly woman's – more like someone's half her age. He followed her through the living room and into the conservatory at the back of the mansion.

A pot of tea and two teacups – one empty – stood on a wicker table next to a recliner.

'I won't offer you any tea,' she said, 'as I expect you won't be staying long.'

So much for Highland hospitality. 'Where's Sandy?' he asked.

'Out fetching the newspapers. No one delivers them any more.'

'No.'

She settled into her recliner, snapping her dressing gown around her legs to hide them from his prying eyes. Then she glared at him. 'So what's this all about? I was expecting to hear from Andrea.'

'About Katarina?'

'Why do you keep calling her Katarina? Her name's Katie.'

'I thought you and Andrea rarely spoke to each other.'

'I'm still her mother, for goodness' sake.' She removed the tea cosy and topped up her china cup, and Gilchrist had the strangest sense of having just been dismissed. He watched her take a dainty sip, return the cup to its saucer with the tiniest of clatters, then look up at him as if surprised to find him still standing there. 'She's not well, you know.'

'Who's not?' he asked, just to limit the confusion.

'Andrea. That's who we're talking about, aren't we?'

'She's not been well for some time, I understand.' He thought he caught the tiniest flicker of uncertainty, as if she sensed the conversation was heading towards an inevitable conclusion. 'Perhaps something happened to her in her childhood?'

She returned his gaze with an unnatural coldness, eyes flat and lizard-still. 'You've been speaking to Rachel,' she said.

'Why do you say that?'

'Because I told her you would.'

Gilchrist jolted at the sound of the man's voice, and jerked a look across the room. He had not heard the Range Rover return – windows in the conservatory must be triple-glazed – nor any door in the main building opening or closing. Not even the irrepressible sounds of the old house, with all its creaks and squeaks from years of settlement and use, despite its recent refurbishment. But there stood Rutherford, in the doorway, arms by his side, face flushed from the early morning chill, a light in his eyes that warned Gilchrist to be careful.

And not a newspaper in sight.

CHAPTER 33

Rutherford entered the conservatory.

Despite Gilchrist's earlier take on Rutherford's secondary role in the Davis family hierarchy, he was left in no doubt that the man of the house had returned to take his place at the head of the household.

Rutherford barely cast a glance at his wife, who said nothing as he crossed the tiled flooring. Her face had hardened, aged ten years in as many nanoseconds, and her lips pressed white, perhaps from being caught in the act of almost spilling a secret. Rutherford strode past Gilchrist as if he were nothing more than a shadow on the wall, then flipped off the tea cosy, dropping it to the floor, and filled his cup. Tea splashed into the saucer, over the table. Then he picked up the cup by the rim – his workman's fingers too thick to fit through the delicate handle – and took a slurp.

For one worrying moment, Gilchrist thought he might throw the empty cup across the conservatory, just to test the quality of the triple-glazing. But his lips jerked into a smile that vanished as soon as it appeared, and he leaned forward to return the cup to its saucer, turned his head to the side, and pecked Vera's cheek.

She seemed neither surprised nor flattered by her husband's meaningless flash of affection, and dabbed at her lips with a tissue that appeared from nowhere, which she then used to soak up his saucer's spillage.

Rutherford eyed Gilchrist. 'Is that your BMW outside?'

'Want me to move it?'

A pause, then, 'You're alone?'

'Why do you ask?' Gilchrist said, and had a sense from Rutherford's eyes that some calculation had just been made, a decision reached.

Rutherford smirked. 'So you spoke to Rachel?'

'Did she call you and say I had?'

'We don't communicate like any normal family.' He flicked a damning glance at his wife. 'I couldn't tell you when I last spoke with her.'

Gilchrist could. Six days ago, according to Dick's records. On his Rumford landline, not the Rutherford mobile. A short call that lasted all of twenty seconds. And maybe even more recently than that – like yesterday, after his own call to Novo had struck a nerve?

'How about Kevin and Annette Kirkwood?' Gilchrist tried, just to try for a reaction.

Which came in the next instant.

Not from Rutherford, but from Vera, who reached for her tea and rattled the cup from its saucer as she lifted it to her lips. Even then she had to use both hands to steady it, her long fingers as narrow as spider's legs. Then she glanced at Rutherford, and Gilchrist sensed that something ominous had just passed between the two of them.

'Let's talk outside,' Rutherford said, 'I'd like to show you something that might help you to understand.' Then, before Gilchrist had time to reply, he turned and strode to the back wall, where he opened a glass door and bruised through it on to the rear lawn.

A rush of cold air followed his departure.

Gilchrist nodded to Vera, who seemed incapable of lifting her eyes, then strode after the hastily departing Rutherford.

A line of flagging stones dotted the lawn around the conservatory, then branched off into two lines – one continuing along the side of the mansion that caught the full heat of the morning sun, giving easy access to landscape beds that seemed alive with colour and bees; the other leading to the rear of the garage and a back door that appeared to be the target of Rutherford's urgent focus.

Rutherford pulled the door open, and glanced at Gilchrist before disappearing inside.

The door closed behind him with a clatter as it hit its wooden frame, then was opened again by a quirky gust of wind funnelled between the garage and the garden wall, and tricked into doubling back on itself. Before the door clattered shut, Gilchrist glimpsed a silhouetted Rutherford reaching up to lift some tool or piece of equipment off the garage wall.

Gilchrist reached the garage's back door, stretched for the handle, and was about to open it when some age-old instinct warned him to stop. He lowered his hand, took two steps backwards, and jolted with surprise as the door exploded open with a force that would have knocked him flat on his back had he been standing next to it.

Rutherford erupted from the garage like a caged bull breaking free.

Gilchrist had time only to stumble back as an axe-head scythed in front of his chest, close enough for him to hear the rush of its urgent whisper. Another manic sweep by a wild-eyed Rutherford would have taken Gilchrist's head off if his heel hadn't caught on a tree root on the lawn and sent him sprawling backwards.

He landed on his back with a heavy grunt that blasted the air from his lungs, and managed to avoid being cleaved in two by rolling on to his side as the axe-head buried itself into the lawn with a heavy thud that shuddered the ground.

Rutherford tugged at the handle once, twice, but the axe-head had caught on a root, and Gilchrist saw his chance. He rolled back over, covering the axe-head with his body, trying to grapple the handle from Rutherford's desperate grip. But his sudden action and his own body weight tore the handle free from Rutherford, the axe-head from the root, and slapped it flat on to the lawn.

Still on his side, Gilchrist lashed out with his leg, catching Rutherford below the knee. But at that angle, his kick was too weak, not powerful enough to tear cartilage or break bones, and Rutherford only grunted in surprise.

Gilchrist jumped to his feet for the final confrontation, but Rutherford turned and stumbled towards the garage. And Gilchrist saw that he was going to find something more reliable than an axe.

No time to think.

Just move.

Now.

Gilchrist put his head down and charged.

Rutherford had his hand on the handle when Gilchrist crashed into him from behind with a force that should have sent both of them through the garage wall. But the wall sprang back at them; Gilchrist trapped Rutherford's legs against one of his own and flipped him over his shoulder on to the ground.

Rutherford hit the lawn full-length on his back, with a grunt so pained that it sounded terminal. Before he could recover, Gilchrist fell on top of him, punched as hard as he could into the solar plexus to take the wind from him. Rutherford gawked like a landed fish, but Gilchrist was in no mood for tossing him back. He took hold of Rutherford's shoulders, surprised by the compact strength of tight muscles, rolled him over and pressed his knee into the middle of his back. Rutherford grunted, but Gilchrist pressed harder until he heard a burst of breath that emptied the older man's lungs and seemed to power his body down as if he'd been switched off.

'You're under arrest,' Gilchrist gasped, his breath coming at him in hard hits that burned his throat and fired his chest. Despite the fight being over almost before it had begun, he was stunned by how hard the struggle had been, how close he had come to being killed. If he had followed Rutherford into the garage, he would now be dead.

He reached into his back pocket for a pair of plasticuffs and, in doing so, angled his body just enough for his peripheral vision to catch movement, a shadow of sorts, reflected in the conservatory's glass façade—

His mind screamed.

Panic shot through him like an electric shock.

He released Rutherford, pushed himself back, knowing he was too slow, too late, as Vera stepped into view, face contorted with anger, arms held high, the axe already swinging down at him in a death blow that would split him in two.

He shouted, 'No . . .' and turned his face away from the blow.

The axe thudded into his body with a thump that splattered his face with blood.

He lay still for a second, too afraid to move in case he found he could not, waiting for the pain to kick in. He had heard about the numbing effect of fatal injuries, when the human body was brutalised beyond recognition and the brain counteracted the pain. The fact that he was able to think like that told him the axe had missed his vital organs at least. But its blade felt cold and smooth, and he dared to open his eyes to see the sleeve of his leather jacket sliced open, the head of the axe buried deep into flesh.

Vera screamed at him then, a demented rush of words, wild and hard and painful and cruel, and she slumped to her knees with a groan that sounded as if it had come from the heart of hell itself.

Gilchrist tried to push himself upright, but the axe had buried itself into Rutherford's back, taking part of Gilchrist's jacket sleeve with it, effectively strapping him to the dead man's body. Vera made no attempt to remove the axe and carry on with the job of finishing him off. Instead, she just sat on the lawn, her dressing gown slipping open to reveal skinny legs, her face pale and drawn, lips mouthing something that could be a prayer or whispered gibberish. Her gaze, for the moment, was riveted on Rutherford's body, on the axe that stuck out from his back like some misplaced animal horn.

Gilchrist slipped off his leather jacket and let it fall over Rutherford.

He inspected his arm, ran a hand over it, flinched at a tender part where the axe had shaved off a layer of skin. The blade had sliced through his jacket and shirtsleeve, lengthwise. A half-inch to one side would have stripped his arm of muscle. An inch or so more would have cleaved bone.

He placed a finger on Rutherford's neck, but felt no pulse. A glance at the axe-head buried deep into his back confirmed the blow had killed him instantly. He slipped his hand inside his jacket, removed his mobile, pushed himself to his feet – on shaky legs, he had to admit – and dialled the Force Contact Centre, all the while keeping his eyes on Vera, just in case she had a sudden change of heart.

But she sat there on the damp morning grass, her frail body slumped and broken, her gaze shifting around her, staring at everything but taking in nothing, as if her very heart had dissolved and slipped off into the cool air.

CHAPTER 34

At 2.30 p.m., the discovery of wee Katie Davis was announced to the media by Chief Constable McVicar at a press conference held in Glenrothes HQ. He praised the efforts of Fife Constabulary, and in particular those of Senior Investigating Officer, Detective Chief Inspector Andy Gilchrist, and his team – no specific members were named, which irked Gilchrist as he eyed the TV screen.

Despite the clamour from the media scrum for more details, McVicar kept the press conference short, asking everyone present to show constraint and give Mrs Andrea Davis the privacy she needed and had respectfully requested. As the investigation was still active, no further comments could be made, but McVicar closed by giving assurance that all guilty or associated parties would be found and brought to justice.

Then he turned his back on the cameras and strode from the room.

Gilchrist switched off the TV.

'Surprised Greaves never put himself up there,' Jessie quipped. 'A golden opportunity like that to show himself off? Thought that was a no-brainer.'

Gilchrist said, 'You ready?'

'Yeah, let's get some nailing done.'

Rather than have all suspects held in custody in various jails around Scotland, Vera Davis, and Kevin and Annette Kirkwood, had been brought to Glenrothes Police Station for further questioning. The Met had Rachel Novo under surveillance, but she had not surfaced from her house after leaving her office at short notice yesterday.

Vera Davis would be charged with murder and attempted murder, but her involvement in her granddaughter's kidnapping was as yet unclear. Surprisingly, or so Gilchrist thought, she was represented by Simon Copestake, who stood when Gilchrist and Jessie walked into the interview room.

Copestake gave Gilchrist a firm handshake, and Jessie a slack one.

Vera, on the other hand, followed Gilchrist's every move with silent disdain.

Gilchrist returned her sullen gaze – her sense of loathing almost tangible – while Jessie busied herself with the formalities, noting date, time, names of those present, and advising Vera that she was being formally charged with the murder of her husband and attempted murder of a police officer. She didn't even blink, leaving Gilchrist with the feeling that he had never before sat face-to-face with such a cold-hearted individual.

He placed his hands palm-down on the table, and stared at her, trying to give off a healthy dose of loathing of his own. 'You knew,' he said to her. 'Didn't you?'

Copestake leaned forward. 'Could you be more specific? Perhaps tell us what my client is alleged to have known?'

'Before I arrived at your home this morning, you knew Katarina had been found.'

Vera returned Gilchrist's gaze with an unblinking stare. 'Her name's not Katarina. It's Katie.'

Gilchrist corrected her. 'Her birth certificate states Katarina Davis, no middle name. The father is unknown, and the mother is Andrea Phyllis McPherson Davis.'

Vera blinked at the mention of Phyllis McPherson, her older sister who drowned in a swimming accident at the age of ten, then lowered her gaze to the table.

'Her twin sister Rachel's birth certificate gives her name as Rachel Gwen McPherson Davis.' The mention of Vera's mother's name generated no reaction. Gilchrist pressed on. 'So how did you know?'

Vera glanced at Copestake, but remained silent.

'For the record,' Jessie said, 'Mrs Davis has refused to answer that question.'

'Your husband, Sandy, was prepared,' Gilchrist said. 'He knew I'd be visiting him.'

Again, not a glimmer, so he decided to nip closer to the bone. 'I've not been able to work out your motive yet,' he said. 'But believe me, I will. You could of course help immensely by telling me why you and Sandy took Katarina away from Andrea.'

Vera lifted her gaze and snarled, 'It's Katie, for God's sake. Nobody ever calls her Katarina. Why do you keep calling her that? And we didn't take her from Andrea. Why on earth would we do such a thing?'

'I know Sandy was involved.'

She shook her head, glanced at Copestake. 'This is preposterous.'

'Do you take sleeping pills?' Gilchrist asked her.

'What's that got to do with anything?'

'Just answer the question, please.'

'I do. Yes. Sandy snores.'

'So you wouldn't have known if Sandy had left your home while you were asleep.'

She tutted. 'That's preposterous.'

The only thing that seemed preposterous to Gilchrist in all of this was the fact that the woman facing him had tried to cleave him in two with an axe, but killed her husband instead, and showed no signs of regret or remorse at what she'd done. And now, here she was, to any onlooker acting as if it were some misunderstanding. It made you wonder that maybe Dougal Davis was not the evil bastard he'd been portrayed, but a man of sound reason whose sanity had been driven to the edge by a cold and heartless wife.

Gilchrist tried a different tack. 'You love Katie, don't you?' he said, hoping that the change of name might warm her iced heart.

'What grandmother wouldn't love her grandchild?'

'Can you remember when you first saw her?'

Even that thought could not shift the scowl from her face. 'She was several months old, as best I can recall.'

Gilchrist cast a glance at Jessie, but she appeared just as confused as he was at how long it had taken Vera to see her beloved granddaughter. Or maybe Andrea had kept her birth a secret. Which pushed another thought into Gilchrist's mind.

'When did you find out Andrea was pregnant?' he asked.

'Hah,' she said, as if livened by the challenge. 'The first I knew about it was when Rachel called to tell me I was a grandmother.'

'Rachel? Not Andrea?'

Her eyes shimmied left and right, as if puzzling at the trick in the question. Then she frowned. 'Andrea's not well,' she explained. 'She suffers from depression. If she'd been living at home I would never have allowed her to have a child of her own.'

Gilchrist sensed Jessie's unrest. He half turned his head and gave the tiniest of shakes – he was not finished yet. 'Andrea never called because she thought you might not approve of your grandchild?'

Vera tutted.

'Or of her being a mother?'

'Andrea a mother? God help us all. She's not fit to be a mother.'

Jessie pressed forward, eyes dancing, as if she were contemplating leaping across the table. 'What gives you the right to decide whether any woman should be a mother or not?'

'I know my own children—'

'Oh for God's sake, don't make me laugh.'

'Why you *insolent bitch*—'

'Let's stay focused,' Gilchrist cut in, and slid a photograph across the table. His team had been busy since Katie's discovery, reviewing CCTV footage and tracking movement via the ANPR system. 'We have CCTV footage of the Kirkwoods' Porsche in the small hours of the morning of Katarina's disappearance.'

Copestake pulled the photograph to him, then frowned. 'What does this prove?'

'And CCTV footage of Sandy Rutherford's Range Rover, also in the small hours of that same morning.' He slid another photograph to Copestake, who looked at it, then shoved it back. 'That wouldn't be you driving, would it?' Gilchrist asked Vera.

'Of course not.'

'Because you'd be sound asleep,' he said. 'You take sleeping pills. We have a copy of your prescription. Would you like to see that, too?'

She tutted, but Copestake said, 'I would.'

Gilchrist waited while Jessie opened a folder and pushed the copy across the table – to be read and slid back. Then he said, 'We also have CCTV footage of both the Porsche and the Range Rover, at roughly the same spot, but heading in opposite directions.'

Copestake held his hands palms-up. 'Is there a question any time soon?'

Gilchrist offered a dry smile. 'We believe they were driving to meet each other at a prearranged spot somewhere off the M74, on one of the country roads out of range of CCTV cameras.' He leaned forward. 'To make the exchange.'

A smile almost tickled Copestake's lips.

Vera stared at Gilchrist, dead-eyed.

'We haven't yet worked out exactly where the exchange was made. From the times on what footage we have, best bet would be on the B7078 somewhere between Lesmahagow and Abingdon. But we should have a better handle on that later today.'

'At which point,' Copestake said, 'my client will then be cleared of any involvement in the kidnapping of her granddaughter.'

Jessie stirred. 'I wouldn't go so far as—'

'By your own admission, my client was at home, in bed, dead to the world, sound asleep from her prescriptive medication.' He nodded to Jessie's folder. 'So she could not have participated.'

'Not physically,' Gilchrist said.

Copestake spluttered a laugh. 'Oh, forgive me, my client was there only in the form of some manifestation in her husband's mind—'

'She was the brains behind it,' Jessie said. 'Although from the looks of her, it's a wonder she's got any brains at—'

'How *dare* you,' Vera snapped.

'You set it up,' Jessie shouted. 'You didn't think your darling daughter had it in her to look after a child of her own—'

'Have you seen her? Have you seen the way she behaves? Men in and out at all times of the day and night—'

'Because she'd had no love in her life under your roof—'

'She was incapable of raising a child, for God's sake. Don't you see that?'

'And you were?'

Jessie's question hung between them like foul air. Vera's face paled, and her lips whitened. Then she said, 'Do you have any children?'

'Andrea was sexually abused,' Jessie snapped, ignoring the question. 'By her father. But you knew that, didn't you?'

Vera turned to Copestake and said, 'Do something, Simon. I don't have to sit here and listen to this diatribe, do I?'

Copestake gave her a tight-lipped smile, then turned to Gilchrist. Something seemed to flicker behind his eyes, and Gilchrist knew that the next words out of his mouth would be a fabrication, albeit wrapped in legal mumbo-jumbo.

'My client clearly has no involvement, physical or otherwise,' Copestake said, 'in the regrettable abduction of her granddaughter, Katie. Without any evidence, your inappropriate questions in an attempt to fluster my client into making some damning statement against her are, in my opinion, nothing short of verbal harassment—'

'Get real,' Jessie said, only to be silenced by Gilchrist raising his hand.

300

'In the unfortunate matter of her husband's death,' Copestake pressed on, 'my client has assured me that she lifted the axe only to protect Detective Chief Inspector Gilchrist from further assault, and that her husband had a reputation for being violent, and had in fact spent several years at Her Majesty's Pleasure for serious assault—'

'That's not how I saw it,' Gilchrist interrupted.

'That may be as it seems,' Copestake said. 'But whichever way you look at it, my client saved your life.'

Jessie slapped the table and pushed her chair back. 'Jesus *fuck*,' she said. 'You'll be telling us next that daughters being raped by their father is just teaching them the facts of life—'

'*You impudent bitch—*'

'Interview over at 2.57,' Jessie said, and switched off the recorder.

Copestake smirked as Jessie stomped from the room, while Vera reached for his hand and gave it a motherly squeeze.

'Your client will remain in custody until her court hearing,' Gilchrist said, 'at which time she'll either be further remanded in custody by the court, or released on bail.'

'This is ridiculous,' Vera snapped. 'Simon. Do something, for God's sake.'

But Copestake's grim look told her he could produce no results this time.

CHAPTER 35

Annette Kirkwood's eyes were swollen, as if she'd been on the binge for a month. To her left sat her solicitor, Jane Whetlow, wearing the same black jacket as she had at their first meeting – still too tight.

Whetlow glared at Gilchrist tight-lipped, as he and Jessie took their seats.

'My client denies any involvement in Katie Davis's abduction,' Whetlow said, eyeing him over the rim of her glasses, her wire hair brushed back so tightly it looked as if it hurt.

An image of a badger about to bolt from its sett flashed into his mind.

'Something amusing you?' she asked him.

'You remind me of someone,' he said, and watched her eyes narrow, as if not sure whether to take his comment as a compliment or an insult. Then he turned to Annette, and said, 'For the record, do you deny abducting Katie?'

'I do.'

Jessie said, 'So what did you think happened? That a baby appeared all of a sudden on the beak of a stork with your name on it?'

'Of course not,' she said. 'I thought it was all above board—'

302

'Hubbie goes out at midnight? Returns home a couple of hours later with a baby in his arms? And you think that's normal?'

'I . . . we've . . . we've never had a child before,' she said. 'We've been unsuccessful with a number of adoption agencies. So I wouldn't know what's normal or not.'

'Interesting,' Jessie said. 'Want to tell us why you were unsuccessful?'

'I don't know why. We couldn't find the right match, I think.'

'Nothing to do with the fact that your husband's got a criminal record, is it?'

'Of course it isn't. Why would you say that?'

Gilchrist could tell from the indignant look that Annette was unaware of living a lie; that she knew nothing of her husband's conviction for fraud in his last job in Edinburgh, his last position as an employee, the reason he returned to Dumfries and set up an accountancy firm, despite losing his professional licence and being struck off the Institute of Chartered Accountants. His current business practices were in effect illegal.

Gilchrist leaned forward, his elbows on the table, a signal to Jessie that he would take over from here. 'So tell me . . . why did you leave Michelle with your mother-in-law?'

At the mention of the child's adoptive name, Annette pressed her hand to her lips and closed her eyes. Tears spilled down her cheeks. She shook her head and sobbed as if every intake of breath was her last. But to Gilchrist it was all an act.

And to Jessie, too, who let out a hefty sigh. 'Wake me up when she stops, will you?'

Her insult had the effect of pulling Annette together. She sniffed, removed a crumpled tissue from her sleeve, dabbed at her cheeks and nose. 'We were going on holiday.'

'Corfu?'

'Yes.'

'Whose idea was that?' Gilchrist asked.

She sniffed again, dabbed her nostrils dry. 'Kevin found some last-second deal that was too good to pass up.'

Novo's phone call to Kevin had done the trick. But they'd made one glaring mistake – going overseas. They could have taken a holiday with their new baby daughter anywhere in the British Isles. Instead, they had chosen to go overseas, but in doing so could not run the risk of trying to go through Border Control.

He knew the answer, but asked anyway. 'Why not take Michelle with you?'

'She doesn't have a passport.'

'So you were prepared to leave her, this child that you and your husband had tried so desperately to have for so many years, even though you'd had her for only a couple of days?'

'Kevin said it was too good a deal to miss—'

'You must've been heartbroken,' Jessie cut in. 'You're the regional representative for Maycom, an international clothes distributor. Do much business, do you?'

'It's slow at the moment.'

'And before this moment? Was it slow then? Or better?'

'Not really. It's always been slow, I suppose.'

'I'll bet it has,' Jessie said. 'So before Maycom, what did you do?'

'I worked from home, selling items on eBay. Mostly knick-knacks, toys and things – and second-hand clothes. But Kevin would give me the occasional book-keeping work to do, that sort of thing.'

'Which of the two cars do you drive?'

'The Porsche,' she said.

'Is it a business car?'

'I think so.'

'I see,' Jessie said, and sat back to let Gilchrist continue.

Gilchrist pressed closer. 'So tell me, Annette, why store Michelle's toys in the attic?'

'I . . . it was . . . Kevin said we should.'

Gilchrist had asked himself why Kevin Kirkwood had been sweating when he'd first answered the door. The suitcases had not been packed, and all the rooms appeared clean and tidy. So he'd instructed a search of the attic and found a pile of scattered toys and clothes that looked as if they'd been thrown up there.

He engaged Whetlow in a long look of disbelief, then focused again on Annette. 'So, let me recap, Annette, can I? Your husband, Kevin, left home on Sunday, around midnight, and returned in the small hours with an adopted daughter. And last night, he said he'd found some holiday deal in Corfu, too good to pass up, and you had to leave at short notice, except you couldn't take your brand-new baby daughter with you. So you phoned your mother-in-law and arranged for her to look after her, the child you'd been dreaming of for years, then Kevin threw all her clothes and toys into the attic before starting to pack the suitcases.' He bared his teeth in a brief smile. 'Is that about right?'

'Yes.'

'I haven't missed anything, have I?'

'I don't think so.'

'Good.' Gilchrist held her gaze. 'Do you watch TV?'

She frowned, wary of his question. 'Not really.'

'You never watched it at all in the last week?'

'Not really. I'm too busy for that.'

Jessie chuckled. 'Me too,' she said, which brought a glare from Whetlow.

'You have three TVs in your home,' Gilchrist said. 'Every one of them works. The first one we tried, the one in the master bedroom, was set on the BBC News. Do you recall watching the news at all?'

'Not really, no.'

'Even the one in the kitchen? That was set on the BBC news channel, too.'

She shook her head. 'No.'

'And the big one in the lounge? Did you watch that?'

'We're seldom in the lounge.'

'So that's a No?'

'Yes. I mean, yes, it's a No.'

He nodded to Jessie, who opened her folder and slid a number of photographs across the table.

'CCTV footage of your husband, Kevin, and a Mr Sandy Rutherford driving to meet each other on Sunday night,' Jessie said to her. 'Do you know Sandy Rutherford?'

'No.'

'Katie's probably in the Range Rover's boot.'

Whetlow scowled as she studied them. 'These prove nothing of the sort.'

'Keep looking,' Jessie said. 'There's also footage of them driving back.'

Annette lowered her head, struggling to hold back the tears.

'I don't blame you for wanting a child so desperately,' Gilchrist said. 'But whose idea was it to abduct Katie Davis?' He watched his words burrow into her system. 'Someone must have come up with the idea, Annette. Was it you? Was it Kevin?' He let several

306

seconds pass, then leaned in closer and whispered, 'Or was it someone else?'

She lifted her head and stared at him, eyes wide and brimming, as if knowing she had no option but to tell the truth, the whole truth, and nothing but the truth.

Gilchrist said, 'Help me, Annette. Give me a name.'

She glanced at Whetlow, pursed her lips as if to seal them for good, then levelled her eyes at Gilchrist. 'It was Rachel's idea,' she gasped. 'Rachel Novo.'

Gilchrist pushed his chair back and stood. 'Charge her,' he said.

Annette gasped, 'What?' and turned to her solicitor.

But Whetlow could only shake her head.

When Gilchrist contacted the Met, he was surprised to be told that Novo was on her way to Scotland, having boarded a flight to Edinburgh. He flicked his mobile on to speaker, and signalled Jessie closer.

'We've passed the surveillance assignment to Lothian and Borders,' the Met officer said. 'Have they not been in contact with you?'

'Not yet,' Gilchrist said, reining in his anger. He should have been the first person the Met called before passing anything to Lothian and Borders police. 'You got a name for me?'

'Sorry, sir. They said they would contact you directly.'

Gilchrist bit his tongue, then ended the call.

His first thought was to arrest Novo the instant she landed in Edinburgh. But an idea was blossoming deep within his mind, niggling away, demanding recognition. Novo's flight to Scotland had surprised him. But again, nothing about Novo should surprise him.

'Novo couldn't have heard about Rutherford's death or her mother's arrest,' he said. 'Not yet. Could she?'

'I don't see how. But even if she had,' Jessie said, 'she's never spoken to her bitch-for-a-mother for well over a year, and I can't see her having any sympathy over her stepfather's death; even less for her mother's arrest for his murder. So I don't get it.'

Even as Jessie's logic dug into his mind, another thought was nudging to the fore.

'Why now?' he asked. 'Why fly to Scotland?'

'Not for the weather, that's for sure.'

'Maybe Novo would be sympathetic to Rutherford's death,' he tried. 'But what if she was much closer to him than anyone ever knew.' He glanced at her, saw he had her attention.

'So you're thinking he's some old stud who's giving her one on the side?'

'Not necessarily, although I wouldn't discount it out of hand. He abducted Katie and made the exchange with Kirkwood. We're pretty sure of that. And it was Novo who arranged the . . . *adoption*,' he said, clawing the air, 'with the Kirkwoods. But did Kevin Kirkwood know Rutherford? I don't think so.'

'So you're saying . . .?'

'That my mention of the name Rumford – not Rutherford – jolted Novo into action. That they could have known each other for a long time. That she flew to Scotland before she knew anything about Rutherford's death.' He stared into the distance, let his thoughts tumble into place. Then he focused his attention on Jessie. 'If I didn't know any better,' he said, and almost smiled, 'I'd say we've flushed her out.'

'So, she's flying to Scotland to do what?'

'That's what we need to find out.'

'I can't wait to cuff the bitch.'

'No. Don't. Not yet. Let's just keep an eye on her.'

'Tell me you're joking.'

'Don't sound so deflated,' he said. 'Maybe the fun is about to start. Get on to Lothian and Borders, and tell them to keep tabs on her when she lands.'

By 5.15 p.m., Jessie had established that Novo had taken a BA flight from Heathrow to Edinburgh, then a train to Gleneagles. But Gilchrist was almost lost for words when she told him Novo had slipped her Lothian and Borders surveillance.

'They lost her in Gleneagles?' he spluttered.

'Apparently.'

'But there's nothing in Gleneagles,' he pleaded.

He tried Vera, but she had no idea why Novo was in Gleneagles. And Andrea was no help either. She'd been taken by ambulance to Ninewells Hospital after being found unconscious at her kitchen table, suspected of having taken an overdose. She had not yet been reunited with her daughter and, despite being told Katie was alive and well, had remained in a disconsolate state of depression. Social Services had been contacted, and were discussing taking action to remove Katie from her mother's care.

So Gilchrist tried another route.

'Do you have that list of properties managed by Rutherford's company?'

Ten minutes later, he and Jessie had addresses of three residential properties close to Gleneagles – two in Auchterarder and one in Blackford. A call to the property management company's manager, Shari McKay, confirmed that both Auchterarder properties had long-term tenants, but that the Blackford property was rarely rented out.

'It just sits there gathering dust, does it?' Gilchrist asked her.

'Mr Rutherford's a golfer,' Shari said. 'He stays there when he plays Gleneagles.'

From the tone of her voice, Gilchrist realised that she knew nothing of Rutherford's death. But he didn't want to complicate their conversation, and said, 'Is anyone renting it at the moment?'

'I've no idea—'

'You run the business, and you don't know if anyone's there or not?'

'It's Mr Rutherford's personal property—'

'But it's on the company books, isn't it?'

'Yes, but only Mr Rutherford rents it out.'

'Which brings us back to my question. Is anyone renting it at the moment?'

'Would you like me to phone Mr Rutherford and—?'

'No.'

A pause, then, 'I could call the property and find out if someone's there?'

'No need,' Gilchrist said. 'We'll make our own way there.'

He suggested Shari meet them at the Blackford property, but she had several meetings to attend. So he arranged to collect the keys and security code for the alarm system from their main office in Perth; but he did not have it in his heart to tell her of Rutherford's death.

Then he ended the call.

At 7.33 p.m., he and Jessie drove into Blackford.

They found Rutherford's property at the north end of the town.

Gilchrist drove past, checked the windows – curtains open – then parked out of direct line of sight of the house, about a

310

hundred yards away. Before exiting the car, he said, 'Let me get the latest from Mhairi,' and phoned her on the car's system.

'I was just about to call you, sir.' Mhairi sounded out of breath. 'Jackie's uncovered some troubling stuff about Dimitri Novokoff.'

'Troubling?'

'Yes, sir. She's found out that Novokoff was never a partner in any microbrewery business in Maroochydore. He never even went to Australia. I was going to mention it earlier to you, sir, but I wanted to check it out first.'

'So he's a liar,' Jessie said. 'Is that why Novo divorced him?'

'That's what I wanted to tell you, sir. Novo didn't divorce him.'

'She didn't?'

'No, sir. She's widowed.'

'Dimitri's dead?' A cold frisson flushed Gilchrist's skin. 'What happened?'

'Apparent heart attack on a private beach in Tangier. But he was with Novo when he died. They were the only two on the beach. Because he's Russian by birth, and his father was a diplomat, his body was flown from the country before a post-mortem could be carried out. It turns out that Novo was held in custody for a couple of hours and questioned by the local police. But there was insufficient evidence to make an arrest, so they released her. When the Russian Embassy threatened to interrogate her, she sought refuge in the British Embassy and was flown back to the UK the following day under Embassy protection.'

'She must have had some political contacts to pull that off,' he said.

'I think her father might have had something to do with that, sir.'

'What about Novokoff's father? Did anyone contact him?'

'I don't know, sir, but this is when it gets interesting.'

311

Gilchrist turned up the volume. 'We're listening.'

'Jackie confirmed that Novo spent five days in a hotel in Marbella within one month of her husband's death.'

'To do what? Meet Novokoff's father? Or someone from the Russian Embassy?'

'We don't think so, sir, but it's the dates that are significant.'

Gilchrist risked a look at Jessie, but she looked as confused as he felt.

'Novo's medical records around that time confirm she was pregnant.'

'And Dimitri was the father?'

'We don't know that for sure—'

'So what happened to her child? Did she have a termination?'

'No, sir. She gave birth.'

'So she must have had the child adopted,' he said, still prying.

'Not directly, sir.'

'Did Novokoff's family claim the child and take it to Russia?'

'No, sir.'

Gilchrist eyed the dashboard; he cast a glance along the street, then back to the phone as he struggled to work out what Jackie had found, why Mhairi was calling, then thought he saw his slip-up. 'How is a child not directly adopted?' he asked.

'Novo had the child,' Mhairi said, 'but under the name of her twin sister, Andrea.'

'Jesus,' Jessie hissed.

Gilchrist slapped the dashboard. 'So Katie is Novo's daughter?'

'It looks that way, sir.'

Which explained why Andrea had kept in contact with Novo, and also her call on the morning of Katie's abduction to tell Novo that her daughter was missing. But he was still at a loss as to why Novo would arrange for Rutherford to abduct Katie in the first place.

'Anything else we should know?' he asked.

'That's it, sir.'

Gilchrist almost cursed. 'Get Jackie to focus on Rutherford. And see if she can find out any more on that hotel in Tangier – who else was staying there at the time of Dimitri's heart attack. And get her to text me the instant anything comes up. You got that?'

'Yes, sir.'

Gilchrist hung up as Jessie let out a rush of breath. 'Jesus. I thought my family were a bunch of nutters, but this lot takes the biscuit. You think Vera the grannie knows the details?'

'Nothing would surprise me.'

'We need to ask her.'

'On the other hand,' Gilchrist said, reaching for the door handle, 'if Novo's where I think she is, you can ask *her* instead.'

CHAPTER 36

Rutherford's Blackford property was a two-storey detached stone building that had undergone extensive external refurbishment – vinyl windows, fasciae, guttering; joints freshly grouted. Sheer blinds on the downstairs windows provided privacy from nosy passers-by. Upper-level windows sparkled clean.

But no movement from within.

Gilchrist confirmed the address, but found no nameplate on the door frame.

'Keep an eye on the upstairs windows,' he said, and waited until Jessie stepped back to the edge of the pavement. He rang the doorbell, heard it chime from somewhere deep in the hallway. 'Anything?' he asked.

'Not yet.'

Two minutes later, he tried again. 'Any luck?'

Jessie shook her head. 'I don't think she's here.'

Gilchrist felt his hopes deflate. He'd been certain this was where Novo would be. But he waited another courteous minute, then slipped the keys from his pocket, slotted the Yale into the lock and gave a twist.

The lock turned over. He pushed the door open.

The first thing that struck him was the heat, as if the thermostat had been turned up all day. The second was the silence – no beeping from the alarm. Had the last person forgotten to set it? Or was someone at home?

The heat warned him that it had to be the latter.

He stood still, held his arm out to prevent Jessie from entering.

'I don't hear the alarm,' she said.

'Might not've been set.'

'You smell food?'

Gilchrist inhaled, caught the faintest hint of coffee.

'She's here,' Jessie said.

'Well, someone is,' he agreed, hedging his bets.

'Maybe she's through the back,' she said, and pushed past him.

Gilchrist closed the door, eased it back on its lock.

By the time he turned around, Jessie was halfway along the narrow hallway.

He caught up with her as she stood in the kitchen doorway.

The kitchen appeared to be two rooms knocked into one, which overlooked a lawn and an expansive wooden deck with no balustrades, as if someone had laid planks over half the back garden. Trimmed hedges over twelve feet tall – leylandii cypress – were as good as brick walls for restricting nosy neighbours. Dusk was falling, and shadows darkened the farthest reaches.

'Not much of a view,' Jessie said.

Gilchrist could only agree, but wondered if the garden had been designed more for privacy than for horticultural elegance.

'Window's open a touch,' Jessie said.

'And that's a fresh brew on the counter,' he said.

Jessie walked to the window and scanned the garden. 'Maybe she's out walking the dog.' She turned to face him, her mouth tightening as her gaze locked on something over his shoulder—

'Breaking and entering's against the law.'

Gilchrist turned at the sound of Novo's voice, felt his blood chill at the sight of her. He was no expert in guns, but if he were a betting man he would put his money on the gun aimed at his chest being a Makarov – a Russian pistol. And the steadiness with which Novo held it warned him she was an experienced marksman – or was that markswoman?

Maybe Dimitri had been a useful husband after all.

'We were given the key,' he explained. 'And we did ring the doorbell.'

'Why are you here?' Novo's blonde hair, no longer tied back in a bun, brushed her shoulders. Her white blouse was open at the neck and a diamond pendant pulled his eyes to her freckled cleavage. Too much sun, he thought. Not like her twin, who looked positively pale by comparison.

'To talk to you,' he said.

'About what?'

'One guess,' Jessie said, and the sightline of the Makarov's barrel shifted from Gilchrist's side as Jessie stepped away from the window.

'Katarina's your daughter,' Gilchrist said, and watched his words work through Novo's mind to end in a creased narrowing of her eyes.

'I see I might have underestimated you,' she said.

'No mights about it,' Jessie snapped. 'Did you really think you'd get away with it?'

'Get away with what? There's nothing illegal about having a child brought up by your twin sister.'

Gilchrist thought Jessie looked stung, as if she knew Novo would always be one step ahead of her, always smarter. 'So you admit it?' he said. 'That you're Katie's mother?'

'I've never denied it.'

'You also never offered it as an explanation of your involvement.'

'Why should I? You're the police. You work it out.'

'You could have save hundreds of wasted man hours—'

'Don't be ridiculous.'

'You have a licence for that gun?' Gilchrist tried.

She smiled at that, then realigned her aim, the gun as steady as ever.

Gilchrist resisted turning his head away from the dark hole of the barrel. 'Put it away,' he said, 'so we don't have to arrest you.'

Novo returned a vacant look, and for one disconcerting moment Gilchrist thought she was just going to pull the trigger and to hell with the consequences. 'If I do, will you tell me what led you to here, of all places?'

Gilchrist had been held at gunpoint before. Even though he had the impression he was being toyed with, he knew better than to argue with any trigger-happy gunman. 'I'd like to know – why?' he said. 'Why did you have your daughter abducted?'

'I didn't.'

That had always been a worry of Gilchrist's, that Annette Kirkwood had coughed out Novo's name simply to deflect police attention away from her and her husband. But Novo's answer was too fast, too assured. It lacked surprise, as if she'd been prepared,

317

and couldn't wait to spit out her primed response to prove her innocence.

'We know Sandy removed Katie,' he said. 'And took her to Dumfries.'

'Good for you.'

Again no surprise, as if Novo had already known Katie was in Dumfries. He thought back to their meeting in London, to his bold accusation that she knew of Katie's whereabouts, and to her consequent clamming up against his onslaught of questions.

'You keep in contact with Sandy,' he said. 'We know that.'

'He's my stepfather. Why wouldn't I?'

'Because you don't communicate with your family. Your words.'

'Maybe I don't consider Sandy to be part of my family.'

It seemed surreal to be having a conversation with a gun pointed at him. But he knew it was often easier to obtain answers when the person being questioned believed they were in control – or, in Novo's case, above the law.

'So why did Sandy abduct Katie?' he asked.

'I wouldn't know.' A smile tickled her lips. 'You'd have to ask him.'

'It's convenient for you that he's dead,' Jessie said.

Novo's gaze slid away from Gilchrist to settle on Jessie, and something in the cold blackness of her eyes told Gilchrist that here was a woman who would stop at nothing to get what she wanted; maybe even kill to keep whatever secret she was hiding. Which seemed to bring him full circle, and beg the question – why?

He felt his heart flutter as Novo adjusted her aim once more, this time pointing the gun at Jessie's stomach. And it struck him then that, with the leylandii hedges, Novo could pull the trigger and no one outside would see a thing. Which provided an answer that seemed so simple he wondered why he hadn't thought of it before.

You could sunbathe in the nude – a rarity in Scotland, he would be the first to confess – or make love on the lawn, even hold a party out there in the middle of summer, and no one would see you. Which was the whole point of a secret rendezvous, was it not?

'This is where you and Sandy meet,' he said, aware of Jessie turning her head to question him.

Novo looked puzzled, too, and not as confident as seconds earlier.

He was questioning himself, if the truth be known, but once you stripped the problem down to its basics, there really was only the one answer.

Novo shifted her stance, jiggled her gun at him, a silent demand for his answer.

'I thought you were going to put the gun down,' he said.

She pointed it at him with outstretched arm, then opened her hand, an invitation for him to take it from her. Which he did, finding that it was a plastic lookalike that had certainly done the trick – scared him and Jessie almost into submission.

'It's a fake,' he said to Jessie, and placed the gun on the kitchen table.

'Jesus fuck,' Jessie cursed. 'I should arrest you for—'

'For what? Trying to protect myself from what I thought were two burglars?'

'Right, that's it.' Jessie stepped forward, reaching for her plasticuffs.

'Arrest me.' Novo held her hands out together. 'Go on.'

But Gilchrist raised his hand and caught Jessie's eye, and she returned to her spot by the window. Then he looked hard at Novo.

'You never phone your mother,' he said. 'But you phone your stepfather.' He looked at the kitchen units, the spotlights in the ceiling, the grouting in the tiled flooring. 'This is his house, a place he kept secret from some people.' He returned his gaze to her. 'Like your mother, for example.'

Novo chuckled. But it sounded false.

'You didn't force your way in,' he went on. 'You have a key, which tells me you were close to Sandy. But how close?' He let his question dangle in the air, just to gauge a reaction. But Novo was not for biting, so he said, 'Were you having an affair with him?'

She guffawed at that. 'I'm not that bloody desperate,' she said.

He watched her eyes dance, and in that fleeting moment had a sense of his rationale being turned upside down, as if all the rules in the world had been swapped for a new reality. Until that moment, he had thought Andrea was the disturbed child, the weaker twin who had suffered irreparable mental harm at the hands of a sexually perverted father. But now he came to suspect that Rachel was every bit as damaged.

Still, he had to push.

'Maybe not,' he said. 'But Sandy had his uses.'

'Did you catch old Sandy with his trousers at his ankles?' Jessie chipped in. 'Giving his lover one?'

Gilchrist thought Novo's cockiness wavered, an indication that Jessie might be close to the truth. But he was still missing something.

'Were you blackmailing him?' he tried. 'Was that how you got him to do your dirty work? Abducting Katie, and delivering her to your friend, Annette? We know that, too. That you and Annette went to university together.'

'I didn't order Sandy to do any such thing.' Novo tilted her head, as if she'd heard a noise from behind. 'Let's talk in the lounge.'

'Oh, lovely. Tea and biscuits?' Jessie quipped. 'Milk, no sugar.'

'In your dreams, you little trollop.'

For one unsettling moment, Gilchrist thought Jessie was going to launch herself at Novo, and he caught her eye again, watched the moment pass.

But Novo's abrupt change in manner puzzled him.

In the lounge, he walked to the far wall and stood with his back to the window. He was intrigued at how Novo's eyes never stilled; how they searched the air around her, as if looking for something. Or . . . Or maybe . . .

Maybe wondering about the time?

'You're expecting someone,' he said.

Novo smiled, a narrow parting of her lips, more pain than pleasure.

'Who?' he asked.

'Patience is a virtue,' she said. 'It won't be long now.'

Gilchrist agreed. It wouldn't be long . . . until he arrested her.

She was toying with them. He had too many questions, not enough answers, and his mind continued to spit up more. Why was Novo here? Why this house? Was Sandy the key? Was she having an affair with him? From an incestuous relationship as a child, to another as an adult? Or did stepfathers not count in the statistics governing incest . . .?

'Was Sandy easy to blackmail?' Jessie asked.

Novo sneered and said, 'I've never blackmailed anybody.'

'What did you have on him?'

'You're clutching at straws,' Novo said.

'I'm not the one drowning,' Jessie snapped, and gave her a twitch of a smile.

'Did you take photographs of Sandy?' Gilchrist tried.

'Why would I do that?' Novo said.

'Photographs are always good for blackmail.'

She tutted at that, and shook her head, but Gilchrist thought he was homing in.

'So where do you keep your computer files?' he asked. 'Not on a hard drive; probably a memory stick.' He watched her eyes give a nervous twitch. 'You must take your files with you whenever you fly off somewhere. Like China. So a memory stick would be useful. You must have one with you.'

'I sometimes wonder about the police,' she said. 'Poking and prodding and searching for answers when there's none to be found.'

Gilchrist nodded, unconvinced. They could search her personal belongings once they had her in custody. And he would bet the barn that they would find a memory stick and, on it, maybe photographs of Rutherford in some compromising position. But for the time being he was content to bide his time, just listen to Novo.

'We have CCTV footage of Sandy driving Katie to the Kirkwoods,' he said.

Novo shook her head, uninterested.

'And I was surprised to hear that your late husband, Dimitri, died in Tangier.'

That comment brought a stillness to her being, as if she were holding her breath to see what else he could surprise her with.

'An apparent heart attack. But there are drugs on the market that do that now.' He watched his words push deep into her mind, and thought it strange how she seemed to liven – rather than sink into sadness – at the memory of her dear departed.

Something caught his eye then, a shadow at the window, almost at the same moment as his mobile vibrated. He retrieved it from his pocket as the doorbell rang, and Novo turned and walked from the room.

He eyed the screen – a text from Jackie; a list of names, one he recognised, which had him frowning. He read on, searching for the gist of the message, and felt his heart give a flutter as he realised that this was a list of guests at the same hotel in Tangier when Dimitri was found dead on the beach.

Mumbled voices reverberated in the hallway, giving him time to send a text to Jackie, asking her to check the guest list at another hotel. Then he had time only to make eye contact with Jessie as a man's voice – its polished tones vaguely familiar – echoed from the hallway.

The door opened and Novo entered the lounge, followed by Simon Copestake.

Jessie's frown turned into a grimace. 'We've been waiting for your solicitor?'

Novo ignored her, smiled at Copestake. 'I believe you've met everyone here.'

'Yes.' Copestake nodded to Jessie, then Gilchrist, and said, 'You look perplexed.'

'Just wondering what you're doing here,' Gilchrist replied.

'To provide legal advice. What else?'

What else indeed? thought Gilchrist.

Which he might be able to answer if he knew why Copestake's name was on the list of guests at that Tangier hotel.

CHAPTER 37

'My client tells me you've been harassing her,' Copestake said. 'That you entered her place of residence unannounced. She's instructed me to file a formal complaint.'

'Quite the family of formal complainers,' Jessie quipped.

Gilchrist returned Copestake's courtroom stare, seeing for the first time in his blue eyes how handsome he was – white smile, square jaw, trim build; how he could bowl over a widow bereaved of her husband; and how a holiday romance in Tangier might blossom into something more serious – behind everyone's back.

'You should remind your client that I'm the SIO in a missing child case—'

'Who has now been found, thank God—'

'And who turns out to be your client's biological daughter,' he snapped. 'A critical piece of information that she never once considered passing on to us.'

Give Copestake his due, he didn't flinch, even though it was likely that Novo had not told him that either. 'She was not compelled to do so for personal reasons,' he said.

'She had a moral obligation,' Gilchrist said, 'and she could now be charged with obstructing the course of justice. She impeded my investigation—'

'You've since recovered the child, so I fail to see how my client could be accused of impeding anything.'

With Copestake, Gilchrist knew he was up against a solicitor with a sharp mind and a tongue to match, so he pressed on, testing for feedback. 'Nor did she disclose the fact that she knew her stepfather had abducted Katie and taken her to a friend of hers.'

Novo tutted, which almost caused sparks to fly from Jessie's eyes.

'My client denies all knowledge of that.'

'She can deny it all she likes, but the facts speak for themselves—'

'What facts?'

'We're standing in her late stepfather's home, to which she has ready access—'

'Doesn't prove a thing. She had a good relationship with Sandy, God rest his soul.'

God rest his soul? Gilchrist felt a flush of anger surge through him at the memory of the axe, the shuddering thud as it hit flesh, the warm splatter of blood, and found his fingers touching the bandaged spot on his arm where its blade had shaved skin.

He forced their discussion back on track. 'Rutherford didn't know the Kirkwoods,' he said. 'So how did he know they were looking to adopt a child? Or who to contact? Or where to deliver Katie?'

'You would need to ask Sandy that.' Copestake smiled. 'Which is now impossible to confirm one way or the other—'

'We're looking into his phone records.'

Copestake's gaze shimmered to Novo for a brief moment, then he said, 'I'm sure doing so will help your investigation.'

'And we've already applied for a search warrant for this property,' Gilchrist lied.

'Here?' Copestake looked amused. 'What are you hoping to find?'

'Photographic evidence.'

'Of?'

Still searching, Gilchrist pushed deeper. 'Evidence that will explain your client's hold over her stepfather.'

'Really?' Another glance at Novo. 'Such as?'

Despite his worry that Annette Kirkwood had given him Novo's name in an attempt to divert police attention, Gilchrist didn't want to spell it out to Copestake: how Novo was the common link between the Kirkwoods and Rutherford; or how she'd arranged her daughter's abduction – she just *had* to have – if Annette had indeed told the truth.

So he said, 'Evidence that would explain how Rutherford knew the Kirkwoods.'

Without missing a beat, Copestake said, 'My client's mother knew Annette Kirkwood as a child. Her husband was Sandy Rutherford. No one can legislate for pillow talk, so I still fail to see how you can connect my client to this . . . this regrettable incident.'

Gilchrist held Copestake's smirk for a couple of beats, then glanced at Novo who had remained standing beside the hallway door. Something in her look, the smug one-upmanship, the silent condescension, had him thinking there was something wrong with this event; that the arrival of her legal representative was . . . was . . . what?

Unusual? Timely? A set-up?

Only then did some neural tumbler slot into place.

'So tell me,' he asked Copestake, 'why are you really here?'

Copestake responded with a gruff sigh. 'To offer legal advice.'

'For a fee?'

'That's between me and my client.'

'From Edinburgh?'

'Excuse me?'

'Edinburgh to Blackford is a good hour's drive. But here you are, in Blackford, and only fifteen minutes after we arrive. You were just passing through when your client called?' Gilchrist said, his voice laced with sarcasm.

Copestake's eyes blinked with confusion. But for only a moment, as his fast legal mind sorted through the danger in Gilchrist's question. 'I was on my way to Perth to collect some personal effects for my client's mother,' he said, 'when I received a call from my client telling me she was being harassed by Fife Constabulary rattling on her door. And believe me when I say this, Detective Chief Inspector, I *will* be filing a formal complaint.'

'Convenient, don't you think?'

'What is?'

'That you just happened to be driving to Perth.'

'More good fortune than convenience, I would say.'

A quick glance at Novo – eyes dancing, body tensing – warned Gilchrist that he was moving ever closer to the nerve centre. 'Let's say for argument's sake that you weren't going to Perth, but were driving to Blackford to meet your client. Here. In Sandy Rutherford's secret home. To which your client has the key.'

Copestake gave a puzzled grin. 'I don't accept that. It's purely hypothetical—'

'As hypothetical as you being in Tangier when Dimitri Novokoff had an apparent heart attack on a private beach?'

Copestake almost jolted.

'Or in Spain the following month?' Gilchrist said, taking a chance on that question without hearing back from Jackie about the other guest list he'd requested.

For once, Copestake was speechless. He turned to Novo, as if seeking help.

'This is bloody ridiculous,' she said. 'I'm getting out of here.'

Copestake reached out for her in the passing. 'Rachel. No. We can—'

But she brushed him off, strode across the room and into the kitchen.

'Where do you think you're going?' Jessie shouted after her, and followed.

The speed with which events unfolded took Gilchrist by surprise.

As he pushed past Copestake, he caught the metallic clatter of a kitchen drawer being opened, and Jessie's voice screaming, *'Don't—'* He entered the kitchen just as Novo thrust an outstretched arm into Jessie's stomach, the pointed blade of a boning knife glinting under the kitchen spotlights, its handle gripped tight in her hand.

Jessie barely managed to sidestep the attack, grabbing Novo's arm. A snap of the wrist released the knife, and a twist of the body had Novo on the tiled flooring in zero seconds flat, gasping with pained surprise.

Then Jessie cuffed Novo, telling her in a voice loud enough to be heard across the street that she was being detained under section 14 of the Criminal Procedure Scotland Act 1995 for police assault. She then cautioned Novo, and Gilchrist thought of telling Jessie just to up it to attempted murder. But he stepped in, helped Novo to her feet, led her back into the living room while Jessie called for a support vehicle. Hands cuffed behind her back, lips little more than a white line, face bruised where she'd hit the floor, Novo looked as if she'd chewed nails and was preparing to spit them out in molten fireballs.

Copestake stood helpless, face drained of blood, shocked into silence by the turn of events. 'You should be careful how you answer this,' Gilchrist said to him. 'But I'll ask you one more time. Why are you here?'

Copestake looked at Novo, held her gaze for a long moment, then lowered his head and walked from the room before her eyes could turn him to stone.

Gilchrist followed him into the hall, up the stairs to the upper floor where he opened a door and entered what appeared to be a home office. The room had a warm feel to it, like the leftover heat from a party. A table – complete with two opened laptops, phone set, printer and an assortment of office bric-a-brac – faced a wall covered in framed photographs of properties; presumably the late Rutherford's pictorial portfolio. A two-seater sofa backed against the opposite wall, fronted by a coffee table of engraved wood.

Copestake sat on the sofa. 'I'll tell you what I know,' he said.

Gilchrist slipped his mobile from his pocket, switched it to video mode, and placed it screen-up on the table. Not the best sound recorder, but it would do.

'I'm going to record this. Okay?'

Copestake's gaze shimmied to the phone. 'Sure. Go ahead.'

Gilchrist gave a brief introduction for the record, then stood back and waited.

Copestake wrung his hands. 'I can't tell you how many nights I've lain awake and rued the day I ever set eyes on the Davis family.' He looked up at Gilchrist. 'I can't represent Rachel. I can't represent any of the family any more. I won't allow myself to be dragged any deeper into this . . . this . . . '

'Illegal mess?' Gilchrist offered.

Copestake grimaced, shook his head. 'No. No. Not illegal. I would never knowingly be involved in anything illegal.' He dry-washed his hands. '*Never.*'

'But you suspected something wasn't right,' Gilchrist nudged.

'Yes, I did, yes.' Copestake seemed relieved. 'But I couldn't be sure. The whole thing with Rachel . . . ' Another shake of his head. 'It's just . . . it's . . . it's difficult.'

Gilchrist thought he saw the problem – well, maybe just one of them. 'Are you in love with her?' he asked.

'*God*,' Copestake said, as if surprised. 'I'm head over heels for her. Who wouldn't?'

Gilchrist nodded in fake agreement. 'But you didn't drag me upstairs to tell me all about your wedding plans.'

'No. No. You're right. Yes.'

'Tell me about Tangier,' Gilchrist said.

'Tangier?' Copestake ran his tongue over his lips. 'I was there.'

'I know you were.'

'I mean, not with Rachel. Not then. Later.'

'After her husband died?'

'Yes,' he said, and stared at the floor, then out through the window, as if searching the far distance. Whatever he focused on seemed to help, for he steepled his fingers to his chin, looked up at Gilchrist, resolution settling behind his eyes – the moment of truth, the clearing of the lies, the legal mind back in control. 'How much do you know?' he asked.

'About?'

'About Rachel,' Copestake said. 'And her . . . her history.'

Gilchrist felt as if he was swimming around in the dark. But Copestake sounded as if he were probing. Why? So he could manipulate his response; feed Gilchrist only as much as he deemed safe? So Gilchrist decided to proceed with caution.

'I'd be lying if I said we know it all,' he ventured. 'Not *yet*, anyway. But experience tells me it will only be a matter of time until we do.'

Copestake nodded, as if at Gilchrist's sage advice, then said, 'I'd always had my suspicions. But that's all they were. You understand? Only suspicions.'

'Of?'

'Of Rachel's involvement in her husband's death.'

Gilchrist narrowed his eyes. 'Why?'

'The way she behaved. It wasn't normal. She was . . . how do I say it . . .? *Relieved*. I would even go so far as to say she was *happy* that he'd died.'

'You need to do better than that,' Gilchrist told him.

Copestake nodded. 'They'd been arguing. Rachel was upset. She'd been crying most of the afternoon. That's when she first came on to me.'

'As in – tried to pick you up?' Gilchrist asked, just to be sure.

'Yes.'

'Go on.'

'We'd had a few drinks the night before. In the bar. Just the two of us. Dimitri had gone to his room early. Rachel told me she wanted to leave him, and wished he would die.'

'Who were you there with?'

'Someone I'd been dating for a few months. She'd gone to our room, too. It was late. After midnight. Closer to one, I think.'

Gilchrist didn't press for a name. That could come later. 'You're not married?'

Copestake shook his head. 'Separated. Two kids.'

'So you were up for it, then? Having an affair with a married woman.'

'I was besotted with her. I still am. But . . . '

After a couple of beats, Gilchrist said, 'What are you trying to tell me?'

Copestake wrung his hands again. 'I think I saw her do something to Dimitri's drink.'

'Where?'

'On the beach.'

'You were there?'

'In my hotel room. I was watching her.'

'Good eyesight.'

'Through binoculars.'

Well, there he had it. Copestake a Peeping Tom. 'This is the day after you had a few drinks with her in the bar?'

'Yes.'

'Did you tell anyone what you'd seen?'

Copestake's lips pursed white. 'No.'

'Why not?'

Copestake tried to return Gilchrist's stare with a determined look of his own, but his resolve failed, and he lowered his head. 'I couldn't be sure. I had my doubts. I started questioning myself until I didn't know whether I'd really seen it, or just made it up.'

Gilchrist suspected that it wasn't doubts Copestake had back then, but his eye on the prize. With Dimitri out of the way, all he had to do was keep quiet and he could collect the prize any time – a month later, to be exact, on a trip to Spain.

'Are you prepared to testify to that?' Gilchrist asked.

Copestake pressed his lips tight, shook his head. 'I couldn't. I'm just not sure.'

'And what about Katie?' Gilchrist said, keen to keep the ball rolling. 'Did Rachel ever confess to you that Katie was her daughter and not Andrea's?'

'No,' he said. 'Not once.'

'So you knew nothing about her blackmailing Rutherford to kidnap Katie?' he asked, just throwing the question out there, even though he needed evidence to confirm that.

'Nothing.'

'What I don't understand is – why did Rachel have Katie kidnapped at all?'

Copestake rose to his feet, as if to reinstate authority in the matter. 'Because Andrea's bipolar and her condition is worsening. She's now a danger to herself. She self-harms. Simply put, Rachel was worried for Katie's welfare.'

'And in your opinion, do you think Katie's life was in danger?'

'I've been Dougal Davis's solicitor and friend for over fifteen years now. I've seen him at his worst, and his best.' He squeezed his hands. 'Regrettably, most of what the press say about him is true, and the damage he's done to his family is unforgiveable. But I tell you this, I wouldn't wish his daughters on anyone.'

'I thought you were besotted with Rachel.'

'I am, I mean . . . I *was*.' He stared hard at Gilchrist. 'But she suffers from bouts of depression. Not as bad as Andrea,' he rushed, as if that explained all. 'When Rachel's in the right mood I've never met anyone like her. But catch her on the other side, and the Devil himself would run.' He turned and stared out the window, but even from the upper level the view was restricted by the leylandii. 'I was going to tell her this weekend that it was over.'

The doorbell ringing from downstairs brought Copestake back with a jerk.

The police support vehicle had arrived.

Copestake said, 'I've never spent any time with Sandy Rutherford, so I don't know the man. But despite Dougal Davis's reputation, I've found him to be an excellent judge of character. He never took to Sandy. Called him a thieving gypsy.'

Gilchrist nodded to the laptops. 'Are these Rutherford's?'

Copestake shrugged. 'I wouldn't know.'

'You don't recognise them as Rachel's, then?'

Another shake of the head. 'No.'

'We'll confiscate these,' Gilchrist said. 'Rachel must know the password.'

'What do you hope to find?'

It was a direct enough question, but the answer seemed more obscure. 'Something that might tell me how she blackmailed Rutherford into kidnapping Katie for her.'

Copestake gave a tight-lipped grimace.

Gilchrist eyed both laptops, then switched off his mobile.

CHAPTER 38

Despite Gilchrist having his hopes raised, Rutherford's laptops turned up nothing incriminating. What folders and files they managed to access contained nothing more than property surveys, maintenance reports, construction quotes, subcontractor correspondence – plumbers, electricians, brickies, roofers. He instructed the IT Section to dig deeper.

Tom Paton, head of IT, suggested the laptops had been used only for Internet access, or for drafting correspondence and reports for copying on to memory sticks. But Gilchrist's memory of Novo not answering the door, the latent warmth of the upstairs home office, told him she'd been taking care of something important.

'I suspect Novo's deleted them,' Gilchrist said.

'We're scouring the drives for shadow copies, sir. If any files have been deleted, we'll recover them.'

A search of Novo's personal effects turned up her memory stick, which he handed over to the IT team.

'I presume it's password-protected,' Paton said.

'It is,' Gilchrist said. 'But she's saying she can't remember what it is.'

'Not to worry, sir. It'll just take us a bit longer.'

The following morning, Gilchrist received a call from Paton. 'Still working on it, sir, but we've found a number of shadow files that were deleted yesterday. Not sure if they would be of any interest to you, but I can email them to you.'

'As soon as.'

'Doing that right now, sir.'

By the time Gilchrist accessed his email account, three messages had come in from Paton, each with an attachment. He opened the first, which contained nothing but images of property interiors, many of the same rooms shot from different angles. Gleaming kitchens, granite worktops, tiled flooring, man-sized fridge-freezers, cabinets of every material and shade that hid integrated dishwashers, tumble driers, fridges and freezers, all competed with bathrooms big enough to hold parties in – fully tiled shower cubicles, glass-walled wet rooms, claw-feet baths, roman blinds. On and on the images went, until Gilchrist wondered what he was missing.

He opened the next emailed attachment, and grunted a curse when he saw it contained similar images. He tried the next – more of the same. Image after image flickered past: each house, room by room, then another, and another, repeating in what seemed like an endless stream. Why Novo had interest in deleting these from Rutherford's laptops was beyond him.

He glanced at the time, his stomach reminding him that he'd skipped breakfast. He stretched his arms, rolled his head, all of a sudden exhausted by the meaningless waste of criminality. Why had Novo attacked Jessie? What had she hoped to achieve? His and Jessie's appearance at the Blackford property had shocked her to the core. Had that been the nudge that finally tipped her over the edge? But for someone who, until her attack on Jessie, had shown such controlled restraint, it almost seemed out of character.

Copestake had said that Andrea was bipolar, but Novo suffered from bouts of depression. What if they were both bipolar? Was that what they'd witnessed? Or had Copestake lied to save his own hide? Or was there some other reason? Had he really intended to break off his relationship with Novo that weekend? Was he only an innocent party whose professional expertise had inadvertently pulled him into the heart of a dysfunctional family?

Gilchrist's mind was crackling with ideas – too many, too fast, and all too confusing, particularly on an empty stomach. The thought of a creamy pint had him forwarding Paton's emails to Jackie, with a message asking her to find out why Novo might be interested in Rutherford's properties.

Then he called Jessie. 'Thirsty?' he asked her.

'Can't,' she said. 'I've promised to take Robert out for lunch.'

The mention of Jessie's son jerked Gilchrist's mind back to Novo's attack. Jessie could so easily have been killed. 'I should've been there,' he said to her. 'In the kitchen. When Novo went for you.'

'I was ready for her. I caught the look in her eyes as she pushed past you.'

'I should never have let her leave the room like that.'

'I don't think any of us had a choice.'

'You handled it well,' he said.

'Does that mean I can ask for a pay rise?'

'Don't push it, or next time I won't help you.'

She chuckled, a throaty rasp that somehow reminded him of how loving a mother she was to her son. 'Go and take Robert for lunch,' he said. 'I'll catch you later.'

No sooner had he ended the call than his mobile rang again – ID Tosh.

'What the fuck're you at, Gilchrist? You send me a text asking me to call—'

'I sent you a text *telling* you to call.'

A moment's silence, then, 'Oh, I get it. Trying to throw your weight about, you skinny runt—'

'You need to watch that tongue of yours, Tosh—'

'I'm in town. And you and me need to talk. Where do you want to—'

'The Central Bar. Five minutes.'

Gilchrist killed the call, disconnected his laptop, and spent the next ten minutes trying to settle his nerves – Tosh had that effect on him – before striding from his office.

The Central was buzzing with a weekend rush.

Tosh was seated in a corner booth with a short tumbler in front of him, which glowed with a golden liquid as inviting as whisky. Without a word, Gilchrist took the seat opposite and opened his laptop.

'Going to show me some porn?' Tosh said, and took a sip from his glass.

'You wish.' Gilchrist turned his laptop so that the screen faced Tosh.

Tosh frowned, flickered a grimace at Gilchrist as the image on the screen danced and shuddered in silence, before settling into the silhouette of Grange Mansion. Then it adjusted in focus until two people filled the screen – Tosh and Gilchrist; Tosh facing the camera at an angle, Gilchrist with his back to it.

A woman's voice cut in, clear and sharp, the volume turned up loud enough for a group of students seated at the nearby table to look up in surprise . . .

Touch me once more, you smarmy bastard, and I'll fucking have you . . .

A female student at the next table pressed her hand to her mouth, while her friend looked on in puzzled amusement. Others, too, turned in the direction of the vocal argument, as if anticipating a fight breaking out.

Gilchrist was aware of a general silencing in the bar.

Tosh glanced at him, then back at the laptop. 'What the fuck . . .?'

You know your problem, Gilchrist? You fancy yourself. You think shit doesn't stick to your shoes. But you're a loose cannon. You're reckless. If it wasn't for you, Stan the man would still be around . . .

'It's coming to the good bit,' Gilchrist told him.

Fuck you, Gilchrist. I'm your worst fucking nightmare. You'd better believe it. I'll get you, I fucking promise. But you won't know when it's coming, or where. Just that it will be fucking coming. And it'll be lights out. Period . . .

The woman's voice died.

Silence hit the bar like a thunderclap. Then someone laughed, a glass chinked, a stool scraped the floor, and the general hubbub eased up in volume to full flow again.

'She's a professional lip reader,' Gilchrist explained. 'And threatening a senior officer with deadly intent is a sackable offence.'

Tosh's fingers crushed his tumbler with a grip that looked strong enough to shatter the glass. His lips pressed white, and his puffy eyes shrank to beads that danced with madness, as if trying to work out where exactly on Gilchrist's face he should smash the tumbler.

'Don't make matters any worse, Tosh. You can still keep your job and your pension. Just not in Fife Constabulary.' Gilchrist retrieved his laptop, turned it to him, and closed it. 'I've made two copies and filed them in a safe place.' He jerked a half-smile across the table. 'I haven't shown this to anyone yet.' Then he glared into Tosh's fuming gaze. 'But if you're still sitting here by the time I come back with my pint, I will.'

Gilchrist pushed away from the table and walked to the far end of the bar.

He ordered fish and chips and a pint of Deuchars. From the corner of his eye he saw Tosh stomp on to Market Street, and felt a sudden release of nervous energy so strong that his legs began to shake. He'd been concerned about how Tosh might react – blow a gasket, start a fight; but even though his ploy appeared to have worked, something warned him that he had not seen the last of the lunatic. Rather than have Tosh fired from the Constabulary – his earlier thoughts – he came to see that his hold could be much stronger if he kept the CD as a perpetual threat over the man.

To force his thoughts from Tosh, he phoned Jack while his beer settled.

'I'm having a pint in The Central,' he said. 'Thought you'd want one.'

A pause, then, 'Don't order it until I get there.'

Next, he phoned Baxter, but was dumped into voicemail, and left a short message.

His fish and chips had just been served when Jack pushed through the swing doors, made eye contact without a smile, and squeezed through the crowd at the bar to Gilchrist's table at the back wall. He sat opposite him, without a welcoming smile or a customary high-five for a handshake.

Gilchrist slid his plate towards him. 'Like a chip?'

341

Without a word, Jack picked up a couple, popped them into his mouth.

Gilchrist sipped his pint – almost done – then removed a twenty from his wallet and slid it to Jack. 'I'll have whatever you're having. And order some food for yourself when you're at it?'

'Deuchars, is it?'

'You talked me into it.' But even that failed to elicit a smile.

Gilchrist watched his son slide his way to the main bar, six foot tall and thinner than Crouch on a diet. Black stonewashed jeans that could be held up by anti-gravity sat below boxer shorts that had seen better days. A loose T-shirt spotted with multicoloured splatters of paint hung from too-bony shoulders. A quick tilt of his head as he downed a shooter – vodka had always been Jack's go-to drink – then the empty glass shoved across the counter before he carried two settling pints to the table.

He pushed one to Gilchrist, dug into his pocket and spilled some loose change on to the table. 'Thanks,' he said.

Gilchrist eyed the pittance. 'Expensive pints.'

'Had a double voddie at the bar,' he said. 'I'll give you the money for it,' and dug his hand into his jeans' pocket.

'It's all right, Jack, don't—'

Jack slid a tenner across the table. 'There you go.'

Gilchrist finished his first pint, placed his glass on the table with care and slid Jack's tenner back at him. 'Keep it for the next round,' he said.

'No. You keep it. Me drinking shooters obviously pisses you off.'

'It doesn't piss me off—'

'Then why mention it at all, man? For fuck's sake.'

'A joke that came out wrong,' Gilchrist said. 'That's all.' He took a forkful of fish and diverted his eyes from Jack's gaze. But it was no use. He returned his cutlery to his plate and said, 'What's got you fired up?'

'You don't trust me, Andy. That's what's got me fizzing.' Jack took a mouthful of beer that almost drained the glass.

Gilchrist eased into it with, 'I think you're upset about being arrested—'

'I'm upset about being fucking *entrapped* and questioned like a criminal.' He finished his pint with an angry flourish, snatched the tenner from the table and rose for the bar, just as DS Baxter arrived.

'Sit,' Baxter said to him.

'Go fuck yourself,' Jack snapped. 'I'm having a pint.'

Baxter clamped a heavy hand on Jack's shoulder. 'Sit down, sonny.'

Jack took hold of Baxter's hand and eased it from his shoulder. Then he squared up to him. 'I'm buying myself a pint, *mister*. And once I've done that, I'll come back to the table and sit all over that fat fucking face of yours if you'd like.'

Gilchrist said, 'Make sure you get one for Ted.'

Baxter grimaced. 'That's very kind of you, Jack. Mine's a Stella. Pint.'

Jack turned to the bar, while Baxter pulled a stool next to Jack's and raised an eyebrow at Gilchrist. 'Getting tough in his old age.'

'Hungover, more like.'

Baxter forced a chuckle. 'Got your message.'

'Any good news?'

He showed some teeth. 'I'll wait till your lad gets back with that pint.'

Gilchrist nodded, cut off another slice of fish and forked on a couple of chips. He'd never seen Jack so incensed; never seen him confront anyone, let alone a DS in a public bar. Jack had always been the first to turn his back at any sign of trouble. But as he watched him alone at the bar, placing his order, he came to understand that for Jack it was all about being believed and trusted. How many times had he accused Jack of taking drugs, only for Jack to hang up on him and for Gilchrist to be proved wrong? Too many, came the answer. And now an attempt had been made by a fifteen-going-on-twenty-something Tess McKenzie to lure Jack into Sammie Bell's drug chain, and in doing so entrap him into underage sex.

No wonder his son was fit to be tied.

Jack shuffled back from the bar and handed Baxter his pint of Stella.

'Thanks, Jack. You know how to keep a man happy. Up yours,' he said, and took a mouthful that half drained it.

Jack sipped his Deuchars and said, 'Okay, I'm sitting,' and Gilchrist felt his heart go out to him. No more tough guy. Just a young man frightened of what lay ahead, and whether or not he would have a criminal record assigned to his name for the rest of his life.

'Right.' Baxter placed both elbows on the table, like a conspirator about to reveal all. 'Your toxicology results are clean.' Then he turned his strongest DS look Jack's way, and said, 'I've just had another chat with Tess McKenzie.'

Jack swallowed a lump in his throat and sipped his pint, the tiniest of tremors in his fingers as he waited for the verdict.

'She says you never touched her.'

Jack shivered a sideways look at Baxter.

344

'What do you say to that?' Baxter asked him.

Gilchrist stepped in to prevent Jack from sticking his foot in it. 'What he's always maintained, Ted. That he never laid a finger on her. Right, Jack?'

'Right,' Jack said, then buried his face in his pint.

'She's also identified a couple of Sammie Bell's gofers,' Baxter said. 'If you'd be willing to have a look at some photos, Jack, tell me if you recognise them, it could help us nail them, big time.'

'Would I have to testify in court?'

'Would be helpful if you could. But no one's pushing you.'

Jack took another sip, then nodded. 'Okay. I'll take a look.'

Gilchrist said nothing while Baxter and Jack argued over a time for him to visit the Office, with Baxter reluctantly accepting tomorrow, which brought a grim smile to Gilchrist's face – Jack's way of getting revenge on the way Baxter had treated him.

Then, job done, Baxter finished his pint and pushed to his feet.

'Not staying for another?' Gilchrist said.

'The wife's got me wallpapering. Halfway through the hall at the moment. It's doing my nut in. If I don't finish it today, she'll leave me in no fit state for another pint. Ouch.'

Gilchrist tilted his pint. 'Catch you.' He watched Baxter exit on to Market Street when his mobile rang. He felt a flush of surprise at the ID screen – Becky. 'Got to take this,' he said to Jack, and walked towards the side exit on to College Street.

He stepped outside and made the connection.

'This is a surprise,' he said. 'Where are you?' A couple of beats of silence on the line warned him that this was not going to be a let's-make-up-and-start-again call, and he found himself pressing his mobile hard to his ear.

'It doesn't matter where I am,' she said.

345

He thought her voice sounded small, strained, as if she were too weak to talk across all the miles that separated them. 'How are you feeling?' he said, and wished he'd thought of something more meaningful to ask. 'I mean . . . are you . . . are you coping?'

'What do you think?'

With Cooper, it had never been an easy journey. He'd often taken their bantering as nothing more than ritual sparring, sexual manoeuvring; two lovers jostling with each other before the inevitable surrender. But he could not fail to catch the hard bite in her tone.

'I think you're struggling to come to terms with it,' he said. 'Losing the child you'd never been able to conceive when married.' He listened to the silent hiss of electronic ether, and stepped to the side as two students jostled past, oblivious to his presence. He watched them totter down College Street arm in arm, trying to remember when he had last done that – only last month, he realised, with Cooper. They'd seemed so close then, even confessed their feelings for each other – well, only he had, now he thought about it, told her he loved her. But for the life of him he could not remember Cooper's response.

'You need support,' he said to her. 'And I'm happy to—'

'I don't need support. I need time.'

He almost pulled his mobile from his ear, not wanting to hear the words he knew were coming.

'I need to take a break,' she said. 'Get away.' She paused for a couple of beats. 'Make a fresh start.'

Again, he knew the answer, but still had to ask. 'You're not coming back?'

'I'll be back in a few days,' she said, 'to carry on with my work.'

He waited for her to continue, but she seemed to have passed the conversation baton to him. 'And what about . . . us?' It was all he could think to say.

She gave a sigh, not of boredom or irritation, but of regret, sadness, resignation in what she had to tell him, perhaps. 'I'm sorry, Andy. I can't. It's just that . . . if we carry on . . . if we . . . it'll be a constant reminder of . . . of—'

'I understand,' he said. 'It'll take time.'

Another sigh, this time with a hint of annoyance at his failure to understand.

'If you need anything,' he said. 'If I can help in any way—'

'Please, Andy, don't.' Another beat, then, 'I'm so sorry.'

The line died.

He kept his mobile to his ear as he looked skywards. To anyone watching, he could be one lover listening to the romantic whisperings of another. He watched a patch of blue appear for a fleeting moment before being swallowed by swelling clouds that seemed to soften at the edges as they turned misty.

He lowered his mobile and hung his head.

Then walked back to North Street for his car.

CHAPTER 39

Gilchrist opened a bottle of The Balvenie Doublewood and poured himself more than a fair measure into a crystal glass. He dropped in a chunk of ice and felt a wry smile tug his lips – *Whisky's a warm drink*, his mother used to proclaim, then contradict herself in the next breath with: *You pour it* over *the ice, son, no' the other way about.*

He took a large sip, relishing its rich sweetness as he rolled it around his mouth.

On the drive back to Crail, he'd phoned Jack and apologised for having to leave so suddenly – after Cooper, he would have been poor company – following up with a promise to take him and Maureen out for a night some time during the week – take your pick. Oh, and can you take my laptop home with you and I'll swing by your flat and pick it up later? Jack had enthused about starting a series of abstract paintings based loosely on human features, the kind of thing Chloe used to do, the first mention of her name in over a year, a really positive sign. Removing the threat of going to jail for having sex with a minor would do that to you.

Gilchrist sat at the dining table and switched on his old Dell computer, surprised to find that the next sip drained his glass. Nothing for it but to have another. He was pouring out a large one – was there any other measure for whisky? – when movement at his back window caught his eye. For a moment, his heart stuttered, then settled when he recognised Blackie on the sill, brushing her body up against the glass.

He removed a packet of Perle Ocean from the kitchen cupboard and opened the back door. 'Here, puss, puss,' he said, and sprinkled a scattering of moist cat food on to the back step, his first attempt to lure Blackie from the garden shed into his cottage. But she eyed him with feline disdain from her spot on the sill, obliging him to close the door and return inside.

Back at the table, he watched Blackie slip from the sill, out of sight.

Well, at least it was a start.

He logged into his email account to find several paper-clipped messages from Jackie. He opened the attachments one by one and worked through them – copies of letters, excerpts of medical records, prescriptions, flight schedules, tax returns, bank statements. He puzzled at what appeared to be an excerpt from a Final Will and Testament – how had Jackie accessed that? – and felt a frisson of excitement sweep through him when he recognised the name of the executor – Hughes Copestake Solicitors. You would never believe what turns up when you least expect it. He read through the attachments again, then once more, the mental fog lifting, clearing by the second, revealing possibilities that had been blinded to him, up until that moment.

Then he pushed his whisky aside and called Jessie.

He told her what Jackie had emailed, explained his thoughts, testing his logic as he bounced ideas off her and she off him. Ten minutes later, he thought they had what he needed to start the ball rolling, maybe even set it alight.

'I'll call Glenrothes,' he said, 'and set up an interview.'

'Robert's staying over at a friend's,' she said.

He caught the excitement in her voice. 'Would you like me to pick you up?'

'Is the Pope a Catholic, or what?'

Gilchrist and Jessie entered the police station and almost shuddered to a halt.

Copestake was walking towards them, jacket over his sleeve, shirt collar open. His eyes hung heavy and dark, as if he'd not slept for a couple of days, or been on the binge for a week. 'Rachel called,' he said. 'What's so important that an interview couldn't wait?'

'She's already wasted enough of our time,' Jessie said.

Gilchrist pushed past Copestake with, 'This way.'

Novo was already seated in the Interview Room.

Without a word, Copestake took the seat next to her.

Gilchrist and Jessie sat opposite and, without introduction, Jessie switched on the recorder and proceeded with the interview formalities.

Then she sat back to let Gilchrist take over.

'I thought you weren't going to represent any members of the Davis family,' he said to Copestake.

'My client's not had sufficient time to find alternative legal representation.'

'So you're it until she does?'

'You'd have to ask my client that question.'

'Are you happy to continue to be represented by Mr Copestake?' he asked Novo.

'Just get on with it,' she said. 'I'm tired of fooling around with you.'

Jessie said, 'In case it's slipped your mind, you're going to serve time for assault—'

'That has yet to be proven in a court of law,' Copestake interrupted.

Jessie smiled. 'Isn't that what I just said?'

Copestake raised an eyebrow in disbelief, which warned Gilchrist that the man could not be trusted to tell the truth regarding Novo's attack on Jessie in the kitchen – *he'd found his client being cuffed by DS Janes for no apparent reason; and no, he hadn't seen the knife in his client's hand, nor had he witnessed her alleged attack.*

Which could just be the start of it.

Gilchrist began with, 'Your mobile records show two numbers stored in Contacts for your sister, Andrea: one for her regular mobile, and one for her other mobile that she seems to use exclusively for calling you.'

'So?'

'So why would you only ever call Andrea back on her regular mobile number, and not the other number, the one she uses to call you?'

'Habit?'

'You don't think it strange that your sister has two mobile phones?'

'Why would I?'

'Or a mobile phone account in Katarina's name?'

Novo gave a smile that failed to touch her eyes. 'If she didn't want anyone to know she was talking to me, it makes perfect sense to me.'

And to Gilchrist, too, he had to agree. He changed tack with, 'Tell me about Spain.'

'What about it?'

'When you and the family solicitor, Mr Copestake here, spent a quiet five days in a luxury villa overlooking the Mediterranean, not long after your husband died.'

'She was grieving,' Copestake said.

'I'm speaking to your client,' Gilchrist reminded him.

Novo gave him a dead-eyed stare. 'I was grieving.'

'That's understandable, with your husband of only eighteen months having died so unexpectedly in Tangier.' He noticed Copestake ease back in his seat, as if not wanting to admit to something he'd said earlier. 'We found the prescription medication.'

'What prescription medication?'

'OxyNorm.'

Novo blinked, gave the tiniest shrug. 'What's that got to do with me?'

'It's an opioid painkiller. But fatal if you take too much. It's what killed Dimitri.'

Copestake jerked to life. 'You can't possibly know that. No post-mortem was carried out on Dimitri—'

'Are you sure of that?'

'His body was flown to Russia before . . . ' He shut his mouth, as if stunned by the angry tone of his voice.

Gilchrist held his gaze, let the silence build for several seconds, then turned to Novo. 'You'd been to Spain before,' he said, 'earlier that same year. A weekend in March. Another in May.'

'If you say so. I'd have to check my passport.'

'You were accompanied on one of these trips by your solicitor, Mr Copestake, while we believe he met you in Spain on another.'

'And your point is?' Copestake asked.

Gilchrist kept his gaze locked on Novo's. 'That the two of you were having an affair long before Tangier.'

Novo shrugged. 'So?' If she'd had a cigarette to hand, she would have blown smoke in his face.

'Let's get back to the prescription medication,' he said. 'Did you know it was your stepfather's?'

Novo frowned. 'No.' But for just that split-second, Gilchrist caught her surprise.

'The villa belonged to Sandy Rutherford,' he said. 'Indirectly, of course. But not a lot of people know that. Especially the Inland Revenue.'

Novo narrowed her eyes. Copestake stilled.

'Does the name RD Enterprises mean anything to you?'

'Should it?'

'You tell me.' Gilchrist returned her blank stare.

She tightened her lips, gave an almost unnoticeable shake of the head. 'No.'

'I would remind you that anything you say could be used against—'

'I said *No*.'

He could sense Jessie's tension by his side; almost feel her desire to demand the truth. But he played it down with, 'Why did you have a key for Sandy's house in Blackford?'

His non sequitur almost threw Novo, but she recovered smoothly. 'Sandy and I had an arrangement. He let me stay in some of his properties when they were not being let out.'

'And the villa in Spain was one of them?'

'Yes.'

'And the house in Blackford another?'

'Obviously.'

'Even though your mother never knew?'

'Never knew what?'

'That Sandy let you stay.'

'No. Yes. Jesus, what's the question? She never knew he let me stay. Does that give you an answer?'

Gilchrist flashed a smile. 'Were you and Sandy having an affair?'

She tilted her head back and laughed.

Copestake coughed a laugh, too, just to keep the side together.

Then Novo recovered, and eyed Gilchrist in disbelief. 'Please tell me you're joking.'

Well, it was a long shot. So he moved on. 'Are you computer literate?'

'Why?'

'I ask the questions. You give the answers.'

'I get by.'

He nodded. 'Spreadsheets, word processing, that sort of thing?'

'If you say so.'

'I don't say so, I'm asking.'

'As I said, I get by.'

As a Lloyd's high-flier, Novo would be far from computer illiterate, Gilchrist knew, but she was acting it, as if in anticipation of his next question. 'You would know then that if you delete files from a computer, they're not permanently deleted. They leave shadow copies that can be retrieved.'

'Fascinating.'

'Our IT boys located shadow files on Rutherford's laptops. One of them has a list of properties owned by RD Enterprises.' Despite Novo's uninterested look, Gilchrist sensed a tightening in the room, as if the air had stilled and was building up an electrical charge. 'One of these properties is that luxury villa in Spain,' he added.

'Is there a question any time soon?' Novo asked.

'Sandy often took your mother to that villa,' he said. 'But, during one of these trips, he slipped a disc and was taken to hospital, where he was prescribed OxyNorm. For pain relief.' He paused for her response, but Novo was an expert in the art of deception. He had come up against some of the most formidable liars on the planet – cold-hearted killers who could convince you the knife had slipped, or the gun had gone off by itself, or the blunt instrument in their hands really belonged to someone else and they were just keeping it warm until the police arrived. Novo could hold her own against the best of them.

Copestake, on the other hand, had beads of sweat forming on his upper lip.

'During one of your trips to Spain that year, either one, it doesn't matter, you found the OxyNorm still in the bathroom. Left by Sandy when he flew back to Scotland.'

'You don't have to answer,' Copestake advised Novo.

'I haven't asked a question yet.'

Novo smirked. Copestake grimaced.

'So,' Jessie interrupted, 'while in Tangier, Dimitri was given a drink laced with, oh, I'd say maybe ten or more capsules of OxyNorm – enough to kill him. It's morphine-based, so the poor man wouldn't have felt a thing, just drifted off to sleep and never woken up. If you had to choose a way to go, that would be it, I'd guess.'

'I'm still waiting for the question.'

Gilchrist eyed Novo. 'Did you give your husband that fatal dose of OxyNorm?'

'Don't be ridiculous.'

'Well, someone did,' Jessie snapped, giving Copestake her toughest stare.

'This is preposterous,' he said. 'Nothing but conjecture.'

'Is it?'

The open question seemed to confuse Copestake, as if he knew he was being duped, but couldn't figure out how. But Gilchrist was fascinated at the ease with which they could both lie – and convincingly, at that. Maybe it was time to do some lying of his own.

He returned Copestake's gaze and decided just to go for it. 'You slipped up,' he said to him, 'taking me upstairs in Blackford.' He sensed, rather than saw, Novo shift in her seat to watch Copestake. 'You never should have told me to review the files on the laptops—'

Novo gasped, 'You did *what?*'

'I did no such thing—'

'If you hadn't, I doubt we would've been as focused on them as we were.'

'This is *nonsense.*' Copestake glanced at Novo, shook his head. 'I would never—'

'When your client attacked DS Janes,' Gilchrist pressed on, 'you were quick to jump ship—'

'Rachel, don't believe a word—'

'She would be charged with assault, and you needed to distance yourself from—'

'I really have to complain—'

'Pointing me to Rutherford's laptops and telling me they

356

contained files that would explain why your client coerced Rutherford to abduct Katie was your red herring—'

'This is utterly preposterous—'

'As it turned out, you needn't have bothered. RD Enterprises purports to be a limited company owned by Sandy Rutherford and Vera Davis, but it's not registered with Companies House, so it's flying beneath the Inland Revenue's radar.'

'I am instructing my client not to—'

'Shut up, Simon.'

'Rachel. I have to—'

'*Shut it.*'

Gilchrist held his eyes on Novo and waited until she appeared to have recovered her composure. 'You threatened to report Rutherford's dealings to the taxman if he didn't do as you wanted,' he said. 'Because you never trusted Sandy, did you?' He let a couple of silent beats pass, then added, 'And you're wondering whether or not to trust your lover-boy solicitor.'

Copestake stirred in his chair, then stilled when Novo raised her hand.

Gilchrist kept his focus on Novo, watched his seed of an idea germinate – from the tightening corners of her lips to a darkening shadow behind her eyes – before locking itself in her mind with final resolve. Self-preservation is arguably the most powerful emotion of any living species, and he almost heard the neural tumblers click into place as Novo's thought process worked to its conclusion. Then she looked hard at Gilchrist, and he knew from the fire in her eyes that the moment of revelation was upon him.

'I'll make a deal,' she said. 'But I want a new solicitor.'

Copestake reached for her arm. 'Rachel?'

357

She shrugged him off with an angry glare.

'Rachel—'

'Fuck off, Simon. I mean it.' She pushed at his chair to distance herself from him.

'For God's sake, Rachel, what're you saying? We—'

'It was your idea—'

'*Rachel*—'

'I told you I wanted no part in it—'

'For God's sake, you're—'

'Terminate this interview,' she snapped. 'Simon Copestake no longer represents me.'

Copestake's face had paled. His mouth moved in silence, and his tongue darted in and out of pressed lips, as if preparing to dry-swallow a pill.

Gilchrist stared at the two of them, stunned by the speed of their collapse. But with such a pair of slippery suspects he needed to discuss strategy before deciding whether or not Novo's semi-slipped-up, half-confession in front of Copestake had been deliberate; nothing more than an attempt to make herself look innocent by shifting the blame his way.

He thought of challenging her there and then.

But instead reached for the recorder and said, 'Interview terminated at 15.53.'

CHAPTER 40

The following morning

CS Greaves took Gilchrist's hand in his and gave it a firm shake. 'Well done, Andy. I understand Katie Davis is unharmed and in excellent health. The Chief's already been on the phone twice, wanting to call a press conference this afternoon to blow the Constabulary's trumpet. He had a personal interest in the case, if you remember.'

'I do, sir, yes.'

'Childhood friends with Vera Davis, of course.'

'Of course.'

'He was asking if Mrs Davis is still in custody.'

'She is, sir, yes.'

Greaves frowned. 'I'm not sure the Chief likes that.'

'I'm sorry to hear that.'

'So you're saying there's . . . nothing you can . . . eh . . . you're prepared to do?'

Gilchrist thought silence his best option.

Greaves frowned, then harrumphed, 'I see.'

'Would I be expected to attend this afternoon's press conference, sir?'

'That depends on the Chief. In light of what's going on. With Mrs Davis, of course.'

'Of course.'

Gilchrist turned for the door. He was about to step into the corridor, when Greaves said: 'One other thing . . . '

Gilchrist paused in the doorway.

'Big Archie would like you to give him a call.'

No longer Chief Constable McVicar, but 'big Archie', to remind him that this was personal to the man. 'About the press conference?' Gilchrist asked.

'You'll have to phone him and find out,' Greaves said, and gave a narrow grin.

Gilchrist closed the door behind him, firmly, and hoped Greaves got the message. He had always known McVicar to be a man of integrity, an honest man who played by the rules, someone who never cheated. But Greaves's parting words had him thinking that Vera Davis – or maybe the whole Davis family – had something over McVicar.

By 11 a.m., Gilchrist and Jessie had Novo's written confession – well, her side of the story might be a better way of describing it – and Copestake in custody under suspicion of the murder of Dimitri Novokoff.

Copestake now swore by his statement that he saw Novo slip capsules of OxyNorm into Dimitri's beer. The fact that he'd never mentioned the specifics before did not sit well in his defence.

'How long had you and Rachel been seeing each other?' Gilchrist had asked him.

'My marriage was over years ago.'

'So how long, exactly?'

'Five years now, I think. I can't really remember.'

'And your firm provides legal services to other members of the Davis family, even Sandy Rutherford?'

'I can't say for certain. I'd need to check our files.'

'I can assure you that your firm does.'

Copestake gave a bored shrug. 'If you say so.'

'Did it never trouble you that you breached client confidentiality?'

'I did no such thing—'

'You prepared Andrea Davis's Will, so you knew all the details—'

'My firm holds executorial authority for many clients—'

'And that her fund would revert to her sister, Rachel, provided her daughter, Katie, was not alive at the time to inherit it.'

'I wouldn't know.'

'You seem to have selective memory loss.'

'I can't possibly remember every single detail of thousands of legal documents.'

'You put Rachel up to it,' Gilchrist said.

Copestake choked a laugh. 'No one can put Rachel up to anything. Least of all me.'

'Money's a powerful persuasion, though. Millions of pounds in Andrea's fund. And it would be yours, too, once you married Rachel.' He focused on Copestake's eyes, but his best courtroom face gave nothing away. 'You never were going to call it off this weekend, were you? Your relationship with Rachel.'

Copestake tutted.

Gilchrist decided to press deeper. 'Your firm also handled Rutherford's affairs. So you knew all about RD Enterprises not being registered with—'

'That's nonsense.'

'Do you deny any knowledge of RD Enterprises?'

'Of course I do.'

'We have copies of title deeds for a number of properties with covering letters on your company's letterhead.'

'That would be from our Spanish office,' Copestake said. 'Nothing to do with me.'

'Except that you seem to know that RD Enterprises handles property in Spain.'

'I . . . that's . . . ' He shook his head. 'Wasn't that what you said?'

'We haven't found anything with your signature on it,' Gilchrist said, and shrugged. 'But we've already applied for a warrant to secure your Spanish office's records, so I'd say it'll only be a matter of time.'

That silenced Copestake. He clammed up, giving a repetitive 'No comment' to every question after that. But Gilchrist felt confident that they would find sufficient evidence in Rutherford's laptops and Hughes Copestake's files to build a watertight case against him.

On the other hand, Novo had continued to maintain her innocence, last night blaming Copestake for first suggesting 'getting rid of her husband' when they'd had an earlier weekend in Spain. But she remained adamant that she'd not taken him seriously, and knew nothing of his alleged involvement in Dimitri's death.

'So, what did you think Dimitri died from?' Gilchrist had asked her.

'Heart attack.'

'Were you not suspicious, particularly after your lover-boy Simon had shown such murderous intent in Spain?'

'Why should I? Dimitri was always complaining of chest pains.'

'We've checked his medical records and his heart was fine.'

'I don't care what his records say. I lived with him. I know he wasn't a well man.'

'And what about Katarina?'

Novo had continued to deny culpability in her daughter's kidnapping – her cryptic phone call to Kevin Kirkwood being only a suggestion to take a break sooner rather than later – and had refused to answer any more questions on her husband's death until her offer to strike a deal was accepted in exchange for having all charges dropped.

But Gilchrist had other ideas that morning.

He entered the interview room behind Jessie, and took a seat opposite a hatchet-faced woman in her forties, with silver hair gelled so thickly it shone like a helmet – Novo's new solicitor, he presumed. She slid a couple of business cards across the table.

'Ellie Stevenson. I'm representing Ms Novo.'

'You're from England?' Jessie said, eyeing the card.

'My firm provides legal services to Ms Novo's employer.'

'I see.'

Stevenson smiled. 'Let's get on with it, shall we?'

Jessie switched on the recorder.

Once the introductions were over, Stevenson began with, 'My client denies any involvement in the unfortunate abduction of her sister's daughter—'

'Your client's sister doesn't have a daughter,' Jessie said. 'Katarina is—'

'Legally, Katarina Davis is the daughter of Andrea Phyllis McPherson Davis. I have a copy of the birth certificate if you'd like me to show that to you.'

'We have our own copy,' Gilchrist told her, and steepled his hands. 'Go on.'

'And my client also denies all additional charges associated with the alleged murder of her late husband, Dimitri Novokoff. After careful consideration, she is prepared to give evidence for the Crown in exchange for waiving all charges against her.'

'She attacked me,' Jessie said.

'Allegedly.'

'No allegedly anything. I was there.'

'So was my client.' Stevenson smiled at Jessie.

'What the hell . . .?'

Then Gilchrist thought he understood. 'You're going to argue that she's unfit to plead,' he said. 'Is that your ploy?'

'I prefer the word *defence*,' she said. 'In the words of Hume's *Commentaries* – to serve the purpose of such a defence in Scots law, my client's disorder must amount to an absolute alienation of reason.' She turned to Jessie. 'Can you give me any reason why my client allegedly attacked you?'

'I was about to arrest her for being complicit in the kidnapping of her daughter—'

'To which I would argue that she had a child, Katarina, to a loving husband, Dimitri, who frequently complained of pains in his chest, and who sadly died while on holiday of a suspected heart attack. And that her twin sister provided a caring and loving home in which to raise my client's daughter. So there was no complicity, and hence no reason. Which is why you should consider striking a deal.'

'Caring? Loving?' Jessie said. 'Have you seen her sister?'

'I understand she's in hospital recovering from some sort of stomach bug.'

'Stomach bug? She overdosed,' Jessie said. 'And stop twisting the facts. In one breath you're saying Andrea Davis is legally Katie's mother, and the next that she's providing a caring home for her sister's—'

'Mother: legally yes; biologically no.'

'Oh for crying out loud.'

Gilchrist raised his hand to bring the tiff to an end. But just from that first exchange, he saw how formidable Ellie Stevenson could be in court. From bitter experience, the words of an old solicitor friend of his sprang to mind – *There's justice, then there's the law, and often the twain never meet* – reminding him that no case was ever a dead cert, no matter how sound the evidence. All he could do was glean as much evidence as he could to strengthen the Fiscal's case. And to do so, he needed to press harder.

'Do you have proof that your client is unfit to plead?' he asked Stevenson.

She shuffled through her paperwork and removed two sheets, which she slid across the table. 'An excerpt of my client's medical records that confirm she's taking medication for depression. By the time we go to court, if you decide to go down that road, I'll have reports from two independent psychiatrists confirming she is unfit to plead.'

'So you're happy to tell your client that she's mentally incompetent?' Jessie said.

Stevenson smiled. 'If I have to.'

Gilchrist looked at Novo, at grinning eyes that mocked him, at a smug smile that struggled not to stretch into a full-blown victory grin. Here was a woman, a mother who had abandoned her only child and in all probability was complicit in the murder of her husband, her child's father – for what?

So she could advance her career? So she could dominate her male associates and run a company division in China? Had the world changed that much since his parents' generation, when all anyone wanted was to have a stable family and raise their children to be honest and moral members of society?

But he had one more criminal point he needed to prove.

He nodded to Jessie, who opened her file, and slid a document across to Stevenson.

'What's this?' she said.

'Andrea Davis's Last Will and Testament,' he said, then nodded to Novo. 'It leaves everything to her daughter, Katie.'

'Which means what, exactly?'

'That if Katie died, or was presumed dead, meaning if she was abducted and never found and was then declared dead, everything would be left to her twin sister, Rachel.'

'So what are you saying?' Stevenson asked.

Jessie said, 'That's motive for abduction right there, plain and simple.'

'So she could inherit her sister's estate?' Stevenson chuckled. 'You're forgetting that Andrea is very much alive—'

'With a history of self-harm,' Jessie said. 'She tried to take her life yesterday.'

Gilchrist leaned forward, a signal to Jessie that he would take over. He needed to control the interview, bring it back on track. He stared hard at Novo, then said, 'Your father sexually abused you.'

'Is that a question?' Stevenson said.

Gilchrist held up a hand to keep Stevenson quiet. 'Rachel,' he said, 'I know it must've been hard for you. You've kept it to yourself all these years, how your father abused you. But you

366

confronted him when you were only twelve, so I know you're strong and can talk about this now.'

Novo lowered her eyes, tightened her lips.

'You held a knife to his neck,' he said. 'Told him if he ever touched you again, you would slit his throat. Your own words.'

Stevenson reached for Novo's arm. 'You don't have to answer that.'

Novo raised her eyes, shrugged her arm free. 'I've nothing to hide,' she said, then eyeballed Gilchrist. 'Yes, I said that to my father. And yes, I would've slit his throat when he was asleep. Believe me, I still would.'

From the fire in her eyes, Gilchrist had no doubt that she meant every word. 'But you didn't anticipate your father's reaction, did you?'

'What reaction?' she said. 'He did nothing. He's never laid a finger on me since.'

'He may not have reacted physically,' Gilchrist said. 'But he changed the wording of his Family Trust Fund.'

Something seemed to flit across Novo's face at that comment, a shadow of sorts that touched her eyes and downturned her grin into a scowl.

He held Novo's bitter gaze as Jessie slid another document across the table.

Stevenson snatched it from her.

'The details of the Davis Family Trust Fund,' he said. 'A considerable sum of money accumulated over a couple of Davis generations, with this most recent version having been drawn up by Hughes Copestake Solicitors. For estate planning, it appears that Dougal Davis was not quite as savvy as his predecessors, having transferred it all into Vera's name, his first wife, presumably for sound business reasons, but had then to snatch back his half of it in his subsequent divorce settlement.'

He nodded to the document. 'Note the dates.'

Stevenson did, then frowned at him. 'So what are you saying?'

'That the remaining fifty per cent of the fund – two million pounds back then, plus or minus a hundred thousand or so – then owned by Dougal Davis, was subsequently put into the name of Andrea Davis.'

Novo's eyes narrowed, and a tremor quivered her lips, as if her nervous system was only now reacting to the injustice of having been written out of the Family Trust Fund all these years ago.

'The dates,' Gilchrist reminded Stevenson.

She stared at the document, then said, 'I don't see the significance.'

'You'll find that within one month of your client threatening to kill her father, Dougal Davis had the Family Trust Fund redrawn to exclude her.' He turned his eyes on Novo. 'And when you and Andrea reached thirty, the age at which you should have had joint access to that fund, only then did you find out you'd been excluded.' He hardened his voice. 'How did that make you feel?'

Novo shook her head.

'You must have been hurt beyond all reason,' he pressed on. 'Were you hurt enough to seek revenge?'

'No comment.'

'And to make matters worse, by that time the fund had grown to just over 5.7 million, effectively cutting you out of almost three million pounds.' He paused for a couple of beats. 'How did you feel when you found out it was all to go to Andrea?'

'No comment.'

'We've spoken to Simon,' he said, and caught her glimmer of uncertainty, the rising suspicion that she had been found out. Even though Copestake had not confessed, Gilchrist pressed on, taking full advantage of his upper hand. 'I believe you did know,' he said. 'You knew *exactly* how much money Andrea had access to. Lover-boy Simon would have given you all the details.'

Novo shook her head.

'How did that make you feel?' he asked. 'Did you feel bitter at having been cheated out of your share?'

'No comment.'

'You must have been enraged,' he said. 'You must have been mad with anger; so mad that you decided to devise some way to claw it back, didn't you?'

'No comment.'

'*Didn't* you?'

'No comment.'

Gilchrist lowered his voice, changing his tone to one of reason. 'Did you never think of discussing it with Andrea?' he asked. 'To find out if she would be willing to share her pot of gold with you, her loving twin sister?'

'Don't be ridiculous,' Novo snarled. 'Andrea's never worked a day in her life. She needed every penny of that fund to see her through.'

'What I don't understand,' he said, 'is why?'

'Why what?'

'Why would you need the money?' He opened his palms at the absurdity. 'You earn in excess of a hundred thousand a year, with a five-figure annual bonus. You inherited fifty thousand pounds from Dimitri's life-insurance policy, as well as clearing off the mortgage on your London apartment.' He leaned closer. 'I mean,

I could understand your bitterness, your rage, but it's not like you needed the—'

'It was never about need,' she snapped. 'It was about correcting an injustice—'

'Rachel,' Stevenson interrupted. 'I have to warn you—'

'I was the one he sexually abused. I was the one who suffered. Not Andrea. She was her mother's pet—'

'Not according to Andrea,' Jessie said. 'She was abused, too.'

'But I was his favourite,' Novo pleaded. 'I was special.'

'So special you put a knife to his throat to make him stop?' Gilchrist said.

'To make him stop abusing Andrea,' she gasped. 'It was me he wanted. It was me he started with. Not Andrea. It was only when he began to pay more attention to Andrea that I threatened him. Don't you understand that? Can't you see? It was me he loved.' She shook her head. 'He never loved Andrea,' she whispered. 'He said he loved only me.'

Then she lowered her head and let tears spill on to her lap.

Gilchrist pushed his chair back, then eyed Stevenson. 'All deals are off. Your client will remain in custody and held under the terms of the original charges for complicity in the abduction of her own daughter, and in the murder of her husband, Dimitri, as well as the attempted murder of a police officer.'

Stevenson's lips compressed to a scar.

Novo tried to look at him, but failed.

CHAPTER 41

Back in his office, Gilchrist checked his voice messages, hoping to hear from Cooper, even just a short call to tell him that she would be in Bell Street at the beginning of the week. But he listened to his messages one by one, not surprised when her voice never surfaced. His email account was just as void. He checked his mobile, but nothing there either, then decided to put it off no longer and made the call.

'McVicar speaking.'

'CS Greaves said you wanted me to call, sir.'

'Yes, I did, Andy. Thanks. Yes. I wanted to ask you about the charges you're pressing against Dougal Davis's ex-wife,' he said, his voice booming. Gilchrist could not fail to catch the inferred importance of the matter, the distancing of McVicar from the case by his mention of Dougal Davis – as if that was going to change his mind any time soon. 'I believe you've still got her in custody, Andy.'

'I have, sir, yes.'

'Seems a bit harsh, does it not?'

'She knew, sir.'

McVicar paused for a couple of beats. 'She knew what, Andy?'

'That we'd found Katie, sir. Before anyone from the Office spoke to her.'

'Well, was that—?'

'Sandy Rutherford had been warned that I was on my way to Perth to question him. I suspect he thought I was going to arrest him. If he hadn't known, I believe he wouldn't have attacked me, and would still be alive but in custody, as opposed to his wife now being in custody for his murder, sir.'

Silence.

'I don't know who made that call, sir, but I will be looking into that. In light of recent events, I think custody is where Vera Davis should remain. At least until after the weekend.'

'I see, Andy. Well, in that case, I'll leave it with you.'

'Thank you, sir.' But the line was already dead.

Novo's records had confirmed she'd not called Rutherford after Gilchrist had asked how she knew Alex Rumford. So, he'd checked Vera Davis's records to confirm that she'd taken a call shortly after Gilchrist had phoned McVicar and Greaves from Dumfries to tell them Katie had been found. That call to Vera had come from an unregistered mobile, an unlikely source, Gilchrist knew. But you did not become Chief Constable by—

Two hard raps at his door.

Startled, he looked up, and pushed himself to his feet as Jack entered.

'Was just passing by,' Jack said.

'As one does.' He shook hands with Jack – a firm father-to-son grip – and had the toughest time not pulling him into a hug. 'How did you get on?'

'He got on terrific.'

They both turned to face Baxter standing in the doorway.

'Jack identified the other two members of Sammie Bell's gang. And they've both got form.' Baxter's eyebrows pushed high. 'Lots of it. How they managed to stay off our radar for so long beats me.'

'Where are they now?' Gilchrist asked.

'We found some CCTV footage of the pair of them outside The Keys in Market Street, then driving off in an old Renault. We managed to get the number plate, and the latest on the ANPR is that it's parked on Lindsay Road near Ocean Terminal in Edinburgh. Been on to Lothian and Borders Police, and I think we'll have them in custody by the end of the day.'

'So you're going to have reason to celebrate?'

'Talking of which.' Baxter glanced at his watch. 'Got a date with a gorgeous blonde.'

'Your wife?'

'Right first time.' Baxter winked at Jack, then turned and walked along the corridor.

Alone again with Jack, Gilchrist said, 'You must feel relieved.'

Jack puffed out his cheeks. 'Relieved doesn't come close, man. I tell you, I was really shitting it. I thought that was it. And Tess, too.'

Gilchrist felt his heart slump at the mention of her name. 'You're not still seeing her, are you?'

Jack mouthed a surprised 'What?' and tapped the air with clenched knuckles. 'Hello, Andy? Anybody in? Hello?' Then he grimaced. 'No way, man. But I've managed to convince her to talk to her parents.'

'You have?'

'It wasn't easy, let me tell you.'

'But it's what she needs to get back on track. Some help from her parents. Right?'

'Yeah, well, parents are important.'

'And parents pay for lunches and buy you beer,' Gilchrist said. 'Come on,' he added, 'how does The Central sound?'

Jack laughed. 'Thought you were never going to offer.'

Gilchrist powered down his mobile, and put an arm around his son's shoulder.

ACKNOWLEDGEMENTS

Writing is a lonely affair, but this book could not have been published without help from the following: Jon Miller, ex-Superintendent, Tayside Police; Gayle Cameron, Police Scotland; Kenny Cameron (retired), Police Scotland; and Inspector Graeme Cuthbertson, Police Scotland, for police procedure; Sheena Fraser, Advocate, Faculty of Advocates, for assistance with all things legal; Tony Kingsbury, for golf knowledge in Crail; Heather Holden-Brown and Jack Munelly of hhb agency for encouragement and advice when it was needed the most; Penny Isaac, for copy-editing and occasional arm-wrestling over that pesky comma; Grace Vincent, Amanda Keats, Clive Hebard and many others at Little, Brown Book Group, who worked tirelessly behind the scenes to give this novel the best possible start, but especially Krystyna Green, Publishing Director, for tough-love editorial advice and for once again placing her trust in me; and finally, Anna, for putting up with me, believing in me and loving me all the way.

This book is a work of fiction. Those readers familiar with St Andrews and the East Neuk may notice that I have taken creative

375

licence with respect to some local geography. Any resemblance to real persons, living or dead, is purely coincidental.

Any and all mistakes are mine.

www.frankmuir.com

CRIME AND THRILLER FAN?

CHECK OUT THECRIMEVAULT.COM

The online home of
exceptional crime fiction

KEEP YOURSELF
IN SUSPENSE

Sign up to our newsletter for regular recommendations,
competitions and exclusives at www.thecrimevault.com/connect

Follow us on twitter for all the latest news @TheCrimeVault